P9-EDE-758

WITHDRAWN
UTSA LIBRARIES

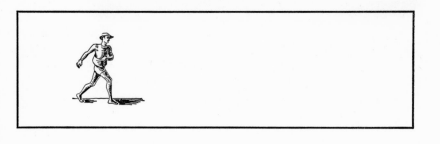

BY R. V. CASSILL

THE PRESIDENT   PRETTY LESLIE   CLEM ANDERSON

THE EAGLE AND THE COIN

FIFTEEN BY THREE *(with Herbert Gold and James B. Hall)*

THE PRESIDENT

R. V. CASSILL

SIMON AND SCHUSTER - NEW YORK - 1964

ALL RIGHTS RESERVED
INCLUDING THE RIGHT OF REPRODUCTION
IN WHOLE OR IN PART IN ANY FORM
COPYRIGHT © 1964 BY R. V. CASSILL
PUBLISHED BY SIMON AND SCHUSTER, INC.
ROCKEFELLER CENTER, 630 FIFTH AVENUE
NEW YORK 20, N. Y.

FIRST PRINTING

LIBRARY OF CONGRESS CATALOG CARD NUMBER: 64-14427
MANUFACTURED IN THE UNITED STATES OF AMERICA
BY H. WOLFF, NEW YORK

LIBRARY
University of Texas
At San Antonio

. . . but for him I could forget the blood, but
for me he could forget the innocence . . .

Vespers—W. H. AUDEN

PART ONE

1

MAJOR ROYCE MORGAN came out of the Army in 1945 expecting soon to be the twelfth president of Wellford College. That is to say, since the war had finally and decisively blunted his faith in the educability of the human species, he was finally ready to accept the career of an educator.

The presidency had been offered to him once before, in 1940, when his father died. Harvey Pelham Morgan had occupied the office entertainingly for more than thirty-five years. The name of Morgan had become so substantially identified with the College that in the following decade half the people who had heard of Wellford would probably have said that some Morgan or other was *still* president there. The other half presumably supposed it had been raised out of virgin prairie in six days by that boyish father figure, Winfred Mooney, in the boom times after the war.

In 1940 Royce had been just twenty-nine years old. He could have stepped into office at Wellford like the heir apparent in some untroubled constitutional monarchy. That he couldn't make up his mind to take the job then may have indicated sheer mental laziness. He liked to "square things" in his mind before he took decisive action, and waiting for the human situation to square is a luxury hard to distinguish from sloth.

There were, of course, reasons that argued against his return to the home town. But probably the very ease of carrying on in his father's name and position was his chief motive for refusing the offer made at that time.

He felt that his father would have disapproved of his return to

Wellford, particularly if the move were to be permanent. Old Morgan had gone from Roosevelt to Roosevelt relentlessly preaching the strenuous life. Annually he amused auditoriums full of captive underclassmen by admonishing them to "leap from your seats and contend for your lives." With glittering blue eyes and a mustache like the flexed bow of an Indian hero, the old fellow used to set on students gawping about the campus and admonish them to read the lesson of harmonious strife spread out even on the campus green. "See those pines, boys? Those branches that seem to droop look to me like the barbs of an arrow not merely pointed, mind you, but *aimed* straight up. I've been here long enough to watch that tree *fight* its way winter and summer up to that grand height."

On his deathbed the old man was reading Wittgenstein and, marvelous to say, was finding the admonition to struggle among even these positivistic aphorisms—though he felt that the Viennese ideas were "just what Democritus said" on the Aegean long ago.

Royce had never been among those Wellford undergraduates sermonized from Whitman and T.R. by his father. He had gone to prep school and college at places which would count more heavily in an educator's career. (Neither he nor his father had ever seriously questioned what Royce's profession was to be—once he got things squared away and settled down to it. He was groomed, simply, to become the next generation's Robert Maynard Hutchins.)

He was raised in a great faith and, as a matter of fact, rather overprepared for the responsibilities of an educator. Named for Josiah Royce, whom his father had idolized in his student days at Harvard, Royce's inheritance of pragmatism topped off in the view that the least pragmatic course in the world is to waste one's own life. If it was taking him longer than most young men to find out who he was and get the full inventory of his personal resources, that might be because he had more of them to count. And he understood that those resources were not altogether his own to waste. His Grandfather Blackburn had been a famous conservationist; Royce took personally some of his aphorisms about a man's stewardship of the bounties temporarily entrusted to him.

So his modesty came to consist chiefly in a certain impersonality toward himself—as if, he thought wryly sometimes, he were a prize cow put in his own charge for feed and raising, though owned by the world at large.

He took it as natural that other people should define him—himself a fact of nature, their definitions natural laws more or less approximating the truth even when in apparent contradiction. He well remembered having been told that Deirdre Prentice said of him in his boyhood, "All Royce Morgan needs is time." That was a doting comment. Its implication was that all the qualities of a good, even a great, man were already present and proportioned in his character, waiting only the proper test from the world to harden them and show them off. When his wife said, "All you needed was to be exempt from time," there was apparently an equal approximation of the truth in her remark, though it was made much later than Deirdre's and was in no way doting. She said this in one of her queer moments of clairvoyance, when she seemed resigned to the failure of their marriage—its failure, at least, to be an adequate vehicle for her love.

When others, like Deirdre or his wife, defined him thus, he did not so much try to live up to their definitions as strain to see how well they showed him to himself, as if that self were always inscrutable to him, more so than to them; and his expression was habitually marked by that smiling gravity of one who waits for the disclosure of what should not be mysterious at all—the quizzical expression of great men before their turn in history comes round. It was an expression faintly comic in his adolescence and again in his later years. Nevertheless it was very impressive, like a mark of inborn authority. People tended to quiet down near him, as if they were listening with him to whatever he was trying to hear.

In return for this natural deference, he conceived himself ultimately their servant. He was a carrier on whose back they could load their most precious burdens. A pack mule, a trustee, a guardian —it never mattered to him much what he might be called. And when he was a young fellow, it never occurred to him in his good humor to doubt that the world—ah! the universe itself—would be hungry to swallow the goodies he brought in his educational pack.

Before the war he simply believed in the manifest destiny of the human spirit to overspread the universe like butter on a hotcake.

Of course it was the luck of having been born in Buchanan, Illinois, that conditioned him to this optimism. The luck of his parentage, his friends, his wonderful girl who, without too much anguish, became his wonderful mistress—that incredibly generous (but, alas, almost featureless) sexual cornucopia from which his future seemed to pour as from an overturned grail. "I loved her mindlessly," he said, straining to listen, as if he expected the universe to approve or disapprove this characterization. Good or bad? Well, good or bad, it turned out to be less than eternal. His love piled up on the shoals of his mind like a boat hitting a reef.

Everything he began with—optimism also—turned out to be too good to be true. So did he. The time came in his good-natured bounty when he had to leave Buchanan to find out whether his optimism might be the one thing needed in more misanthropic centers of culture.

Jilting his wonderful girl, Carole Prentice, was a practical and symbolic way for him to say goodbye to the home town. When thinking set in—as it had to for someone so expensively educated—it became plain to him that Carole would be exactly the wife he needed if he were to follow a path of lesser resistance, doing what his father had done instead of what his father admonished. Carole was the ideal wife for the president of little Wellford College, and he was obliged to be something more than that.

So, at his convenience, not Carole's, he turned her into a pillar of salt and left her looking back at a girlhood totally formed by her expectation of someday marrying him, and therefore useless to her as preparation for anything else.

He had none of the good excuses—none good enough for *her* to go on living by; that was the crux of it—for jilting her. He had not become restless, tired of her, or uncomfortable with her. Just the opposite. She had always quieted him and made him content. She still did. That was the threat he was fleeing, a life too comfortable to force an examination.

12

But though he had thought his move over for a very long time and satisfied himself of its necessity, he had to live afterward with the guilt of presenting his decision to her without warning. As a matter of fact, they had just finished a thrilling, habitual, and mutually satisfying intercourse in a Chicago hotel when he told her that this time when he went back to teach his popular course in American History at Columbia it might be "better" if they stopped writing and made no more plans to see each other.

She wasn't even quite surprised by his announcement. (As a pet lamb used to the hand fondling the curls at its throat would not have time to be surprised at the blade drawn lovingly across its jugular and the stunning spill of blood emptying its brain—so *he* would think of his act later at bad times.) She had no practice in being surprised by anything Royce told her. She was so used to taking what he said as a normal, sensible explanation of holy writ— merely something she hadn't learned *yet,* just as she hadn't learned yet how the capitalist system worked, though her aunt Deirdre had more money than anyone in Buchanan.

She merely lay there, full of his semen, grateful for the many privileges life had given her so far, and tried to sympathize with his wish to be rid of her.

She didn't argue or shriek. She said, "I suppose I'll understand where we went wrong better when I get some, goddamn it, perspective on it." In the lonely, on-dragging time of the rest of her life. She said, "I've always taken things too easy, without *examining* my rights. It's true. I'm such a farmer, really." She said, "I might have called it off if you hadn't, darling. I've seen we weren't quite *right.*"

To which he replied, "No, no, no," because he had made up his mind to take on his own back all the guilt of this parting—and still supposed he could.

She hardly cried in that room. But at one point she asked, "Is there someone else?" Then the mere baldness of this question seemed insulting to the person she loved so respectfully, so she quickly added, "I'm sure you've thought everything out and there isn't anything I could say you haven't already taken into account. But it would be easier for me to know. Have you met someone in New York you're in love with?"

He deliberately answered "No" because it would have misrepresented his larger motives to say "Yes." He wanted to be free of her because he was afraid of the sloth to which even the shockingly recent delights of the bed lured him. He was a big, strong young man and it always troubled him to lie in such well-padded delight while others, weaker than he, were on their feet taking the dead cats the world threw in their faces.

He wanted to be free because—like any bad young lecher, which he was not—he had already had her. The grotesque (and in his memory forever shameful) circumstances of this farewell were an appropriate miniature reproduction of their whole premarital exhaustion of the novelties marriage might have given—might have given if they had met in their early twenties instead of in kindergarten. There were no mysteries in Carole. The hymen, after all, defends most of the mysteries a girl of average mentality has for a young intellectual.

He supposed he knew what she would look like at forty or fifty as the wife of the hollow administrative type he hoped not to become. She would almost certainly still look nice then, very stately, clean, and genial, still firm and athletic. After college, while she was waiting around Buchanan for him to come and claim her formally, she had learned to fly. She would still be flying sport planes and smiling shyly like Amelia Earhart, smiling on everybody, as if humbly convinced they deserved her smile merely because they were not so lucky as she.

He knew that in thirty years the cast of her mind would still be charitable. As charitable to the well-meaning and tawdry as to the excellent and hard-won and beautiful. From her idealistic Aunt Deirdre—or from life itself? from privilege and health?—she had learned that tolerance was the greatest of virtues. And though Royce knew better, he dared not imagine teaching her anything else.

No doubt she matched and represented his better self. Even so, his better self had no future except to resist change as well as it could. He had heard the drummer of change. He believed in it then. He couldn't stay.

"Then you've got to love me one more time," she said in their Chicago hotel room. "Love me." Her voice was a heartbroken imperative. It was the only time he would remember when she had asked something for herself from a relationship in which she had been charitable so long.

He had said No, there was no other woman because that seemed to be the part of the truth he owed Carole. As a woman she would have seen another woman as the most important factor in his departure, whereas Priscilla London truly seemed to him more like a symptom of the times and mysteries with which he meant to engage. When he married her in the year after he deserted Carole, he rather supposed that he was marrying the glamour and terror of intellectual restlessness. Priss was an artist who thus far had expressed her anguish in a half-dozen media and, if not personally neurotic, was a fair personification of the urban neurosis that scared the Midwesterner in Royce.

"But, darling," Priss had said in those days, "women aren't as representative as you pretend. They're *fesse et tetons* and this and that, and for a big, voracious lug like you, that's almost more than you can bear."

"Since A. Lincoln died, no one likes candy more than Royce Morgan," he admitted. He was intellectually rather proud of his sensuous indulgences. Amid all the guilt he felt at ditching Carole, he had never admitted any guilt for having so many times enjoyed her voluptuously. The guilt was more abstract than that.

Priss said, "You'll go in over your depth if you try to make women *stand* for something. Though me, I'll stand for anything. Try it."

He had told her about Carole and himself—not everything, for one never tells everything; the tonality of sense and grief is simply not to be reproduced, though much of the attachment of lovers depends on its intensity—and she said, "I honestly can't grasp why you think Carole's simple and I'm complex. I may seem like some kind of bohemian to you, but no one seduced *me* when I was fourteen, and when I did get it, I took it pretty casual. She's deep, that girl."

"Fourteen," he mused. "But she was starting high school. . . ."

Priss began to laugh as she liked to laugh at his best deadpan jokes.

"I mean that kind of thing was *done* in my time in Buchanan. *Ça se faisait à Paris.*"

"Pa-ree, Illinois," Priss choked.

"It's the Midwest that's deep," he said. "It's America's Middle Europe and no one knows what will come out of it."

"You!"

"Yes, if you want to see it that way. I'm deep. But Carole's not. She's just faithful. When someone is faithful to a person or a situation that's vanished or changed, they may seem complicated to you, but Carole's truly not."

"Then you really are," Priss said, wrapping him with honeymoon arms and legs and demanding the oblivion that the creature in passion is supposed to know. And of course—enough to satisfy her— he abandoned conscious memory of his farewell to Carole in this intense salute to his lawful future. But in forgetting the paradox he completed the form in which it would present itself to him when he, goddamn it, got some perspective on it: that enjoyment of the flesh is most a marriage when it is intended to be a farewell. Carole, who had never intended to trick him, had tricked him good in making him enter her body "one more time." Then poignancy had been welded to pleasure and nothing on earth can ever quite throw down that combination. He *might* be true elsewhere to other things. He would *have* to be true to that moment of marvelous contradiction.

So he would never be free of wondering how he had been able, how he had had the impudent recklessness before God, to choose between a woman who demanded so little for what she gave and one who—body, soul, and psyche—would always demand a little more than, at best, he had to give. He did not see fully from the beginning how Priss London would goad and spur him when he halted at a wall too high to jump or a ditch too wide to get over— not *fully,* but if ever a woman wore spurs to bed on her naked feet, it was Priss. And his first great intuition about her was of the supra-terrestrial, almost cosmic, scope of her neurosis. During the war, on transports or naval ships, he used to intuit the Pacific Ocean, how it swept its emptiness south from the tiny atolls toward the Indian Ocean and the South Polar waters, the globe's open back door to empty space. In this intuition of waters he would recognize Priss and smile as well as a man can at such a recognition.

He smiled at the choice he had made and never denied it was his own. And though he was never happy again as he had often been happy with Carole, he took the riddle of that choice as his guide. He consulted it as his oracle, and its first major service to him had been to tell him loud and clear he ought not become president at Wellford when his father died.

After his ill-explained refusal, he got an unbearably generous letter from Carole's aunt. Deirdre Prentice was chairman of the Wellford trustees then, still hale and confident in her late fifties. The offer had come from her in the first place. Now she was extending herself—with something of Carole's ill-fated tolerance—to cancel Royce's trivial scruples. She wrote:

If you have any suspicion, my dear Royce, that I am trying to bring you and Carole together again, will you do me the kindness to dismiss it? Whatever estrangement there has been between you two must not be allowed to intrude where the good of the College is concerned. I have heard—I am sorry it was a rumor that brought the news—that you have been married recently. Very well. I wish you all happiness. And you must understand that Carole would not wish, in any way, to complicate your new relationship were you to please us all by coming back where I do believe you want to come. I think you are one of ours and that you belong with us.

You would please an old woman who loves you if you could believe me utterly sincere in what I have just said. If I have overstepped the bounds in referring to a delicate personal matter when I should only have spoken of business, I hope I have the credit with you, as a very old friend, to ask your indulgence. I wanted to leave no stone unturned because of false conventionality.

The effect of the letter was to solidify his conviction that he should not go back to Buchanan again, even for a visit. And when he got Carole's wedding announcement a little later, he was troubled with the hunch that she was—a little belatedly, more in remorse that she had been in his way than for any practical result—getting herself out of the way so he might still come home as president.

Her husband was killed in Italy in 1944. News of this came to Royce on Saipan and he grunted a strange little laugh as if knowing that the poor husband was timely dismissed, having served his purpose. The issue of their lives was still strangely between Carole and himself, though they had married others. And he still felt that only the future accomplishments of the liberty he had asked of her could justify the disappointment he had given her. The accounts were not closed.

But there on Saipan, in combat where he was more observer (and rather more fatefully the observer) than participant, all the optimism he had brought with him so far dropped from its zenith. One day his feet tangled in the fresh guts of a Japanese soldier. As he sat on a green hillside later, eating with undiminished appetite from a mess kit that rested on his stained boots, it came to him with the immediacy of a revelation that none of the moral accounts of his life—or any life at all—were ever *going* to be squared. The account books, rather, were merely tossed away like garbage left floating behind a ship in convoy. The very intensity and good health of his faith in education made him accept its final proposition like a sign in the heavens: *Nothing counts.* He no longer believed in anything, except that life had been sufferable *so far.* Between morning and evening of an otherwise insignificant day his education delivered itself like a flash of lightning discharging a long-accumulated potential of energy.

On that day the Midwestern stagnation he had been escaping began to look like an oasis. He was educated enough to hear the great warning—"far enough." He wanted to go home.

By 1945 his belly was full of the dreams and lies of Washington (where in '41 and '42 he had helped form AMG units before he went

18

on active duty as a major in the Army) and the hysterical intellectual fashions of New York (where he had taught and studied for nearly seven years).

In his marriage he no longer saw a promise of intellectual challenge. He saw instead that his lovely, troubled wife needed very badly to get out of the rat race that had first made her glamorous to him. Their first son had been born in '41. For the boy, at least, there should be a certain time to frolic and run before his education, in its turn, showed where the flat world dropped off into the void. On the wide Buchanan verandas of Royce's boyhood there might still be a time of green innocence before education set in. It was for the boy Lot (whom he still hardly knew, whose temperament could hardly be guessed from the blending of such a mother and father) that the decision was made to go home.

For himself Royce might have preferred to go settle in the Dordogne, in one of the little towns near Albi that he and Priss had visited on their honeymoon. The impulse that makes hermits was on him. He might have followed it to make the life of a hermit scholar in France.

But along with the presidency supposedly waiting for him in Buchanan there was the house in which he had passed some good years as a boy. The good old house with an orchard behind it on the river bluffs and a nonconformist, gingerbreaded stable out in back had belonged to his three maiden aunts. The ladies were gone to California now and wanted him to have the house for his own, if he ever needed it. They would have hated to sell.

He remembered hot, thunderstorm-threatening afternoons on the great, vine-shaded porches of that house, the sprinklers turning on the lawns like girls wrapping themselves in silver capes under the twilight maples, and quite a menagerie of legends and Midwestern spooks that had once whispered to him in the halls and stairways of the old house. That, at least, he could secure for Lot, hand it over unchanged from the time of the father to the time of the son.

There were many obvious reasons why he ought now to give up his aborted pilgrimage and go home.

"But Carole . . ." Priss said, before Royce made any decisive move to take his family back to Wellford. "She was in that other country and the wench is not dead."

Not dead, but rather conveniently married again. This time she had married Navy and was "settled"—as the word from Buchanan had it—in Honolulu.

"But Carole . . ." Priss said obstinately.

"Women are not, as I recall being told, representative. Therefore she's no ghost," Royce said. The woman had been generous in requiring him to love her "one more time"—so it would not be forever. The uses of the flesh authorized the uses of other flesh, and beyond the abandoned flesh might hover the airs of sentiment, but they determined nothing.

"I never supposed that Carole counted," Priss said, "as Carole. All I had to worry about were your mad, self-inflicted Morgan scruples."

"Now that I'm over them, normal life can begin."

"And you're over them for good?" She seemed pleased to think he might be.

And he allowed that he was indeed. So they went back handily in the very teeth of the commandments that had sent him forth. The teeth were blunt. The old bear of conscience was blind and easy to trick, a tame old creature.

But Royce didn't go back as president. That would have to wait just a little. The name of Morgan was still fragrant in Buchanan in 1945. Deirdre Prentice was still eager for his return, still a grand matriarch of the town, and still on the Board of Trustees, but no longer chairman. Though the presidency was open again after two short wartime incumbencies, Royce could no longer expect the office by virtue of being the only son of Harvey P. Morgan. The trustees had voted to make no new appointments for the year ahead.

For that year Chancellor George Hand was in charge of the College. It was his advice and invitation that brought Royce back as an officer. He was confident that if Royce accepted, for one year, a post as dean of studies, thereafter a Morgan would once again occupy the mansion at the heart of the campus. It seemed as good as settled. But not yet settled.

So for that year Royce and his family lived in the big house where he had grown up among doting relatives. The small town made Priss nervous. Not intolerably. Lot, their son, took carelessly to the verandas, started Royce's life over again, as far as one could see. All well there.

As the year drifted, Royce shaped some tentative policies for the times to come and—aside from refurbishing old acquaintances with people who slightly sickened Priss—left the practical politicking to George Hand, as George advised that he should.

At last, later in life than some, Royce was building his house where the sand seemed solidest. He caught himself resembling (except for white mustache and fierce merriment) the huge portrait of his father that still hung in the president's mansion. The day-by-day routine of Buchanan left him unstirred in the complacency he had once dreaded worse than guilt. There seemed no question about the long run. He had time. It was measured, weighed, and now delivered to him.

Then, toward the end of the school year 1945-6, in May, the trustees met. Royce was left with the subtle embarrassment of finding that they preferred another man for president.

An "advertising man" at that.

2

THE NEWS CAME in successive waves, like an exclamatory, over-whelming headline followed by the smaller type of explanation and sentiment.

George Hand brought the headline to Royce's office just below the vacant presidential chambers in Arden Hall. George had lunched with the trustees at a hotel in downtown Buchanan. He got back to the campus grim, angry, and bewildered at three o'clock.

"I can not understand," he said, patting his billiard-ball skull with a handkerchief and thrusting his chin out like a mace threatening the legions of darkness. "I will have to blame myself for a failure of tactics, but I'm not yet in a position to see the flaw."

Lolling back in his swivel chair with his hands folded behind his head, enjoying a huge, lean cigar and enjoying almost more the fresh air of surprise that came with George's announcement, Royce smothered his impulse to laugh. George was taking the upset hard— and perhaps had more to lose from it than Royce himself . . . there-fore deserved solace.

"Why can't we simply blame the force of the opposition?" Royce wanted to know. He had been unhorsed. The thing to do was dust his pants and hobble as gracefully as possible off the field. He was not a man who took defeat very seriously, being disinclined to be-lieve that ostensible defeats or victories, either, had much to do with the fundamental course his life would take. He was big, young, strong, handsome, disenchanted, pampered from the inside out by good nature toward his mishaps, and fortunately too lazy to cry much over spilt milk or try to reshape the past by applying mental English.

But George lived in a world where the realities were primarily moral. Once he had purified his own intents in the crucible of conscience, "the opposition" became a synonym for error or wrong. As a Christian knight he must accept perpetual blame for any failure to overcome it. Besides, he had counted on being the *éminence grise* of Royce's administration, the fox that directed the lion's good-natured paw. It was almost as demoralizing to discover himself an outwitted fox as to be caught with wrong intents.

"I had a majority for you when the business meeting began," he said. "You led six to three, as I had expected. If I had pressed immediately for a vote I'd be here congratulating you now, instead of . . ."

Royce shook his head. "As long as Henry Worth had his mind made up that I was an unsuitable president there was little chance you could hold the majority, I suspect."

"Henry respects you," George said.

Now Royce did laugh aloud at the inadvertent contempt that sounded in that "respects." It was not Henry's contempt, of course. It was George's. For all his moral bias, George could not hold to belief in transcendental victories in the field of practical politics. A lifetime in college intrigues had not taught him any sufficient substitute for winning when the stakes were vital. It was distasteful now to find himself bracketed with a loser.

Royce said, "I'm sure Henry respects me. He's made that clear since I came back last fall. But he respected me more when I was a thousand miles away. The mere fact that I accepted a year of waiting would be sign enough for him that I lacked enterprise—even though that year was, as it was, his own idea—I no longer represent what Henry calls 'vision.' I'm not hot any more, as lesser gamblers would put it."

The analysis piqued George for a minute. "We should have kept you in the wings," he agreed. "If you had taken the offer Reed College made you . . ." He shook his neo-Socratic head and went on darkly, "Henry is a gambler who rose with the times. If there had been no war, Henry would still be a junk-dealer."

Royce smiled at the exaggeration. One smile was as bad as another to George in his fit. "A junk-dealer with his left hand up to the elbow in politics and gangsterism," he cried in pain. His splendidly geared mind often immobilized on fixed ideas, and there could hardly be a more characteristic example than this of stubborn conservatism. What he said now of Henry Worth might have been near the truth ten years before. Recently Henry had shown the only signs of reputable genius that Buchanan could point to in its whole history.

Buchanan had had its other indisputable genius in the person of a Hoosier Sicilian named Datento. In the twenties Datento had made the city a thriving capital of vice and dope. A man rather more far-sighted than his contemporaries, who had founded their empires on alcohol, Datento had seen that the rural millions of the republic were as potentially corruptible as packed city dwellers, that every county seat burned with ambitions for depravity no less exploitable than those of big cities. He had not lived long enough to profit fully from his vision, being dynamited by Chicagoans who, it was said, were afraid that legitimate commerce would follow illegitimate, like traders following missionaries, and therefore feared that Buchanan, a hundred miles away, might become hog-butcher and wheat-stacker to the world unless Datento's enterprise was halted.

Two decades later Henry Worth—not quite raising Buchanan to the rank of competitor with Chicago—had nevertheless made this city, a thousand miles from salt water, a major shipbuilding center. When America was the arsenal of democracy, the junk which he had bought and sold as a young man was replaced by new steel plate from the rolling mills in Gary and Granite City.

Landing craft by the dozens and finally by the hundreds were fabricated in the Worth yards. The hulls made in Buchanan were towed down river, stopping at a dozen points on their way to New Orleans for further installations and fitting, so that the entire Mississippi Valley became an assembly line disgorging these ugly, efficient fleets into the Gulf.

Now that the war was over, the shipyards were being dismantled. Every week of the past year Royce had counted fewer cranes along the riverbank opposite his house. The steel mesh fences enclosed acres of weeds now, where not so long ago welders, cutters, engineers, crane men, and the brute labor hired off the farms of six counties had done their civilian duty. No one supposed Henry was out of business. He would contribute to the new peace as he had contributed to the war, but until he found what new weapons were needed he had all too much managerial gusto for Wellford College affairs. It must have been within the last three weeks that he had found time to scout the country for a president more vital than Royce appeared. Three weeks ago he had expressed no opposition to Royce's candidacy.

"My last hope went when Deirdre Prentice switched," George said. Even three days ago Deirdre had been absolutely committed.

"At the pinch, Deirdre only wanted to be assured that our new president was not a Catholic, with a name like Mooney," George said. "*I* could have assured her that since we were being so reckless as to choose an *advertising man* to lead the college, we could count on his being whatever the circumstances required—Protestant, Catholic, Jew, Mussulman, Confucian, or all of them, depending on the day of the week. Henry said that he believed Mr. Mooney was indeed baptized a Catholic but had been for many years apostate. Was a nonpracticing Christian who would not be embarrassed, at any rate, to take the name of our Lord in his mouth when ceremonial occasions required. That satisfied her! Holy mother! That satisfied her!"

It did not seem to Royce that any such trivial assurance had been decisive with the old lady. Already, in dim outline—as if from conclusive experience with how tediously few possibilities there are for human motive—he was guessing what sufficient reason Deirdre had used at last for pulling the rug out from under him. She had not meant to lead him on—as once he led her trusting niece—but finding him so far led, so temptingly under the deadfall. . . . Often enough in the past winter he had wondered if Deirdre were not creeping into senility, reverting to a girlishness where mere prank and vengeance would exert an overwhelming temptation.

But such probabilities were not to be discussed with George, who liked to keep the apples and the oranges of life in neatly separated groups. So Royce merely said with a fake, comfortable air of impartiality, "Henry wouldn't have picked a fool, George, and I think it's unfair to judge Mr. Mooney through the peepholes of our disappointment. Particularly since we're going to have to work with him."

Surprise flared on George's face like a kindling match. "Royce, you're not planning to stay?" All year George had been whispering where it counted that Royce had had offers of deanships at major universities (which was true enough, discounting the plural) and presidencies of reputable colleges (again true, though an exaggeration that neglected to state that all these colleges were either intensely sectarian, Southern and segregated, or forbiddingly isolated from direct air or surface transportation to New York City, all or any of which characteristics made them unacceptable to Mrs. Royce Morgan, Priss). Whatever the degree of his exaggerations had been, it appeared that further discredit would rebound on George if Royce were not to fly on eagle's wings right out of this benighted and provincial Buchanan.

"I was only thinking of the year coming up," Royce said. Actually he had made no such clear specifications in his own mind yet. He was only marveling how much his relief at not becoming Wellford's president resembled that revelation on Saipan when he discovered the vanity of all human endeavor. And it was tempting to wonder if he had not, after all, come home to Wellford just exactly so this further humiliation could excuse him from the hard responsibilities that had once seemed his mortal duty. He had been a serious man, and such men recoil seriously when the game is revealed to be fixed. Deirdre Prentice was not the only one who might be loping back toward the irresponsibility of childhood. "We're still trying to get our bearings, the family and I," he said, a little irritated at having to form any explanation for the great impulse to relax that possessed him almost erotically. "It's too late to make a move for next year."

"I'll greet Mr. Mooney with my resignation," George said, absolutely in earnest. And God knew he would be in exile if he left Wellford now. For the last twenty years he had made most of the

general policies and the multitudinous daily rulings that gave Wellford its character, leaving to Royce's father and his two short-lived
successors the formalities that they might handle with whatever
grace they could. During much of the time that Morgan senior had
set the tone, George directed the tune.

And through all those years of George's management, Wellford
had been too small and too poor to strike out with any bravery. It
was respected throughout the Midwest somewhat beyond its deserts
—probably because of the Morgan tone, that never admitted defi-
ciencies as long as the spirit was right. The least of George's hopes
had been that it might get up sometime to the level of its reputation. Now, like every other college in the country, it could foresee
expansion and opportunity for change. Enrollment was already up
twenty-five percent from the prewar years. Another fifty percent in-
crease was expected in the fall.

It was to this opportunity that George had directed his strategy.
Counting on Royce to be at least as tractable as his father, he saw
the chance to make a great college. With Royce he had agreed to cut
the deadwood from the key departments. They had gone so far as
to form a shadow faculty of men ready to come when there was
room for them.

Now—exactly because that opportunity existed—it had been
snatched away from George by an industrialist who recognized it
just as clearly and by an old woman who had suppressed her spite
too long.

Gamely he said, "I suppose if you can find it in your heart to stay,
this might not be the last chance for the presidency. I can't imagine
that Mooney, this *Mooney,* will remain long."

For a minute visions of mischief made him blush as he recalled
how he had dealt with the last two presidents to keep the opening
ready for Royce when he came home from the wars. Alistair Parker
had lasted four lean years before he went back to teaching economics
at UCLA. Jonas Leed was "fired by Henry Worth"—in the blunt
phrase of those who understood neither the niceties of academic
parlance or the elaborate snares to be rigged out of academic wire—
after less than a year in office. Of course Leed had been set up like

a duck when George found him unsuitable. Henry had been little more than executioner. There were still strings for strangling in George's fingers, and Mooney might do well to keep some spot in the advertising game to fall back on.

But considering this defeat a postponement was no longer consolation enough. Royce might be young enough to wait. George was not. He was solemnly convinced that the next two or three years would stamp Wellford for the next twenty. Suppose "this Mooney" remained only two years or three (and short of literal assassination they could hardly expect to dispose of him in less time). The great chance of George's lifetime would be gone beyond retrieving. This election had been, for him, decisive.

"You may stay, but I'm resigning," he said, for just a moment failing to cloak his despair in anger.

"No, you won't," Royce said. It was rude to be so clairvoyant, and he did not mean to be rude. But he saw no point in prolonging this moment of transition. As if they sat on a big turntable he saw their relationship swinging around, inevitably altered by the new perspective. George had wanted him for a stalking horse. No more. Now George would begin to resent that the horse had not been moved with enough personal ambition to deliver some kicks in its own behalf. Royce had the name, the youth, the preparation, the advantage of an inside track, and he had failed. For the rest of his life George would have to blame this man as men blame the convenient tokens that accompany bad luck, merely slipping farther from charity in their knowledge that the blame goes wide of the mark, but unable nevertheless to refuse the relief of anger.

While Royce—in all the years he was, after all, going to remain at Wellford—would have whatever blessing comes with knowing, point by point and link by link, all the detail that explained this present defeat. At last he would think he saw how all the disasters of prosperity about to rain down on them were merely transmitted through this present like water through a garden hose, sprung from some source a long way off, prepared beyond memory, fated and necessary, even though the imagination balks at attributing to fate so much trivia and all the silliness that day after day brings forth.

It was, all of it, not merely explicable, but to be explained, now that Wellford had pinned his shoulders again and had him flat where he must listen whether he wanted to or not.

So perhaps even when his lazy heart was congratulating him on missing the election, he already foresaw what was still to be exacted of him and prophesied for himself as well as George when he said, "I think you'll stay and do your best."

"Oh, *that*," George said with unguarded disdain. The best they could now expect opportunity for was the second best of their wish and need. Both of them knew that.

3

AFTER GEORGE BROUGHT the headline fact, Carole Prentice Ogilvie Slater came with the sad story—the human side, so to speak, of the news that Royce Morgan was not to be president.

Royce was at home justifying the ways of the trustees to wife and child in their respective, ambivalent states of shock. Priss was not sure yet whether she ought to sigh or shout, laugh or go blind. Whatever Buchanan, Illinois, had failed to provide her, it had always thus far provided the expected. Now this. The shock opened vistas of excitement. Perhaps now they could go east again, where Priss felt that she belonged. She wasn't happy at belonging east of the Hudson River, but it was one of the stiffeners of her soul. All her life the Midwest had seemed "funny" to her (Royce had seemed funny, too; sometimes in his very simplicity he was as exotic as an Islander and she had reflected that if she had not married him she might very well have married a Negro or a queer)—but a few months in Buchanan had convinced her it wasn't *even* funny. It was just less of everything she was used to, except space. Of course it was comfortable—this good old house that had belonged to Royce's family a long time, the many townspeople who took her for granted as Royce Morgan's wife without much concern for her talents or shortcomings. But she set a low value on comfort. It was Royce, not she, who had gone to the edge of the world at Saipan, looked down and hurried home to be comfortable. Somehow she was jealous of him for having looked at the void or the monsters or the horror or whatever it was he had seen. If he had seen it, it was her right to see too, and she didn't suppose this Midwest would ever let her look on emptiness or pure despair. It would find a way to swaddle her with cradle-to-grave security. So she brightened at the new likelihood of leaving this dullest of Edens.

"All I regret is overestimating Henry Worth," she said. She recalled a party of the spring where that crop-headed tycoon had been more than necessarily attentive to her, had seemed the one man among those she called derisively the "Buchanan chivalry" who had been away often enough to know what style was. She had talked to him about contemporary music and, though he didn't know Copland from Gershwin, he knew how to listen to a bright woman with the right perfume on her earlobes. "You romanticized him for me," she accused Royce, "with all your talk about business as a legitimate field for the imagination, and when it comes right down to it he's just a spear-carrier in Veblen's great American opera."

"George called him a junk-dealer," Royce said mildly. As the accused should, he was standing before wife and son in the afternoon dimness of their cool living room, separated from the handsome Victorian couch on which they sat by a tall martini pitcher, glittering in the modulated airs of a Buchanan May like some symbolic arc of justice.

Of course *he* was not on trial before them. They were merely court-martialing a titular husband and father who had muddled them into an embarrassment with tribes he had pretended to understand.

Lot, who kept munching steadily on olives and crackers, seemed rapt in silent amusement that once again his oversized father was caught short and forced to defend himself against the mere intensity of his mother's emotion. He squinted with pleasure every time she called someone a name. He laughed aloud at the idea of Henry Worth as a junk-dealer—as if he somehow believed that Mother and Father could make people be whatever they called them.

"I can't get over the comedy of their electing an advertising man," Priss said. "So Henry Worth wants to expand the College? They'll make a business of it and it will hum! Imagine the promotion. 'Two pants with every B.A.' 'Tuition *from* nine hundred dollars.' 'Learn now, study later.'"

"Mr. Mooney has done college promotional work," Royce said softly. He was strongly conscious of Priss's stare at his face and at the moment rather pitied her for forgetting that his face never showed anything. As he often did, he was submitting the overt man for her to blood herself on, pinch, pummel, bite, and scratch—figuratively speaking—while from within he watched with caution lest she break her nails or teeth. "I believe he's just recently launched a syndicated column about educational problems."

"Mooney!" Lot said, helping himself to more crackers and chuckling as if the name itself were a sufficient disgrace to satisfy his mother's requirement for revenge. He was persuaded, completely against the grain of her liberal precepts, that she was a witch whom no one dared seriously cross.

"Why does he want to give that up?" Priss demanded brutally. For a minute she found her peace in the thought that the impostor was giving up the delights of Manhattan to serve far from the light. But she was not, after all, the queen or witch Lot took her to be, and she needed something substantial to repay her for the loss of something she had not much wanted.

"You say George expects to get him? To . . . ?" Her long red fingernails worked busily on the stem of her martini glass. At thirty, Priss was an exceptionally handsome woman, without the faintest trace of what Buchanan valued as naturalness. Even the beauty of her skin—which she never made up heavily—and of her lean, fine breasts, too firm to require support, had the qualities of an artifice, had something that distinguishes overbred animals from mutts well loved by the popular heart, as if breeding were somehow a less legitimate tampering with nature than rouge or trick brassieres. And her narrow, painted nails were like metallic extensions of the mechanism within. "It might be worth staying to see."

"George won't."

"You said he was mad enough."

"That's exactly it," Royce said. "The anger won't last, because anger doesn't. He'll stay because he has the habit of marriage to Wellford, the way a certain kind of husband could never consider divorce however impossible the situation."

"Like you. A certain kind of husband like you."

Royce followed the brisk sidestep in her thoughts, but blinked to pretend that he did not. The pretense was useless.

"You'd never leave me no matter how much I deserved it," Priss muttered gloomily.

"Well . . ." No answer could be right. He was wise enough not to give one.

"And that's insulting. It devalues all my efforts to be a good little wife. Why should I accept dirt like this from the trustees knowing you'd be just as faithful if I got on the phone and called them turds?"

"I promise to leave you when you falter," Royce said. "Only it would be better to stay off the phone."

"Oh, I won't say a word. They'll get no satisfaction from me." Her warrior eyes said they could still expect trouble. "One might stay to help George with the Judas bit. I'd do my part. We'll have a year to tie old Mooney in knots and throw him back. Really, Royce, I'm not a rebel but I'm a born subversive. What I can't stand is that your father held on for fifty years to make something of Wellford and you let an advertising man come along and turn it into a business without lifting a finger."

There were many things that Priss couldn't stand, but this naming of a single flaw in the otherwise unassailable universe gave her the rare force of simplicity. Like George Hand earlier in the afternoon she seemed to be operating on a higher moral plane than Royce could scramble to. Plainly he was to be left the scullery work of dealing with practicalities. Plainly it was no longer his privilege to remind Priss of winter nights in Buchanan when she had felt—not only felt but made her feelings articulate—that she had been innocently condemned to Siberia. Expelled, she was now at liberty to declare Buchanan her happiness and one desire.

Royce said, "If we—you—can bring him down in a single year that would be just sweet. But I have a hunch he's coming to stay, and as of next week, or soon, I'll let my friends know that I'm job-hunting."

"It's good for me," Lot objected. He meant that Buchanan and the house where his father had been a child were almost essential to his character development, and in this view he was merely re-peating the arguments that had persuaded him out of New York at only four. He still inhabited this house as uneasily as a penguin ad-justing to a Florida zoo. Until very lately the mere size of their yard had produced symptoms of agoraphobia in him and he saved money in a piggy bank to get back to Washington Square. But plainly he understood that his mother was onto a good trick for sweating the old man and he followed her lead with love.

"What's good for you is to stop soaking your olives in my martini," his mother told him. "What am I? Some sort of corrupter to the Morgan men? If your daddy says we're leaving Buchanan . . ."

"You will sacrifice yourselves and follow," Royce said.

"*That* could be borne, but I'd like to quit when I'm at least even with the game," Priss lamented. "Bad enough I've got stretch marks from Lot, now I'll bear the marks of provincial hypocrisy to my dying day. Deirdre Prentice. *That* Deirdre . . . ! All winter she's fondled you. . . ."

"Not quite literally."

"As if you were still some royal little boy! It's sickened me, and now to find out all the time she hated you for rooning her niece."

"I'm not obliged to believe that was her motive."

"So she goes to the meeting and blithely stabs you."

"In the ass," Lot said with a bray of precocious merriment. His voice was a pure explosion of excitement, of participation in a dance of feeling. Nevertheless, while he shone with glee, two odd vertical lines appeared in his forehead like lines of pain.

"Lot!" his mother said with that indulgent horror native to women whose character it is to be mothers of only sons. "Lot, you ape."

"Blithe!" Royce said. He put his forefingers to his brow as if he expected to find lines like Lot's there and to erase them if he could. "You misunderstand Deirdre totally if you suppose she did this blithely. You can be sure she prayed over it."

Then for the first time in a great many years his face showed what he truly felt. He had just seen a ghost. He really saw her.

Carole Prentice was at their screen door. Had she been there long enough to hear herself characterized as "rooned"? Perhaps. Perhaps not. Anyway her face was a mask of submission to time's all-ruinous caprices and to any low characterization the Morgans chose to give her. She stood arrested in soft focus past the gleaming mesh with her hand upraised to knock, more humiliated that they would know she had overheard, even, than by what had been said.

Frozen there, unable momentarily either to run or knock, she was accomplishing exactly what a ghost would accomplish, a ghost come winging home from two disastrous marriages to show herself in a crucial disequilibrium of time where a major decision would be made by overwhelming trivialities.

What she had come to say was important enough to her. The unhappy timing of her arrival was too much. She might have been equal to apologizing for her aunt's defection from the grand old Morgan cause. If she had come even an hour later, the likely decision for Priss and Royce to leave Buchanan might already have been taken. Her appearance—its unmistakable ghostliness—settled Priss's determination to stay in Buchanan. To stay not merely until "this Mooney" was subverted out of the presidency, but until the ghost of times she never shared was finally expelled from Royce's cagey heart. Click. The future was determined.

"Come in. Ah, Carole, come in," Royce begged.

They had to revive her with gin before she could say much. She was sweating and glowing beet red from the impossible contradictions of her presence with them. (Priss would say later, "She came like a girl who means to claim the hymen she lost wasn't hers.") She gulped two ice-cold martinis like spring water, smiling and silently waving her hands. Her eyebrows rose and fell as if in a cartoon of some creature breathing its last. She alternately blushed and whitened and shook her head as if *now* only gestures could be trusted for honest communication. Her eyes widened like a scared fawn's while Royce introduced her to wife and son, and though she said she was delighted, just delighted, to see them, it was clear

35

that the one thing that might have made her mission tolerable was to have found Royce alone. ("Since she plainly wanted to take your head in her oversized lap and let you cry it out," Priss said.)

The Morgans knew, of course, that Carole was here to say that, yes, her Aunt Deirdre had betrayed Royce by a senile and vengeful whim. Since, yes, this vengeance had probably been taken in Carole's name, Carole wanted desperately to repudiate it. Presently they would begin to talk to the point. With Royce's help they would find words to make the dilemma bland. With words any escape is possible. Until they came, the dilemma was being celebrated—danced, you might say—by Carole's twisting between its horns.

She couldn't say she was sorry without making things worse by declaring just what she was sorry for. So she literally writhed while she took on alcohol. The writhing was, to Priss's swiftly judging eye, indistinguishable from the bumps and grinds of a belly dancer. It was clear to her that Carole's moral distress—projecting and attracting a veritably buzzing swarm of sympathies to and from *both* Morgan males, most likely—was the sublimated equivalent of a bitch in heat. However spiritual and abstract Carole's effluvium might be, its action on a damned Morgan was predictably erotic. And Priss understood finally what Royce's descriptions of his childhood sweetheart had nicely obscured.

Alas, her female eye saw profusion in Carole where in herself she saw only the ideal female average, a specimen cornstalk against a bursting granary. She saw Carole's brassiere and girdle strained like spinnakers filled with the south wind. It did no good to remember that Royce conceived his guilt against this woman in literary, metaphysical terms. Any red-necked hired hand would have seen the terms were insufficient. And it did no good to suppose maliciously that without the cunning straps and stitching of the brassiere those grand breasts might fall to the zodiac of Carole's navel, since, for one thing, the navel they would fall to was no doubt exactly like a heap of Illinois wheat surrounded by Biblical lilies. And for another thing, sixteen years ago, when Royce first saw and nibbled them, they had certainly not been fallen at all.

The neck that flushed and paled was a superb column. If Carole's short haircut was unbecoming—as it was indeed—and her suit was all wrong, the faults merely emphasized the grandeur good tailoring and hair styling could so easily bring out. No ghost had ever before come calling with such rosy, plump calves under generously dimpled knees. Lot was staring at them thoughtfully as he took very tiny nibbles from his new olive. The lines were deeply etched in his young forehead.

Him too, Priss raged to herself. He'll fall into the love his daddy left gaping open like a grave in the April rain. She was all too clairvoyant before a tableau like this. The moment was on her when she saw the inescapable design of her life like the stylized scene on an urn. It was a design of love, but love forever inappropriate and never fair.

Nothing fitted. Not in what she saw that day and never forgot. She loved Royce for being big and handsome, physically extravagant and physically mysterious, while he loved her for the riddles of her envious heart, or for the answers riddles ought to have but damn well often don't. And—just to perpetuate the failure of symmetry on this particular urn—Carole, who ought to have loved him as Priss did, for the pure joy of taking a grand physique between her knees, loved him for being pure enough in spirit to be the ideal leader of Wellford College.

The three of them should never had got in a room together, let alone into an antique design. The centrifugal force of ring-around-the-rosy was already building up excruciatingly.

"I've just had it out with Deirdre," Carole said at last. She wasn't going to fail the duty that had brought her here, not any part of it.

"But, goodness," Royce said. "Goodness, we had no idea you were even back in Buchanan." He was not unwary. He was edging back from the quicksand of emotion. "Great. It's so great to see you. Changed, but not much."

"I've heard so much about you," Priss said, rolling her eyes and calling on unseen witnesses to forgive her for this parody of understatement. Yet she was smiling and solicitous, too. It was her gift to mingle tones bewilderingly.

Piteously Carole asked them to believe that mere *hours* ago

Deirdre had conscientiously meant to vote for Royce. Carole had driven her to the hotel for the trustee meeting and one of the last things Deirdre said before she left the car was, "We'll have to have the Morgans over for a private little celebration when it's settled."

She accepted one more martini and composed herself with an effort so transparent it was worse than abandonment. "The very worst thing . . ." (She must have meant about Deirdre's misplaced vote.) "The worst thing is that Deirdre is going to die. She has cancer of the throat. She's been hoarse and coughing."

Royce made a little sound of compassion. Lot suddenly sat up straight and listened keenly for what would come next. Priss stared.

One of Carole's hands flopped up from the majestic curves of her lap and fell again in the hopelessness of trying to order her account of the catastrophic disorder she must somehow report. Then she turned to Priss, as if to a stranger she might summarize what it was impossible to give fully to Royce. "You see, Deirdre, my aunt, who was like a mother to me, was never in any formal way at all part of the College. She was—I suppose you'd call it—a friend of Royce's father. He shaped her ideas. Deirdre was always a good woman. . . . Wasn't she, Royce?"

"Good," he said.

"But all the things that were . . . *higher*—is that the word, Royce? Well, *higher*, she got from him."

"Or brought to him. Devoted to him," Royce said. He was stricken by the prospect of the old woman's death. He wished, as his habit was, propriety and quiet for her now in her time of dying. He was beginning to guess that the gist of Carole's report would be the depiction of a troublesome impropriety and chaos in his old friend's mind.

"Who's dead?" Lot asked.

"Nobody. Hush," his mother said and put her arm around his small shoulders as if he were the one among them who most needed protection.

Carole said to Priss, "Well, she knew that Royce would carry on the sort of things his father did, would have the same ideas about the College. She came home very tired from the meeting, and one of the things she said first was, 'Well, I'd better change my will. I'm not going to be buried in the circle of friends.' You know. She was wild. But she said it so calmly."

Royce's father had provided a special circle to be set aside on a knoll in the Presbyterian Cemetery. It was a very old agreement that someday the fine, thin bones of Deirdre Prentice would lie near those of Royce's mother; of Dr. Gottfried Paulus, the least militant socialist who ever fled the Kaiser's tyranny, the least dogmatic Hegelian the world of philosophy ever knew; of Herman and Marie St. John, who were Royce's godparents; of Vivian Jennings, whose husband still muddled the affairs of the English Department; of Helen Stack, who died young with her talents as a composer still unheralded by anyone except Harvey Pelham Morgan and those he could browbeat; of Genevieve Duhamel and Elizabeth Carter. (More women there around the old man's grave than men. The darling old fraud would have it so.) Now Deirdre was counting herself out. She believed that she had deliberately excluded herself—consequently she must have acted with incredible passion in denying Royce.

"Well," Royce said, "we'll have to talk to her about that. Of course she has to see this doesn't . . . well, it doesn't go beyond her rational decision to vote as she saw fit." But of course it did. Nothing was plainer to all of them. So he inherited the duty of isolating it, trimming away the roots of connection if he could so an old woman might at least rest in peace. This was the first of the unquestionable duties that tied him to the stake in Wellford.

"Of course it doesn't," Priss said. "It seems so much more important to her than to us. Of course we'll be going somewhere else and this won't even hinder Royce's career. She mustn't change her plans."

"I wasn't easy with her," Carole said. "I told her what you just said. She wasn't hurting Royce. She was betraying herself."

And there—somewhat obliquely, but awkward and bold enough —was the truth, from one who ought to know. In the pinch Deirdre had *meant* to hurt Royce. Hereafter the old lady might be persuaded that she didn't *really* mean to, but the act that counted was now a matter of record here below and up in the lofty regions where Deirdre had chosen to mark her spite.

In those ministerial tones that presidents sometimes need, Royce said, "But the worst of it is . . ." He nodded to remind them that the worst thing was Deirdre's approaching death—and he reminded them of this because it would not do to think that the very postponement of her spite until she approached the end might be more ghastly than death itself. A specter had to be exorcised—that of an old woman wrestling lewdly with a simple but unseemly fear of going out before she had left her wound on good things she could not take with her.

He said, "That's why you're back, Carole?"

"No."

"No?" He should have known she would not come here to play the ghost unless she were driven to play it to the hilt. Quickly he braced himself for more shovels full of chaos.

"My husband was killed," she said. On her face was a look not so much of sorrow as of guilty embarrassment. Priss, at least, read the expression correctly. "Slater was kind of a wild man. He got his Cadillac out on the runway and hit a fighter coming in. That's the real story. It wasn't even in the Honolulu papers." She made a queer, gallant face that asked, What can you do?

To Priss it seemed (she thought this instantly, without the need to reflect and without the need ever again to correct that brilliant first insight) that what you did was kill off husbands who might have kept you from where and what you really wanted to be. She thought of the two recent presidents of Wellford who had been so trickily dismissed from the scene because they stood in the way of Royce's return, and she couldn't help seeing Carole's two husbands as near parallels. What could you do with a woman who killed off military-type husbands so quickly? The guilt on Carole's face had been a pure giveaway of something mighty potent and strange.

Priss said, as if she were changing the subject, "So you'll be staying with Deirdre, of course?"

"Until," Carole said.

"We have to see more of her," Royce said. "As much as she wants to see of us. I've always been a little embarrassed by this 'circle of friends' thing in the cemetery. It's awfully corny, you know. But if it's important to Deirdre, she has to understand . . ." He ended with a grunt of laughter, as if the whole gruesome tangle of past and present was too much for him.

It *was* too much for him. It was too much for anyone, and those like Deirdre, who pretended to let some of the tangle slide properly away into oblivion, were as apt as anyone else to find themselves strangled sometimes by what they intended to forget. But whether a just unraveling was too much for him or not, it was his duty to unravel. What was on him here—what Carole had come flying from Hawaii to put on him—was the task of being the one domino in the row that does not go down when the others are falling. Whether that was possible or not . . .

So that afternoon, when he had expected no annunciation worse than what he had to tell Priss and Lot, was the first time he glimpsed clearly how he must end his life. He had tried to ease back out of it and now he saw—for whatever he would make of it—that there was no way back. He was at the geometric center of a thicket, and every direction was forward. No wonder he laughed.

Just then, to confirm something else—though she probably supposed she was making up for having brought so much gruesome news at once and blurting it out so that Royce, at least, would miss none of its significance—Carole's eyes fixed on Lot's handsome little face.

With love so spontaneously frank as to be indecent, she said, "He does look like *you*." While that *you* flooded the room like the keening of a maenad who has seen the print of a goat's foot on the rug, Lot cowered, and Priss came to the decision that only years and God's plenty of circumstance would fully illumine.

For her part, she was going to stay in Buchanan until this thing was fought out, this weird triangle. All at once she knew how very sick she was of fighting a ghost. Here—and only here—was her chance to have a flesh-and-blood and plainly vulnerable woman for an antagonist.

It remained to be seen whether old Deirdre Prentice would lie at last in the "circle of friends." And it remained to be seen which of the two, Carole husband-killing Prentice or she, would go into the connubial earth with deadpan, hardly-worth-it Royce Morgan. Or who wanted to most.

She saw now clearly that the years of her marriage—which meant her *life,* damn it—might have been wasted, sapped by some quirk in her husband that could only stand visible in the world personified by another woman.

He had preferred her, but not with a single heart.

Surely such a man was not worth winning. He would never give more than half at a time, him with his obligations hanging around his neck like albatrosses and leis.

No, but the game was worth winning. While Carole stayed in Buchanan, Priss would stay to play with her.

4

THE MORGANS heard from George Hand that Mooney had arrived at Wellford to assume his duties while they were vacationing on Cape Cod with Priss's father. For all that this development was expected, word of it made Priss restless, as if she had just remembered leaving the back door unlocked at home.

She said, "Last winter I thought it would take me years to call Buchanan 'home.' All of a sudden . . ." All of a sudden on a May day she had found that Buchanan was so much her home she could not escape it by coming back to the seashore where she had spent the summers of her eighth to fifteenth years. Carole and Deirdre Prentice were more substantial among her preoccupations than anyone they met here among her father's retinue of arty, well-heeled friends. So was Winfred Mooney, though she had never yet laid eyes on him.

Hardly a day passed when she didn't bait Royce with schemes of Latin-American flavor for overthrowing the new regime before it was well begun. The sooner they got the job done, the sooner they could be on their way. Though she felt Buchanan was her home, it soiled her to feel it.

While her schemes got saltier, the cartoon she drew of Mooney was progressively fitted with the rags of contemporary life that appalled her most. He was Madison Avenue and Creeping Commercialism. He was Propaganda and Usury. He was the man in the Brooks Brothers suit who asked each morning what his friends had done for him lately. She pictured Henry Diogenes Worth as having gone about the country with his lantern looking for the Purely Dishonest Man—and finding him naturally among the hucksters of New York.

This entertaining and intermittently serious diatribe was supported by her father. Father London was a painter who had begun his career wisely by marrying money. The money had lasted longer than Priss's mother, so he was able, in blithe defiance of changing fashions, to go on as the last surviving Cubist because "not all the possibilities have been exhausted in that vein yet." He had been an expatriate in the days of Juan Gris, Hemingway, the Crosbys, and the *Transatlantic Review* in Paris, and he knew everybody who was anybody in that seedtime of American arts. His Bohemia was never less than comfortable, but he had rioted with the Surrealists at the first showing of "Le Chien d'Andalou" and had to his credit—besides his achievement as a painter—such midwifely services as persuading the American Country Club in Paris to finance a little magazine for Henry Miller. Wealth had indulged him in opportunities to kick against every prick he saw. And of the embarrassing comedy at Wellford he advised Royce, "Tell them to kiss your ass."

Royce valued the advice aesthetically if he found it wanting in practicality. He loved his father-in-law, and he thought the whole anti-Mooney hullabaloo a nice safety valve that kept Priss from talking (and perhaps from brooding) too much about Carole and her dying aunt.

"People like your Mooney never look for the content of time," said Bergsonian, white-whiskered London, who had never respected the form of it. "They figure how a thing runs and make it run faster, whether it's natural resources they're wasting—denooding the forest land"—merrily smacking his pink lips when he thought of anything being "denooded"—"or thinking up some new gimmick in the arts." For his own timeless part, it would always be a spring day of 1924 in Paris with the canvas on his easel forever modulating some problem Picasso had posed and been too impatient to finish. "My advice is to get out right now. Head for the territories with your boy. They'll turn your College into a production line."

Royce had thought he was heading for the territories when he got his family out of New York less than a year before. There was nowhere farther to go. When he moved next time, of course the jump would have to be onto an educational production line already functioning. "Mooney hasn't turned it into anything yet," he argued mildly. "According to George Hand's letter, he's quietly looking things over. He seems to be taking most of his meals—he's a bachelor—at Joe Chapin's lunch wagon, where the students eat. I think we might take this as a sign of plain living and high thinking."

"That's a trick to take George in," Priss said. "George simply doesn't have it in him to trust anyone who spends more than fifty cents for breakfast. I think someone besides Henry Worth ought to look into this man a little. Royce . . . ?"

"I'm much too lazy. You have friends in New York who probably know something about him. Why not run down and ask what they know? Only . . . wouldn't it be too bad if any of them spoke well of him?"

"Not my friends," she said with a contented smile. Nevertheless she made no effort to investigate Mooney's record on her own. Her vindictiveness didn't require a factual basis—probably because Mooney was not its true target. She still played with the notion that Carole was the real usurper in their lives, and probably she cared about the College only as a schematic representation of unmentionable rivalries.

There were no letters from Carole, though she had promised to let them know if Deirdre worsened radically during the summer. In spite of their intent, Royce and Priss had not seen the old woman after the election. Royce went on hoping that some genial face-to-face encounter might be possible while Deirdre was still on her feet.

One hot day as they were driving down from Provincetown, Priss said, out of a silence, "She's a Giorgione woman. Carole."

"You mean she's too fat to look well in a bathing suit."

"I wasn't thinking of that," Priss said in some irritation, "though her tiny head on that immense body . . ."

Royce warbled as if he had bit into something unexpectedly sweet.

"Papa would say she was eminently paintable just because she has such jugs." Cubist he might be, but Father London chose his models

45

with Renoir's eye. "But I was really thinking of the Giorgione painting and of Carole in a background like that, with a lute player behind her and this endlessly voluptuous greenery and hills with a
thunderstorm sky and lightning on the hills like something she'd
made happen."

The description and analogy were typically Priss-obscure. As
queen of the half-real, she had just hinted what she meant to have.
She wanted the landscape of his youth, wanted somehow to own
Carole-and-Royce in their summertime as people don't even own
the objects of their own memories. Libido trembled like a compass
needle pointing at a never-never north, and he could only pity her
for the wish he inferred.

"I've wondered whether you and Carole are going to be friends,"
he said.

"Friends?" That idea had never even occurred to her, though
she could, if she had to, suppose that in some conventional sense
they would treat each other as friends. Friends wasn't the right
word, though. Neither was enemies. Let the relationship grow into
a name of its own, she felt. It would have an odd name—one that
only the female followers of Royce Morgan would ever have any
use for. "Sisters?" she said with a laugh. Presently she said, "Well,
we're in the same sorority."

A second—long and faintly incredulous—letter from George
Hand said that as of August 1 Winfred Mooney was occupying the
president's mansion. He had, at least, moved into the bedroom
where the housekeeper slept in the elder Morgan's day. In fairness,
George approved this austerity. He also managed to convey, through
a veil of courtly prose, an image of an awe-struck Mooney orphan
who didn't yet dare believe that Wellford's seasoned pomp (modest
though it might be, really) was at his disposal.

More surprisingly George expressed cautious approval of Mooney's
first twitches on the administrative reins. Estimates of the fall enrollment had been revised and now revised again. Enrollment would
likely be two and a half times what it had been in '45-'46 if housing

and classrooms for so many students could be found. And maybe they could. President Mooney was showing "remarkable ingenuity" in planning temporary dormitories, offices, and classrooms.

Incredulity was at its peak in George's assessment of the way Mooney tucked into the problem of enlisting an adequate faculty to face the hordes. Apparently he was not going to hire teachers by the head. In the face of exploding enrollment he had fired Clifford in Botany; Jennings, Kahler, and McGraw in English; Huefford in Math; poor Miss Tabor and her sister-in-law (who had been the entire staff of the Art Department since about the time John Singer Sargent died); Kingsman in Chemistry; and the football coach.

That meant *all* the deadwood Royce and George had talked of easing out of the key positions in the next few years was gone in one ruthless sweep. Compunctions and personal loyalty which might have slowed Royce had not stayed Mooney's hand. The newcomer's ruthlessness must be put down as an admirable thing.

Where Mooney would get replacements for so many teachers— and more yet to meet the bigger enrollment—was far from settled.

He lacked Royce's wide acquaintance in the academic world and probably had no way of distinguishing a scholarly sheep from a pedagogic goat. So, in recruiting new faculty members, he would have yet to rely heavily on Royce in the foreseeable future. And if that did not quite put him at the mercy of subversion, it nevertheless indicated how his authority would always be bound and limited behind the scenes. To some extent he was already declaring his dependence on as yet unpledged loyalty from Royce. At this juncture, nothing could have been more apt to enlist that loyalty than just this careless exposure of a weak side.

"Yet President Mooney intends to keep the size of classes below last year's maximum," George wrote. "He has put us considerably in the red by offering premium salaries and attractive futures to many men you and I had picked out, so he may bring it off, though we'll have to tolerate holes and patches and a deficit for the coming year."

He reported that the administrative staff was working very hard—

47

presumably trying to keep up with the Mooney whirlwind. But no, there was no reason why Royce should cut short his summer and come back to help.

Well. Where now the scarecrow figure of a Madison Avenue slicker that Priss had so confidently drawn? She sniffed over George's letter and said, "So the little corporal is giving you rabble a whiff of grapeshot? George came around even quicker than you predicted."

"It looks that way from here."

"Do you still want a closer look?"

Whether he wanted it or not was hardly still in issue. Soon now they would be going back where everyone except Priss—and Carole perhaps; that remained to find out—had accepted the *fait accompli*.

"I've always valued the surprises that come from patiently waiting to see," Royce answered her with an infuriating meekness, all the more infuriating because it refused to declare itself flatly as either sincerity or joke.

"Anyway, I'm getting anxious to see him," Priss admitted.

"You've talked as if you had."

"Oh, I've *seen* him. I merely want to check the appearances against the reality. Aren't you anxious?"

"To see what we'll all make of the coming year? Yes."

"What he is will determine. So you do want to see him."

They got their wish on the evening before the fall semester began. Mooney had been in Chicago and later in New York after they reached Buchanan. So they had no private meeting with him before a reception he held at the mansion for faculty, trustees, and important townspeople.

It was a splendid September night when they approached the mansion by the central campus walk. Already students lurked and ambled in shadowy groups with here and there a young profile or a mane of shiny hair catching the lights from dormitory windows or the student lounge. The heightened, raucous note of traffic around the campus indicated very many more of them nearby.

"The hosting of Buchanan chivalry," Priss said of the loose column pressing toward the mansion. She was prepared to condescend to them all—the more so because they would necessarily be amused (however they hid it) at Royce's coming as mere guest. She saw Henry Worth and his wife bulling into a group ahead of them and lagged back. She could be polite to the others. Perhaps not to him.

Halfway to the presidential steps they came up with Carole and Deirdre—or Carole marching beside a wheel chair containing a wasted wraith who must be Deirdre, since it could be no one else. The encounter was dreadful, though none of them had the courage to admit it. Rather they must greet each other as if everything were as it should be. The time was already past when frankness was allowed them, and Royce felt the cheat of her haste, as though her dying might have been a trick she had used to get ahead of him while he was away.

In the arbitrary light on her withered face her eyes seemed immense. Her smile hardly counted, but the eyes burned with something like fanaticism. The sober, steady force of her lifetime's will had become uncontrollably impatient now.

She took Royce's hand in both of hers, while Carole beamed as if over a sufficient reconciliation. "Oh, Royce," the old woman said, "I can't help feeling that something is beginning tonight. The great adventure."

"Yes," he said.

"I've been home tonight. You know I'm in the hospital now. I didn't want to come here straight from there. Carole and I were out among the flowers. And the sundown was so splendid. Did you see it? It made me think of some great, noble life coming to its close, and I thought of many things, Royce. Your father. How he always taught us—and he did teach us all, not just the students—that a good heart and hope and . . . so many good things still to be, Royce, whatever the past has been, whatever ugliness . . ."

"Yes." If she had any answer for the quandary of death, he wanted no more than to support and agree with it. And yet, now more desperately than ever, perhaps desperate for the first time in her seventy years, she wanted the right answer—which gave her a tone of fanaticism, vile and mocking as some odor of waste from her body that cleanliness would not suppress.

"It's as if we only had to open our hands and so many good things would come pouring in," she said. "But we don't. We don't. But never lose faith. We're never ready, that's all. We need *time*." And time sat on the arm of her wheel chair like a hideous bird with its moist talons already rummaging her old guts, stabbing and tickling her throat against the defenses of the drug. She began to talk faster, coughing a little, but raising her voice to a kind of lyric pitch. "Time. And all the things we hoped for that never quite material- ized can materialize. Your father used to say, 'No heaven on earth.' No heaven on earth, and we must be very strong. I have faith that all these young people . . . students . . . It's hard to remember you and I were young, though you're still young and will see many things."

"Shouldn't we go inside?" Carole asked. She had caught some inkling of where her aunt's monologue was tending.

Deirdre's skeletal fingers scrabbled on Royce's hand, asking from his health some reassurance she could never ask for in words. "Now you're back!" she said with a kind of triumph. "The war's over. It's been a terrible time and you all so far from home. I wrote to you, didn't I?"

"Yes."

She turned to Priss, "You must remind him always what strength he has, how big a man he is. We always knew—his father knew— that Royce would pick up the world on his shoulders some day—if pessimism didn't hinder him." Her tone was merry now, as if pessimism were some childhood disease that might keep him home from coasting on a snowy day. "You must remind him. Make him stand up like a giant—*now that he has the responsibility of leading Wellford.*"

It was her joke, cunningly and bewilderingly delivered, so that no one could ever be quite sure whether she had forgotten the whole past—literally losing it in the bewilderment of her condition—or with supersubtle cunning was pretending that she had forgotten the matter of the election and its outcome. Whether this was her manner of apologizing for having turned against him, or announcing that in a transcendent sense she never had—whatever it was, she was not to be examined on her meaning, not here and now certainly. So never. Carole began to move the wheel chair again.

Over the sibilance of its tires Deirdre croaked, "I wrote at Christmastime and you were in Hawaii, I think, and I cried to think of you out there. So far from the good Christmases we used to have. But I never brood about the past. We mustn't. When I'm gone you must never forget what precious things are entrusted to you here, Royce. The task of life is education. Just education. We mustn't fail."

Carole was smiling fixedly, and it occurred to Royce, with some of his old impatience toward her, that she couldn't distinguish between these heartbreaking vagaries and the hardheaded, generous things Deirdre had used to say.

He thought it unwise, considering all the others who would remember what Deirdre was choosing to forget, that he and Priss go into the mansion with her. So he let them go ahead while he hung back to talk to faculty and faculty wives he had not seen since June.

When at length they approached the high, white wooden steps leading up to the porch, they did so just as Winfred Mooney came out.

In the last of the twilight with festival lamps gleaming inside and behind him—reflecting from his pure white hair as brilliantly as from a mirror among the white pillars of the mansion—he seemed like one of those figures that step out of Swiss clocks to announce the hour, a figure of contrivance whose panoply the environment of Time has polished. He was simply too perfect—too perfectly the physical stereotype of a college president—to have been produced by human design, even his own.

A look of anxiety puckered his brows (darker than his hair) as he sorted faces from the advancing streams of guests. The effect was as strange as if a lacquered figure should have been touched with worry. He stood there for a full minute, searching as if he were expecting someone who could never reasonably be expected in Buchanan. Then, either recognizing no one or not wanting to stage his meeting with them outside, he went back through the door.

51

"Royce!" Priss whispered shrilly. She was shaken with spontaneous laughter, bent against her husband's arm. "He's one of those men from the carnival they make up and pretend he's mechanical."

"Shhhhh!" Her characterization was too precise to risk its being overheard.

Yet she would not be hushed. "Like a carnival performer. But prettier. Oh, they got the right man. He's perfect."

There was no doubt about her being overheard. Now the rumor would go that Mrs. Morgan had said . . . But she had not spoken for effect. She was a clairvoyant delighted to recognize what common sense would be a long time in admitting. She had been right all along. Royce, with his moderation and meekness—exactly because of them—was far behind her.

"That white hair!" She laughed ecstatically. "It's Platonic. It's absolutely what they wanted and he knew they would. He's ideal. I'll bet he bleached it for the job."

And so—as those with common sense would have to learn much later, most of them except Deirdre—he had.

5

AFTER THAT first meeting at the reception Priss couldn't say flatly whether she liked Mooney or not. Of course she had been prepared to dislike him. Such preparations have a way of exhausting animus before the right time to express it arrives. Mooney was what she had come to see. Even a long look down her nose at the rest of Wellford or Buchanan society was far, far short of fascinating.

She circled him in the big drawing room under the shining candelabra which the Class of '07 had donated to the ideal of presidential ostentation. With the smile of a dean's wife, she went on soft feet over the maroon carpet—like a timorous child, like a hunting leopard—back and forth, always behind or at a side angle to the white-haired performer. She listened for his voice while she laughed at what the faculty wives had to say to her.

Once—she was clinging to George Hand and to all appearances paying him close attention—she overheard Mooney misuse the word *authoritarian* for *authoritative*.

Quickly as a spy who has caught an awaited signal, she led George over to the punch table. They were reasonably isolated for a moment and she said, " 'I've heard from an absolutely authoritarian source that the Rockefeller people have their eyes on Wellford.' " She lifted her cup to her mouth and peered up at George over its glittering brim—a trick of flirtation she had hardly used since college.

"Have they?" he asked—and wondered for the rest of the evening why she laughed at him then. "I've no doubt a number of people will have their eyes on us to see what we're up to," he sighed. "Hope they don't get too much sand thrown in them." He peered grumpily around and asked where Royce had got to.

"Don't know. We always operate separately. More dangerous that way."

She meant to be dangerous to Mooney, meant perhaps, when she talked to him, to let him see he wasn't entirely safe here. But she was a bit disarmed in having overheard his mistake. A chink had opened already in his bland armor; now there was less challenge.

When she actually got around to talking to him she found him taking pains to get on her good side. People who did that put themselves in peril of her immediate contempt. But he did it skillfully enough for the requirements of this first meeting. At a well-chosen moment he said, "I hear you're an artist," without smirking in the usual Buchanan style. He would have erred badly in saying, "I hear you're artistic"—as Henry Worth once had said—or even, "I'm told you're interested in the arts."

"I'm a homeless one, if I am," she told him.

"You danced with Martha Graham's troupe," he said, precisely informed and too tactful to marvel over this intelligence.

She nodded. "And I've painted in my time. I used to play a pretty good jazz violin. Oh, I'm artistic." She didn't mind parody if it came from her. "But if you're asking, Do I dance? No. You dance from here." She slapped her softening belly. Once the gesture would have sounded like the collision of pine boards, now it was a small hand slapping a firmer elastic. "I lost it when I was pregnant with Lot, whatever it is that makes you dance. I suppose I painted because I envied my daddy. I always compete with the men in my life."

He offered her a conspiratorial smile, as from one performing artist to another. "What I'm really getting around to is that you do ceramics."

Priss looked interested. Last year when she had assumed that Royce was going to be Wellford's president soon, she had refitted the stable behind their house as a ceramic studio. The need for a new art—for another of those forms of competition with her husband that she understood as glibly as an artful woman could—had wilted after the election. She wasn't sure she would ever put her hands in clay again, but she was more than ever eager to dip them in certain lives, and she was interested to see how far Mooney meant to draw her into his plans. Far enough to checkmate Royce? If he saw the need to do that, it meant he was afraid of her husband.

"You've heard what's happened to our 'art department,'" he said sadly, as if a volcano had scattered a layer of ashes over Miss Tabor and her sister-in-law. "Well, Bojac, Dr. Bojac, that trim gentleman over there with Chancellor Hand—you haven't met him?—you know he's the new head—and incidentally told me many nice things about your father, whom he met at Wellfleet—thinks we can get going nicely, thank you, painters and all, but was lamenting a weakness in craft. When someone mentioned *you* . . ."

"Using my studio?"

"Temporarily." He was matching her tone beautifully, sparing her the gush she had heard him pouring for Mrs. Worth and the loftiness he had had for Deirdre and Duane Armitage (Armitage Mills).

"It sounds like mobilization." With the compliment she made him lower his eyelids like Napoleon overpraised for Austerlitz.

"Using *you*," he said. "There simply won't be either an instructor or a studio for ceramics for at least a year or two."

"Do you suppose we'll be here that long?" she mused.

"You'll be here when I'm gone."

She saw his eyes flicker like jewels catching an accident of light, knew that he was recklessly questioning her about what neither of them would risk in open speech. They were playing with fire, and in that moment at least they recognized the incendiarist in each other.

"We might make a bet on that," she said.

"Ah, we can't predict the future," he laughed. "Anyway, it's a job if you want it. We're not going to play by the rules here."

She shook her head, refusing. "No. I think this winter I'll start a novel. I have an interesting idea for one." The idea was gathering form right now. When their eyes met it had been like looking in a magic glass that reflected her worst self (or sibling thereof) and

55

she was suddenly kindled almost beyond endurance, wondering which of them would be able to use the other for ends that were mutually wicked. If she wrote a novel . . . in it she would make him her murderous alter ego. If she spent her time on a novel it would keep her sheltered where he could not use her.

"The offer is permanently open," he said joyfully.

She didn't track him any more while the reception lasted. She had found him and the discovery soothed and stimulated her like a drug. It added something regal to her manner. She went confident as an empress among the lesser guests, even returning to Deirdre and Carole with exactly the right note of solemn cheerfulness. She dazzled Dr. Bojac and made George Hand admit to himself his provincial experience of women. Her manner refuted any suspicion that Royce and she were here on terms less than they would have chosen.

The best of it was that Royce observed and understood. On their way home he said, "You were more your old self tonight."

"Than?"

He meant to say "Than since I came home from the war, or even before Lot was born," but warily said, "Than a long time."

"Hmmm," she said, snuggling against his arm as he drove, as if taking his approval neat. Her new excitement was not falling away into shreds of dreariness. She was going on and on with her novel about Mooney. Reams of invention strewed out with every block they drove past.

"What we may understand, if we choose," Royce said, "is that if one doesn't expect too much of Buchanan one might get more."

She chuckled to think how much—however vague or tentative its shape might be—she was beginning to expect. "I expect lots," she said.

She was not more herself suddenly, for there had never been a self, but selves—good and bad, merry and depressed, cunning or benevolently clever. She was a player who had never handicapped her pace by dragging along those parts of a self that could not be fascinated by the object in view. Tonight she had met a man whose very presence "in Royce's place" had reminded her in a flash that selfless ambition can have its triumphs. Her elation was like the dancing she had had to give up.

And what did it matter how deep in malice her fantasies were driven? She had recognized Mooney as bad enough to accomplish the gutting she would hereafter dream of with wicked pleasure. He wasn't the devil, because there isn't one; nor an incarnation of him, because the devil is too smart to risk taking on the corruption of mortality. But bad enough to—somehow—snarl the promises still extant between Royce and Carole. How this would be accomplished was not in her novel yet. It was enough to guess it could be done. The guess made her a sweeter companion for her husband, and that was what mattered, was it not?

"This little moment, at least," she said. "In this little moment I adore being just where we are. I adore you, old Royce."

Above the treetops of the suburban street the moon seemed to be running in pace with their car. She watched it move like a coin dropping into a velvet purse. Then its outlined craters reminded her of the pockmarks on the face of Mrs. Henry Worth. She thought how precisely Winfred Mooney (and she, she, his wicked sister) would have calculated the values attached to those relics of acne in girlhood as he decided the tone he would take with his patron's wife. This intimacy, the sharing of her thoughts with him, delighted her almost to giggling.

Royce slowed the car to turn into their driveway. "We'll celebrate tonight," she said.

"Celebrate what?" he said with his grave irony. Well, of course this was the night of his rival's triumph, but, being Royce, he would go along with a celebration of their homecoming. Ahead of them, speckled with moonlight and velvet shadow, was their own great lawn. In the house, lights were burning downstairs in anticipation of their return. Upstairs in the maid's window, next to Lot's room, a crack of light showed under the blind. Odors of grass and the sound of anxious crickets received them when he stopped on the gravel and walked around the car to help her out. Everything essential seemed to be as it had been since Grandfather Blackburn's time.

"I suppose this house is my main reason for having chosen to stay," he said, just as if he were answering a question. He, too, had been busy with a private dialectic as they drove from Mooney's.

When they were inside and had built a little fire in the living-room fireplace in front of the couch, she said, "We're going to celebrate you."

He brought tall drinks for them and stooped to kiss her. With his lips still moist from her kiss, he said, "What about me?"

"Your *youness*."

"It sounds like something I should keep decently covered with clothing."

She was impatient with his modest joke. Modesty was his evasion, and as her passion mounted she did not mean to let him evade. "I'm not the only one who recognizes it. Everyone there tonight . . ."

"Admired the way you carried it off for us."

"No. You. I was only putting on an act. You can't fool people essentially. They recognize . . . essences. What Deirdre said about you."

"Poor Deirdre's so afraid," he said, sitting beside her, but, with the thought, staring morosely into the fire.

Priss did not mean to discuss Deirdre's wasting. She was busy with seduction and nothing could be less to the point than talk of death.

She said, "Wouldn't it be *funny* if she was right in saying now you had the responsibility of leading Wellford? Not as president, she meant, but *really*. As the *man*. That's what I meant that everybody saw. Seeing you and Mooney together clarifies everything. He's *nothing*. To think we ever worried! At best a man like that is tolerated in his notion that he can run anything."

"Then why are you so worked up by him?"

She was as shocked as if a knife had been inserted under her ribs. He was staring at her without censure or worry, merely with the kind of bewilderment one sees in the eyes of a fine horse or dog. He didn't know *why*. He was asking in terrible sincerity. But he had known that it was Mooney who had set off the excitement which was—until this jolt—becoming increasingly erotic. And Royce wasn't supposed to know things like that. She never underestimated his intelligence, but she counted on him to be slow in perception.

"Damned idiot," she laughed. "I keep saying you, you, you, you. I suppose I'd built him up to be some kind of superhuman dragon, and it's a relief to find he's just straw."

"He's what we'll make him. Or let him be. If we let him be straw, I suppose that's all he can be."

"Aren't you relieved? Don't you feel you can breathe again?" But she was tense with anger at having been caught. She set on her husband with the unfeminine eagerness that had baffled him in their courting days—something long dropped from their marital habits. Her hands worshiped the great span of his ribs, and she twisted her head to stare up at his face. A method actress, she thought of one time she had fallen hard from a pony and was picked up from the turf by the barrel-chested riding instructor whom the other ten-year-old girls could only adore from a distance. She had never felt so tiny, so imperiled, or so grateful for rescue (if you'll lift me, Royce, I'll forget Mooney and Carole and be only your wife) —nor felt how easy it is to twist one's own peril into a whip—as when she had made him pick her up. She had been scared in her fall. When she heard the other girls twitter their envy from a pony-back circle as she was lifted, she felt only the thrill of power. And now she could make her husband do what she dreamed. He was not safe from her, merely because he guessed that Mooney had begun their celebration for them.

He loved her. More, far more than that, he saw a self in her while she saw none. For a little while as they kissed, as she felt the responsive excitement shiver his body, she might almost have renounced her sick wish for revenge. Earnestly she prayed to him, "Love me!" She set his hand between her legs, spreading them for his caress.

The command, phrased this way, apparently embarrassed him. He suddenly remembered that they had drinks which might spill if they weren't careful. He drew a little away from her and cocked his head as if listening for any sound of Lot prowling or the maid not yet settled.

She would never know how her words at this minute had managed to echo the command Carole once gave him. But they had been so close to release just seconds before that she could sniff Prentice somewhere in the woodpile of his busy thoughts. She was furious now in proportion to her previous willingness to yield. She went for his fly with greedy hands, her nails bright as already stained knives working mechanically. "Oh, fuck me so she'll hear," she said.

"Barbara?" Barbara was their maid, a farm girl from Buchanan County who learned nothing from what was told her and everything from what she overheard.

"Carole! Who else? And smelly old Deirdre, too. Sometimes I think Carole's in this house, the way you pussyfoot and creep at me. Since she showed up last spring. Don't you think a woman can tell the difference?"

He truly supposed this woman could. He was abashed, caught in a delinquency, justly accused, though he could not be sure exactly what his fault should be called. He had glimpsed Mooney in her thoughts, she Carole in his.

His wife was no less beautiful in her rage. "Don't you remember the times in New York before you went overseas? Come roaring at me! She's not here. She can't hear unless you make her."

"Well," he said. "Well . . . perhaps we'll both be sweeter in the morning. A night's sleep. Not now. God, Priss, Priss, it ought to be an act of love."

But he sat still while she undid his belt and tugged trousers and shorts down from his thighs.

"Can't you?" she hissed.

"I *can*," he said in a kind of dismal detachment, seeing more than feeling his body respond to the stimulus of her intensity. Where was the treachery? No more in her clawing for justice, her due, than in the idiotic response of his flesh. He felt like a big cat tricked by the lion tamer's little whip and cap gun—but tricked beyond his capacity to oppose the trick, so he followed her upstairs to roar at her command. If that was what she wanted, he had no grounds for refusing.

Since he had known her she had had great faith in sexual resolutions. In practice if not in theory she had separated them from love before this and the best of them (the most intense, therefore best) had often come in the midst of ill-stated quarrels like tonight's. She believed in orgasms—mutual, multiple, and "big"—in default of a belief in God. Some sort of magic they might have, but her need was for unburdening and salvation, and usually they only helped her sleep.

Tonight they helped her sleep in a house that wouldn't be hers by a gift of love, the house too complexly mortgaged to be given ever. And anyway she didn't want the house, she wanted—more than ever since she had seen Mooney—Royce's hoarded past, the Giorgione landscape of it with Carole the lady among the gypsies by the well of childhood.

There was no way to get it. Winfred Mooney's clever eyes had told her that. Better than cry sour grapes at what she couldn't have, she might still sour them in the bowels of the revelers who ate them so long ago. She slept with the consolation that she might do so. She was going to marry Carole to that horrid phony.

The house, mortgaged or not, was still Royce's, to console him in his sleep according to his different conscience. His boyhood holidays and convalescences had usually been spent here rather than in the presidential mansion on the campus. In his early years it was a house of women, occupied by his mother's three sisters. Even before his mother's death it was customary to bring him here when heroic cookery or prolonged steaming were indicated. His entire tenth year was spent here while his mother languished in an Arizona rest home and then died. Her coffin had been set in flowers by the front stairway, in spite of his father's wishes that she be buried from the Wellford mansion.

That funeral was one of the few occasions Royce could remember when his aunts had rebelled successfully against the old man's stately determination. And because for that once they succeeded, he thought for a long time that death was a comfortable thing, where a lady might lie down to rest in such an aura of homey, beflowered attention and respect as her dry-eyed sisters gave her then.

He had not gone with the coffin to the church nor to the cemetery.

He remained right in the kitchen with Aunt Mildred, drinking Ovaltine and reading a detective story during the funeral services. It was only when the scruples of adolescence began to tighten that he guessed he had done something monstrous, that something monstrous had been done to him, by this discreet evasion of the truth. Even then he did not have to face the wickedness of his omission alone. Aunt Grace anticipated his afterthoughts, and before they were well enough formed to bite severely she confessed to him that she "had never felt right about it." It had been his mother's firm command to spare him "all that hypocrisy and ugliness that goes with a funeral" and her sisters had stood by that direction. "Only, there may have been more hypocrisy in minimizing the occasion than in facing it for what it was. We didn't give you full credit for your manliness, Royce."

That was the temper of the household as he remembered it. It was errant on the side of comfort to the point of spoiling him (and inducing a sybaritic hypochondria which he had trouble breaking during his military service); nevertheless it was unremittingly concerned lest he fall short of the ideal of manliness better represented to the ladies by their father than by his. Grandfather Blackburn commanded a company in the Philippines when America was building her empire and was killed in the Argonne forest, where he commanded a brigade of National Guardsmen. Royce's aunts—and perhaps his mother, too, bless her divided loyalties—always hoped he would follow Grandfather's path to West Point "someday." Aunt Grace and Aunt Linda lived long enough to see him wear a major's leaves and the Silver Star ribbon during the war. That must partly have made up to them for his decision that he was only an educator.

Because of their military ideal, their house had been a place of liberty and adventure as well as an eider-downed nest. It was in the basement here that he kept his air rifles, his soapbox racer, his model airplanes, and the steel traps he bought for himself in his seventh year when he was determined that the Buchanan suburbs must be as rich in pelts as the Hudson Bay country. His father came on him once that year setting a large trap in the shrubbery by the Wellford Chapel steps. "Boy," he said, with an air not so much outraged as appalled (or just not so much amused as determined to miss no occasion for one of his famous quips), "Boy, if you were to catch some stoo-dent there—and mind you the Wellford stoo-dents are on their honor to stay out of the vegetation—I expect he would just chew his leg off and escape anyway. Take those engines of destruction to your aunts' back yard if you must play with them. And mind you, be careful of your fingers. Ten are not too many."

Once Royce built a canoe in the carriage house between the green Packard that seemed immortal and the red Chevrolet that was one of a yearly changing succession of knockabout cars. On summer afternoons he portaged the canoe down the bluff to the sand shoals of the river below. His target range had been in the orchard where the bluff broke from its crest (there were no houses below them then and no shipyard on the other shore, either). From near the same vantage point he flew models of the *Spirit of St. Louis* and various Spads and Fokkers toward the down-river haze. Once Tom Jaffe and he started to build a man-carrying glider that was to race on bicycle wheels down the slope until it had enough velocity to become airborne. Fortunately, they were diverted from the project by the gift to Royce of a Model A roadster with a rumble seat, a gift that carried with it an obligation to divert his talents from aircraft design to girls. The glider had never been finished, but the skeleton of one wing still hung in the loft of the carriage house, the wood brown as an old soupbone now and probably brittle.

Later, in the days when he was an Eagle Scout and before he was wise enough to see the flaws of altruism, he had run a sort of summer camp for the poor (and sometimes hoodlum) Tenderfoot Scouts of Buchanan who could not afford two weeks at Lake Nopekhah in the regular Scout camp. He was in prep school then, and through the school year was missing Buchanan badly. Or more probably he was already missing the vanished prime of boyhood and had found this expedient for clinging to it a little longer.

For two succeeding summers they pitched pup tents in the orchard. His scrawny troop and he marched and cooked over the river valley as far south as the town of Moult and as far east, up the river, as Indian Road. They swam from a raft he had put together out of oil drums and a chicken house floor. Sometimes he let them steal watermelons and sweet corn. (Never chickens.) He let them wreck his canoe and felt a certain propriety in its destruction, since he would never need it again for exploration. They broke the last of his target arrows shooting at stones in the river, lost his compasses, field glasses and a Daisy pump gun he had owned since he was eight. He didn't even bother to bawl them out for their carelessness. He was letting the physical form of his world go as its substance got solid inside his memory.

As a despot not at all beyond corruption, he probably learned more from them than they from him. In return for some vain skills in knot-tying, map-reading, and the preparation of Mulligan stew, he learned a lot about the mores of Buchanan slums. Those wise twelve- and thirteen-year-olds tempted him belatedly to start smoking. They fascinated him with the lore of Datento's operations and seemed to know (what the state police never found out) who had planted the dynamite that blew his bedroom and him to smithereens. They shamed the innocence of his seventeen years with campfire tales of each other's sisters or their own. He never had much impulse to explore the lower depths of Buchanan—he knew all about low life from novels and sociology texts—but for the first time it began to occur to him he had missed some of the pleasures of boyhood in enjoying others so richly. Those kids woke an envy that was only appeased when he took Carole Prentice's maidenhead upstairs on the hardwood floor of Aunt Grace's bedroom.

For there had been darker liberties encouraged by this house than the emulations of that "soldier, author, and conservationist" Grandfather Blackburn. In his teens Royce seldom took a date home to the mansion, where he lived with his father and a housekeeper. Especially if there was necking to be done, he brought the girl here. On very many evenings—some afternoons, too—he fondled Buchanan's better-class daughters in one of the gliders or porch swings on the giant, vine-shaded porch that circled the house like a ballet skirt.

Hot afternoons of approaching thunderstorms, while the insects hummed in the vine, the glider springs sang like sleepy sirens, the sprinklers pirouetted on the dimming lawn, and from the far side of the house Aunt Linda's radio played while she dozed on the couch. And among the glider cushions this girl or that—all matrons now— had teased and coached him in the junior-grade art of love. By night, after dances in the high school gym during the holidays or at the country club, this matron-to-be or that might come here with him for coffee and brief conversation with his aunts before those discreet ladies retired upstairs, leaving the sofa—in summer those gliders and swings again, always again those night-perfumed gliders—unobserved for athletic necking.

He would never have put his arm around a girl in his other home at the mansion. He did his intellectual work there, and he was a well-showered monk of the library in that compartment of his neatly divided existence. To have kissed one of those easily kissable girls anywhere in the mansion would have shocked him far more than it would have shocked his father, supposing the elder Morgan had witnessed it.

But here in his aunts' house the necking was hardly less innocent than the taste for learning spurred by his father's platitudes. It was innocent because all parties—and especially his presumptuous aunts —presumed it would be. So it had been. Clear as a parable stood a recollection of opening his eyes during a session of summer necking to peer at the flesh his lips were nibbling—only to see the tanned sleek skin of his own forearm. It was silly, all silly and embarrassing too, in mature recollection. But nothing worse.

Of course he understood the theory of sex. From Georgina Mason or from someone else he knew about the KYVs in Buchanan's North High. He was on their side. In his mature view it was altogether desirable for those girls to keep their virginity until they married.

So how, then, account for the grotesque extravagance with Carole? Probably the root of it lay in a corruption of the intellect instead of in sensuous stimulation.

Of all the girls he had known in his sociable adolescence Carole was the one who appealed most to his chivalry. She lived then—as now—only eight blocks down on the other side of the street. He had begun to dry her tears when she was three and he was five. And her tears had seemed to him, even at first, seen through the gross screen of infant sentimentality, to be angelic. That was not too strong a word for the feeling she kept alive in him, and it may have been that intolerable feeling he chose to crush when he violated her.

All this was not to say that she was particularly different from the other girls with whom they both grew up. Of course she wasn't. She was one of the crowd. She had the same phases, tastes, crushes, manners, vacations, and clothes—and probably about the same number of boy friends. After puberty she was not even the prettiest girl among those Royce knew well, though before twelve she had been. It was her fate to be a real beauty at the time when, for a woman, it counts least.

Once Carole had been unbearably lovely and sweet. Add to this that around her hovered the romantic aura of bereavement. Her parents had died together in an auto crash about 1924. True, Royce's mother was dead as well. But that seemed a fully accommodated circumstance, quite in the natural order of things. Morgans and Blackburns died with good conscience and good spirit and that was that. One felt that Carole's parents must have screamed in the wreckage, quite unprepared to leave their lovely duckling daughter and their own good lives. Perhaps Royce heard a story to that effect. At any rate, Carole's loss had a persisting quality of rawness, of harsh whimsicality, that would not let it be accommodated in his generous world. One felt that.

His aunts always arranged something special for her in their holiday celebrations or at birthday parties. Their motives were that "the poor chick will be particularly lonely at a time like this."

There could hardly have been a more factitious excuse for charity. Carole was provided for. In fact Deirdre must have been worth any half-dozen of ordinary parents. Carole was popular enough, too, in grade school and junior high. She lived better than comfortably and was exactly as fully occupied as she wished to be on any given day or week. Like Royce, she was an only child, and like him she was mothered by female relatives.

But people always liked to be solicitous of Carole, even then. Royce overdid it cheerfully for years. He simply never doubted until he was seventeen that her happiness was his grail. He would have felt honored to give his life in protecting her from those ineffable threats that seemed to buzz around her taffy curls like furies in the nursery.

Yet one summer afternoon when his aunts had left them playing badminton together in the back yard while they went downtown to a movie, he lured her upstairs. To prove he was as well-rounded a youth as the little bums in his Scout patrol he sacrificed all the merit of guarding her so long. What judges required this proof?

He remembered forever how breathlessly they crept up the polished stairs and how their white sneakers whispered as they went to Aunt Grace's bedroom. Royce took one look at the prim chenille cover on the bed and at the hospital whiteness of the pillows. His nerve began to fail.

"Get down," he said from a dry mouth. He put his hand on Carole's shoulder and pushed gently. He thought she was shrinking to infant size as she knelt.

How loyally and unquestioningly she dropped to the floor! Her blind smile looked like a veil over a skull. Her elbows screeched like hoot owls on the waxed floor as his weight straightened her full length.

There was hardly a question of pleasure in that brief coupling. It would be hard to imagine any shared act in which there could be less of the personal. Her pool-tanned pelt and taffy-colored hair seemed exactly the same color as the wood on which she lay. She neither flinched nor kissed him nor looked at him. The accomplishment was all his—as if some hunter had truly come upon a nymph imprisoned in the grain of pale wood and had known nothing better than to ravish it.

Only, when it was time to steal back to their game, she said, "I'm bleeding." When he heard that, he would have been glad to be hit by a bullet or by lightning.

After that—yes, for nine years after that, a period that even in his present memories seemed prolonged out of all likely proportion, prolonged with the leisure of prehistoric times, ages of the dinosaur, having hardly any quality of history, of change or progress—his unclassifiable union with Carole had continued. Not a marriage, it was nevertheless some odd and prehistoric parody of marriage, a domesticity of young, leaf-eating dinosaurs, an adolescence so deeply colored by their dependence on each other that the rest of their lives would have to show those tints, one way or another.

Nine years . . . of what? Well, of pleasure, for one thing. Pleasure not to be ignored in any summary or counting of debts. For nine years, however infrequently they might be together for some of that time, he had counted like a traveling husband on the weeks or summers when he would be home with Carole in Buchanan and they (once or twice at least in each visit) in bed. There had been no pleasure in that first coupling. Pleasure soon enough appeared to complicate the snare, for them both.

But it was not for pleasure's sake that Royce had let the anomalous relation go on. Conscience had been hit hard when the girl said she was bleeding. It rang like a bell. He had done what conscience could not tolerate—so he did it again, as if by making the sin more common he could discount it. He could not live with the accusing image of a fractured virgin. Between himself and the ineluctable hour of his treachery, he had placed the easier figure of an accomplice who "liked it" as much as he. A willing Carole served as cushion and defense against the haunt of a ravished girl-child. The healthy Carole, who stopped bleeding promptly enough, sheltered him against that icon of maidenhood who, in his bad dreams, would bleed throughout the prehistory of his adolescence. She cried in soft confusion when he first tried to explain what he "meant" by treating her as he had, but gave up tears when she found it was going to be a matter of course.

The overt crisis had been brief enough. Many scarecrows vanished with it. Presently Aunt Grace's serene bed itself became the scene of their trespasses. The float he had built and anchored in the river was used for unscoutlike purposes. While Carole was still in high school they sometimes made love in Aunt Deirdre's basement. One night Royce slept there after Carole went upstairs to her bedroom, risking discovery as if on purpose to exorcise his fear of what Deirdre would think *if* she knew. Later, of course, he was pretty sure that Deirdre had known, almost from the first. And finally he believed, too—for it was the best way to grasp the whole meaning of that age of dinosaurs—that his prim, wise, game aunts had (in effect if not on purpose) intended it so on that sultry afternoon when they left the children playing in the yard. And had they not tolerated this savagery by their white-haired boy (those conservative guardians) so he could accept with complacency later those knowledges that would have wrecked a truly civilized man? Hadn't they blooded him like a dog? Weren't they training him for the approach of barbarisms that they were merely too comfortable to name, those old women who knew how to enjoy a world they no longer trusted?

Before as well as after his break with Carole he had indeed "thought this all out." And every time he had thought it out, in outline or in detail, the reckoning had come out with appalling evenness, as if everybody's guilt rode in such perfect balance with everybody's satisfaction in the situation (tacit or moaned aloud) that only a willful violence could possibly break the imprisoning equilibrium. She grew on what he robbed her of—for nine years of illicit growing.

She had not been the only woman in his life during those nine years, nor he the only man in hers. A dozen willing girls had taken a historic place between the day he ravished her and the settlement with Priss that ended his sexual wandering. In the first of his New York days he had been an ardent, over-rationalized satyr, not only keeping a show girl for mistress while he still expected to marry Carole but keeping her for the well-considered purpose of working out a solution to the dilemma that Carole presented to him. On her side, as he pretty well knew, there had been a few lovers along the way, and though that quasi knowledge had given him irrational anguish at the time, it had not provided any solution either.

Those anguishes, which must have been jealousy, over her college indulgences were so far gone now as to be almost beyond memory.

With them, unhappily, had faded those sensual memories which once had kept a balance in his feelings about the girl. What had been sensual—and therefore "all right"—had become abstract by the same banal process of time that dries an animal pelt for the taxidermist. In the abstract what he had done to Carole was not all right at all.

For nine years—the mind groaned with that *nine*—he had kept her from making a shape of her life, which now that she was thirty and twice widowed seemed unlikely ever to have much shape at all. He had begun to grieve over that when she came home to Buchanan last spring. The grief had fixed and frozen tonight when he saw her pushing Deirdre's wheel chair, as if her still fragrant, healthy female body were a draft animal not only for the old woman's physical wasting but harnessed also to that inevitable despair that waits for the changeless in a world of change. While they were going, the nine years had been paid for with love and love-making. There was, in the nature of things, nothing but remorse left to pay for their loss now that they were gone. In the calm of a house in Buchanan one was returned to thoughts like that.

It was not by any means merely Carole's presence in Buchanan that kept reminding him of his embarrassment for the way, once, he had said goodbye to her. Like the rest of his sentiments, that embarrassment was all the more intense for being dissociated—by almost seven years now—from the hopeful intentions that had plunged him into it. To have broken with Carole by seducing her into approval of the break—that, in the abstract, was not only almost as bad as having lured her upstairs one sunny playday, it was almost the same thing, so that the generalization of a guilty memory saw a continuity, unbroken, in his whole conduct of the affair, now unrelieved by the times when her hot hide and heart had hinted forgiveness sufficient to his fault.

Bad enough that, but the historical fact was only tinder. Priss threw in the spark, a born incendiarist who could leave nothing alone, Pandora's favorite daughter who took all reticence for a personal challenge. If Royce was now in some never-to-be-slackened moral embarrassment toward Carole, Priss would set it to music. Yes, she meant for Carole to hear them in what Carole would have to understand was happiness.

Oh, he was in the middle, right in the middle. Somewhere between nine years with Carole and seven years with Priss, located on a golden chart where years were only divisions, the private moral task assigned to Royce Morgan was pinpointed.

While he slept in his well-loved house, responsibilities grew on him and returned like barnacles fixing on the hulk of a capital ship built a little too late for action.

PART TWO

6

ONCE IN THE COURSE of Mooney's first year as president of Wellford, George Hand permitted himself the liberty of saying to Royce, "I can't claim I know exactly where he's going. I can't say I like the fellow, but everyone else seems to find him admirable. *They're* all pleased with him."

And that, as it seemed to Royce, was a masterly appraisal of the Mooney method of making illusions work. The faculty, as a group, was sure that the students, townspeople and trustees liked him. Individual faculty members were sure that the rest of the faculty liked him. Carole, who would eventually become articulate on the subject, inclined to the view that Priss liked him. Priss was sure, in her Machiavellian humors, that Carole would like him well enough to be taken.

Henry Worth thought the right people in Buchanan liked him.

The other right people thought that Henry liked him.

So nearly everyone supposed he *ought* to admire since the others did. But there was a universal difficulty in forming a direct impression of the man as a basis for either like or dislike. It was as if when one looked straight at him one saw nothing—an empty chair, a door opening and closing by itself, a gift to the college fund materializing out of thin air (or out of the unsolicited generosity of the alumnae, which amounted to the same thing). He was, one felt, a process, not a substance, an act of prestidigitation, not an administrator, a *happening,* not a man with appetites or idiosyncrasies or a good square butt to sit on when he was tired—or scruples or objectives of his own, either. From the first the bargain that he offered to everyone

75

else was, Let me get my hands bloody or dirty if necessary to Get the Job Done, while you keep yours clean to gather the benefits. But *let me.* . . . What the Job was, exactly, no one had yet found the occasion to ask.

He stuck in the mind like that abstraction of the philosophers, pure utility, or maybe like a genie that Henry Worth had summoned by rubbing a dirty old golden lamp. If one tried to look at him directly, one saw only the physical man, or not even that, but only the daily masquerade.

Under his splendid white-as-starch hair there was a young man's face (he said he was thirty-five when he came to Wellford and he could not have been lying, one way or the other, by more than three or four years). A pink face with eyes like jewels so valuable that he had developed a permanent crinkle of the lids to veil them from a greedy world. Not quite fat, he had the pleasantly sleek look of a creature fattened to demonstrate his master's opulence to the whole world. And his tiny hands, as pink and clean as his face, handled official documents like a riverboat gambler dealing. To think of them bloodied by the requirements of his position was to think metaphorically of assassinations that would never come to judgment in a common court.

When he came out of the president's mansion about nine each morning with a Homburg riding jauntily on his white top, crossing to the old-fashioned arched doors of Arden Hall, he issued like today's newspaper, hot from the press, disposable by bedtime, perhaps, but nevertheless part of a permanent or even immortal series. All things to all men (and all circumstances, too) Mooney (or the Mooneys) had infested Wellford like an Asiatic horde. Everyone felt that, though the naked eye saw only a single figure in passage from mansion to office; so it was the naked eye that seemed to be in error. Willy-nilly, people believed in the very many Winfred Mooneys (and the contradictory Mooneys) reported by all the other witnesses.

"It's my impression that the students have found a hero," Priss said, fingering that impression to determine if it had a potentially lethal edge. "He's a regular *guy*." She had heard, then, of the cake-eating episode, one of his earliest dramatic triumphs.

Half a dozen veterans of Iwo Jima and Okinawa had formed the habit of carrying lunches to the campus and near Thanksgiving the head librarian had discovered them eating between the bookstacks on the top floor of the library. Miss Halstead saw disrespect for literature and an unfortunate precedent. She was also frightened to peer into the cavelike gloom among the books and see the gleam of chomping teeth as these lightly transformed infantrymen gobbled their dry dessert.

So she set on them with unfortunate shrieks, much too much like the stereotype old maid driving kids off her porch with a broom. The young men not only resented being shrieked at, but heard in the shrieks an opportunity to tease. They came back the next day reinforced. Probably there were twenty or more married veterans, who lived too far from the campus to go home for lunch, eating their imitation C-rations among the stacks when Miss Halstead came on them, this time threatening disciplinary action and maybe a Cossack charge by the rheumatic old campus police. One of the veterans was supposed to have called Miss Halstead something salty. She replied (and the epithet became a kind of honorary one at once) that he was "a cake-eater." They dispersed that day with giggles.

The thing gathered steam over a weekend. Some girl wrote an editorial in the weekly student newspaper, rather feebly but emotionally linking the test of strength to (1) the student housing crisis, and (2) the natural resentment of veterans at encountering chicken after they were discharged "into the free atmosphere of a college."

Monday at noon Miss Halstead swept into the stacks flanked by two creaking members of the campus police whose pistols (alas) were drawn and trembling in their hands. She saw that the lunching veterans were more numerous than in the previous week. She alvanced without a pause.

Then she said (all over the campus for weeks to come students, and particularly coeds, would be overheard mimicking her intonation), "Why, President Mooney . . . !"

For there he was, one of the guys, a white-haired old veteran himself, just setting his teeth in a pink-frosted piece of cake, not merely rebuking her stuffiness by his presence, but flinging it back like slop in her not insensitive face.

Her intonation (and even she would realize it full well as soon as she withdrew in haste to her office and began to sob) had been exactly and precisely that of a bloomered spinster enraptured yet horrified at coming on a man in her privy.

"Why, President Mooney . . . !" the coeds sang in parked cars when they slapped importunate hands away from their hems and elastics. "Why, President Mooney . . . !" sang voices from occupied cubicles in men's toilets when someone tried the door. The voices sang it out of the shrubbery and across the athletic fields. Miss Halstead heard.

She brought her mortification to Royce. She came to him, as she explained rather oddly, because he was "closest to the president." And she wanted—deserved—to be told what President Mooney "meant" by popping out at her from an ambush of unruly students. Odd that she should speak of Royce as closest to Mooney, for as any old hand at Wellford would know, the chancellor was second in command, at least on the official table of organization.

Royce supposed he knew what she meant—"close to being president" was what she might more correctly have said. Like others in the college family she had seen the embarrassment of his failed expectations. Now in the grip of her own embarrassment she had come to him as a fellow victim.

"If he had spoken to me about it, made his wishes clear . . ." she lamented. With some stiff pride she said, "I conceived it was my duty to handle the matter myself without troubling anyone higher up. Him."

And how should she be answered according to her desert? That probably President Mooney had also acted from delicacy? Had not wished to give her a formal order to back down from her position, but rather had felt the whole contention might be dissolved in good humor by his illustrative prank?

Well, this was not among the matters where Mooney had confided in him, and the conjectures he had to offer the poor woman could be no more than balm for an irremediable hurt. He knew on the authority of overhearing Mooney's secretary that the president had not premeditated his appearance with the rebels. He had been walking near the library when someone yelled, "Come on to a picnic," and he had impulsively gone. But that sort of account did not explain what was "meant," either.

Royce advised Miss Halstead to forget it. Probably after this show-down the veterans would go back to lunching in the student lounge as they were supposed to.

She said she *couldn't* forget it.

He heard in her absurdly suffering tone the echo of "I'm bleed-ing," and ruefully concluded he had enlisted one more in the Buchanan company of the victimized, of which he was honorary captain, all embarrassed.

But in the other camp the students had glimpsed one of the Mooneys as a folk hero—those who heard about it secondhand at any rate. Those who had actually been with the president in the stacks when he put on his show had been made nearly as nervous as Miss Halstead.

Invariably his popularity spread in that leapfrog fashion; always, so to speak, more quickly established in the bleachers than in the boxes behind home plate. It was always thought to be more firmly established in the more numerous elements of the institution—that is, more among the students than the faculty, more among the faculty than the administration, more among the administration at large than with Royce or George Hand. (Among Miss Halstead's darker motives in bringing her trouble to Royce must have been the not unsupported notion that he was waiting his chance to get Mooney.)

Before the year was out it was taken for granted around Wellford that the students adored the new leader. (Taken for granted by whom? It must be that things taken for granted go to the liveliest grabber, and that was Mooney. *He* took it for granted, and knew— if he knew nothing else—how to use one grant to wheedle another.)

He came to their football games and the swollen dances that over-flowed the old fieldhouse in that year of inflation. He danced with the candidates for beauty queen and advised the boys who were making the selection. At a chapel with the full student body in attendance he produced architectural renderings of the proposed new dormitories and cottages for married student veterans. "Room rent will be consistent with what you're paying now," he boomed, juggling the daydream renderings like prompter's cards before their eyes, "*and* the mattresses will be as comfortable as those in the Coolidge Motels."

Many of the faculty missed the allusion at first. The students got it—and roared a ragged laugh of response. The Coolidge Motels were gaining a *sub rosa* reputation of hospitality for student fornication. Their president was letting them know how he winked at the natural and inexpungeable habits of boy with girl, and was not the prude that his white hair and position might indicate. He took it neatly for granted he would be loved for this sly lapse of dignity.

Those on the faculty who caught the innuendo, and gnashed worn teeth over it, might well remember that it was his hands which were reddened and his plump round shoulders on which rested the guilt for tolerating the motel phase of The Undergraduate Experience. Theirs the profit from undergraduate contentment expressed loudly enough by this laughter in chapel.

From early in the year Mooney began to leapfrog his popularity out beyond the boundaries of the campus. On the day of Wellford's first big football game with Forest University, he caused himself to be driven before the multitudes in the bleachers in such a car as had never been seen even close to the playing fields of Wellford. He was chauffeured by a freshman named Tommy Barker.

Wellford was trailing by fourteen points when he appeared at half time. Royce, who was sitting high in the stands with Lot between himself and Priss, was detachedly speculating how at this very moment, when the skies were so miraculously sweet above ground, Henry Worth was down in the subsurface locker room with the boys and the new coach. Perhaps Henry, who still cared, was waving Melanevski's contract. And if things had been otherwise, it might have been Royce's presidential duty to be down there interposing himself so Henry would not kick the poor man's ass, even though he might tear up the contract.

A pennant-rippling breeze swept the Morgans in their high perch, an air smelling of the frosts beyond Lake Michigan in the balsam forests, an air dashed with the spice of automobile exhaust and the Prentice Packing Plant as the whites in a Van Gogh painting are tinted with acid yellow or green. The majorette strutting the turf with two rows of sleigh bells across her tits, browless under her busby, drove a shining baton from left to right like a juvenile Circe pointing out swine, and behind her the sweating Wellford Band played "The Wellford Fight Song." (A great half-time joke for Priss: Forest—14, Wellford—Fights.) She was so delighted with Wellford's disadvantage she was almost as open as Royce to the splendor of the American day, almost as thankful for it.

"Sweet," she said.

"The uses of adversity," he said, earnestly thankful not to be down there calming Henry.

"What's that?" Lot asked.

He was pointing. At the open end of the football field a mammoth car was suddenly present, as if by autumnal enchantment, under the red and brown maples. It was a Rolls-Royce Silver Cloud, vintage about 1938, but it looked like more. It looked like the incarnation of Britain's finest hour, an Arthurian mechanism returned as promised not only to stand immaculate and unperturbed under the rage of the Luftwaffe but to shed even those defeats and miseries of age or time that otherwise not even British pluck could stand against. A chariot of Victory, not unworthy to ride the prow of a stone boat commemorating Samothrace.

It drifted along the snow-white sidelines in front of Wellford rooters. While the stout-legged coeds and lanky boys gaped, it seemed to plant itself like a luxurious tank on the firing line, beside the players' bench.

From a gray door that opened with the massive silence of a bank vault's door, Mooney stepped onto the grass. His Homburg sat tilted on his head like an opened visor. He was not smiling. It was not the moment for that. He started to raise his hand, whether to make a V sign or lift his hat to the crowd no one ever knew.

He hadn't time to complete the gesture. At that second Buchanan County farm boys and the sons of Gary foundrymen came charging from the locker room. And as they passed him their scarlet jerseys and white helmets seemed all at once refurbished. And no doubt Mooney did the refurbishing just by reaching out to the boys in appeal and command.

An absolutely unprecedented roar went up from the Wellford and Buchanan sports-lovers. Jubilation, amusement (a Rolls-Royce with chauffeur is, among other things, *funny* to Midwesterners), the simple joy of yelling in a vast company—whatever the shout meant, it announced something new. The passion for sports had been lively for a long time in Buchanan. That day it became a spiritual hunger.

Mooney put his arm around Coach Melanevski's shoulders and they walked to the bench like Feeble Virtue supported by an angel. Mooney sat with him on the bench through the second half. His car remained where he had got out of it. And this was as unfair as if Forest U had been threatened with a cannon.

The visitors were massacred after that. Before the third quarter was over one could see that Forest tacklers were actually cringing away from Wellford's invincible blockers and ball carriers. Once their quarterback was seen to stare hopelessly at Mooney's car when he should have been watching the pass from his center. Wellford recovered the ball ten yards behind him.

The final score was fifty-three to fourteen. Priss computed it otherwise. "That man could be president," she said on the way out of the stands.

Useless to remind her that he already was. "Of the United States," she said wonderingly, perhaps for the first time conceding to herself that she might have some trouble managing him for her special purposes.

Royce had been made inexplicably gay by what they had witnessed. He clowned with Lot as he led the family through a splendid dust-fog and swirl of falling golden leaves toward their mere Packard. "What did you think of Gingwertz' punting, hey, boy?" For the hell of it and for anyone to see, he flung back the skirts of his topcoat and poised on his left toe while he kicked the right one up between his extended hands. "We'll get out the old football, huh? And I'll see if I can still boot one that far. I'll teach you how to spiral them that way, huh, Sport?"

Lot said, "Daddy, if you had got elected would we have that car?"

A saddening question, because to answer it truly was to strike Romance down from its place in this twilight.

"No," he said. Whimsically he thought that if Priss were not there to overhear he might have said Yes. She held him to the truth whether she respected it or not, and she knew him too well to expect that the heart's answer would ever be the truth from him.

"Like Hitler coming to a rally," Priss said.

Turn about, Royce held her to the truth. "Oh, *no*. No, no, no. Didn't you hear *who* yelled when they saw him? Oh, it was American. You know it was more like Sheridan rallying the troops at Cedar Creek."

"I didn't know he *had*," she said. "Anyway, they all think he's a cutie pie."

There was no one to contradict her that night at least. Coach Melanevski got a little drunk at a reception in the presidential mansion and phrased the widely shared feelings of the hour when he told a sports writer that President Mooney was "darn near godlike" in his ability to inspire men with confidence. Well, perhaps Henry Worth had literally kicked him like a dog in the locker room at half time, and it was easy to appreciate his relief at the subsequent change of fortune.

Still waiting for a response in himself, or even for any clear-cut Mooney policy to clarify enough so he might judge whether or not *he* liked the man, Royce concluded that George Hand had settled once and for all in admiration. More than that—in trust. For just after Christmas Wellford College bought real estate adjoining the campus—some shabby three-story apartment buildings and a couple of eroded fields.

This was not a huge deal. Royce supposed that a fair price might have run in the neighborhood of seventy-five thousand dollars. He further supposed that the price must have been substantially lower than that—a bargain snapped up—because the transaction was made in haste, without either summoning a special meeting of the trustees to approve it or waiting to put it on the agenda of a regular meeting. That is, it was handled out of liquid funds and credit, and though the decision to buy was obviously Mooney's, George had to approve the diversion of money and command Jake Nutley, the treasurer, to put it on the line without delay.

Surely the College needed the land, if not for its immediate program of building dormitories, then for the foreseeable expansion of the next five or ten years, when real estate prices would probably be higher.

Surely it was a sound stroke of business, apparently more conservative than otherwise, but the very suddenness of the stroke set up a ripple of following uneasiness. The small businessmen of Buchanan, who were still among the College's chief creditors in that year of renaissance, talked it over among themselves. Guardedly, each passed on some information about how long it had been since the College had made him any substantial payments. Quite a while, they agreed—and though there was, reassuringly, a Republican Congress in Washington, these were the men who had put it there to batten down the hatches against the general postwar recession they still expected.

But they calmed themselves by recalling that the new president at Wellford was well liked and strongly supported by Deirdre Prentice as well as by Henry Worth. The Prentice money came from meat packing, and Buchanan had been packing meat since it became a city. Miss Prentice would never tolerate maneuvers by the College that might harm the plumbers, the laundries, the wholesale grocers, contractors, electricians, and office-supply houses who were owed most of the money. Henry Worth had such a big interest in the

84

First National by now that if the College slipped into crisis, the bank could bail it (and them) out promptly. It was never quite clear to those people just how little either Miss Prentice or Mr. Worth had been consulted about the real estate purchase.

Some of the well-paid new members of the faculty caught up the anxiety as the businessmen were letting go of it. In February there was quite a little talk that there might be a one-year moratorium on one-ninth of their yearly salary (or one-eighth or one-tenth, the wild guess varying according to the academic discipline of the worrier, the economists guessing less, English teachers foreseeing the worst). They healed themselves with the recollection that the small businessmen of Buchanan depended so much on the College for the cream in their trade that they were bound to extend credit until the College leveled off. And when Mooney got on the road to go after gifts and endowments . . . With such a likable operator telling the Wellford story, the long-run picture was bright, bright.

So Mooney skated over the thin spots of his first big, independent move as president. When things began to quiet it was apparent to Royce that if George Hand "couldn't say" whether he liked the new authority, it was merely expedience that kept him from a flat declaration.

There was something of the hunting dog in Royce, and it simply bewildered him not to be able to get a scent of the real man inside or behind the multiple façades. He could agree with Priss on the easy formula that Mooney was all things to all men, but this only bewildered him the more, since Priss, whose scent he thought he had fixed in the cadre of his intuitions once and for all, seemed to place such a different value on this than he could.

"But if he's nothing at all—nothing in himself—how can he lead people along at such a clip?" Royce argued.

"Aha," Priss said, as if she knew. As if, being a woman, she knew. He concluded she had recognized something womanish in Mooney, but since he was too good to admit to himself how this womanish thing operated in a real female, he learned nothing about Mooney from that.

Nor anything from Mooney himself in those first few months. All things to all men, Mooney faced honesty and openness with honesty and openness. The big thing between himself and Royce was the mishandled race for the presidency? Very well, at a tactful time Mooney spoke of it.

On one small-scale social evening in the mansion the two men got to talking about the portrait of Royce's father that still hung in the drawing room.

Royce had always, honestly and openly and even to his father's face, made fun of the painting. With academic gown and collar seeming to balloon in a strong wind, the painted figure looked more like a patriarchal Bat Man than the ingenuous old sage it should have depicted. So, Royce suggested to Mooney, why not retire it to the storage loft above the basketball court?

"Nope. Never," Mooney said.

"You're going to redecorate, though."

"When we have the money," Mooney said, wincing as if in honest remorse at the debts he had already piled on the College. "The plans are already in the works. A couple of boys from a Chicago firm have been through the place like termites and they're ready to go. I've already fought the battle of your father's portrait with them. They're not to budge it, or reframe it either. That old man's face helps me more than anything when I have a tough decision."

Royce winced in his turn. "He looks like the arch-Philistine himself in this picture. He wasn't actually that bad."

"We won't see any more like him," Mooney said. "That's the face of Old America. Of a time. Of an age. It really is." To show his taste, as well, for Young America, he said, "Don't be too hard on Pop. The face resembles you quite a little, you know." He watched for a sign of agreement that failed to appear. "Your wife's an artist. What does she think of it?"

"Mmmm. She sees it as a pattern of what I shouldn't become."

"I suppose she didn't want you to follow on as president here," Mooney said. He chuckled at the ambivalence of woman's nature.

"She wanted it and didn't want it."

"Of course."

"We were agreed, anyway, that I wasn't to repeat my father's pattern in any case. That's the keystone of our marriage." And then Royce paused with the chill of indulging in more openness than was quite safe. He had a sense that Mooney's neutrality (natural enough on a matter none of his concern) was enticing him to denounce Priss, to go on and say, Maybe it was a mistake. . . . Mistake, mistake—a keystone trying to support itself in mid-air. . . . And if he said that to *Mooney*, what honor was left for him in the game they were all playing?

"You're both wrong about *that*," Mooney rumbled. The tone was manly and deep-throated, perfect for candor between men. "That's why, for the time being, I fit better in the job of president than you would have."

That was fair enough. Royce grinned, bobbed his head in a type of salute. "I think you do."

Then, maybe a little more boyish than manly, Mooney began to disclaim the baldness of his statement. "There are times when I think that. Other times I feel like an impostor here and I've wondered if you didn't resent my . . . being whisked in ahead of you by Señor Worth."

"I don't feed much on resentment."

"I'm sure you don't," Mooney said, with a slow uptake of flattering amazement. He reached up to slap Royce on the shoulder. "That's why you won't resent my saying what I read in that portrait. I believe your father had some supporting faith you're denying yourself."

"He did his best and didn't worry."

Mooney nodded. "And you worry. Very quietly, so the rest of us won't know you're doing it. Yes, I suppose you do. As far as I can tell—you know I've learned a lot about things in Buchanan since I came—you could have been president if you'd wanted to consolidate your gains. But you'd rather be an onlooker. Not that you don't contribute immensely. Anyway, I'm darn glad you decided to remain. Heaven knows why you did." A roguish smile, deep and toothless. "Why?"

There was no deceit in answering, "I still don't know." But Royce was stirred to candor by the other man's excellent counterfeit of it—so stirred that he might have said, Why, to find out who you are. . . .

There was only once in that first year when Royce could feel securely that he surprised the real owner of the Mooney personality troupe. That was at Deirdre's funeral.

The good woman had outlasted the schedule set by her doctors—probably out of sheer terror and revulsion, though even Carole appeared to believe her aunt had accepted the terminal pain, fogginess, and death with resolute bravery. And all on her own she had decided that she would be buried in old Harvey P. Morgan's circle of friends, whether she deserved to be there or not. It was too horrid for her not to believe it made a difference where her body lay.

A great part of Buchanan had come to the church funeral services, and not because the town had grown up with the Prentice Packing Plant, either. On an east wind, the packing plant smell still tainted the air, winter and summer, an odd sniff of prosperity and rotten flesh. Deirdre had nothing to do with that—more with the west wind, maybe. Men, women, and children (even Priss, even Lot, like others who had had no great contact with her) thought they knew her, or that they must know her, since they lived in her town. Suddenly, in the circumstances of loss, it seemed to everyone there had been a uniting mother spirit who had walked their streets through all their lives. She had been no ministering angel to the poor, but they loved her (or remembered now that they had) for her hardy conviction that, being Americans, they needed only justice and education. She was the lady who "you know, *supported* the College and donated the bandstand."

The smaller crowd that followed the hearse to the Presbyterian Cemetery included mostly people with money, her own sort, and they loved her though she had never given them justification for their vulgarities in commerce or the waste of their leisure. They loved her for adherence to a manner of life they would have called "old-fashioned"—meaning that even the careless could see it had been devoted to a plain ideal of a "free folk on a free soil" that they had given up the hope of buying. She had always shamed them a little by her life and they had stayed out of her way (she hadn't many close friends since old Morgan died), but at her death they welcomed this shame, as if by a small acknowledgment of it they could reclaim what they had squandered.

She was a great woman, the pastor told them, and told them they were gathered to admire the sundown colors of a noble life. They knew better. They were here to watch the earth obliterate the last protestant against its broken promises. And under the decorum, horror and dread of the future had their silent moment.

When the coffin went into the earth, Carole, who had been standing at the graveside, bolted at a swift walk to where the Morgans stood. Her face was unmarked with tears. She was too shaken for that. Instead her mouth sagged in the kind of smile seen on an anesthetized face.

Her mouth opened completely. It was clear she wanted to ask Royce something. Then she knelt and took Lot in her arms.

"You loved her, too. Didn't you? Didn't you?" she asked.

The boy squirmed in her embrace. He looked questioningly at his father, What am I supposed to say to that?

"Carole," Priss said. "We want you to come home with us this evening. It's only, it was only not being quite *sure* how it would be taken, how it would . . . how Deirdre . . . you know, that we haven't seen more of you all this winter. But come home with us. Please come."

And—of course, because it was Carole, still drugged with the promises her aunt had at last shaken off—there was an indecent excess of gratitude on Carole's face as she nodded her acceptance. It was as if she felt that the spoiling flesh in the grave over there was her shame, that she could hardly understand why anyone would want anything to do with her, related as she was to that thing that had to be covered so deep out of sight. Death's little orphan saying thank you to life. . . . Royce wanted to slap her and Priss too. Something odd was going on that he hated. He wanted to grab Lot and run from the two women.

Probably this anomalous topsy-turvy of his sympathies set him up to respond as he did to Mooney that afternoon.

As they walked slowly toward their car with Carole they passed the president being set on by Mrs. Henry Worth, the lady still scattering tears like an overtaxed lawn sprinkler. She had his lapels and was going to make him answer whether "there had ever been any woman who quite lived up to Deirdre Prentice."

Royce saw Mooney arch a dark eyebrow, stare beyond his questioner with an expression of absolute nonpresence, and repudiate all his debt to the heartbroken vote that had made him president by saying, "Madam, I hardly knew the woman."

For once, Royce thought, a statement from the heart, though that heart was as empty as interstellar space. The hollow truth echoing clean among their despairing pretenses. Clean as a bayonet.

Royce liked it—and for a while after that supposed he liked Mooney.

7

CORRIDOR LIGHTS sparkling on a narrow tile floor, a woman pre-occupied with how to balance her resentments against the high-mindedness of her calling, inattentive until the whisper of sneakers behind her slips through the screen of mature judgment and touches off fears disposed of half a century ago.

Miss Halstead was attacked one night as she prepared to leave the library alone after closing time.

Or she thought she had been attacked. She had certainly been knocked down by someone—either someone running past in criminal haste or (she remembered, she was sure she remembered) someone who had knelt over her and tried to lift her skirts.

At twelve-fifteen on the night of March 22 her screams were heard by a night watchman, who found her tottering down the outside steps, bleeding from a cut on the temple. Her gray hair had been pulled into writhing star points, and she hardly paused for breath between screeches.

The watchman understood that she had been raped, so he called for a police ambulance and sent her off to the hospital, where through the night of her delirium she named President Mooney himself—and then several others—as her attacker before examination proved her sexually intact and drugs carried her off to sleep.

Royce heard about it first the next morning when Mooney asked if he could please come up to the presidential offices—right away, if he wasn't busy.

For once Mooney was aghast. He was slumped in his big green leather chair. Below his black bow tie his white shirt crumpled in a dozen large diagonal wrinkles, as an adult's shirt would crumple if worn by a small boy. His head wagged in dumfounded resignation when Royce came in.

When he had given the bare, yet contradictory, essentials of the story, he complained first about the dean of students, in whose province fell such vagaries of student life as raping librarians. "Bungle Parker, foursquare Jeff Parker. He won't do, Royce. He can't take authority."

Royce made no comment. The judgment seemed to him a fair one and he had wondered before this how long Parker would survive in the new disorder.

"All year," Mooney said, "I send him out to *do* something and he brings me *reports*. You know the way we've had to farm out our students all over this side of town until we get dormitory space. Of course it makes for a lot of studding and back-seat bingo, what you call it." He grimaced as if with earnest distaste for the idea of boy in girl. "I put him in a car and told him last fall to go around the girls' housing that has special approval this year and see that there aren't any studs upstairs. I told him to shoo them out of the Coolidge Motels as often as he had to, only see that no one got picked up by the sheriff or the town police. You know, he brought me *reports*." Mooney opened a drawer and laughed as he threw a fat manila folder on the mahogany. "There! I suppose this material might be useful for any paternity suits that may arise from the student body, for he's got here not only a complete record of who was with whom and how many times but practically how many bumps it took the fellow to finish off." Again the pink mouth puckered with disgust, surely heartfelt. "What I did *not* need was a Peeping Tom who would crouch outside the window until the rascals did their deed and then come and *report* it all to me. This morning at *five* he called me to announce that Miss Halstead had been ravished in her own library by Tommy Barker. He was going to hang up the phone after his announcement, as if now that his *report* had been made he could go to sleep."

This was leading somewhere. Mooney did not delay one of his

points unnecessarily. "If Tommy is taken down to the police station for questioning this morning, the whole student body will know it."

"I presume he will be cleared?"

"I called him at home. You know he lives at home and not in student housing. I asked him if he was even *in* the library last night. He wasn't."

Since Royce had some slight acquaintance with Barker from the old times when the boy had mowed the lawn for his aunts, he considered it probable that Tommy had not been in the library since he matriculated. He said, "I don't suppose the stain on his reputation from being questioned will be a deep one. If Miss Halstead accuses him it might be better to let the police check his alibis."

"Can you think of any reason why she'd choose to name him?"

Very easily Royce could. Miss Halstead unquestionably shared the old prejudice of his aunts that anyone who came from Bronkley, the Buchanan suburb that spread around the Prentice Packing Plant like a village of serfs around a castle, was not only a probable rapist but one who would rape his betters and tell the details in a Bronkley pool hall. Further, Miss Halstead, with a card-index mind, would know the Barker family from afar (as she knew something about everyone in the county as well as in Stratford or twelfth-century Florence) and probably knew that someone of Tommy's blood was or had been in the pen at Joliet for an identical crime. Further (Royce was adding one pathetic two with another) Miss Halstead would know that Tommy was now chauffeuring for Mooney and might accuse the man for the unforgiven outrage the master had perpetrated in the cake-eating crisis. Poor woman, poor Philomela, with no tongue to name her true ravisher.

"Royce," Mooney said, pleading like a brother. "I want to ask two things of you. First, will you take on the job of dean of students? In addition, that is. We can't spare you from Studies—oh, no. Second, will you put on your coat and go right now and talk with Miss Halstead? I'm really concerned about Tommy's reputation, and I feel it all the more intensely because he's a *poor* kid. . . ."

Royce felt he could certainly do no less than go to Miss Halstead—since she had come to him once and now needed help again.

It was apparent beyond question that only one person in the world would ever know whether there had been an intent to ravish Miss Halstead when she was run down in the library corridor. The poor lady herself would never know, and when her own wildly contradictory guesses settled, she would find equal doubts at every compass point of her memory. She could leer in her own mirror like a cynical police sergeant and whisper, "Maybe you only fell and bumped your head, dearie. Maybe you were all alone when it happened." It was Royce's task with her merely to make her understand that her vacillating convictions did boil down to uncertainty. For this she was not grateful to him, nor he at all proud of himself. Dirty work was its own reward in this case.

Miss Halstead went back to her job after a day's rest in bed. But she was on the skids now. Everyone knew it. The Faculty Library Committee, over which Royce presided wearing his dean of studies hat, was convinced she ought to be replaced at the end of the academic year. They had a number of real complaints against her, but they drove these home by recounting that she had once shown her senility by gasping, "Why, President Mooney!" and once *invented* out of pure old-maidishness an assault by some student or other. She was also said to be "hysterically" attached to the Dewey decimal system against the more progressive Library of Congress book-numbering method. It was recommended that she be replaced by her first assistant, a fruity little mustached vermin named Clackfart who had come with a Ph.D. in library science.

Royce accepted and then sat on the recommendation. But Miss Halstead knew it had been made. Her knowledge spun her faster on the vicious circle so that her increasing unpredictability tended to justify the charges retroactively.

This time when she came to Royce she said, "I could kill that man." She meant Mooney, but she could not explain exactly why he deserved a bullet in the head. She just hated him as she had never hated anyone in her sixty-two years.

There was nothing to be done about her hatred. It was beyond reason. It was to be her pension for serving thirty-five years amid the labyrinthian record of man's inhumanity to fellow creatures caught at a disadvantage.

But he helped invent another job for her. After that year she would be in charge of "Surveying the Wellford College Resources for Extension Studies."

Then he tried to avoid her because she became increasingly, tiresomely voluble in her efforts to trace back to Mooney the moral responsibility for all that had happened to her.

Yet—inadequate logic aside—he knew as well as she that Mooney was responsible for her fall, and that he was there to catch her (and Mooney's other victims) before they hit the ground.

And it was to his knowledge beyond reason—to intuition, instinct, and, yes, to unsupportable whim itself—that he had to turn when the choice was offered him to kick the ladder from under Mooney's climbing feet or to help him climb.

Mooney had apparently over-reached himself, after all, in buying the real estate. He had paid about twice the seventy-five thousand dollars that would have seemed to Royce a fair price for the buildings and land. He had paid it quickly because the owners had another offer from a huge brush company that wanted to build a Midwestern factory there, that close to a railroad spur and that close to the supply of pig bristles from Prentice Packing. He and George Hand had calculated (correctly, as far as could be determined by subsequent events) that if they had asked the trustees to approve the purchase they would have been turned down. At any rate, when the trustees heard how much cash had been put on the line, they were scared and angry (even, probably, Henry Worth, though in the circumstances presented he maneuvered like British cavalry protecting the baggage wagons to secure his own advantage). In effect they told Mooney he was on his own, to sink or swim with the deal he had made so rashly without their advice.

Beyond question he had expected the trustees to swing in behind him when they were confronted with a *fait accompli*. Both he and George Hand had expected Henry to use his voice at the First National to raise a loan whether or not the rest of the trustees would mortgage old college property to underwrite it.

Henry went out of town and stayed away while the bank president told Mooney and Hand that the bank would finance the new real estate with a straight loan of seventy-five thousand against the property as security.

So the other seventy-five, which had bled temporarily out of every fund in the College, all at once threatened to be more of a bloodletting than the College could stand. Agility, great financial agility, at least, was demanded to get through the next few months.

Mooney's cardinal advantage showed then. He didn't care. He had looked into the future and seen inflation. He had made his bet that what now seemed an outrageous price for the real estate would seem something quite different in a few years. And anyway, this above all, he was gambling with someone else's money. If they didn't like it, they could fire him. That attitude stripped him like an acrobat ready to go up for a triple somersault.

He called in the small creditors who, around Christmas, had worried about how long they would have to wait for their money. Sitting behind his desk with his arms folded and a cigar holder stuck in his rosebud mouth, he asked them, without preliminaries, to cancel Wellford's indebtedness to them and "start from here with a clean slate."

For a minute there was an uneasy scraping of feet in the presidential chamber. Then Bob Consolo (Consolo's Meat and Produce, creditors in the amount of $4,218.65) said, "Mr. Mooney, I think you mean an extension, a . . . not pressing you, a . . . holiday, a . . . sort of moratorium."

"I mean a cancellation," Mooney snapped. He rolled back in his green leather chair and blew cigar smoke at the ornamented ceiling. His Homburg was lying on the edge of his desk, and now the creditors saw a pair of gloves peeping from under it. They could hardly escape the suggestion that the man was quite ready to walk to his Rolls-Royce and drive home to New York.

Adam's apples bobbed across the room and someone tried to laugh. "Well, now, look here . . ." someone said.

Then there was silence again as everybody counted the rainbows forming in Mooney's cigar smoke.

Somebody said, "I'd like to see George Hand. I'd like to see Jake Nutley and have them explain in dollars and cents just how this is going to work out for us."

Mooney sighted along his cigar and holder. He smiled impudently at them. He did not bother to say that they would all be driving Chevys instead of Buicks or Packards if they had to do without College trade. Everyone here knew it. Why bother to put it in words? "I consulted fully with both Mr. Hand and Mr. Nutley before I made this request," Mooney said. He was telling them that he might go down but that they would go down with him—and telling them they cared more than he did. "I am the president and I take full responsibility," he said. And only sticks and stones would ever hurt his bones.

"I'm also prepared to offer you an alternative," he said, making it clear that they should understand there was only *one*. "The First National is prepared to discount all your bills at seventy-five per cent. *With* . . . the proviso that hereafter the bank will act as clearing agent on all purchases the College makes from your firm. Now I realize you're all going to have to do a little paper work to see where you'd come out on such an arrangement. And frankly I want those of you who would come out ahead to take it. . . ."

So, they understood, without any paper work required, would the F.N.B. and therefore so would Henry Worth, for through the foreseeable future they would be dependents of the bank if they accepted. That afternoon the little men looked up the gun barrel and saw the eye of Bigness staring right over the sights at them.

Bob Consolo growled with anger. "We're kind of used to having a college in Buchanan . . ." he said. But beyond the implied threat to take Mooney at his dare and sink with him—hell, carry the College down, too, while they were at it—he was not yet ready to speak. Only, when he stared at the cigar smoke, he seemed to be watching an effigy burn.

"I guess we'll let you know," he said. And since none of them yet had a better defiance to hurl at Mooney's insolence, they followed Consolo out in silence.

Then, for forty-eight hours and a bit longer, the shape of many futures wiggled indecisively. It was not really in the cards that Wellford College would fold and sell its buildings for an old soldier's home, nor that the small businessmen would thereafter become indigent. Yet one could see the edge, see great gaps between better and worse and wonder how to avoid falling. Toward the end of those hours Bob Consolo came to Royce's home.

Royce had never thought of Bob as a friend, though they had known each other since grade-school days. Both now, for somewhat different reasons, were members of the American Legion and frequently had chatted in passing at Legion smokers, probably because Bob had wanted to stay in good with anybody connected with the College. Even after last spring's pratfall, Royce was somebody. Further, both of them had laid Carole Prentice in days long past—which Bob knew (though Royce did not) and counted on (all other guidances failing before Mooney's surprise attack) as a link of brotherhood against some common peril.

"They'd damn well like to nut Mooney," he told Royce, expressing the consensus of his fellow sufferers in the confiscation.

"But are afraid they'd lose money by so doing."

Consolo laughed hollowly. "The question of money is involved in it, but that's not the whole thing. They're pissed off at Worth, too."

"But have no plans for castrating him."

"Not right now."

"Well, if the wish to parade with testicles on a pikestaff is not your main ambition, then it sort of comes down to a question of whether you're willing to take the gamble Mooney proposes. It must be clear enough that you might come out ahead in the long run if you go along with the College and don't get entangled with the bank."

Bob moaned in the collective voice of those he represented. "It would take most of us five years to show a profit on College trade if we accept his terms."

"It might."

"And then . . . here's what several of us have said: What's to keep Mooney from pulling the same thing again *in* five years? Or less? See, there's a feeling around that Henry Worth put him up to this just *so* we'd run to the bank. That he means eventually to shake us little fellows out and take over everything. Do you think Henry is behind this?"

"No," Royce said. He didn't suppose it was worth Henry's time to maneuver this way on the limited Buchanan scene. "I think that if the College were to find itself in desperate straits in five years, you could count on President Mooney to save it by whatever means were at hand."

Bob put his hand on Royce's knee—evidence of his own earnestness and a way of measuring Royce's. "That's really the way you see it? Saving the College? But what we'd like to know—among other things, of course—is whether Mooney will be here."

Royce disengaged his knee by standing up and going to the sideboard of his study for a bottle of bourbon. It sickened him a little to feel a hand trembling so passionately for money's sake.

"I think he'll be here."

That did not seem to be the guess Consolo wanted. He had come in the hope of getting some inside tip that would let him and the others like him avoid the gamble—for which feebleness Royce would have withheld the tip if it had been his to give. He might have cheered if he saw them muster the nerve to go for their tormentor with a sharp razor. He certainly would have sided with them if their concern for the College were anything but a pious second thought. As things were presented, he was still neutral.

"We can't see it clear," Consolo said. "The boys and I have argued it this way and we've argued it that. In a bigger town we'd know what to do."

"Or if Buchanan starts to grow . . ." Royce teased solemnly. Ah, yes—in five years, two years, one year the alternatives might be easy.

Trade might flourish so they could tell Mooney to shove his proposition. On the other hand, the College might be so populated with flush students that the canceled debts would not be missed. But the time between *then* and *now* was the maddening curtain that Mooney had twitched like the barker at a kootchy tent.

Consolo said, "All we've been able to hold onto is that most of us will stick together and either take Mooney's offer or sue."

"Or get your money from the bank?"

"Maybe," Consolo admitted, hangdog. "Anyway, we're this far agreed to all meet it the same. Even that won't hold up much longer. Someone will chicken out and then it'll be every man on his own. So I'm going to ask you as an old friend—and I think the boys will take your word—shall we go along with him?"

Now the bet was Royce's, though he saw no conclusive grounds for choice. It was not unlikely that if he said "No," the resulting uproar and the mere bother of suits against the College might raise enough trustees against Henry Worth to get Mooney out. But on this one occasion when the opportunity was there, something balked in him and said, Too soon. The curtain of time ahead tantalized him, too. Maybe in a year he would know whether Mooney should have been thrown out now. But the arguments pro and con that he had finished with himself to his own satisfaction balanced evenly so far. There was no practical imperative.

If Mooney should be toppled, Miss Halstead would be avenged and (he saw at least this much of future probability with grim clarity) all the future Miss Halsteads fated to go down in Mooney's path would be spared. It would satisfy some deep need to see the bank and Henry Worth kicked in the snout as they tried to get their feet in the trough. But these moral attractions did not yet tip him to decision.

Poor Consolo got his hands on Royce again. That revolting clutch made some kind of answer necessary, for whether either of them could fully interpret it or not, the hand on the shoulder said, Look, Carole was still your girl after I made her, so you've got a better right to decide than I. Here was a straw clutched out of the invisible past, when there was no other basis for faith. It was Bob Consolo's appeal to an authority beyond Royce's ambiguous position in the College and town.

Since Royce could not understand the basis for such an appeal, what probably moved him to an affirmative was just a recollection of that day when Mooney appeared in his Rolls during the game with Forest.

Now his decision recognized that appearance as Mooney's only pledge: I'll give you whatever you really want. Intuitively Royce trusted in the fulfillment—and all his fears were that the cheering crowd, the dazzled individuals, from Coach Melanevski all the way down to Lot Morgan (and pawing Bob Consolo) would choke on what they were granted.

But if they wanted it . . .

"Yes," he said. He had no right to deny people what they wanted most, so . . . he had no right to deny the man who would most likely give it to them. "Take it. You'll make money in less time than you think now. Mooney's got big plans."

"You mean in our place you'd . . . ?"

He was not obliged to answer that. Instead he smiled in a way that reassured his petitioner, drank off his bourbon decisively, and repeated, "Cancel the bills. Take Mooney's offer."

He would have been very unhappy in times to come if he had been really sure that it was his advice—or command, or urging, or whatever the right name was for it—which made the small business-men of Buchanan ride with Mooney. But of course there was no way to be sure. He only felt that his advice had been consistent with the way things would have worked out anyhow. He had merely confirmed that Mooney, better than anyone else on their small Buchanan stage, voiced the dictate of the times.

So he went on being neither happy nor unhappy, waiting and watching an ascent that he would only once again have a chance to block. He had concurred in the future. Henceforward, neither happily nor unhappily, he was one of the wheels of the juggernaut

—and therefore all the more responsible (simultaneously at that) for its victims. Therefore more divided. Therefore unable to hold out any tangible help.

There was nothing more for him to do for Miss Halstead, withering from her rape. He sided with her. He stood with her. Then? To stand with did not necessarily permit or require an action, any more than to despair implied an emotional display.

But standing at least meant staying. When a good offer came from the California university system that spring, he did not even mention it to Priss. He stayed to stand with the others even if that meant no more than a rueful and brief smile, as at the end of Melanevski.

The coach turned ugly when his contract was canceled in May. Drunk again—this time in the American Legion ballroom with his arm around Bob Consolo—he was heard to call Mooney a "two-faced, two-timing bastard."

Evidently the godlike power to inspire confidence had given Melanevski an inflated view of his share in Wellford's coming glory —which in Mooney's still uncontradicted view would be too great to afford a place for a born second-rater like Melanevski.

8

When the Morgans began to see more of Carole after Deirdre's burial, her diffidence had, indeed, the distressing, exaggerated humility of one who might have overheard their bedroom passages—a person not so much possessed by her own guilty secrets as guilty for possessing someone else's.

The immediate cause of her demoralization was of course the horrid wasting of her aunt. Carole had come flying home because she needed to lean on the sturdiness that once seemed everlasting. She came back to have the freckled old hands bless her for murder. She had married Bill Slater without love, had lain with him as his wife, had borne him no children, and with all her female instinct knew she poured excesses of hooch into him—having fun—so that someday he would be paid off for sporting another man's forever loyal woman. Whatever she might tell herself or listen to, the deaf female that inhabited her knew she was Royce Morgan's. So it was obligatory (even though unforgivable) for the very sheath that lured and accepted the trespass of "husbands" Ogilvie and Slater to spew their heat back coldly and send them to die. There was, of course, a male world of Panzers and F-6-Fs and careening Cadillacs. This machinery had done the visible disposing of bodies. An 88-millimeter projectile from a tank's cannon had scattered Ronald Ogilvie on the Italian turf. The prop of an F-6-F had carried out the sentence against Slater for his lese majesty, taking off his head as briskly as any headsman would have done it for a dishonored queen.

Carole neither understood nor trusted that male world and its machinery very much, though she could operate some of its machines better than the next person. What she understood was how her loins had condemned two men, and she came home to get Deirdre's virginal approval for that. Not that they would in any circumstances have spoken of it this way. The female principle in them was as mute as it was deaf to ordinary speech. Yet Deirdre in her strength would have found ways to applaud the achievement of widowhood, since she, too, had believed with the ponderous inertia of the heart in the marriage between her niece and Royce.

Carole came home for that, and found instead that the first bedsores were beginning to harass Deirdre like a flock of jackals attacking a lion's victim while it still lives. For Carole there was something more ominous about the earliest peppering of sores on the skin than in the cancer performing its secret ministry unseen.

Worse, Deirdre's vote against Royce repudiated a tacit understanding between young and old woman which had underwritten the nine years of anomalous relation with him—as if a true marriage were being retroactively denied.

Deirdre said, when the two of them had it out right after the election, "You blame me for second thoughts, and perhaps it would have been easier to go on just a little longer spoiling him. You blame me, though he treated you like a *plaything*." The bitter accents from her aunt were the worst betrayal Carole had known in her life, and her aunt's word stuck in her ear like a bean. How much easier if Deirdre had said "whore"—since that would have been a scarecrow word, borrowed uneasily to serve the occasion of anger. But *plaything*—the contempt and despair therein came from the roots of Deirdre's life; she saw everything staked on seriousness and work. How much better to have been caught years ago playing under Royce and whipped for it or shamed and locked up than to be told so late how much tolerance she had wasted.

"If I was a fool that's not altogether Royce's fault," she said, but she knew that she was beaten in the argument as she had been beaten in life—because the rules were changed on her while she remained faithful. In those things that counted most for her she had been most a fool.

The bedsores, when they began to spread like flowers in a benign season during the last months of Deirdre's illness, seemed purposely to remind her she had counted on the old woman's living forever.

They were Carole's obsession—*hers*. For the doctors the masculine work of doing what they could to slow the cancer and block the big complexes of nerves; for her the incessant, breath-holding opposition to the sores. Even when Deirdre was in the hospital, which, after October, was most of the time until she died, and when there were nurses to change the pads and unguents and to roll the finally power-less body, the clusters and banks of sores were Carole's garden. They were hers to dream about and wake from each morning in a terror of anxiety. They were for her to tend like some little girl in a nursery rhyme: Mary, Mary, what itching, pustular abominations grew in your garden while you slept? In a kind of enchantment she peered over the nurses' shoulders when, in the hospital period, they lifted the dressings to disclose whether the garden thrived or withered. And tending the sores seemed to repeat some obligation her aunt had laid on her long ago, warning her in a warm strong voice that if she were negligent the crimson-headed, violet, and gold of the garden would suffer instead of her for her fault.

There were some victories against the sores, at least in the summer months when Deirdre could get about, first on her feet and then in a wheel chair. Meticulous cooperation between the women, some unspoken harmony of will, restored patches of baby pink and deli-cate skin where a sore had been conquered. Carole would believe that because one area had healed, her aunt was getting better. The cancer didn't seem to matter.

But then elsewhere, though usually at least tangential to the healed area, a dark spot would appear. First it would be delicate as drifting smoke, like a shadow that might be either below or above the skin. Then it looked like a bruise under the skin. Then it was brighter and blossomed, like something bursting through into Carole's con-sciousness, turning toward the terrible sun of her guilt.

It helped, of course, that the old woman matched every inroad of her disease with some lie about the life that had brought her to it and had finally pinned her flat in the packing-house stench of her own meat. She forgot that she had voted against Royce for the same reason she denied her bad nights when Carole came to her at dawn. So she forgot that she had ever had any reasons for voting against him. The past was idealized because the present absolutely had to be.

On the night of Mooney's reception, when they met the Morgans on the walk, Deirdre had been as high on her lies and morphine as any Bronkley drunkard on cheap gin. She had not so much been reconciled to Royce. She had just failed to recognize him clearly in the middle-aged man who stood in front of her with his legal wife beside him.

Later, in her pitifully brief intervals of lucidity, she stopped admitting that Royce Morgan had ever grown past the age of twelve. She liked Carole to bring old snapshots to the hospital, and one of her few regrets as they talked about twenty years ago was that there weren't more photographs including "Dr. Morgan's boy."

"He was like a king," she said tearfully one day.

"Who?" Carole asked, thinking it possible Deirdre meant old Dr. Morgan.

"Why, Royce," Deirdre said, as if surprised that anyone could wonder.

"He was only a child."

"A child, yes. You know the old times were not good, either for men or women. And confusion. If we wanted something, we were too old to enjoy it when we got it. But there had to be a time." She stopped as if she had perfectly and lucidly completed her thought.

"A time for what?"

"To be where."

"Where?"

"All right."

"I'm sorry," Carole said. "I understand, darling. I understand. You gave me such a good childhood."

"Where," her aunt nodded affirmatively. "He was a king." Tears rolled down the bony gullies of her skull. "The old times were not good," she said—meaning surely the times *before* the old times where her hope was absurdly anchored still.

And Carole, leaving the hospital that day, clung to the ornamental limestone risers beside the door, supporting herself a little while as she tried to focus on the pigeons flying over the brightness of snow. Through clenched teeth she said, "This isn't good for me. You ought to know it isn't good for me."

Cancer may or may not be a communicable disease, but the confusion of dying is. Charitable onlookers said that in nursing Deirdre as she did, Carole was displaying the well-rooted toughness of her character. They either did not know, or in mercy had to ignore, how she began to drink desperately and more heavily than ever to pass the nights of waiting.

And that—as it never is—was not the worst. The old woman's death forced her to think again of many things she had let drift almost out of her memory. From their panicked reassessments ruined women catch the inspiration to commit their worst follies all over again.

In the years since Royce told her he was on his way—onward and upward—she had formed a tissue of acceptances and healthy commonplaces to cover the wound. She had lived a life at least superficially normal. Early in the war she had gone cheerily into the WAFs because she liked airplanes and felt better to be helping out. She had liked people. She had been "in love" each time she married. That had seemed only right to her—just as it went on seeming only right to her that Royce had broken away if he "had made a mistake." (And she could think that he very probably had. The idea that she was, after all, a "born farmer," born, alas, a little out of place, was stubbornly set in her, set to grow and flourish for the rest of her life.)

She believed conventionally enough in love as an exchange between parties, an evenly shared possession that grows with mutual respect as two loving people get to know each other better—from which it would follow logically that Royce and she had not truly loved each other, that she had not known love as nature intended her to know it.

Therein logic erred badly—though it gave her a formula to repeat to herself as often as she needed it. It erred, for love in her, in her big juicy body and in her emotional needs that were out of all proportion to her reasoning control of them, was simply a tyranny, with herself as its single subject. She loved. There was no doubt of that any more than there is that a steam boiler puffs. But to suppose that this energetic outpuffing of love was meant to be part of a reciprocating mechanism turned out to be a nearly deadly assumption. In fact it *had* been deadly for a couple of husbands who were rash enough to guess that huffing and puffing of love was for them— that when the dragon came out of the cave it would want to be petted. They were shown better.

Of course she had enough common sense to know she was not literally their murderer. Their deaths were accident and the chances of war. Still she felt that trying to focus this awful love of hers on them was a process that might have killed them before her eyes. They might have died in the conjugal bedroom if the process had gone on long enough.

She knew that after each of them died, love and the need to love had gone on unabated in her (just as it had after she sensibly slaughtered her expectations of Royce Morgan). So it must have been a very bad error to suppose these things were created by anyone outside herself. When Deirdre died, Carole's ruin was completed with the knowledge that loved ones have no more responsibility for the growth of love than a sucking baby has for the production of milk in the breast.

Her breasts were pained with love after Deirdre's death, and there was no one suitable to be in love with. The very impulse to fall in love with another man frightened her—seeing what that had come to before. Besides, if she were going to fall in love with a man again it would probably be Royce, and though her life was ruined in all its larger promises, the ruins still had a pattern that steered her away from him. She was loyal—therefore must not love as far as he was concerned.

The right man might yet come. There was a good deal still to attract enough men to give her a sporting choice. She was just a little past thirty. She was not exactly pretty, but she might seem something much better than that to men with a taste for big women. From Deirdre she had about half a million dollars in property and hard, beautiful cash. It would take a very cunning man to guess the state her demoralization had reached, for she had learned it was a duty to keep grinning, and the shell of dutiful observations was intact, still quite intact. She was thought to be taking her trials gamely.

Besides, just as some men might especially like a big, plump girl, some might like her kind of demoralization.

So there was time. So there was hope. If life had never been built on its own ruins before, it would long since have disappeared. In the meantime, since she couldn't help loving, she fell in love with the Morgan family as a unit.

It was stacked cruelly in the cards that she should love Priss. Fundamentally the choice was to love or to hate, as it always is between one lover and her successor if they are in contact at all. Especially after three deaths, Carole lacked the conscience to hate anyone. *Ergo* . . .

Royce had chosen Priss over her. He was wise. Therefore every past and present deference to his judgment encouraged her to love.

Priss had asked her "home" from Deirdre's grave. Therefore she must have penetrated deep into the secret of Carole's homelessness.

Further, Priss loved her—which says nothing of the quality, constancy, or commitment of that love, but only that it was there to be sensed. Carole's capacity for wholesome wonder and respect flattered Priss as hardly anything else in Buchanan could, and Carole was valued according to that measure.

The two women were a good deal together in that spring after Carole was freed of Deirdre. Carole was given a large history of Priscilla London Morgan.

Carole said, "Oh!" to most of what she heard. "Oh!"

Anyone who could be moved, as she was, to wonder and respect by the decorative "themes" of the Country Club dances was ordained to gape like a fat elder sister at Priss's recollected triumphs in art. From Deirdre, out of Harvey Pelham Morgan, Carole had a simple faith in the arts. "They carry you out of yourself," she said. Anyone who knew how to enthuse as she could over the renditions of

Brahms and Saint-Saëns by the Wellford Pro Arte Orchestra was meant to burn pure white when she was told about Priss's days with Martha Graham, or the times Priss had studied painting with Beckman and Ernst, or played with a jazz group admired in Greenwich Village circa 1936.

"Oh!" Carole said to all these glamorous accomplishments. Only why had Priss ever given them up? "You ought to at least play your fiddle for Lot," she would urge, blushing. "I'd love to hear you play. I never could play anything except the triangle."

"Triangle?" Priss, for such questions, had a tone of condescension so sugared that it passed for a flattering reply to flatteries.

"A triangle is a piece of steel that goes *booing* when you hit it. They let me carry one in the North High Marching Band," Carole remembered. "Oh, it was silly. I guess it should have been humiliating. But Deirdre always told me it was *something*. She used to say, 'At least it's something!' "

"Someday you get your triangle and I'll get my fiddle and we'll go through the streets," Priss said.

They would never do anything so showy in Buchanan, of course. But since Carole needed occupation (Priss's rationalization) and Carole had to be kept handy on a tether (Priss's obsession), they must immediately start on something. So they went into ceramics "seriously."

Mooney had repeated his appeals to use the studio and Priss's services. She thought: Wouldn't he sniff a little harder—and catch a more important scent—if she and Carole could soon tease him with a bit of commercial and artistic success? When her father came to Buchanan for a spring visit, she enlisted him to get the project rolling.

Father London didn't give a damn for "jugs," as he called them, and he was no longer much impressed when his daughter made a new start on anything. He used to hope she would find herself each time she started something new. Now he only hoped she would hold onto herself, at least long enough to give Lot a straight start in his life, for he was crazy about the little boy.

This may have been one of the reasons he so quickly asked Carole to marry him. His acquisitive eye saw not only a rich widow (he was not likely to undervalue the happiness of marrying for money; that wise stroke had made his life) but saw the flickering promise of something splendid developing between her and the child.

He liked to watch Carole, in taut slacks and loose violet sweater, trundling Lot around the Morgans' yard on Royce's old bicycle, leaf-shattered sunlight falling on them like a shower of mythic gold. He sat there enjoying the wobble of Carole's ass, savoring the supramotherly way she indulged and checked the brash, bright kid. It would have been disloyal of him to think that because this girl was a more natural mother for the boy than his daughter that she ought to have been Royce's wife instead of Priss. But the judgment was too definite to throw away altogether, so he compromised it foggily by daydreaming that he could provide the boy a sweet grandmother and himself a dandy, comfortable lay by the same maneuver.

Shyly, with a take-it-or-leave-it gruffness, he offered his daydream to Carole—and was jolted rather stiffly to find that her response was neither a happy affirmative, nor amusement, nor astonishment, but fright. He had never frightened anyone in his whole life before, and it shook him up.

To make things worse, Priss heard of the proposal—from Carole, who timidly wondered if the old man had been joking or what—and vilified him for it.

"Daddy, if that woman falls into bed with any more of the men in my life I'm going to have myself sewed up and go to a nunnery."

"You mean Royce . . . ?"

"Well, not *now*, of course. You know how fastidious Royce is. And I don't mean Lot, either, though there's something kind of sloppy in the way those two carry on."

"Something very nice."

"Very nice then," Priss said with a skewering smile. "I mean Royce lost his virginity, or whatever boys have, to that one and I'm learning belatedly to my surprise that it makes some kind of metaphysical difference."

"But I thought," her father said slowly, "that you liked Carole." His painter's eye had liked the look of this Midwestern household and preferred to take it simply, at the value of its handsome surface, a value somewhat enhanced by the presence of Carole as *friend,* with no ambiguities dangling from that word. He should have known that where his daughter was involved there would be a labyrinth under the paintable surface and that Priss lived her true life down in the labyrinth with intrigues always in progress.

"I like Carole fine," Priss raged. "Just where she is. No closer, no farther, *please.*"

"You're trying to manipulate her," he said in bewildered despair of guessing either how or why, only sure that he wished she would not.

"How can I?" Priss said, holding up her hands in a fury of innocence. "I can't make her do anything she doesn't want to, can I? Tell me how I'm manipulating her. You can't. Furthermore it was boorish of you to joke about marrying her when she's really, really, really sick in the gut from everyone dying on her. She's not *quite* so sunny as she acts around strangers."

"I may be a stranger, but I wasn't joking," Father London said. Nevertheless—helpless as a muscle man against a tiny judo expert— he let go his loverly daydreams and lapsed into being Grandpa, who helped the girls with their ceramic project.

He didn't like jugs. He only liked cubist paintings and high living. But in the month of his stay he turned out to be an efficient organizer and executor. So, happily, was Carole.

Sneering at amateurism, Priss wanted to bring out a line of tableware—"not just *vases,* for heaven's sake"—that could be put into quantity production if her experiments went well. She brooded over her conceptions and designs, sending Grandpa and Carole off again and again to Chicago. They were to find someone who would build a kiln "more professional than these little plug-in jobbies." The old man knew people at the Art Institute and the Institute of Design. Carole knew—or rather her banker and lawyer knew— engineers and contractors who ordinarily would not spare the time to advise a couple of women starting their own shop.

Priss refined her templates and molds, a handsome young witch incanting over her retorts. The other two ordered equipment, directed carpenters, electricians, and the mason who built their kilns, and for a while the Morgan stable hummed like a war emergency.

This went on with the lively accompaniment of talk that Carole would be—or was being—drawn toward the designing end of the project. "That's the reason for the whole thing," Priss explained earnestly to Royce. "Heavens, not just to turn her into a businesswoman or give her some way to spend her money." Carole was financing the kilns and remodeling, and insisting on it with an unhealthy fervor, as if paying off a psychic debt. "I'm trying to find something creative for her. Why must you always try to choke the creative?"

"Is that what I've done with you?" he asked with grief.

"Who's talking about me? I'm happier than I've been for years. Can't you tell that something's *going* for me? Can't you tell, sweetie? I'll show you," she said with fevered affection. "I meant for Carole. Don't you think you came near enough to spoiling her life so *we* owe her a way out now?"

"If we had it to give."

"Don't you trust me? What have I done wrong?"

"Nothing."

"Then why do you wag your head as if I had? What do you want me to do? Call the whole thing off?"

"I want you to go ahead."

"Try to sound like it then."

"Yes."

Her brows lifted maliciously. "Is it that you want to screw her again and I'm getting in your way by being her friend?"

Here was an invitation to fight back, at least to counter with an equally massive denial. But he said, "I'm not very good at handling these extreme terms. Can't it be the truth that I have *some* lingering ambivalences about Carole—guilts, if you like that word; frustrations, if you like that—without finding them so overpowering I have to believe them the full truth of my life?"

"Oh, I always know what you're going to say by now," she cried impatiently. "Get off your goddamn horse. Have at her. Who cares? Daddy's trying. Help yourself. Did you know Daddy asked her to marry him?"

Royce knew that Priss had not often called her male parent "Daddy" since puberty, and when she did there was emotional broken glass scattered somewhere nearby that the barefoot would do well to watch out for.

"It doesn't surprise me greatly," he said. He felt a swift onset of fatigue, like a chill, as if more than he already knew—more than the secret fates had yet unwound—was anticipated by this roundabout pattern of quarreling. Without knowing exactly why, he felt great pity for his father-in-law, as for a man looking at green meadows from a prison window.

"Oh, nothing would surprise *you*," Priss said. Then, her black-mail collected, she softened. "Really, my love, recovery is setting in. We're making our readjustment to civilian life and all that sort of crap. Carole does have talent. You must see some of the things she's starting to do with clay."

"She has a talented teacher," Royce said, staring at the years to come. "Promise me, honey, one thing. Be careful of her."

"I intend to, honey," Priss answered offhandedly.

Royce saw a few pieces of pottery that Carole ran up in the studio under Priss's talented guidance. They showed exactly why Carole had played the triangle—only the triangle—in the marching band. A determined child with ten thumbs could have done as well.

As a matter of fact, Lot was learning to throw a pot far more quickly than partner Carole. Some evenings Grandpa London, Lot, Carole, and Priss all deserted Royce to work in the unfinished studio. The old man did fine things and was bored with them. Priss restricted herself to finicking with designs that might be popular. Lot was the natural star of these evenings, and Carole was delighted that it should be so.

One evening she came in with the boy to Royce's study, walking behind him, beaming uncontrollably in her pride.

"What you got?" Royce asked, shoving books and papers aside on his desk and taking in his big hands the clay thing the boy had brought to show him.

Carole could not contain herself. "It's an urn! He didn't have any template or even pictures to go by, but he'd seen it in a book. It's an *urn*!"

Lot cocked a scornful eyebrow at this gushing flood of maternal emotion roaring over his head. "A Grecian urn," he said.

Turning it in the lamplight, Royce saw it was, well . . . well, hardly that. The sticky thing had lumps and bulges, and anyone but a mother should have seen that if Lot hadn't used a template, perhaps he should have. The design was scratched crudely. After all, a five-year-old had done it.

And yet, yet the spirit was not invisible. It spoke through the clay. Whether or not the palpable design contributed the major effect, or whether Carole's unrestrained presence with them there woke some ideal possibility and just for a moment tugged away the veils of event and circumstance, Royce felt a queer catching of his throat, a second of ecstasy as if he were in the presence of something realer than his life.

He held the damp thing like a globe on his fingertips, breathed hard, and said, " 'With brede of marble men and maidens overwrought.' It's wonderful, Lot. Wonderful, wonderful, wonderful."

"Gimme, gimme, gimme," Lot said, dancing with the praise he could not quite accommodate. "Mommy's gonna fire it tonight and I can take it to kindergarten if it doesn't crack."

"Maybe . . . maybe, maybe you shouldn't try to fire it," Carole said. She knew what could happen to clay from which not all the air bubbles or impurities have been cut. She knew that Lot was very often too impatient to prepare his clay well before he began to throw.

For an instant the boy hesitated. He was too thrilled with the beauty he had made, the headiness of triumphing like this in his father's eyes (to say nothing of the eyes of his kindergarten buddies, known in anticipation) to want to risk all that in the hot kiln. And yet . . .

"It's got to be fired," Royce said gently—as if for the second time in Carole's presence he were saying the most dreadful of sentences. It shook him that once again, and after all he could be said to have learned, that the decision had to be exactly the same.

"It's gotta be fired," Lot said reproachfully to Carole. Who once again bowed her head to authority.

For some reason that would never be fully understood, the over-wrought maiden Carole remained sitting in Royce's study when Lot went back through the house and across the young grass of the lawn to the studio. Both she and Royce bent their heads and listened (a little breathlessly, afraid that in the dark crossing somehow he might stumble and dash the urn to pieces) until they heard the tone of voices—not the words—from the studio signifying a safe arrival.

Then they still sat on with bowed heads as if listening—well, listening to the mysteriously renewed maples in the dark outside that whispered in some everlasting wind, hearing far off the horns of a processional, a lowing of garlanded heifers, treble song, joy itself leading them to betrayals and their present age. To loveliness betraying them, and yet . . . They remembered what had been good and knew no more what to do about it than they had known before.

"He's a good boy," Royce said huskily.

Then her head came back, mouth open and opening wider, and her eyes burning like damnation. He was afraid. He was afraid simply that she was going to say what she might have said one other time: No, goddamn you, no, you're wrong. Put your cock in me and stay. You can't leave me.

He almost heard that.

But instead she cried like a medium, "He's a king." Her own cry seemed to wake and shame her. She knew it was Deirdre's sick passion that she echoed here. But since her aunt had lived all her life in the disciplines of virginity and had been dying when she finally permitted herself the expression, Carole could not claim the right to speak this way. "I mean . . . he's so nice and proud in a nice way, he makes me think of a storybook king." Having to tone down and falsify what she really meant shamed her.

"Well, we mustn't let him hear that," Royce laughed. He saw spring lightning glimmer above the dark horizon across the river and waited for the sound of thunder. Before it came, he said, "Gee, I haven't kept up with what you toilers are doing out there with your mud pies. Let's go see."

He knew Priss was timing Carole's absence—not only her minutes with him but the extraordinary opportunity of the occasion—with a measure more sensitive than a clock. He had never had a keener sense that Priss was watching them, that now she was close to seizing what had to be kept theirs alone, kept from Priss even at the cost of denying to themselves its existence.

That night when she came with Lot to his study was the high-water mark of Carole's intimacy with the Morgan family. For a moment she and Royce had stared at a muddy urn in the boy's hands and had intimations of the figures that belonged, by right, on its globy surface. An intimation—and then denial.

Something happened a few days later that served—still cryptically, of course—to give them the means to dramatize the necessary cleaving of what they were forbidden to share.

To initiate the dramatic sequence, Lot peed in his pants in front of his kindergarten classmates. His parents never quite got the story clear of how this "was allowed"—as Priss said in her outrage—to happen. "He's a *little boy*," Royce said. "It isn't a question of its being *allowed* to happen. It *will* happen to little boys." "That satisfies *you*? That explanation?" "No," Royce said, who all his life was committed to wondering what nature meant. Here again he would have to fall short of finding out.

Anyway, it appeared that Lot had been reciting. He knew a Mother Goose rhyme, and since poetry is powerful stuff, it may be that the rhythms and the rhymes sounding in the ducts of his head said more to him than the silly verse could possibly say to his squatting peers. Some men there are who cannot hold their water when the bagpipe blows i' the nose. . . .

His father could guess how those queer, characteristic indentions would have appeared on his forehead like the print of invisible huge fingernails. How Lot would have still been listening to something else, some unearthly euphony, when the hot gush wet his seersucker shorts and the yellow, frothy puddle spread its perimeter toward Miss Kenneth's hand, paralyzed on the hardwood floor by sheer unwillingness to believe what she saw.

Miss Kenneth called Priss that morning—to ask if Lot had come home, since, gee, he hadn't returned to the classroom after she had sent him to the lavatory. Priss called her a "stupid, twenty-two-year-old bitch unfit to be a teacher" and roared over at top speed to pick up Royce from his office. Together they cruised the green streets between their home and the school, back and forth, peering behind hedges and lilac bushes, up and down alleys.

"Where's your father this morning? Does Lot know where . . . ?"

"You mean he'd look for him instead of me . . . us? Father's home, maybe out in the studio. And Lot's *not* home."

"Let's look there again. Maybe he's got there by now."

But he hadn't. Mr. London was just waking up, fixing his breakfast in the kitchen. When he saw Priss's face he said, "What's happened? What . . . ?"

"*Nothing* has happened," Priss said with deadly anger. "We're looking for Lot, is all, and if he isn't here . . . Come *on*, Royce."

"Nothing serious," Royce said to his father-in-law. He smiled and Mr. London shook his head.

"We'll look down by the river," Priss said, and since she was still driving the car, they went down there, careening onto a driveway fifty yards from the water's edge, frightening a man watering his lawn.

They ran along the bank of the river, through muddy swales and over stretches of damp stones. Bushes lashed their faces. Priss lost a shoe and kicked the other one off. Her gaze was turned constantly toward the brown blue drift of water past them.

But overhead the branches moved in a weaving motion. The smell of mold and greenery was healing, and at last even Priss was reassured. She stopped and took a deep, shuddery breath. "He wouldn't have come down here just for . . . some little thing."

"If he had it would only be to be alone awhile. We'll go back to the house. He'll show up." But now that Priss was sure, Royce was not. He felt like a man compelled to hold back all the waters of the world, the great South Pacific itself, with the flat of his hand. He felt compelled to a gesture like that a soldier would make as he died on the beach at Saipan. He said evenly, "I'm sure he's there by now."

Mr. London came hustling to meet them when they turned again into the driveway. "It's all right! It's all right!" he called. "Lot's over at Carole's. He ran away from school and went over there. You're supposed to call."

"I will," Royce said. The hand that had blocked the flood relaxed.

"Not you. Me," Priss said. Shod again, she clattered her heels dramatically across the boards of the porch. The sound they made was happy and martial, anxious and glad. "But why didn't he come home?" was the first thing she said into the phone.

Carole sensitively took the question as a reprimand—which in all probability it was. She had gone too far, merely in being Lot's chosen sanctuary. She had hung up his shorts to dry in the back yard. She had given him ice cream to eat in one of the cushioned wicker chairs on the sun porch. And somehow she had grossly usurped another woman's rights, her friend's rights. She had better stand farther away or she might do more unintentional harm.

No one said that Lot's accident was a turning point. It was unlikely that Carole herself ever called it that. But afterward she came to their house less freely. She lost interest in the ceramics. What had not been clear became clearer—that she had nothing more to contribute to that venture. She thought it might embarrass Priss to maintain the fiction that she was still needed.

Like the sores she had sometimes driven from Deirdre's skin, the more ghastly emotional consequences of the past winter were vanishing. She began to see more of her old acquaintances. She scheduled a few dinners and cocktail parties at home, the first of them on evenings when at least her friend Priss would represent the Morgan family there. Sometimes Mr. London came, too, and jousted in the role of a bohemian with Buchanan business people (who had outpointed him two to one in fornication and other vice, who were philosophically nihilist in comparison to his old-baby optimism, whether anyone realized this or not).

She appeared at a few college functions, and under Priss's occult stare chatted a time or two with President Mooney. All Buchanan thought she was "coming out of it" and admired her as much for forgetting the horror of her attendance on Deirdre as for having endured it. When it was known she meant to spend the summer in Hawaii, there was some speculation that she might sell out her Buchanan interests and stay. A lot of people would in her place.

But still, as that spring ended, she didn't seem quite "to know what to do with herself." As a piece of obvious self-therapy she bought a surplus Piper Cub. She had flown a good deal during the war. At least it would pass the time to go on with her flying.

Twice in the splendor of late May she took Lot with her on flights down the river valley and home again with a great circle up close to Chicago. Maybe she was showing the young king his kingdom— not an acreage so much as a season, a great green season most readily visible from a certain altitude. He came back each time like someone who has been dreaming. Strange things went on between the two of them alone up there in the yellow-winged Cub.

At the end of the second flight Father London and Priss waited for them at the airport in Priss's new convertible. The afternoon was hot and muggy at ground level. Mr. London shed his jacket after a while and presently his red bow tie. It was as if he were stripping to prepare for frankness.

All at once he said, "You accused me of joking when I asked Carole to marry me."

"Weren't you?" she asked languidly. She was peering into the domed sky as if it were a crystal ball she held between her palms.

"I don't know," he said with a little grunt of exasperation at himself. "Maybe I'd just like to paint that . . . that *stuff*."

Priss laughed at him fondly. "God never meant you to be a cubist. Why have you tortured yourself so long?"

He didn't bother to reply that his life had been the opposite of torture. That was too obvious, even to Priss, who was seldom distracted by the obvious.

"Was she joking with me when she said she was going to marry this Mooney fellow?"

"*What?*" Priss's teeth came together with a click.

"That doesn't suit you *either?*" Mr. London said acidly.

Priss was recovering herself. "I'm merely bowled over. I mean, congratulations on being the first to hear! When will the good tidings be announced to the rest of the commoners?"

Her father shook his head impatiently. He had something to tell as straightforwardly as it *could* be stated, and he saw no excuse for adding unnecessary misunderstandings to what was already complex enough. "The other day when we were coming home from Chicago she told me the whole story about how her aunt was involved in this fiasco of Royce's. She told me more than that. About the way *she* was involved."

"Did she tell you that Royce was, as they say, intimate with her—sort of whenever the brute wanted to—for *nine years?*" There. She had the family skeleton dangling on a string like the souvenir of a Mexican fiesta, and didn't the little fellow jiggle comically?

"You gave that one away to me a while back," he said.

"You're welcome, I'm sure."

"Carole may have been alluding to it. I got what she meant. But, honey, she knows that's all long ago and forgotten."

"The Gulf of War yawns between." Priss yawned.

"And there's no use holding grudges."

"It isn't exactly a grudge that Carole holds. . . ."

"What then?"

"I don't know." With her hands she drew an urn shape in the air. Something ineffable. She would not tell him about the Giorgione landscape.

"You can't name what she holds, so it's *nothing*. It's not right to resent what you can't even name. Carole is spotless . . ."

"Dad, you ought to marry her. Don't take no for an answer. I mean, tuck her under your arm and drag her back to Wellfleet."

". . . and you merely attribute designs to her. Your designs, most likely. You draw them on her like tattoos on a circus lady and blame her for them."

"So you insist. Have you ever heard me utter a malicious word to or about her?"

Still the old man was not to be deterred. He had never trusted Priss for anything except to be herself, and if that was usually at least sufficient, there had been times when it was not. She had scared him sometimes; the habit of fear returned to prompt him now. "Don't let her marry that rascal, Priscilla." He had given up calling her Priscilla in the same year she quit calling him Daddy.

Priss chewed on great concerns while they silently searched the sky for a sign of Carole's plane. They watched a DC-3 come in from Chicago and drag its clumsy tail up the runway toward the hangar.

"And when does Carole expect this wedding to take place?" she asked.

"I told you it was, as far as I could tell, a spoof. Though she isn't very much on jokes. You're spitefully trying to blunt my story, and it has a leetle moral point to it even for one as smart as you."

Priss laughed. "Oh, Jesus, you used to go all to pieces when I was a smart aleck. So I worked it up. It's your fault. Why didn't you beat it the hell out of me with a club like a decent father, or drown me?" While she spoke she meant it. In a minute she would not.

"Yes," he said regretfully, taking her hand in his soft and hairy paws. "The point is that Carole feels you—the Morgan family—got an unfortunate deal. That Royce was humiliated. And all that."

"She couldn't stand it if *he* were. What about . . . ?"

"Whatever she's going to do, she feels it's almost her duty to help straighten things out as they should be."

"Marrying Mooney would help?" Priss shook her head and threw the red herring of obvious realities. "If he needs one thing to really establish him as lord mayor it's to marry the Buchanan Packing Plant and have all that pretty money to play around with."

"She doesn't think so."

"Carole's not a great student of human character. As witness her weakness for me."

"I suppose not. But she wasn't analyzing Mooney's weaknesses.

She has the terrible notion—this is what she really tried to joke about—and it was funny—queer—that she's a husband-killer. Carole as vampire!" He snorted at the absurdity, which seemed to snort back rather terrifyingly, right into his face. "Her marriages must have been pretty bad."

"I guess they were."

Her tone broke the old man up. "Goddamn, but women are hard on women! I would like to cry."

"Sorry, Pop. You've gotta remember to whom you are addressing your human sentiments. Me, I'm an unnatural friend, unnatural mother . . ."

"I never said that."

"Who's got him up in an airplane this afternoon? Who remembers all his *Reader's Digest* type sayings? Who told Royce the kid was a king . . . of all things? An unnatural wife . . ." More red herrings for the dear old seal who wanted so much for her to be good *and* herself at the same time.

They were herrings, weren't they? The red chunks of meat she was tossing?

"I didn't mean to criticize you, baby." He searched her face hopefully for a sign of tears. If there were tears he could wipe them away. There weren't any.

Contritely, impatiently, she said, "I know Carole had terrible marriages and I can guess why, damn it. And anyone but a smart aleck would cry along with you, Pop. But. So? So she thinks she might ruin old Mooney or lure him off to live the big life in Hawaii with the pineapples. . . ." She shook her head in doubt.

Then, far away in the northeast she saw the sun catch a flaw in the sky. She lost it. Saw it again, larger and growing larger. It was Carole's plane, carrying her son. The very minuteness of the little wings up there against all space brought home to her suddenly how much she trusted Carole, after all. Trusted at least some large competence and some power, even if it was only the power of money.

Then it occurred to her with the same fantastic abruptness that, yes, it was possible. Carole might be swept into a marriage with Mooney, even without her intervention. Some other forces—all that erotic money, for example, to tempt the man—might move to the same end as her sick dream of marrying the woman to someone Royce would, beyond all other men, despise.

She clutched her father's shirt sleeve. A thrill of terror went through her as she understood that Something up there, watching from however far back in space It would have to go to be invisible, corresponded exactly to the malice and unspeakable envy that had eaten her heart clean away.

Something . . . She wanted to flee right home to Royce and ask him to kill it. Instead, of course, she waited for Lot and Carole, to greet them with hugs and laughter.

9

"IT's SORDID," Priss said.

"It's morbid and turbid."

"Who are *they*?" Lot demanded from the back seat.

"They are two blackbirds. Like Heckle and Jeckle," Royce told him, shivering away the headed grass leaf with which the boy was tickling his ear. "You have great faith in my driving, buddy, or you wouldn't try these distractions."

Priss snatched the grass away. "White horse!" she exclaimed. There on their right a dirty and yellowed white mare watched them skim the singing highway past her umber and ocher pasture. Priss licked her right thumb and stamped it in the gloved palm of her left hand.

"I saw it first," Lot said.

"But you didn't stamp it," Priss told him. "Watch for graveyards. They count twenty. Well, it is sordid, although the word amuses you, sweetie. The president of Wellford can't marry that tramp!"

"You older ladies of Buchanan will forbid it," Royce said gravely. "You and Mrs. Dawson and Mrs. Firehurst and Mrs. Olmsby are, if I understand you rightly, concerned about the tarnish on the College if Mooney marries a lady of the theater."

"This time he's going too far," Priss warned. She did not, for the moment, mind being bracketed with the older ladies. This role gave her exactly the tone of indignation appropriate to Mooney's latest outrage. After a summer of mysterious flittings and reappearances, a week after school began he had brought to the campus—not only to the campus but to the mansion itself, where she occupied the redecorated guest suite—a blowsy "opera star from Chicago" called Magda Farona. Madam Farona appeared to the best judges of the matter to be well into her forties. To those like Priss who maintained, "But there *are* no opera stars in Chicago," her development recalled Mae West sooner than the deep-chested divas of the Metropolitan. But Madam Farona had indeed entertained the Wellford students and faculty one Friday night in the chapel with "Highlights from Wagner," a couple of songs of Mahler's, and encores of "The Last Rose of Summer" and "The Wellford Fight Song"— a program that had made Max Jarrell of the Music Department pound his head with astonishment, though he said the lady had a "first-rank" voice. Royce supposed that really the woman must have skipped sometime, somewhere, along the edge of fame, only to miss it because of some impertinence like drug addiction, mischance in love, or some psychic pathology whose symptoms would be revealed only in the misfiring of her whole life. She's one of us, he thought to himself, rather liking the lady, rather constipated with melancholy these days when he thought of himself, Priss, Carole, and Mooney, too, becalmed in their backwaters.

Madam Farona had entertained the public one night—but by this time she had been resident in the mansion for almost two weeks. Coeds and faculty wives were all twittering rumors of romance—because most of them lacked character to rumor anything more sinister, and Mooney's bulldog housekeeper dampened anyone's tendency to fancy the worst. Built like old Mae West the singer might be, fresh from triumphs before the crowned heads of the underworld she *could* be (at the farthest stretch of speculation), but if she were the Whore of Babylon herself the Protestant Mrs. Clifton would see that nothing untoward was done in her mansion.

Mooney had gone out of his way to let the audience know Magda Farona was an old friend of his. He had gone over the heads of the Music Department in arranging her public appearance. So when she lingered eleven days, then twelve, after her concert, light female minds imagined Mooney in love. Priss and others saw sordidness.

"I can't believe Mooney will marry her," Royce said that late October afternoon as he drove home toward Buchanan. "He's just teasing you all again, experimenting to see how far he can make people go in their speculations."

"Why?" Priss asked.

Royce shrugged, "Well, he *likes* to play with the world. It's his toy. He doesn't care about it the way the owners would. I'm sure he was ready to let Wellford's creditors foreclose last spring—as they wouldn't have really, perhaps—and go somewhere else without even bothering to remember he'd been president here. He likes to see what will happen if he lights a fuse. Any fuse."

Lot, watching for a twenty-point cemetery to put him ahead of his mother, said, "How would they know if someone was dead, Daddy?"

"Listen for his breathing. Feel for his pulse."

"No. I mean, if somebody died in that house." In the rear-view mirror Royce saw that the boy was pointing at a farmhouse set all by itself on a hilltop amid a morbid glory of red, black, and yellow leaves. The late-afternoon sun fired its windows. A slow flight of crows in the chill acetylene colors of the sky above it moved like the pallbearers dismissed from a grave. It was easy to see (hard not to see) how the house on an Illinois hill would seem to a child's eye a house of death. So lonely. So silent at the end of a perspective.

They had driven over to Galena that afternoon because Priss and Lot had never seen the Grant house there, and Priss—who didn't care much about Grant but was enthralled by the idea of Dick Diver "biding his time like Grant in Galena" in Fitzgerald's novel—had wanted to sniff the source of the simile. What she found had not stuck to her ribs. So on the way home she got to "talking Mooney"— as half the College referred to one of its pastimes—and got her son meditating on graves and death.

Royce said, "If someone died in that house, after a while the neighbors would wonder why they didn't see him. They'd come and when they went in they'd know he was dead."

Lot chewed his lip. "Well . . ." He did not want to be compassed by an answer, for his mind was called out toward infinity by the loneliness of late afternoon. He had not found Grant in Galena either, though he had stared at the musty rocking chair where Grant rocked while cancer grew in his throat, and had glanced impatiently at the old battle flags and medals. "No," he said competitively, "I mean if *everybody* was dead, how would *anybody* know?"

"That's a good question, sport," Royce said. "The Greeks used to go around and ask each other that in Greek. I don't recall that they ever got an answer to it."

He was thinking that when they drove into Buchanan, after Lot had been delivered to Barbara for his dinner and bedtime books, he and Priss would go for dinner at the Ringleby Dawsons'. Over martinis, in front of a nice football-weather fire, he and Dawson would talk about Grant and the cabinet scandal and the Mississippi Valley campaign and the History Department budget and promotions for the new men Crawford and Blues, while Priss condescended so nimbly to Mrs. Dawson that the lady would hum like a happy teakettle. She would think that Priss had established exactly the right tone for conversation between a dean's wife and the wife of a department head. And none of them would know that they had died.

"Maybe the Martians would come and find out," Lot said. Now that he had stumped the old man, he was willing to give ground and be reasonable.

His father laughed immoderately—so much that his mother frowned her bewilderment. Let it be known that she deserved an explanation.

"The Mooneys would come," Royce said happily. "Don't you see? They'd come with their Madam Farona's and just fool around with us. To see if we were alive."

"You get too much pleasure from your mental life," Priss said severely. "It's time we straightened up and did something." What she meant to do was turn up the volume of community disapproval so loud Mooney would have to ditch that yellow-haired singer and look for a more suitable wife.

That was her intent. She didn't have to bother. Madam Farona took her trunk back to Chicago and after some interval Mooney confided to Royce—*perhaps* only to Royce, one confidant never knew whether he was the sole secret-sharer or part of a mob individually pledged to keep Mooney's secrets from each other—that his old friend Magda was a terrible lush. The trunk she had brought was mostly full of booze. After the concert she had opened her trunk, and had lain for three weeks in the mansion unfit to move, a risk to *be* moved by day or night.

"I took a hideous chance in asking her to come," Mooney said. "There were times while she was here when I was sweating blood that the word would get out—or *she'd* get out. Henceforward I owe a great deal to Mrs. Clifton for her loyalty. Loyalty's the priceless virtue, isn't it? And I wanted to give Magda some kind of a helping hand. Poor girl is on the skids."

From this confidence, profound but still carefully circumscribed, no hint as to that life before in which Mooney had become poor Magda's friend . . . or got his Rolls-Royce . . . or even found friends who would stake him to it. He gave not so much the shadow of magnitudes still undisclosed as simply a peep down a very deep well shaft.

Royce was obliged to agree about loyalty—insofar, he thought, as there can be agreement between the hypothetically dead and the hypothetically Martian.

Had playful Mooney found how a loyal action can serve a second function? Had he not used the protracted and speculation-inviting visit of Magda Farona (née Mary Fox of Boston) to signal that he was, in spite of the strictures of his position, marriageable? In the market? On the market? Ready (or nearly ready), eager (though still unhastened as to choice), and prepared (though his kingdom was not yet finished) to take unto himself a consort?

As Mooney's second year went on, Royce found that these questions asked themselves. It appeared to him that Mooney was too exalted—and too busy—to court, but that he had signaled to all Buchanan that now he might be receptive to a suitable offer.

Magda left behind her a biding question. Freshman coeds who had unquestioningly assumed that President Mooney was as old as

God unfroze to the realization that, while he was neither young enough, callow enough, nor impulsive enough to stoop to *their* callow youth in making his choice, he had at least enough spunk in him to be called an eligible bachelor. Buchanan mothers who had only read about "eligible bachelors" in slick fiction or Chicago society pages decided, between relief and anxiety, that he was yet too old and too prominently positioned to be either threat or promise to their daughters of a nubile age. More or less as a chorus these mothers chanted the prophecy that if Mooney married in Buchanan —as he probably wouldn't, they thought—then it was likely he would choose either Carole Prentice or Celeste Armitage, both of splendid family and both thought to be in want of a prominent husband. Celeste was three years younger than Carole and had not been married. Yet Carole was thought to be the more likely prospect— perhaps because in the river-bottom silt of common speculation on the matter there still lay the memory of the years when many mothers had taken it for granted that Carole would someday be the wife of President Morgan. Pure old-woman stupidity honed off the edges of distinction between one man and another, one time and another, and the silty public mind was comforted to expect what it had always expected for Deirdre Prentice's niece.

In her role of visitor to faculty wives, Priss brought home some inklings of how Buchanan and the college family viewed the matter.

One day Royce found her in their front hallway before the Victorian mirror in its mahogany stand, unpinning her hat. The smell of cold had come in on her fur coat. The mirror picked up December reflections through the front-door pane. It was a pool of incandescence in the comfortable gloom. Priss rocked before it like the silhouetted priestess emerging from an oracle with tidings.

And said, "Celeste Armitage is going to announce her engagement next week. To a brewer. From Louisville. They understand that this is a concession."

"They? Concession?" Royce helped his wife out of her coat, saw her smile in the mirror like a rip of light, as if all the luminosity reflected from the snow outside were showing through her as it showed around her silhouette.

"Why, she's giving up the race to Carole."

"Race? Good God, there's no race. I haven't noticed Carole running anywhere."

"*They* have," Priss said, playfully tapping his midriff and edging past him into the living room, where Barbara had made a fire. "Or, if not running, then drifting. You've noticed it too, Royce. Heaven knows I tried to give Carole something to paddle with. I mean the ceramics thing and . . . well, going out of my way to be such friends with her. But she drifts. She doesn't go away from Buchanan and there's nothing for her to do here. Except marry Mooney, of course. It's so logical."

"*Logical?*" Even a grave and sober man might squawk the word in such connections. There was not the faintest logic in anything Priss was saying, nor in the process she was probably reporting correctly. There was, however, something more formidable than logic, a subrational movement—an almost inorganic process like that by which a river shifts its bed. Grains of silt were moving toward a configuration as inevitable as it was, by reason, unpredictable. He was old enough to understand that what Priss had to tell him might be so. Women knew about women, he thought. As a historian he believed that historic events were often only convenient labels for great determinations made invisibly.

"So it's all over but the shouting?" he asked. "Carole will marry him?" If he were to ask Carole herself such a question now—but it was part of the configuration that he must not ask—she might not know what on earth he was talking about. Yet somehow she would know, too. Somehow, profoundly, she would be bound in the female confederacy without regard to her own objective interests.

"It's not by any means all over," Priss mocked, easing her lithe body into the sofa cushions. Her thin cheeks glowed from her walk through the cold. "Heavens. I'm sure it will never *happen*. I don't think Mooney will ever marry anyone."

"Then you weren't serious in your indignation about Madam Farona."

"I was too!" A pause while Priss decided which level of abstraction represented the true reality for her today. "Wasn't I? Perhaps I wasn't. But I felt indignant whether there was reason to be so or not, so it's just the same."

"No."

"Yes," the relativist said, enjoying her freedom of movement among contradictory truths if nothing else. "The point is it's just unbearably fascinating to see how in a small town like this such a ground swell gets started and moves. I'm the only bitch of them all who's unkind enough to put it into words." She laughed and stretched lazily before the fire, as if it were her element, from which for a little while she had ascended to be a shopping tourist amid the quaint moralities of the world. "You're taking all my fancies calmly. Is it because you think they're all so frothy?"

Royce shook his head.

"How would you feel if she really did marry him?"

He shrugged.

"Would you let it happen? Would you let her?"

He was on the verge of answering that he had no power of decision in the matter—then saw the trap. If he answered so, Priss would take him in the lie. Yes, it was constantly in his power to go to Carole and take advantage of her aimlessness to send her away—to send her away, at least, from such present dangers as Buchanan contemplated to others unknown. That is, he might muster the voice of authority, might loom in front of her like a very palpable ghost, shout "Boo," and scare her away. But the dead sometimes have intimations that they have died. He knew how and where the Royce who had the right to decide for Carole had died.

So he said, "Thank God for the reality principle. You ladies reading tea leaves may predict marriage. I'm not sure that Mooney will notice he's engaged just because you discern the propriety of mating him and Carole. Why should he want Carole when he's got Tommy Barker?"

Last year Freshman Barker had been only Mooney's chauffeur

and the putative rapist who ran Miss Halstead down. This year . . . Since early December when the basketball season opened, it appeared that Mooney had uncannily picked himself a winner from Bronkley. Of course Tommy had starred at Lincoln High, but that was an inadequate prediction of what he was beginning to do now. A genius was emerging from the wraps (or rather, from the scarlet and white Wellford sweatclothes). On the hardwood courts he was explicating Mooney's promises in language that anyone could understand. To state senators, to bankers and industrialists, to small businessmen still smarting over defaulted debts, to packing-house workers and spastic newsboys, he was carrying the word that Wellford could be big time.

The females of Buchanan might tizzy about the eligibility of the bachelor president. The gents figured that, while he might have sailed pretty close to the edge of tolerance when he was boffing that singer and keeping her right in his house, he sure knew before they did what stuff there was in the Barker kid.

Clear now in retrospect was Mooney's anxiety that Tommy should not be subject to suspicion about the attack on Miss Halstead. Not so clear was how Mooney had seen the full potential of Tommy's talents.

"It's not a prophetic gift," Royce said. "It's just a bird-dog sense for the main chance. It must have started with an if—*if* Tommy became sensational. . . . Tommy's becoming sensational, so now, without needing clairvoyance, Mooney can see chances for the publicity he trusts more than our traditional methods. In publicity he sees wealth for the school, and in a wealthy school he sees the chance to build his monument. In his monument—still far ahead—he sees himself. Will a man in pursuit of himself be diverted by mere matrimony?"

"Not all wives are obstacles."

"I'm not suggesting Carole might be."

"Still . . . I can see his hesitation about her. She's getting to be a terrible lush."

"Nonsense!"

"I can understand you'd defend her, and it's not fair to make out that I blame her for this. I have some notion of what it meant to her to watch Deirdre go. I'm only stating the simple truth."

"You let Lot go flying with her."

"She isn't canned all the time. She's not an alcoholic. I've never seen her when she wasn't quite sober enough to do whatever she'd promised. Granted. Granted. Why do you get so hot when I say the obvious about her? Only . . ."

"I misdoubt the balance of what you call obvious."

". . . wouldn't it be ironic if *he* found *her* unsuitable as wife of a man in his position?"

"Ironic beyond bearing. But why don't you write a novel if you want to give such concreteness to possibilities and anxieties?"

"Oh, I'm going to. Don't worry. You'll all be in my story some-time."

"The point is we're talking about nothing more substantial than a female consensus that he ought to marry. It is known that Carole is unmarried and for the moment directionless. That does not add up to the necessity for either of them to consider the other seriously. I can promise you that Mooney will get more mileage toward what he really wants by bringing in a gaudy subject for rumor like Magda Farona from time to time than he'd ever get out of a common mar-riage. I'm afraid your tea-table speculation has left the man's real genius for managing sensationalism out of account."

"You'd rather talk about Barker, who is a bore," Priss said. "O.K. I've touched your defenses about Carole and I'm sorry. But anyway it's interesting to hear them all guess she *might* marry him. Do you suppose there could be something prescriptive—sort of compulsory—about their expectations? That Carole would feel it was her duty to do what Buchanan expected?"

Whatever he supposed, he was afraid there might be compulsion for a woman who had so little to anchor on as Carole had. Some-one who had been so *cut* adrift.

"I didn't mean to change the subject."

Priss acknowledged this with a drowsy nod. "It's always Mooney, really. Why should people talk about him so much?"

Because they saw in him a show of life they could no longer claim to show themselves?

A few days later—it was still January then—Priss came home to announce, "She's dated him."

"*Dated!*" Royce grunted his disdain for the word, though of course Priss had only chosen it to tease him. The facts were merely that Mooney and Carole had made a couple for drinks and dinner at the Bojacs' and had gone with them later to the showing of an art film in Litchfield Auditorium. Though their appearance together would surely be commented on—and the comment become part of the force of their drift—the only thing that surprised Royce was Priss's hearing of it at second hand. Carole was still coming to their house five times a week—to see Lot or to see Priss if she brought the boy from kindergarten or to see them all if she had an excuse—and when she did not come for morning gossip over coffee with Priss she often called. If she had any secrets from Priss, these were probably secrets from herself as well. But now she had "dated" Mooney, and she had not known how to tell the Morgans about it. It was the sign of a new phase.

"Things are coming along," Priss said. She offered another surprise to her husband. "I'm going to give him the studio." There was something in her tone of the well-practiced courtesan yielding one more favor as a reward for her suitor's constancy or good behavior. "After all, I suppose there's not much point going on with the jugs now that Carole's stopped pretending any interest."

"I'm sorry she has. But you can't force enthusiasms on people. You helped her through a rough time."

"Isn't that a nice thought? You don't believe it for a minute and neither do I. It's just another sign of her will to debase herself."

"You're giving up too. Why should it mean something different for Carole than for you?"

"It doesn't!" she flared. She stared at him in mock wonder. "You big fool, it'd probably ruin you to find out how negative women really mean to be. But the difference remains that Carole's a farmer and I'm not *that*. She's luckier than I."

"She didn't marry a man ignorant of woman's real nature."

She was almost through minding irony from him. Once it might have wounded and set her to elaborate introspection. Now it mainly amused her. "'My other elements I give to baser life,'" she said hammily. "I take the veil. In pure charity I can't compete with my husband and my guide—who proves it by sucking Mooney's ass so long. Oh, I didn't mean that, Royce!"

He knew she hadn't. Her meaning lay beyond human speech. She had merely said the words the way a child discharges a firearm, because he can.

"As long as you withhold such sentiments in front of . . . those who might be hurt by them," he said with terrible, cold, ponderous gravity. His eyes were on her, but utterly blank.

In panic she tried to bluff swiftly away from the moment. "Sure. You're used to my colorful and picturesque manner of speech. Not everyone is. Anyway, *pro bono publico*. With this year's enrollment in the Art Department they need the space if nothing else. Bojac has promised to send Tom LeCoeur out to do the actual work."

"LeCoeur's a painter, isn't he?" Royce knew very well what the young man was. He had recruited LeCoeur from the Art Institute in the previous spring, knew and liked him as well as any of the recent additions to the faculty.

"I'll have to teach him before he can teach them. So you see I haven't really given up anything. I'll be around for most of the classes. He's done a little ceramics. You object to this?"

"I was only a little surprised by the way it was presented to me."

"Well, I've already told Mooney I would. Don't worry. I may be an unnatural mother and Carole would be a better one, but nobody's going to suffer from neglect. Lot—"

"I wasn't thinking of him." He was wondering, suddenly, what else she might recently have planned with Mooney, for he heard in her disquiet the accent of treachery. Yet he knew that she would have said nothing more of great import to Mooney. She would not have discussed Carole Prentice in any way with the man. She would not need to. If he was beginning to see her game, he saw that its cardinal communications would not be made in direct speech. She was giving a little something to Mooney, no doubt, because he was moving in a direction she approved. He had been seen with Carole. He would know now that Mrs. Morgan not only approved but might have more than the use of her studio in store if he held this direction.

"You're angry, aren't you?" Priss said in a contrite voice.

And Royce thought, my God, she doesn't even know what she's doing. Not wholly. Am I to be the only one who has to see it all? He was not so much angry as afraid. On Saipan he had bargained to be the domino that did not go down into blindness and worse with the rest. He had not foreseen all that obliged him to.

At that moment, he would recall years afterward, he had *known* that Carole would be married to Winfred Mooney. Tied to the rock of that knowledge, he heard his wife ask if he was angry.

"I won't do it if you say no," she told him, coming to sit against his knee. She put her fingers under his chin and turned his head so that the blank eyes were on her again. "I can still call it off. Hell, I've got so much to do with my life!"

"I'm sorry for you, too."

"Hell, I don't have to teach. I can write my novel."

Of course their quarrel—if it had been that—was composed with an effective denial that it had ever erupted. Little by little it was accepted that the studio in the Morgans' back yard was committed to the Wellford Art Department for the second semester, and that of course Priss would supervise the classes in ceramics taught there.

Mooney went out of his way to thank Royce—no, to thank the Morgan family—for this service to the College. Not *his* College. Their College. If he saw any of the strings Priss had attached to the offer and was still manipulating, then Royce was very much mistaken in his analysis of the man.

No. It was rather, simply, that Mooney knew the strings were there. Still playing blind, he was guided simply by a confidence that there was always more than met the eye in any circumstance—and that, perhaps, this faith alone would bring him profit.

Of course he had never wanted the use of the studio for its own sake. Then for the sake of what? Because the strings attached led on through the black maze toward where the hero waited with a sword to lop off his grotesque head and horns? Myth might tell where Minotaur Mooney was headed, but there was no way of transposing myth into the language used to settle everyday affairs.

"I'm glad it's been arranged," Royce told Mooney. "As much for Priss's sake as the College's. She needs . . ."

"I know, I know," Mooney said. That was his advantage. To know that Priss needed something so badly that she might sell off her husband for its sake. What it was she needed, he did not even have to imagine, for the moment. When the time came she would let him know.

10

Item: In the 1947-8 season the Wellford basketball team won twenty-two games and lost six, thereby winning its conference championship for the first time since 1934. Thomas Q. Barker of Wellford was nominated All-American forward by sports writers in Buchanan, Dubuque, Nashville, and Lincoln, Nebraska. He was mentioned as a "hope" for next year's All-American by writers in San Francisco, St. Louis, and Brooklyn.

Item: Mrs. Priscilla London Morgan and Miss Barbara Overbeck, returning to the Morgan home on March 18, 1948, at 3:45 P.M., after shopping at the A&P and the RoseJohn Delicatessen, entered the front door to find Mrs. Carole Prentice Slater (widow) on the couch with Master Lot Harvey Morgan. Mrs. Slater was bouncing the six-year-old boy on her knee while she sang:

> *This is the way the gentleman rides.*
> *Gallopy-gallopy, gop.*
> *This is the way the lady rides.*
> *Trittity-trottity, trot.*
> *And this is the way the farmer rides.*
> *Hobble-de-hoy, hobble-de-hoy.*

Upon the entrance of Mrs. Morgan and Miss Overbeck, Mrs. Slater, in the midst of her song, was seen to color beet red, but not to desist from bouncing the boy.

At the completion of the song, Mrs. Morgan remarked to her son that he was much "too heavy" to be bounced any longer on Mrs. Slater's knee.

Master Morgan replied that they had only done this—while awaiting mother and maid—because they "used to do it when he was little" and he had begged the entertainment once more "for old times' sake."

While watching the floor-shaking, mirth-provoking, blush-bringing, rapid up-and-down of the young rider on his steed, Mrs. Morgan had said to herself (silently): Dear God, she's big. Dear God, she's strong as a mare.

At the incantation of the final line (Hobble-de-hoy, hobble-de-hoy) Mrs. Morgan was seized by an attack of dizziness, accompanied with hallucinatory images of her husband (Dean Royce Morgan) riding in similar fashion on the equine body and ecstatic oscillation of Mrs. Slater (née Prentice).

Item: Dean of Studies, alias Dean of Students Royce Blackburn Morgan declined with thanks two tentative offers of appointment from, respectively, Tulane University and Antelope Valley Junior College, the former an offer of a deanship, the latter an offer of presidency. The tone of his refusal, regretful. The reasons given, spurious. Letters of gratitude were also dispatched over the dean's signature to Brigadier General Archibald Greave, 27th Division U.S.A. (Infantry), Professors Hieveland, Buckley, and Kolbinger of Columbia University, and Sergeant Lawrence Wolff, 27th Division U.S.A. (Infantry) Inactive Reserve, resident in Antelope Valley, California. Gratitude was deanishly expressed for instigating these offers of appointment.

Item: On the anniversary of her alleged assault in the Wellford College Library (Grant Hall), Miss Vivian Elizabeth Halstead did issue or prepare to issue to the faculty of Wellford College and to the trustees and to the Buchanan *Courier Sentinel* a mimeographed pamphlet of nine pages entitled "The Case against Winfred Mooney."

Miss Halstead was intercepted outside the *Courier Sentinel* offices by Dean Royce Morgan, acting on intelligence supplied by Hopkins Halstead (brother) and Mrs. Hopkins Halstead, in the sense that "Vivian has got something terrible she is trying to pass around." Intercepted, Miss Halstead tearfully affirmed to Dean Morgan that all copies of the pamphlet were still in her possession (in the trunk of her Pontiac) and that only she, her brother, and her sister-in-law had yet read the charges therein.

Dean Morgan's inspection of the one hundred copies entrusted to him by distraught Miss Halstead revealed that the charges fell in categories: (1) Fiscal Slackness—The refusal to honor debts contracted by Wellford College; the acceptance of kickbacks from glaziers, electricians, interior decorators employed by the College. (2) Demoralization of Academic Disciplines—The discharge of "respected members of the teaching staff and associated services" and the hiring of "green youth, many of whom have not a Ph.D."; displays of disrespect for "learning and tradition" in private and public utterances. (3) The Promulgation of Misleading Prospectuses— Encouraging parents of daughters to believe there was adequate dormitory space for their girls when there was, in fact, inadequate supervision of "emergency approved" housing; causing "the nation at large" to believe that Wellford College was offering a "Veteran's Degree" that could be earned in two years of concentrated study, when in fact no degrees except the B.A. and the B.S. and the M.A. in English were offered. (4) Sexual Deviation and Promiscuity— Keeping his "known mistress" in the presidential mansion; setting "one of his creatures" to the mission of criminally assaulting or "carnally humiliating" the undersigned; entering homosexual relationships with Billy Cox, Lon C. Breckenridge, and F. Milton Santiana (the latter two interior decorators who had refurbished the president's mansion, the former of unknown employment); humiliating secretaries and freshman girls by "obscene utterances."

Questioned charitably by Dean Morgan as to the source of her information—*in re* those instances where the charges were of specific malfeasance—Miss Halstead submitted that "anyone could see" President Mooney did not maintain a Rolls-Royce on the salary he received. She said that Tommy Barker had "bragged in Bronkley" of his assault on her. "Everyone knew" that Clackfart, her successor as librarian, was a "deviant." (There were notes about his amours even in the *girls'* toilets of the library.) She had seen and overheard Clackfart in highly suspicious conversation with the two decorators from Chicago during their work on the mansion. "Billy Cox" was probably a pseudonym of the sort that deviants are known to take. But, if required by his skepticism, she could take Dean Morgan to the very barber who kept the still-dark roots of President Mooney's hair from creeping up into the white. The barber would confirm this proof positive of "inversion." The president bleached his hair "like Jean Harlow"!

Item: Hopkins Halstead returned to the College Extension Service the mimeograph machine his sister had borrowed.

Item: Since the threat of Miss Halstead's publication had been quickly isolated and dissipated, Dean Morgan viewed with charity all the principals involved. For Miss Halstead, the charity one accords the shell-shocked veteran transformed into an arsonist. For President Mooney, the charity of disbelieving all the specific charges of the pamphlet, and of doubting that the general ones were phrased with sufficient objectivity to be admissible in the determination of public opinion. For himself, the charity of thinking that no respect for the free dissemination of opinion could have brought either more happiness or enlightenment than his swift suppression of Miss Halstead's unlicensed printing.

Item: Master Lot Morgan threw and decorated "a Grecian urn" to replace his original creation, which had burst in the firing a year ago. The accident demoralized him so long he had done no more work in clay until he saw his mother busy with the Wellford students, who now came four times a week to work in the stable studio. With her help and direction the second urn was more symmetrical than the first had been. When it had been successfully fired, glazed, and fired again, it was presented to Master Lot's father.

Item: Mrs. Carol Prentice Slater presided at the Easter Tea, offered annually in the presidential mansion. Mrs. Slater was chosen at the suggestion of Mrs. George Hand, whose sentiment was that Mrs. Slater's service as hostess would be a tribute to the memory of Deirdre Prentice.

Item: A lady resembling Magda Farona, opera star, was seen breakfasting with Mr. Henry Worth of Buchanan in the Pump Room of Chicago's Ambassador East by Mesdames Gracie and Poore, also of Buchanan.

Item: At the instigation (or perhaps in emulation) of President Winfred C. Mooney, valued ideas, notions, or projects were, by the majority of the administration and by an increasing minority of faculty and students, labeled "seminal." Upon noting the sudden, widespread usage of the word, Mrs. Royce Morgan said, "Haw haw."

Item: Mr. George LeGrange Clackfart, librarian, was found a position in a Florida university "commensurate with his training and experience." His replacement, Robert (Bob) Donovan, came to Wellford bringing a robust wife and five (5) children, of whom three were boys and two were girls. Mildred (Millie) Donovan was ostentatiously *enceinte* at the time of her husband's appointment. In view of the desirability of maintaining a demonstrable balance of sexual characteristics in the Donovan family (and henceforward among all personnel or premises pertaining to the Wellford Library), Dean Royce Morgan said of Mrs. Donovan's pregnancy, with a thin laugh, "She had better produce a girl." Mrs. Donovan did.

Item: In conference with Colmar Jensen (basketball coach) and William Casey (director of athletics and football coach), President Mooney declared, "You are not thinking big enough." Mr. Jensen, supported by Mr. Casey, expressed doubts about the basketball schedule proposed by President Mooney for the coming season. Each separately and both conjunctively objected that however stellar the performance of Thomas Q. Barker might continue to be, he could not singlehandedly sustain the Wellford Five against the competition of Oklahoma, Nevada, and N.Y.U., top teams proposed as Wellford adversaries by the president. The most Colmar Jensen could concede in favor of the proposed schedule was, "It is a seminal idea."

President Mooney riposted, "Do I have to do it myself?" Mr. Jensen and Mr. Casey were required on this and following occasions to be in attendance at the president's office while, by telephone, President Mooney assembled what was described later by informed members of the Economics Department as an athletic cartel. Sports writers and editors of known disposition were induced and presently obliged to use their influence with top teams that might have had reason for avoiding Wellford. Managers of sports arenas in New York, Chicago, St. Louis, and Los Angeles were offered package deals of Wellford vs. Nevada, Wellford vs. Oklahoma, Wellford vs. N.Y.U. Only in the event of their acceptance did they find themselves under the necessity of adding pleas and inducements to N.Y.U., Oklahoma, and Nevada to accept engagements unilaterally announced by President Mooney.

Mr. Casey grasped the semantics of "seminality" more rapidly than his associate Mr. Jensen. When to him Mr. Jensen white-liveredly pleaded, and not for the first time, "But where will we get a team to go with Barker?" Mr. Casey then proposed to President Mooney that he once more lift the Bell telephone and address himself to Mr. Charles Dowling of Philadelphia, called (on sports pages and perhaps in the locker room) "Dolly." It was Mr. Casey's implication that Mr. Dowling would know where and how rapidly to recruit a team fit to support Mr. Barker through the coming years.

With Mr. Dowling hired as basketball coach, it was then proposed by Mr. Casey that Mr. Jensen be retained to teach boxing, squash, gymnastics, fencing, and cross-country walking. In short, that he be superseded like Dean Morgan, Coach Melanevski, Librarian Halstead, and the Mesdemoiselles Tabor (not to speak of others gone or overrun) by an effective of the new regime.

Item: A Midwestern youth named Billy Cox was arrested for

vagrancy in Provo, Utah. One William Cox was designated salutatorian of the graduating class at Buchanan's Lincoln High. Dean Royce Morgan read of the latter instance in the *Courier-Sentinel*. He did not clip the story.

Item: Upon leaving a student production of *Twelfth Night,* presented in Litchfield Auditorium, Dean and Mrs. Morgan discovered that an April snowstorm had made their expected path from the auditorium to the parking lot behind Arden Hall impassable. Mrs. Morgan rejoiced in the snow as it blew astronomical configurations (exploding nova and compressed centuries of unhindered drift) around the lamps bordering the sidewalk. Dean Morgan reflected on the health of the new grass and crocuses beneath this untimely storm. Detouring, the couple encountered President Mooney and Mrs. Slater walking together toward the presidential mansion. The following interlocution established that President Mooney had enjoyed his evening at the play. Mrs. Slater said it was "Fine. Oh, just *fine.*"

Item: The first of the new dormitories (women's) was completed and furnished ahead of schedule. It was furnished with mattresses inferior in quality to those found in the Coolidge Motels, and with desks, ventilation, closets, and carpeting superior to most of that to be found in the emergency housing.

Item: On April 12 at high noon, in the absence of Barbara Overbeck (maid), Royce Morgan (husband), and Lot Morgan (son) from the Morgan residence at 112 Goodwin Heights, Buchanan, and upon the dispersal of students registered for Ceramics (Art Department 1:17), Mrs. Priscilla Morgan engaged in adulterous copulation with Martin Thomas LeCoeur, assistant professor on the staff of the Art Department. The copulation was, on Professor LeCoeur's part, essentially unpremeditated. On Mrs. Morgan's part, long premeditated, often rejected as unthinkable, as often meditated again with the stipulation that since she could not only think of it but find in it some symbolic focus for obsessive and painful emotions, the moral act (adultery) was for her equilibrium necessary and the physical act (coitus) was for the moral act an indispensable basis. In selecting a partner Mrs. Morgan had been guided by considerations of facility and the emotional neutrality of both participants, since direct emotional involvement would not only lead to boring sequelae but would distract from the central objective sought—the exorcising of past injustices against her marriage committed by her husband-to-be and his first mistress.

Intercourse was achieved in the bedroom occupied for thirty-two years by Miss Grace Blackburn (now resident at Pacific Palisades, California). At the specific insistence of Mrs. Morgan it was performed on the floor where eighteen years previously her present husband deflowered Miss Carole Prentice.

Instead of anticipated-and-in-the-imagination-already-familiar fantasies that during the act past time would be reconstructed in her favor (so that the hymen here surrendered would be hers and not Miss Prentice's), her only escape from the distasteful realities of lying half clothed under a relative stranger was the momentary hallucination that she was being penetrated by a horned and bull-faced chimera, and that this creature was Winfred Mooney, president of Wellford College. Mrs. Morgan predictably failed to achieve orgasm.

From postcoital fright but undiminished gallantry worthy of his Gallic forebears or his recent comrades in the 115th Regiment (Airborne), Professor LeCoeur asked if this April delight could be, the occasion favoring, repeated. Mrs. Morgan replied, "Don't be a goddamn fool."

In postcoital disappointment and the consequent frenzy of reestablishing her person and her home before maid or son returned at the expected hour, Mrs. Morgan regained composure by the cheerless recollection that, since marriage, this was her fourth adulterous deviation, the others having occurred during her husband's service in the Pacific theater. None of them either, in her accounting, had reached its ineffable objective or brought her peace. Mrs. Morgan laughed ruefully to recall that her first adultery had the fantasied objective of magically producing mail from her husband when, during the Saipan campaign, she had been twelve days without word of him. Mrs. Morgan, completing her make-up before her mirror, paused as if turned to stone by some vision therein while she stared and said, "Darling, you ought to kill me. Come home, you sonofabitch, I want to eat you up."

Item: Miss Vivian Elizabeth Halstead (emeritus) of Wellford College left Buchanan to make her home in La Jolla, California.

Item: To Dean Morgan, Mrs. Morgan expressed the wish that "in the near future" the Morgans might have "them" to dinner. Dean Morgan replied that in his view to entertain President Mooney and Mrs. Slater would indeed be a welcome part of the spring social calendar. In view of the fact that his former military superior would in early May stop for two nights in Buchanan, that occasion might serve for a most enjoyable dinner party, of which "they" would make part. He suggested as another guest Mrs. Jennifer Sparling (divorced), a friend of his grade-school days, reputed lively. Not slow to discern her husband's administrative touch, Mrs. Morgan demanded whether General Greave was married. She was told he was a widower, whereupon she gave it as her opinion that Jennifer Sparling was altogether too apt to "latch on" to President Mooney in the course of such an evening, since Mr. Sparling had also served his time in the advertising world from which President Mooney came and "poor Carole" would be stuck with a "stuffy old brass hat." Mrs. Morgan's evident passion ended the argument and prevented Dean Morgan from retorting that Arch Greave had a colt's tooth and a lickerish tongue that would more likely shock poor Carole than bore her.

Item: To Chancellor George Hand came the not entirely agreeable surprise of reading in a national news magazine that "seam-busting Wellford College" out in Illinois had instituted a Veteran's Degree. "The no-skimping B.A. can be earned in two and a half years by young men in a hurry." While such a degree had been a subject of conversation among President Mooney, Chancellor Hand, and Dean Morgan, agreement had been that Wellford would be guilty of fraud in promulgating such a program. President Mooney himself had finally taken the firmest stand against it, but, confronted with the magazine, admitted (after a preliminary sneer at "journalistic irresponsibility") that he had given the story to a stringer in St. Louis while on a fund-raising trip to that city. To Chancellor Hand's question, "Does this oblige us . . . ?" President Mooney answered with alacrity that it obliged Wellford to nothing—not even, he supposed, to answering the inquiries that would pour in from hard-pressed veterans hoping to enroll in the new program. Perceiving how he had nonplussed his right hand, he changed his tone and expressed (in the subjunctive) a regret for the necessity to use publicity conceivably embarrassing to the College, though, as Dean Morgan and Chancellor Hand had heretofore agreed, the general idea was a seminal one. Wellford must be, whenever possible, in his view, seminal in the world of education, and if such a program were beyond its means, the torch had now, figuratively speaking, been flung to stronger hands. (Though in his view no hand was stronger than *Chancellor* Hand. No, sir.)

Item: Estimates of next year's enrollment at Wellford: 2,200 students.

Item: Thomas Q. Barker appeared at the Rotary luncheon on April 28 in company with President Mooney and the newly arrived Dolly Dowling. President Mooney spoke. Dolly Dowling shook both hands over his head in the manner of a prizefighter. Barker blushed when presented with cuff links in the form of gold basketballs. One earnest Rotarian said, "What the kid needs is a shirt to go with them." He did not offer the one off his back, perhaps feeling such a gesture to be inappropriate to the solemnity of the occasion.

Item: Brigadier General Archibald Greave of New Orleans visited in the home of Dean and Mrs. Royce Morgan of Buchanan. He was entertained at dinner on May 7 by the company of President Mooney, Mrs. Carole Prentice Slater, Professor and Mrs. Ringleby Dawson, Professor and Mrs. Milton Bojac, Professor and Mrs. Max Jarrell, and Professor and Mrs. Wilton Emory. Mrs. Jennifer Sparling sat at home and played tiddlywinks; at any rate she sat at home, thus demonstrating to the satisfaction of Dean and Mrs. Morgan who wore the pants in the Morgan family.

In anticipation of embarrassing questions from the bemedaled veteran of high rank as to what he did during the war, President Mooney launched early into a modest and humorous recital of how the firm of Messer and Breton (570 Madison Ave., New York City) had "sold" the war effort. In his view he, Winfred Mooney, had become rather more an editor than an account executive during the period of crisis. To the American public at large Messer and Breton had introduced "some splendid writers—novelists and poets and radio writers, not to mention great writers like Milton, Tom Mann, and Tom Paine." Much historical material that might have remained unknown to the citizenry was, by the occasion and by the stable at Messer and Breton, brought alive into the public heart by the passion of advertising.

General Greave replied that he was indeed gratified by the distinctions between American propaganda and that unleashed by our late enemies and particularly by the infamous Dr. Goebbels.

Upon the departure of the guests, two by two, General Greave, over a nightcap, remarked to Dean Morgan, in Mrs. Morgan's presence, "You and your lady have a good situation here. I sense boom in the air and at last I begin to understand why you turned down Tulane." The remark occasioned firstly certain discursive analogies with the choice by General of the Armies Douglas MacArthur to emphasize the role of the Pacific theater and the Far East in the shaping of the postwar world. "Only . . ." As General Greave essayed a return from his analogy, flattering to the youth and vision of his host, and giving it its present application to the situation at Wellford College, he hesitated tactfully after saying, "Only . . ."

"Only . . . Mooney!" said vivacious Lady Morgan, never reluctant to take the creature by its horns, nor to utter what reticence passed over in silence. "I tried to warn you he was a nonpareil." And though indeed she had, prior to the dinner hour, commented shrewdly on the character of Wellford's president, her delight in the astonishment of the insufficiently warned observer passed common bounds.

"It's hard to visualize Royce taking orders from him," graciously suggested General Greave, blushing as an elderly Southern gentleman may upon observing horns in a lady's hands.

"I suppose my work is rather to put some content into his whims," Dean Morgan explained. Then challenged, "But Mooney works. Tonight you saw the future, and it works, General. This is the age of Mooney, which your victorious arms have won."

General Greave hoped that the thought might perish.

As Dean and Mrs. Morgan prepared to retire into that bed where Miss Grace Blackburn had slept so many peaceful years, Mrs. Morgan expressed the hope that "they" could be invited alone sometime in the near future. "Just the four of us. It is ripening."

She was asked how she could determine love's—or perhaps only matrimony's—progress. She declared, "Because Carole has more and more things she won't talk about, and I want to *see*."

Pantsless Dean Morgan agreed to her wish.

Item: Urging the disgraceful lack of imagination among the hairdressers in Buchanan (and secretly recording Mrs. Slater's lack of imagination in her failure to seek the superior skills available in Chicago), Mrs. Morgan prevailed upon her friend, Mrs. Carole Slater, to permit her the privilege of restyling her hair. During this ritual of preparation (to which Mrs. Slater gratefully and almost cringingly assented) Mrs. Morgan exploited those arcane powers devolving upon the manipulator of another's tresses to induce a state comparable to the effect of sodium pentothal (truth serum) with the end of hearing "from the horse's mouth" what was toward between Mrs. Slater and President Winfred Mooney. She was satisfied merely that, in the responses to her delicate inquisition, Mrs. Slater lied.

Item: On the morning of his nativity in late May, Dean Royce Morgan encountered, on a campus sidewalk somewhat closer to

Arden Hall (Administration) than to Stack Hall (Art, Domestic Science, and Biology), Professor M. Thomas LeCoeur. In response to the dean's observation that this was a day of great beauty, Professor LeCoeur, beauty-lover, replied that Yes, it was indeed, since he had this day received appointment to the staff of Nebraska State Teachers' College at Peru, Nebraska.

Dean Morgan expressed heartfelt regret, the more so that this news should come to him upon his birthday, more yet so in that Professor LeCoeur had been one of the new men on whom the good hopes of Wellford rested, and most because the explosive expression of thanksgiving for the opportunity to be away from Wellford signaled some unspeakable and perhaps unguessable resentment. At the expression of administrative regret, Professor LeCoeur (a man six years younger than the dean and more impulsive, not to say accustomed to wearing a bohemian heart on his undersleeve) said, "How long are *you* going to stand it, Morgan?" Considering the rudeness of this question merely significative, Dean Morgan silently questioned further. And heard, "I mean being screwed by people who aren't in the same league with you and you know it." Considering the verb (inf. *to screw*) not so much offensive in the context as strange, Dean Morgan mildly asked who was, in the artist's view, screwing him, and was answered with a dark nod to Professor LeCoeur's left, perhaps indicating the presidential mansion or perhaps the planet Mars. Then Professor LeCoeur said, sighing, "There's no fathoming the immense gulf between human minds," and without further clarification took his way toward Peru, Nebraska.

Item: As the approach of the June convocation announced the end of this, now his third, year of biding his time on the Wellford scene, Dean Morgan, private and perpetual taker of stock, father, husband, dean, friend, adviser, butt, witness, analyst and Heaven's analysand, idler, strong domino, amateur of history, disengaged lover, and unstung cuckold, took stock and concluded (tentatively): That his talents, if not his manhood, were fully employed by Wellford College, Anno 1948.

His manhood? That which must have been the outcome of genetic, intellectual, and environmental preparations antedating his birth in Buchanan's Mercy Hospital and of his own early cognitions, determinations, essays, intimations, and adaptation to the then prevailing and from the foundations of the earth expanding limitations of reason, as well as to the less discernible but more prescriptive contents of the subconscious (racial or personal), to myths not only of his Midwest but of remote lands and times. That which once with purpose was projected temporally forward to the then unpredictable —and indeed undetermined—present; projected if not with hope, since without prediction hope is unthinkable, then with the confidence a thinking rock might entertain that when it has fallen it will still be a rock (in his case the confidence that in whatever composition of improvised or accidental circumstance he would still be a man). That which, alas, was forbidden on pain of extinction to identify or justify itself by its adequacy to the employment of any transient present whatever, either the present of administrative wisdom, or of domestic harmony, or of libidinous involvement. That which must be owned but never possessed, defended but never saved, honored but never credited.

His talents? For soothing and resettling ancient librarians, female. For patient and tolerant amusement where approval or affection was impossible. For being a good daddy where fatherhood was, in the sense required by the self for emergence from its hermitic isolation, denied. For observing the formalities of Christian and sexual love (agape and Eros) where remained only erotic and ethical fixations upon a future once glimpsed and already antedated, for whose sake he had perhaps immortally frustrated the ideal capacity for love in not one but two women, wife and long-time mistress. For directing extensions in the Master of Arts program. For treading water in the gulf between the minds of his colleagues. For interposing mind, heart, and pants (their still vital contents if need be) between the alien souls in his charge and the more immediate of the disasters for which they clamored.

PART THREE

11

THE MORGANS' HOUSE—that mere physical shell which so mildly, constantly, and capriciously subverted Royce Morgan's attempts to take stock reasonably—never quite revealed its enchantments so clearly as in June weather.

It was a house "that if it had been any bigger couldn't have been wooden," Lot Morgan said, young Lot who was beginning to believe that he had *always* lived there.

Except for the trim, the entire house was clapboarded. Even the stumpy and faintly romanesque arches supporting the porch roof that swung massively around front and side of the house were faced with a ruche of clapboard texture. The long, long slopes of the shingled roof, broken front and rear with so many ample dormers and a transverse second and third story like a collided smaller house going its own way, had the dimensions of an eighteenth-century ship of the line. And in fact there were features throughout the structure (from the compact, paneled, and low-ceilinged study to the proliferation of windows on the side which once had unobstructedly overlooked the river) that retained some recessive traits of naval architecture. It was as if the prospering landlubber who conceived the house had not been quite able to forget the voyage that brought him or his ancestors to the new country.

White on its gently sloping knoll, in the snowy months it loomed like an ice palace among the grand maples and elms of the lawn. When the porch screens were down and snow mounded on the wide porch rails or crusted sootily on the battleship-gray porch floor the house seemed to draw in upon itself like an animal with enough fat on its bones to keep it comfortable through any winter. A boy Lot Morgan's age might crouch some winter afternoon behind the clapboarded railings with his cheek just touching a spot of snow and, staring from the hermitage of his imagination, stare the mild, surrounding suburb out of existence. Then he could see a country rich with savages and benign wild animals.

In spring and autumn when the sparse foliage around the house would dissolve—from certain sidewalk vantage points a block or a block and a half away—the geometry of roof line and corners, the house could look like a giant, ermine balloon grounded until some wind might get under it and sweep it back where it came from.

But in June, when the trees were fully leaved and the sail-sized black screens walled the porch and the light of any hour in the twenty-four broke all but its sculptured mass into patterns of dark (dark green, blue, deep violet, or black) and white, the airy house sat on its knoll like a comfortable ark which life-loving Methodists had grounded on the Ararat of their decent desires. There was a sense about it of well-curried creatures just departed, two by two, for a romp on the grass or a sniff at the orchard and barn of their new environment. The movement of a June breeze along one of the varnished upstairs halls, or heat rising delicately in the back stairwell toward the lofty attic, the scarcely audible throb of the big fans pumping basement air through the heating pipes were intimations, for a boy Lot Morgan's age, of worlds beyond worlds of which these stairways, banisters, closets, kitchen, and flowered walls were a part. It was a house of odors and murmurs, best in June.

And for a boy of Lot Morgan's whimsically judicious temperament, just the *sort* of house where a big gray stud of a car (to which on a football afternoon he had pledged allegiance) should come in a June twilight bringing the sweet lady with whom he once played horse and a snaky impostor with hair the color of God's.

Since they were not his guests and an impulse of repugnance and timidity made him choose not even to greet them, he watched Carole's arrival with Mooney from behind the curtain of his open bedroom window. Fingering his just-bathed testicles, he watched them come up the walk smiling and disappear under the rain gutter rimming the porch roof. He heard his mother's voice ring like the nice little bell his teacher used to get order in the classroom. They wouldn't pull anything on his mother tonight, whatever they had come for. He heard his father's deeper, edgeless voice laughing a welcome, and heard Carole say, "Oh!" as if the roses his mother had arranged in a great bouquet on the cocktail table were, this time, no fooling, more than she could bear. He listened for Mooney, expecting a hiss, but heard only the other three in June-cadenced talk, no duller but certainly no more interesting to him than if he had been able to make out all the words.

He withdrew into his room, put on a light, spun the old-fashioned plaster globe on his dresser, looking for Switzerland where his new stamps had come from, then threw himself face down on the coverlet of his bed, where he had stacked the books he meant to look at before sleeping.

There was one about a white stallion the cowboys could never catch. Another was about everything that had wheels. There was another about birds and he tried to figure out which bird his mother was most like. His figuring came out the same as every other time he looked at the book. Unsatisfactory as it was, she looked like the sleek little sparrow hawk leaning down commandingly from a telephone pole, daring anything to show its head in the sickening greenery of the watercolor field. White-haired Mooney was a raven, of course, because the raven's eyes, the way they were set like a hunter's aiming down a rifle barrel, had always scared him. Carole was the big fat white duck. It made him giggle the way the curved underfolds of the duck's body hung down around yellow legs like something hanging down around something.

He wished his father were the trumpeter swan. But, as it said in his text, there were no more trumpeter swans. All gone now, but oh, Jesus, oh, wow, what a bird it was, like a ton of snow up there in that farthest corner of the sky he'd seen one day when Carole took him flying. It weighed about a ton but it flew, and not like a noisy airplane either, but absolutely silent in the sky, hunting for its mate or a younger trumpeter swan just like it.

Thinking of all that bone and feathers being airborne was like thinking of his father driving Mooney's car. He just wished it were so.

When he put the books aside and turned out his lights, he couldn't hear anything downstairs, so they must all be out in back, maybe in the studio, though he could hear Barbara messing around in the kitchen.

He didn't mean to sleep just yet. He had an idea too good for that, one that wouldn't work in the light. He was going to have them take Carole out in the studio and sacrifice her. The two men would tie Carole to one of the pottery wheels while his mother watched like a sparrow hawk perched on the window ledge. They'd start her spinning and put their hands in her to shape her and make her rise like a big white jug under their molding hands. Or a little white jug—since, as he watched through the third-story window of his fantasy, the spinning whiteness, now fat, now slender, seemed to diminish away like something watched over his father's shoulder in a riverview mirror.

Wherever this fantasy had come from, its silly components were less significant than the unquestioned and unquestionable choice of Carole as victim. He loved her. She bothered him. He hated her. As with nearly everyone she had ever met, probably, her vulnerability was intolerable, whether it was construed to be sexual or of the heart. Therefore, let them, for him, spin her sacrificially away until she became no larger than a white star. And then vanished in the moist breathing of a boy sleeping healthily through a June night.

Down in the stable studio—after round one of the cocktails had been consumed in the screened twilight of the porch—the four adults maneuvered within the social equivalents of young Lot's dream. Unstrung Mooney had expressed the wish to have "a good look" at the place he had visited only on more formal occasions before.

That meant first of all a drink-in-hand ramble to the end of the orchard while Royce expounded on what this view from the bluff had been once, before it was broken and civilized by ten or a dozen houses smaller and more modern than theirs.

Through the evening-darkened greenery of the apple trees they

158

saw the stable as what it was meant to be—a capricious and ornamented afterthought to the sober magic of the house. Its little white towers and cupolas showed in the broken twilight like some mushroom growth, not so much ageless as instantaneous (though it was seventy years old), the projection of every instant's inclination not to conform to past and future.

They must enter this privileged structure by the functional double doors of aluminum and glass that Priss had wanted for the passage of outsize equipment and there turn on lights in a room where shelves of fired and unfired rotundities looked on them like layers of audience in the galleries. Priss leading—this floor was hers, from the plasterboard wall that set off garage space for the Morgan cars to what had once been the harness room and was more recently the office where she and Tom LeCoeur had taken refuge from students. Under an ice-blue light the kilns and wheels looked more like stage property than objects of use.

"And," President Mooney of Wellford boomed, "is some of what I see student work?" Down from a dusty shelf he took an ugly, bisque-fired vase, the size of a football. He set his cocktail glass down to use both hands in his examination. His eyebrows lifted to say, Well, someone *tried*. He laughed tolerantly, and as he looked to Priss for an explanation, the well-manicured middle finger of his right hand began to play unconsciously in and out of the red neck of the thing. "Anyway it shows a certain aboriginal craft," said New Yorker Win Mooney.

"I'm afraid it's mine," Carole said. "Isn't it mine, Priss? But you promised you'd bust . . ."

The hands that held the vase became reverential, protective, as if he were afraid Carole meant then and there to seize it and throw it into the trash. "It has the charm of looseness. It feels good to the touch," he insisted.

"Let me look," Priss asked, but when she tried to take it from Mooney's hand and look for initials or other identifying marks left in the clay, he would not quite let go. "I don't think it's yours, Carole. It wouldn't be on that shelf. . . ."

"It's mine," Carole said, quite insistent on honesty, as if hoping, perhaps, that the tone of the evening would be the undemanding honesty of friends, all candid about their shortcomings.

Yet, there was a kind of touching wonder in the fact that out of the scores of undistinguished student leftovers she should have been able to pick this unidentified shape as her creation.

"Not all its merits are cheaply visible," Royce said.

"Nice," Mooney insisted.

"Clumsy," Carole repeated.

"Not yours," Priss swore. And amid these contradictions the matter was dropped. There was plenty in the studio to distract them— most of all perhaps an aura of professionalism, Priss's contribution, that ignited Mooney and set him muttering about "artists in residence" and other institutional ornaments dear to a forward-looking educationalist. With an avaricious gleam in his eye, he was responding to more than martinis.

He was avidly learning how designs may be etched in slip when Barbara put her head in the door to say the meat thermometer registered one hundred and forty and both ladies rushed to save the roast from an overcooked Midwestern fate. Royce poised to follow them. Mooney asked, "What's upstairs?"

There was only a huge, empty loft now where Lot played sometimes on rainy days, but Royce put on the lights and led the way.

The spiral of wooden stairs they climbed was so narrow and turned on so short a radius that Royce had to corkscrew his spine. And it was as if the displaced spinal cord should remember a serpent's twisting when he recalled how he had gone up these very stairs with Carole (one Christmas vacation when he was home from Exeter) to find their pleasure before he took her to a country club dance. Fortunately fleeting was the thought that he was bringing Mooney up here to show him not only where but how that vanished scene had been enacted.

"You see, there's nothing," he said with a smile.

Nothing much. There was a tongueless coaster wagon on the broad planks of the floor, unutterably lonely in all that space, a low table with pieces of a puzzle spilling over it, a wide, fancy window that was high enough to give a view of the sunset still lingering in the trees across the river, and . . .

"What on earth?" Mooney asked, pointing upward, shaking his head at the improbable surmise.

"*That*," Royce said. "Oh, that. That's a wing." High up among the rafters hung the brown ribs and spars of a wing quite like one that hoisted the Wright brothers off the sand at Kitty Hawk. "A skeleton in the Morgan closet. Yes, you've found it. Tom Jaffe and I started to build a glider once from some plans in *Popular Mechanics*." At one time, he meant to say, boys build model airplanes and gliders just as, he meant *not* to say, they seduce their female playmates. And time carries those phases cleanly away, he wished to affirm. "Damn thing had bicycle wheels and the theory of launching was to discover a road steep enough to get up speed for a takeoff. I believe Tom and I meant to run it right down the bluff toward the river. Fortunately we never got to the point of covering that wing, though we spent most of a winter building it."

"Carole's told me you were great on . . . on Boy Scout things," Mooney said, without the faintest trace of irony. He craned his neck at the never-tried airfoils, either in envy or recognition of some dream that made them closer than brothers. Whatever he may have seen, he had found the occasion, long jockeyed for, to plead openly for alliance, to strip himself figuratively like a wooer.

"Ah," he said with a whispering chuckle. "You lads were going to rush down the bluff and across the river and, God, where would you have stopped?"

There was a sudden, not quite coherent turn toward wistfulness in his voice. "It must have been wonderful to grow up here. It's a great country." He shook his head as if, like the land of dreams, the Midwest had suddenly swum into his ken.

He said, "Some of my friends think that any place that isn't New York is ridiculous. You know such people too. People who can't understand why I'm out here except to advance myself." He shook his head like a sinner looking back. "I had the privilege of a childhood in filthy old Boston. The old daddy said I'd go to Harvard someday—that's the one justification I can remember for our living there, though there must have been other necessities—but it turned out to be Boston University. I despised it."

In the shadow-fringed loft his thought spurted and hissed like a fuse lit by accident. He had not made it clear what he despised—Boston U., or all his past, or his old daddy. But the admission that he had ever had a parent came strangely from him—seeming, as he always had, to have issued full-grown from the times, like a dapper *Zeitgeist*.

He laughed and said with disturbingly naked—even aggressive—humility, "I would have despised Harvard just as much. I don't want *that*." He bobbed his head apologetically as if he understood as well as Royce how much his thought was outrunning his explanation of it. "For mine. For Wellford. You haven't seen—you wouldn't believe how strongly I feel about what education has got to be. It's been so wrong, so wrong. For generations, perhaps, warping youth, frustrating youth, eroding their capacity for . . ."

For? The answer, the object, seemed to be suspended in the silence just beyond the end of a breath. For? For? He did not trust himself to say what for, as if to name the glory would be to profane it.

Nor could Royce in any circumstances have brought himself to ask the word, not even ask by a glance, since he was simply afraid to look at the face from which the inspired voice issued, for fear of seeing a fraudulent grimace. In what was passing for pure confession it would have been too unkind to search for the note of falsity. And whatever the performance of this man was henceforward to be, it would be better to believe that the well-guarded heart was pure.

Mooney took a drink and a breath and said, "It could change life! I'm a disciple of Whitman and the Greeks. I believe in the swarming multitudes within the mind of each person . . . Ah, it's so hard to find anyone one even dares *say* that to. You might well laugh, too."

"No."

"No. *You* wouldn't. I believe you can understand it's not a pretense with me. You know—you with your sharp eye—how I'll trick and scheme and dye my hair to get it. Oh, I do that, too." The words came like a scalding stream from pained lips. How doubt their utter honesty?

If there was still a doubt let it be removed thus: "Even tolerate *you* here. If one thing was clear to me from the minute I came, Royce, it was that I'd never be secure for a minute as long as you were here. And George Hand isn't the only one who advised me to move you along. You've made me very nervous."

Royce shook his head in the not-yet-committed gesture of one who can't believe what he is hearing. Mooney took his sleeve and shook his arm. "Listen, you're the only man in Buchanan who frightens me. Not by your name. Not by your connections. Not even by your intelligence. It's your character. I believe you're a giant, Royce. Your character and your patience. You sit and listen and watch. And you take us all in, and then—pfft!—you have us all. Right where you want us."

"I won't claim to understand the mechanism you're attributing to me," Royce said, not so much reluctant to hear this crescendoing appeal out to its end as wishing he could hear it in the open air. The loft had become oppressive, as if Mooney's passion had exhausted the oxygen. Whatever it meant—and it could not mean what it superficially amounted to—it needed space around it if it was not to be altogether morbid. Lightly he said, "I understand that patience may seem aggressive. Priss has schooled me in that notion."

"I'm not blaming you," Mooney said hoarsely. "No, no, no. Let me get back to the point. I'm playing for everything here at Wellford. I want a great university." He let the word ring, suddenly dampened it, rushed on. "I want to build something that will last a thousand years."

In that year so soon after the war, references to millennial duration still automatically produced associations with the Third Reich. But Mooney sailed right over that hurdle. He knew his giant well enough to know him incapable of easy analogies.

"*You* see what I mean," he said in a kind of ecstasy. "I can boom it. But you can make it . . ." He paused on an indrawn breath, his tongue poised for the word "seminal"—his mind too cunning to use it now.

But in the strange, oppressive isolation Royce heard the word, felt the discharge of passion soiling him like the pollution of a dream he was incapable of halting.

He took a deep, tired, smiling breath. "I'm moved by what you've said. I don't *quite* understand what you want of me."

"Your soul," Mooney said in his bland hysteria. "Your soul for the university. Don't sell me out. Use me as I intend to use you. Get off your horse, Morgan. Come on the road with me. I'll raise the moola." He made a coarse, self-deriding gesture of shilling for money. "You bring the men. The spirit. The young. The faculty. Don't say no, Morgan. The chance will never bring two people like us together again."

"I haven't meant to sell you out . . ." Royce said with a troubled shake of his head. Then drove ponderously and resolutely for the twisted stair that would get them out of here.

The rest of that evening was Mooney's triumph, and it was not so much the triumph of his sincerity in the stable loft (that he had been sincere was beyond Royce's ability to doubt) as the triumphant exploitation of advantages that his brief sincerity had won. There had been no hypocrisy in his flattery. No matter. He used it as if it had been pure hypocrisy. He had found the note and the moment to stalemate Royce at the same time he incited the ladies.

Through dinner he went ecstatically on developing his vision of the University-to-be as he could not have told it elsewhere. It took, perhaps, the sum of Carole's charity and Royce's formalizing sympathy and Priss's sibyl cunning to make a pyramid out of the chunks he had to deliver.

Something had happened. He had a prospect, and he thought it a firm one, of adding a school of metallurgy onto the existing liberal arts structure. Nadige Brass and Copper Tubing of Racine was willing (Oscar Nadige said he was willing) to give them a building and pay staff salaries for a minimum of ten years, the return to be the training of engineers for the parent company.

" 'Let's see the color of their money,' our friend Worth demands," he said with a thrill of defiance in his voice.

"Henry's skeptical?" Royce guessed.

"Henry's worse than skeptical. He's becoming destructive and negative. There's no worse millstone around our neck than Henry Worth. Perhaps it's fundamentally pure jealousy—I understand his type—in that he's done nothing at all since his war profiteering but sit on his money and expect it to hatch."

This assessment did not depend for its force on its accuracy. Mooney was in full swing away from reliance on Henry, and the next step would be some scheme to pack the trustees and get Henry out of the way altogether.

Which could be the motive for this evening's courtship? It could indeed, Royce supposed, but saw himself and his good will required for more than a balance of power in a showdown with Henry.

If they took on a metallurgical school—and if it thrived as one would hope—could it in any real sense be fitted into a unified educational program here? Would it be a bump on the log, an essentially distinct enterprise? Royce found that a serious answer was being solicited from him.

And yet, when he tried to give it, he found Mooney beaming on him, approving not so much the sense of the analysis he made as finding it "high-priced," sounding well tailored, a magnificent label to put on the goods. He saw himself photographed as a man of distinction endorsing a blend of Virginia tobacco and Kentucky horse shit.

No matter. No matter tonight. The color of the Nadige money had not yet been seen. This was a matter that would be settled within the next two or three years. What did matter was the height of ambition looming like a mountain peak when the mere mention of money scattered the obscuring clouds.

These three (or these four, assuming that Mooney's own astounded ears had never heard such visions come out of his mouth) were the first to know the full scope of his wishes. And, in the grip of the creative moment, it mattered very little whether he had been plotting something like this all his life or was making it up on the spur of the Nadige offer.

Mooney was forty-one. (None of the others knew that for sure;

by a process of military intelligence Priss knew that his age was between thirty-nine and forty-two, that his birthday was the Fourth of July.) But that evening he showed himself ageless. He spoke as boy and as sage—pubescent, senile, ripe, naïve, clairvoyant, and heroically blind.

How his jeweled eyes glittered over the red roast and the June-green peas as he compared "a base of twenty-five hundred students," soon to be attained at Wellford, with a kind of bridgehead from which his educational forces could march, countermarch, hop, skip, jump, and fly without the encumbrances that "older places" (Harvard? Yale? Princeton? Chicago? Stanford? The Big Ten?) carried around their hoary necks.

He spread his little hands like a victorious fighter pilot in a newsreel when he told how he and George Hand had just mortgaged last year's real estate acquisition for twenty-five thousand more than the purchase price.

"I got away with *that*," he said with owlish, droll self-astonishment, permitting himself now a tremor of awe, if not fear, like the acrobat's apprentice who has not even dared notice the space beneath until he is off the wire.

"Royce hoisted you over," Priss said—not so much claiming credit for her husband in his practical services as directing the point at Mooney's vanity, and speaking with the privilege of a *very* close friend.

He had not known. It was news to him that Consolo, for the merchants, had ever come asking Royce, What shall we do? But he took it now with absolutely no surprise. He had known—or it was as if he had known exactly—what he could count on Royce to do for him. And it shocked Royce to see himself so predictable to this man.

"Well, hand in hand," Mooney joked. "The way I'd like to play it I'll always need people better than I to fill in the gaps for me, catch me when I wobble, tell me off when I'm wrong. The truth is . . ." and it seemed to stun him touchingly to perceive it so clearly, ". . . the truth is I haven't much to contribute except . . ." He dared not—not quite—say *vision,* so he shrugged the word away unspoken, to let them call his function whatever they wanted. "At any rate, now that we're here, you can see what's next," he said in his imperative half-whisper.

"Well, not to pay debts," Priss said drolly and Mooney whooped with laughter and wiped his eyes.

"Debts pay themselves," he said with sleepwalker's confidence. "No. We're going to build a fieldhouse." His lifted eyes and rising hands described the dimensions he had in mind—as if he were watching a vision of two zeppelins and a whale joggling around loosely under a two-acre fieldhouse ceiling. "Tommy Barker's going to build our fieldhouse," he said. And that was a foregone conclusion.

He dismissed that step, too, as an already certain element of the base—like the infantry of twenty-five hundred students who would shortly be on hand.

"Barker's very good, I suppose. . . ." Priss, skeptical, was not so much trying to puncture the skin of the vision as tease out an amplification.

Mooney sighed like a lover already soundly affianced. "Tommy's *very good,*" he said. "And will beget our fieldhouse, and the fieldhouse will beget a library and a library will beget gifts and endowments of the aged, the gifts will beget and beget and beget."

Royce laughed to himself and Mooney heard it like a cue. "And Royce Morgan will beget the university that people like me are too busy with externals to beget ourselves," he said.

He was not looking at Carole when he said this, but Priss was and she saw the unsuppressible blush rise and fall and rise again on Carole's neck as she caught the sense of Mooney's proposal.

Oh, they all gathered that in essence Mooney was proposing a brotherly sharing of the throne, with himself in the lesser role of go-between, mouthpiece, fall guy, and figurehead.

And Royce, prepared by that reckless wooing in the stable loft, knew all at once that he believed Mooney would stick by what he proposed. He would stick by it for good reasons and bad; he would not even be constant from one month to another in respecting his own bargain. But like a profligate husband who returns to his lawful wife as automatically as he chases every passing skirt, he would in the long run be loyal out of compulsion. It was simply this: In the long run he had to want what lay at the end of the exercise of power. He could not himself conceive what this might be, so he had to ally, as if with a blood oath, to the man who was supposed to know the end. In this case, with Royce.

If there was treachery in the offer, it was not Mooney's. He was—faithful merchant of souls—trying to buy "the best," whatever his cunning told him was the best available. If the pig he sold from his unexamined poke turned out not to be the best, if it turned out to be nothing at all, the responsibility for that fraud would not be Mooney's.

So it appeared to the mind behind the face behind the cigar smoke. Only, Royce thought, puffing his good cigar in the candlelight and trying to detach himself enough to see all four of them as they were composed in a group so he could remember the picture of this trade in years to come—only, it isn't me he's proposing to. He's proposing to the women, one or both. In his big pitch he offers what they want in exchange for my hypothetical soul.

So when he did recall that evening in the years afterward, seeing four people making a monstrous bargain, he saw the one who might have been himself—the skin that might have been the poke for a soul worth their dickering—emptied by the very fact that it was bargained for and yielded. He would never suppose that he was sold to Mooney by the women. He was sold by the failure to imagine before Mooney had what the women might want most from him—sold, in a word, by the impotence he had brought from Saipan.

"We can hope," Mooney said exultantly (when to hope was to set the perfect snare for hope). On the spur of the moment, or spurred on by the moment of opportunity, he named the things they could hope to make of their Wellford, Buchanan lives. And it sounded wonderful.

There was Mooney's genius. It did not lie in discerning how the other man might be bound to him (for the mute configuration of circumstances had made that possibility) but in giving it the human sound of hope, giving an affirmative voice to amoral possibility, so it could become their purpose and therefore their responsibility, like a choice.

From a base of twenty-five hundred students (spear-carrying lambs from Nowhere, ready to march on Cloudland and colonize it) the crusade could distance all pursuers. Mooney would drive the chariot. Royce would sit up high. The ladies . . . wouldn't they adore the speed and the conquest, knowing it was all for the good? Yes they could, so they would. And as the future was being mined with explosives, it sounded better than ever. There was Mooney's genius.

Later the four of them lounged on the screened porch again in the chintz-covered gliders. There were no lights except those that came from the street, gathering starry green reflections from intervening maple leaves or dewy hedge tops, and the slant mellow light falling through a window far up at the corner of the house.

What would seem so strange later—as it would have seemed un-likely at any time before this evening—was their intimacy. For all the propriety of their language, they seemed to loll in a kind of lewd linkage, like perverts in a daisy chain or (the more ancient image) like a knot of vipers tangled for hibernation in hell's own climate. Of course the hospitality of the Morgan house and Morgan booze had made their contributions, but the catalyzing force was surely Mooney's presidential gift for putting folks at ease.

He had tripped them with his humility in respect to Royce's future. He did more. Among intimates he volunteered a winning confession of the bumbling behind the Miss Halstead affair. He confessed his extreme embarrassment at "botching things up" for her back on the day when he took his place with the cake-eaters in the library stacks.

"You made a legend," Priss said.

"Oh, no. Oh, no!" he disclaimed. "The simple truth is—" he took a chortling breath—"I'd never been a college president before. I acted like a smart-aleck boy. It was an absurd thing to do, and afterward I was frankly too paralyzed with embarrassment to stop the wheels that had been set in motion. That was left to Royce." (Who recalled that he had been able to stop nothing, that the juggernaut had rolled on and on.) "Poor old lady. Can't we call her back, Royce?"

He was seen to wipe his eyes, but since he had been laughing all the while he spoke, the reason for his tears was beyond determining.

Nevertheless he had not lamented Miss Halstead in vain. Carole heard the note of self-abasement. Carole saw. Carole *would* make the most charitable interpretation possible, and not merely because she was high on martinis, hospitality, and the flattery of Royce. Each of them, in the spell of the evening, was made to feel that as of now old attitudes were impertinent to their novel intimacy. While Mooney was putting off his masks and showing himself, after all, as human as anyone, it began not to matter what Priss had intended for Carole or Carole had intended to do on her own or what forebodings Royce had entertained about her and Mooney. It was as if all their past intentions and even their schemes had only been guesses at a process that took its own surprising turns in spite of them. So here and now Carole *would* respond to a candor and fundamental generosity Mooney had never been able to expose before.

She was being won there, under Royce's very eyes as it were, and not because anyone had intended it that way—but because it had to happen.

While Mooney's voice played its facile tunes, there fell away one by one the obstacles to her yielding faithfully. Her splendid, creamy shoulders between the blue straps of her dress trembled with laughter at his jokes and slumped in submission at his ecstatic hopes.

And from humility he bounced like a wrestler coming off the ropes to a dazzling (but almost impersonal) arrogance. With the women flanking him he started again on what he had tried to tell Royce in the stable loft. This time he brought it to its point.

What were they really talking about? What were they giving their lives to a college for? What was education for?

"For love," he said in an unstrained, perfectly simple voice. Then ducking, even yet fearing to be misunderstood (he had not been), he immediately tried the pedant's trick of explaining away his clearest communication. "That is, the liberation of the individual in the

Greek sense, unbinding the natural self so the libidinal flow will be
. . . natural. Hell, education isn't to make people complex. It's to
allow them, in a complex world, to be simple."

"Yes," Royce assented, as though he had been asked. The voice he
heard, if not the man before him, had spoken what he had tried
hardest in his life to believe. He would not be reticent when he heard
it spoken plainly. And of course Carole heard his assent, and of
course applied it to her own interpretation of what was being said.

"The erotic college," Priss joked, to keep the moment nimble.

Mooney landed acrobatically on his feet before this mockery. "I'm
not proposing to incorporate the Coolidge Motels into the curricu-
lum," he cracked.

"No, but . . ." Carole said. "No, but . . ." She wanted to agree
with what had sounded so good, so noble. In spirit she would agree,
though she could not match the others in their nimbleness of expression. She would assent once again to what promised to be better than
life. Her hand rested on Mooney's sleeve to tell him, Yes, she agreed.

When they left the house toward midnight, Priss and Royce stood
at the screen door watching them fade down the glooms and
shadows of the walk, then saw them pause awhile before they got
into the swanboat of a car that waited to carry them off.

It was impossible to be sure that Mooney was kissing her there at
the end of the walk, but as if she knew he must be, Priss said all at
once with a terrified shiver, "Royce, what have I done to you?"

She had done nothing. Her loose-built schemes and all the refined
envy of a woman with time on her hands ended where they had begun, in her imagination. They were surely without direct influence
on what was still to happen that night between white-haired Mooney
and Carole.

But she must act as if it were all her doing and hurry her man,
her male, her stallion upstairs to their own bed to make up to him
what he was denied in the loss of Carole, to drive deeper into him
the barb planted by her conspiracy in that loss.

She must open her body to him like an undefended fruit, split for his pleasure and oblivion. Close like a jaw. Accept like a sinner pummeled and trodden into the mud. Demand like a devil. Writhe in her gratifying torment. Cut like scissors in the moment of greatest opportunity.

For an hour on their bed—too warm for even the covering of a sheet—she fought him for some meaningful part in what was happening in spite of her. She led him by the ears to the sewer of her self-disgust. She crouched her whole body like a nude slave at the base of his towering manhood and tongued her adoration, her submission. She broke in the fervor of orgasm, recomposed like an image recomposing on the surface of disturbed water, and took his seed like a vampire.

He tried, as always, to let her find what she wanted—speech where there was only brutal silence, answers where there could be nothing but sensation and fantasy. Ah, he was a lover, and if bodies could, his ought to have quieted hers.

But for the hour of their passion he was buttoned, like the men buttoned within the armor of a tank, inside the hermitage of his thoughts. And there Priss's question—*What have I done to you?*— was cruelly transposed into *What has been done?* He had tried to accept the evening at face value. If not all of Mooney's promises seemed solid gold, the armistice they represented was some cause for rejoicing. The promise of a new beginning had been there. He had heard it, had said his own yes to it. But after Priss's question all the complacencies stacked up as the evening went on seemed to have been stacked on purpose to be collapsed in one ominous clatter. In the uproar of second thoughts (dinning while the bed bounced, like the shrilling of springs in some second-rate brothel) the girl who had walked off his lawn with Mooney was progressively transformed from the family friend, the widow of thirty-three, and the self-appointed aunt of his son, once again into the preadolescent beauty, orphan, and playmate he had almost eclipsed from his thoughts.

She was a child who needed his protection from her own faithfulness, who had asked for the cue to say no and die instead of the cue to say yes and be torn apart. He should have prevented her going the way she went. . . .

He should have prevented it. That was the given task of his manhood, not this sensual, physical pronging. In knowing that he knew that the very act of mounting his wife (yes, even of here getting her with child, as it would turn out he had) was the sign of his impotence.

Which Priss knew too. And she was cheated by this insidious knowledge. So that nothing came of her attempt at magic but that she got pregnant. It was one of the ironies of planned parenthood that Sherman Blackburn Morgan should have been conceived out of his mother's decision to assert her magical control of the world.

At a quarter of two they were finished. Royce Morgan had not satisfied his wife. His wet body lay harboring an image of Carole as a female Benjamin, the last born. The child now delivered by his virtuous silence and his impotence into Babylon . . .

From these appalling contradictions he retired promptly to sleep.

And woke, when the first warm honey of light from the June morning was saturating the curtains, to find Priss fully clothed in a gray dress standing beside the bed sober and alert as if she were ready to go out.

She had already been out.

"Well," she said. "Well, now we know. At least I do and you're about to, whether you want to or not. He stayed all night at Carole's. Imagine, he's parked that dumb car in her garage and closed the door. I had to go in the side to make sure it was there."

"That was brave of him," Royce said groggily. The color of the morning sun sticking over the horizon reminded him of the unfired vase in the studio where Mooney's finger had played. He sat up and blinked in fright.

"It's a very recognizable car," Priss said, as if fornication were an exact science and the comprehension of it a detached mental discipline.

Royce's face showed nothing. "I guess this indicates what Mooney really meant when he spoke of the end of education," he said lazily.

"It indicates what lengths I'll go to," Priss said. "I won't let us just be used. I intend to do some using myself."

"For instance?"

She shook her head in angry bafflement.

"For instance calling a photographer from the *Courier-Sentinel* to picture Mooney backing his car out of the garage of a well-known Buchanan lady?"

"Oh, not *that*." Her notions of revenge remained metaphysical.

"I do not see any practical exploitation of your discovery, Dr. Morgan," Royce said. "Tennis anyone? It's a lovely day. Let us seize it."

"Not that, but there must be something to do. It means something."

He nodded and headed for the shower, where he heard Lot tinkering with the taps. "Be my wife and help me understand," he said.

She shook her head. Her spying trip had been a last clutch for the notion that she was in control, that she still had teeth and claws to use in making a life. She was not in control, but she did have teeth and claws. She would use them here, on him, in default of the good chance to use them on her avowed enemies.

"Fun's fun and let them have it," she said with blithe bitterness. "I guess this does mean they'll marry, doesn't it? It appears to be in addition to good reasons already noted."

He nodded a slow agreement. "I've been wrong about that, too. I didn't think they would. Yes. I suppose they'll marry soon. It isn't in Mooney to waste his effort for anything less. I guess it will be soon," he said, "since last night indicated that Mooney needs more than Tommy Barker after all. Since even he knows there has to be an end in view for all he's able to pull off."

12

THOMAS BARKER, All-American forward in his third year at Wellford, was and was not the same Tommy Barker who before the war
had mowed the big lawn for Royce's aunts. The physical capacity
and Hoosier single-mindedness of the basketball star had no doubt
always been there in potential. Surely the environment of Wellford
in its booming years (not to mention the contagion of big thinking
caught from proximity to President Mooney, the front seat of an
imperial car being perhaps the best place to observe the secrets of
the rear seat) added something definable as the habit of success to
the young man's native endowments. After the war he traveled with
a different entourage than that which used to come out of Bronkley
with him.

His mowing labors for the Blackburn ladies were chiefly memo-
rable to Royce because his whole family came with him to the job.

An ancient blue Essex would swing up the gravel drive on a hot
afternoon of those years. From the rear seat, where he had ridden
beside his lawn mower, Tommy would get out first, a wiry eleven-
year-old with close-set eyes.

After him, his father, his fat older brother, and two small sisters in
coveralls descended. The father would kneel with Tommy beside
the mower, upended on one wheel, while they oiled it and tested the
blades with the amateur cunning of country mechanics preparing a
Model A for a vacation jaunt across the plains to the mythic Rockies
or Yellowstone National Park. The two little girls in faded blue held
hands and covetously stared at the house, while already the fat
brother had found shade to lie in. A perfectly constant smile of

servility and contempt covered his face like something applied for comfort—like a damp handkerchief, perhaps, laid on to keep the gnats away.

By the time young Tommy had made his first mowing circuit of the big lawn, a second car would have appeared. This was a Buick touring car, one of those rolling clipper ships that saw their best days and greatest popularity while Buchanan sportsmen were learning to gamble on the national stock market. It was the kind of car that might once have carried the gangster Datento's girls or his little packages of painkiller to the county fair towns in seven states or down to St. Louis, Sardis, or Cairo on moonlight nights. It was the right chariot for a criminal folk hero, but its depraved rakishness was long gone over into plain decrepitude before the Barker clan got it. Its already aging home paint job covered pits in the original finish visible from the porch when it was parked by the stable. Bolted-on patches of galvanized tin held the outline of the high fenders intact and covered, on the body, what might have been bullet holes put in by some state policeman long since raised to an office job in the capital.

The Buick brought the rest of Tommy's family. These were mostly female, but included two brothers-in-law whose bare arms and round faces showed the caponized sleekness of professional reliefers. The Barker ladies always brought refreshments, and they dispensed them under the big top of the Buick while they watched Tommy earn his dollar ten.

The going rate for lawns in Buchanan was two bits in those times. The Blackburn lawn had been computed to be four times the size of a "normal" one, and Royce's aunts added a dime to the fee to show who they were.

On and on through those primeval afternoons, the lawn mower whirred its chiselly sound as Tommy worked from a vast periphery down to a little green island, square as a sheaf of banknotes, to be obliterated with one last burst of steam and a ceremonial showing of his clenched teeth. As each section of the lawn was finished there would be a moment—and no more—of suburban silence.

Once he got going Tommy never stopped except between the sections divided by flower beds and brick walks. A section finished, he knelt again with his father to test the blade edges with a dirty thumb and shoot drops of oil, darker than opals, into the muck around gears and bearings.

The pauses were so uniform and brief that it must seem to a watcher that Tommy never really changed his pace after the first grass began to shower up over his knees and fall around his sneakers. And perhaps it was the machine-like evenness of his performance— so antithetic to images of boyhood, so contrary to Tom Sawyer's style—that the Barkers came to marvel at, finding it (as Royce had, too) not merely heroic, not merely a laudable show of strength, but a kind of satyr play, prophetic of some tragedy and tragic immolation to come, a dance of boy and machine whose meaning would be fully spelled out only by time.

When Tommy reversed his mower and pushed it (singing its steely song) from the south sections of the lawn to the north ones, the spectators from the Buick trooped shyly after him, carrying sandwiches and lemonade and stationing themselves at the fringe of the orchard to see the last acts performed. Probably from time to time one of the attendant female Barkers offered Tommy drink from a fruit jar full of lukewarm lemonade, and probably from time to time on the hottest days he interrupted his task to bathe arms and neck from the garden hose as the nontoiling brothers-in-law so frequently did. But memory preserved the pure relationship of ideal grasshoppers watching the uninterrupted toil of an ant. One did not remember Tommy's ever having accepted relief. He was the artist and prophet of the clan, and he mowed a lawn they could not even imagine without his dedication.

At least his family never helped with the primary function of cutting the grass. They did, however, serve him somewhat like the *cuadrilla* and the entourage of a matador. They ran ahead of his mower to gather whatever obstacles had been left in his path by the slothful owners of the property—hoses and sprinklers, lawn chairs, magazines, lemonade glasses, and little wrought-iron tables, and all the detritus of bourgeois self-indulgence. All these were tossed helter-skelter on the porch so that, after Tommy's mowing, the porch seemed to have been covered by flood water that had drowned the civilization for which it was made.

It was the duty—at least the invariable accomplishment—of Tommy's attendants to so terrorize Royce's aunts and their guests that they would keep out of Tommy's road. The poor ladies always kept inside until Tommy was through, and if they did not literally lock their doors against the threat of a noyade, they peered out from around their curtains with the air of maidens in a village taken by bandits.

The two little girls in coveralls used to sneak onto the porches sometimes and peer in at one or another of the screen doors until some bawling voice would hail them back to the lemonade jar. One day they crept up a slanting drainspout to peer in a bathroom window where Royce's Aunt Linda had gone to pee. She squawked. They fell ten feet into a flower bed—and in a few minutes could be heard whispering like delicate rodents at the front screen door.

But probably the main motive that brought the Barker family was that of simple awe, and they came as so many sports fans would come later to the old and new Wellford fieldhouses and the arenas of the Midwest and the nation, to pay tribute to a folk hero whose charisma was as undeniable as it was crude.

"There is something about that boy," Grace Blackburn used to say. "Maybe we ought to pay him more than a dollar ten." At a dollar ten per *blade* of grass they could hardly have paid enough for the revelation, and at any price they could not have afforded to understand what Tommy the Mower prefigured. And Royce, visiting in a summer holiday, had warned idly, "If you did, you'd have all of Bronkley up here to watch him. There's a real likelihood that no other male Barker ever earned a dollar ten on any one given day of his life. They're probably up here trying to figure how he does it so they can."

"He seems to be in training for something," Mildred Blackburn guessed shrewdly.

Mooney was the first to recognize what the boy had been training for, the first to suppose that in partnership with him this bony youth might become the greatest normal-sized white basketball player to emerge on the North American continent.

Tommy had had offers of athletic scholarships from several schools bigger and richer than Wellford. No one else offered him enough. After his freshman year and his chauffeuring apprenticeship, probably no other school *could* have offered him enough. When Dolly Dowling and the supporting team that Dolly hired came on the scene in Tommy's junior year, when the star became part of a machinery designed not only around him but for him—as it were *within* him (or within whatever humanoid, name-bearing, photo-genic, high-leaping, from-sports-page-smiling, at-pep-rally-predicting, in-private-vanishing thing was reified by the star-making system of Mooney's devising, anyway)—he (it) could probably not have been transferred to another setting without finding that not only his coach had turned into a pumpkin and his horses to mice but he himself had been transformed back into a prepubescent laborer destined for no employment nobler than pushing a lawn mower on the college green to earn his tuition by unsporting sweat.

The star was made, not born, or ripened or refined, either—though everyone must admit that not just anyone would have served as raw material. (That was where the heart would stick, the stomach twitch eventually—at the hard recollection that within the process there had been a boy. Not a good boy, not a blameless boy.) To his own charge must be laid the fact that somewhere, sometime, irrespective of what was done with him, *he* must have understood how, out of all the multitudes of the earth, he had found in Mooney his proper partner. Those blank, badger eyes of the Bronkley boy must have glimpsed shrewdly that Wellford—never heard of before in the Big Story of American sports—was the Valley of Elah where little David could wind up his sling most picturesquely to let fly at any and all Goliaths. With two little Davids—one to throw sand in the giant's eyes while the other aimed his rock . . . Yes, Tommy had decided on his own responsibility that he could not do better elsewhere.

And yet it was Tommy, too, who would at last put out his boyish hand to derail and confute the career made of, for, and by him, groping as it were, into outright vice in search of that primal right to say "I" from inside a system that had identified him only as Number One.

Before that criminal restoration—not so much inevitable as merely understandable after the event—Tommy Barker had served more truly than Royce Morgan as Mooney's partner in making Wellford College into a university.

Before his Icarian tumble, Tommy's brilliant flight and all the opportunities for parlay that it presented to partner Mooney succeeded in delaying the marriage of Mooney to the widowed girl-child Carole.

Those were great, revolutionary years at Wellford. Mooney was too busy to marry. As everyone could see—each from a different perspective (and the lady from hers, not often flat aback with knees spread for the presidential pleasure and convenience, but often enough to keep the right alive, yes, and the normal expectation, too) —too busy.

What Priss's spying had satisfied her of was still taken, as firmly as it could be, for granted in Buchanan for the next two years. The certainty blew warm. It blew cold. But dozens of onlookers who had never seen the Rolls-Royce ensconced on a May morning in the ample Prentice garage detected in the air some signs of an imminent marriage. It came to be expected that where Mooney appeared informally (excepting athletic events and student functions, where his appearance was in line of duty) his little lamb Carole would be sure to appear as well. And that they should be thought of as a couple was enough to put a sort of picture frame around them that in time became a sort of pen. What drift had brought together, no one thought of putting asunder.

Nor did anyone, probably, say that Mooney was too busy—too much married to Tommy Barker's career—to get around to marrying Carole. They simply saw that this was so.

The seminal fact in Wellford's transformation into a university was Tommy Barker's play. Nadige of Racine had indeed shown the color of its money. The possibility of a metallurgical school had about the same status as Mooney's marriage—it looked as if it would materialize *sometime*. But so far every time the money looked green, prohibitive conditions put off the decision to go ahead. Henry Worth had long since forgotten his reasons for opposing the addition. He went on resenting it like a personal affront. But in the meantime, the offer from Nadige had been dangled under the noses of a dozen other Midwest companies (somewhat as Mme. Magda Farona had been dangled before the eyes of Buchanan womanhood) and they were twitching to show their money of the same fragrant shade.

As Royce could see better than most, prospects of Wellford's big future hung in the air like a thunderstorm, only waiting to be precipitated. He did what he could to foresee its shape and prepare for it—Noah laying on the planking and whistling the animals up as he glances over his shoulder at the sky. Like Noah, he humbly disclaimed any powers to bring or prevent the deluge.

Tommy Barker made it happen. But Mooney's was the veterinarian's and the midwife's hand, dribbler of the seminal juices, receptor of the newborn squalling thing that would finally be shown to the world in the early 1950s—Wellford University. As personal manager of the Barker cult, apologist for the means that would be justified by an end nobody asked to be shown, guarantor that a soul would be grafted onto the newborn "as soon" as its life and survival were assured, Mooney was too evidently in the middle of his maneuver to be interrupted by marriage or any other claim for an accounting.

In terms of practice Royce accepted that as calmly as anyone else. Sold to his bargain, he kept his end of it well. And he kept it practically isolated from the flux of symptoms he could not help noting while the cycle of gestation ran its course.

One remote checkpoint on the cycle was his contact with the students. Among them was a little couple named Burke, who lived in an apartment between his house and the college. From time to time, especially in the cold months, he picked them up and gave them a lift to school.

Burke was a veteran of the ETO. His wife was a homely little chatterbox, the ideal tinder for any spark of furor over sports. Week by week in the first year of Barker's glory Royce watched the husband surrender his skepticism about "all this." The susceptible little woman was winning. Young Burke began to opine solemnly that "Wellford owed an unpayable debt" to Barker for having put it on the map. "We've got national visibility now," he said once, confident that he meant something with those words (which might have come down to him indirectly from the horse's mouth; they had a Mooney ring). "Basketball *in itself* isn't so important," said the spiritually wizened young man, "but there's a lot of alumnae and townspeople who are going to rally and support the college who would have been indifferent before."

"Each one of them will say that basketball isn't important to him but that it's a good thing for interesting others in the college," Royce said.

"What?" Not even little Burke, who was glad to be respectful of the *Dean,* took him seriously when he was most serious, most himself. Burke went on, "Basketball will bring in money. It doesn't matter where the money comes from, and if Barker makes a better school of Wellford, I say more power to him."

As if a student ought to concern himself with such things! Surely expediency, finance, was the administration's worry. It was Mooney's, Royce's, and George Hand's. Surely the point of having a president is to divide labor so that not everyone will have to put on the heavy burdens of authority and compromise. But—just as surely—it was Mooney's accomplishment and perhaps the key of his success to make the whole institution think like a president.

Presently, having corrupted her husband into athletic enthusiasm, Mrs. Burke showed herself sounder than he was. Finally, when Wellford lost the national tournament in Barker's senior year, Royce found with dismay that both of them were suddenly stone cold toward the team, toward Barker, and toward Wellford's athletics in general.

"It isn't as if the team represented us," Mrs. Burke said with a startling gravity. Ah—if she had only said this a week before, when most sports writers favored Wellford over victorious N.Y.U.! She wasn't really turning her coat, Royce thought, nor being a fair-weather enthusiast; she was just, alas, unlucky in declaring herself only when circumstances made it ugly and easy to do so.

She said, "Everyone knows they're a bunch of mercenaries and they're not taking real courses."

Royce said gently, "That's not quite correct. I've had to review their eligibility personally." He knew what they were paid. He had not yet heard—nor had anyone else in Buchanan—the full story of where three of Tommy's new teammates had used up their eligibility in former college play. He still thought then that Wellford had observed the letter of the law.

Young Burke nudged his wife, a signal not to disagree with Authority, and her face got fiery red with embarrassment, but she would not be quieted.

"Well, Dean Morgan," she went on, "whether or not there's any outright crookedness, everybody knows the team isn't, aren't legitimate students."

"You don't have any evidence of that," her husband said with the judiciousness of resignation.

She looked at both the men, almost in fright, as if they had entrapped her. "Evidence!" she said. "How would I have *evidence*?" Her knowledge was of another kind, meaningless in public affairs, painful to clutch in her privacy.

"Then you don't know what you're saying," her husband scoffed —not unkindly, really, but as if to let her off easily.

She did not want to be left off. She pushed her little flaming face around the bulk of Royce's arm and said, "Me! I'm not the greatest intellectual, and I suppose you might chuckle about my opinions. All I know is I never had it easy and it isn't easy to get along on George's GI entitlement, and I'm going to have a baby, and that's all too damned hard unless you can believe an education is truly, truly worth it."

"Aren't you confusing . . . ?" Royce began patiently. And after the chitchat of comforting her was through and he had let them out at their destination on the campus he had to answer to himself that,

Yes, somehow there had been a confusion of the means by which Mooney was securing his base with what should have been the purely private intercourse between each student and his books. Impossible to understand quite how the athletic destiny got so messily involved with humanities and sciences, but there it was—in everyone's mind an unsortable tangle.

He had never supposed it to be essential to the bargain that the disciplines of the classroom or of the library could be kept absolutely distinct from the artificial fervor over sport and its commercial accompaniments. Neither the single mind nor the minds of Wellford's thousands were so hermetically compartmented that one kind of passion could be kept isolate from another. But until the thing had happened, had gone its full cycle and revealed its own concrete and specific terms, he had no better language than anyone else for comprehending what it meant.

A faculty protégé of his, a sociologist named Wallace Emree, started a major project of investigating the Tommy Barker phase of Wellford. Cannily he set the machinery of his discipline to work in an attempt to measure from within, as it were, the shifting tides. He interviewed hundreds over a period of two and a half years—students, faculty, and townspeople. He tabulated athletic receipts and, as well as he was able, correlated them with the expanding College budget. He charted and graphed and had not begun to finish the mammoth work by the time Tommy blew it all apart. Maybe he was making a language that would define the reality. All in good humor he and Royce used to go over his latest findings and attempt to articulate their meaning.

But for all of that it seemed they would have been as well off using the language of fairy tale and saying that—after pep meetings on some snowy afternoon, with the band blowing heartily among the snow-bent campus pines, the "pom-pom girls" cartwheeling madly between the students and the team on the steps of Arden Hall, Tommy up there frowning like a boy potentate amid his entourage of six-foot-six recruits—when Mooney and Dowling with Tommy between them drove away in the gray Rolls-Royce, the impatient heart of the College sent the adventurers to bring back—literally— the Golden Fleece.

Given such expectations, there had to be a day of reckoning. Hearts that had expected the impossible could not be satisfied that all this basket-shooting and showmanship would produce at length would be a towering fieldhouse.

Which, as a matter of fact, was built on Mooney's schedule, ready for use during Tommy's senior year.

With the same eyes that saw Mooney's promises to him and to the College coming true, Royce Morgan watched the Barker cycle. Later he would remember that for all his foreknowledge of how it must turn out, he still could—and did—watch with constant surprise.

For instance there was the night that Mooney collected trustees and College wheel horses in the mansion to announce that ground was to be broken for the fieldhouse. Since everyone knew in advance why he came, the surprise lay elsewhere. Smiling, Mooney said, "There is one bit of additional information which I'm privileged to give you tonight that I'm sure will be more than cordially welcomed by all of you. The Board of Trustees this very last Saturday voted unanimously to call the new building the Harvey P. Morgan Memorial Fieldhouse in reverent memory of that President Morgan who contributed so much to forming the spirit of Wellford."

There was polite clapping. There was Henry Worth's sardonic, good-humored stare leveled on Royce and Priss, measuring them with a practical man's curiosity about how they were taking this loaded tribute.

"I think," Mooney went on, "that not even Dean Morgan was aware that the Board had this under contemplation. Were you, Royce?"

Royce shook his head. He was looking up, across the front parlor of the mansion, at the great, ham-colored face of his father's portrait, finding for the first time ever some expression in the painted blue eyes, round as tulip bulbs beneath the white handlebars of the old man's brows. The painted eyes said, My God, boy, now I'm really done for; now I'm really gone.

His serene death now seemed like a bit of treachery that left him defenseless against something he might have enjoyed as a joke, but which was no joke at all. To have named a chapel, a library, a classroom building, or even a dormitory after him would have been no violation. A fieldhouse full of hired athletes was rather another matter.

"We've had considerable colloquy with the architects who designed our building for us," Mooney said. "It has been worked out that the entrance lobby shall contain a large wall facing the doors. And on that wall I have proposed that we hang in perpetuity this grand old portrait of H. P. Morgan." He gestured up at the square yards of canvas behind his shoulder. And Royce thought that the painted lips tried to speak then, and he took the sense of their complaint to be the exact words of old Hamlet telling his son about that poison in his ear.

In the full tide of his eloquence, Mooney went on, "I'll miss that old man's wise countenance questioning me as I pass through this room. Like Socrates' demon, President Morgan has never told me what to do but only what I must not do when I've looked to him for guidance. And if I've been able to avoid some of the stumbling blocks in my first few years at Wellford . . ."

Royce guessed what he meant was that he owed his nimbleness to the slow-gaited old man. To Mooney the old mouth must have whispered, *Don't get caught.*

That was the wisdom that endured. That alone. But while it was heeded, all provisional qualifications faded. Uncaught, Mooney could be accused of nothing by anyone in that room.

Among the spectators there was, for instance, George Hand, who had once lamented the frustration of his hopes—and had stayed to see them well on their way to fulfillment. Once he had meant to conspire with Royce for them. They were handed over to him more easily than he could have dreamed.

For the College was in good shape. Things had worked out. God was with them . . . while Mooney was uncaught. Let no one scorn the good at hand because he would have wrestled hard for it otherwise.

And there was Carole, too, beaming her confidence that Time was bringing all they needed to their hands. Still unwed, she did not look as if that circumstance worried her. Why should she worry while Mooney was still uncaught?

The uncaught orator said, "But after all, whatever is great, whatever is good, whatever enriches Wellford belongs first of all to the students. They'll see his face and feel his vision constantly among them when the painting hangs in the fieldhouse."

Then Priss whispered cruelly to her husband, "And you know whose picture will hang beside him."

Of course. Though not to be announced that night, it was yet a foregone conclusion that the image of Tommy Barker would complete the installation on the fieldhouse wall.

The winter before there had appeared in the window of a Buchanan department store a colored photograph of Tommy, exactly eight feet high and four feet wide. In shrill scarlet trunks and immaculate white jersey, Tommy crouched on an infinite plane of hardwood. A basketball clung to the palm of his hand like the opaque, dark globe of a blind fortuneteller.

The next fall, when the great zeppelin hangar of a building was dedicated, there it was, this portrait of the ideal Tommy, he who had (already) made Wellford University a practical reality, given national visibility to a little college out in the sticks, consolidated the beachhead of Mooney's dream, he who, almost before the attending swarms of basketball fans had got used to seeing his image there beside Harvey P. Morgan's, came closer than anyone else to halting the tide that bore Mooney's damned boat along so swiftly.

In February of his senior year Tommy was arrested for accepting a thousand-dollar bribe. The money had been paid him for throwing the final game in the national tournament to N.Y.U.

Arrested, he never for a minute denied his guilt. He had taken the money. That was what money was for.

Suddenly a new light illumined the vast, ugly, tinted photograph of him. One saw the expression, under his short curls, of a boy who would forever—until, in Mooney's jargon, the last whistle blew—go on cutting grass for old ladies, astounding one and all with his single-minded concentration on doing the thing that was there to be done.

13

AND STILL the arithmetic was wrong. Tommy had taken the most that was quickest and easiest when he put out his hand for the gambler's envelope containing one thousand dollars. But what was a thousand dollars against what he stood to gain by refusing the bribe, by maintaining for a few days longer the minimal integrity required by the tolerances of big-time sport?

In the hubbub of dismay that roared through Buchanan on the news of Tommy's arrest (roared, for that matter, through the whole nation, making Wellford University more "visible" than even its glories had made it, as a shorn French whore was more visible in the open daylight than ever she was in the nudity of her revels with the occupying Nazis) that question rose like a ghost to trouble the full-throated indignation which might have purged Tommy's erstwhile adorers.

It was known that Tommy had offers to play professional ball after he graduated. Alternatively, he had been offered the manager-ship of a sporting-goods store in Buchanan. In exchange for his name and presence as inspiration to the sporting fry of all ages he would get stock in the store, would have banker's hours, would, in a word, live in a financial, social hammock for the rest of his life. How explain the reckless decision to risk so much for so little?

"He thought he wouldn't be caught," said the hardheaded. And Royce saw the force of such an explanation. It must be presumed in all cases of wrongdoing, however ineptly hidden.

"He was just too dumb to weigh one kind of chicanery against a more probably successful kind," said Priss, who was not dumb and was therefore tempted to blame everyone else's troubles on their lack of wisdom.

She was by no means alone in thus disposing of the riddle. Royce's secretary, Mrs. Agnew, a Buchananite who had known about Barkers all her life, came full circle to about the same view. Mrs. Agnew's sister had been Tommy's fifth-grade teacher and a more distant female relative had suffered some molestation (less than rape) at the hands of Tommy's fat older brother. At the time of Miss Halstead's misfortune, Mrs. Agnew had pursed her lips and out of mere deference to the boss's taste for decorum withheld her conviction that Tommy was, indeed, the assaulter.

That and all she knew of Tommy's young life had undergone a glamorizing change in the cycle of his stardom. What she had considered Barker villainies and sluttishness became for her the school of hard knocks in which Tommy was being prepared to bring Wellford from behind and beat Indiana in the last three minutes of play. His lack of interest in either girls or friends was altered from psychopathology to "reserve." His scrape with the law for stealing metal castings from the Worth shipyard was transformed liberally into the natural impulse of a restless boy too young in wartime for military service. (And after all, the junk-dealers in Bronkley who bought the castings from him meant to sell them right back to Henry Worth. The big top of cost plus sheltered Henry from loss and no harm was done the war effort.)

Mrs. Agnew had never quite joined the Tommy Barker cult that centered in the president's office upstairs, where the receptionist, Miss Jolas, kept a photograph of Tommy forever gazing out from a silver frame on her desk and public-relations man Bill Munster ran something like a campaign headquarters, complete with bar, where all sorts of friends of the College were welcome to come and talk basketball. No. Mrs. Agnew was an intellectual (had a record collection, wanted to live in New York so she could attend "all the plays," and venerated Priss Morgan for her "accomplishments"). But she had run into the hallways with the rest on those mornings when a jaunty Mooney returned from a game away from home with a firsthand account of the latest triumphant passage at arms.

Mooney had a special style for these after-the-game returns to his office. He would appear in the administration building with a newspaper dangling from his dapper coat pocket like a hand-rolled cigarette dangling from an adolescent's lip. One understood that the sports page had been folded to the outside, and that before he got to the relative seclusion of his chambers he would draw an audience of janitors, secretaries, students, visitors, or faculty—sport seeming conducive to democratic mixing—and wave under their noses a photograph of Tommy appearing to straddle the necks of giant guards from Minnesota, Nevada, or whatever other hotshot team had tried luck with him on their home courts.

Mrs. Agnew had grieved purely when Wellford lost the championship game to N.Y.U. 67–68. Wasn't it heartbreakingly close? she asked, sighing and laughing and reminding herself that basketball wasn't so important after all.

Ah, and then to learn so quickly that it was less important than one thousand dollars cash to its chief exemplar. She could explain it in no other way than that Tommy hadn't understood. First that he hadn't understood the pure, high hopes that she and others had sent with him; then, when the enormity of the whole crass athletic exploitation rose from the deeps of her mind like a mythical sea-monster, that he hadn't understood the cold, hard rewards his position offered him. He was too dumb.

That young Barker was stupid as well as criminal was a proposition that Royce was willing enough to accept as presented. But there, precisely, was the moral rub, the booby trap at the heart of the riddle. For in all that would follow as a consequence of the bubble's bursting, in all the impossible decisions between wrong and wrong that would be incumbent on him to make, he would henceforward be tormented by the notion that in spite of stupidity (or by its very wholesome exercise) young Mr. Barker had resigned from a vicious enterprise that everyone else remained indentured to.

So he had taken the money and got caught. That was his separate peace. His escape. Fear no more the heat o' the sun, young Tommy. Home art gone to Bronkley. And thy wages are that the grand manipulators will bother thee no more.

What he had resigned with a simple (albeit criminal) Bartlebyan "I do not choose to" flew to Royce Morgan's hands like the fabled lead basketball.

Someone had to be constant among the shocks that came one after another that spring. And who had to was the man who could. *Ergo,* Royce Morgan was patsy of a situation that might have made him heroic if nobler consequences were in any direction visible. He was the buffer between indignations that suddenly all appeared to be self-righteous when they were not grossly self-seeking.

A certain proportion of Buchananites wanted to hang Tommy, or didn't mind saying so. They weren't going to, of course. But the College had to decide what disciplinary measures it would and could take to satisfy the thirst for blood.

Royce sat in these deliberations with Mooney, George Hand, and Dolly Dowling.

"I like to believe there is not the temperament to hold grudges in our community," George said with his old man's stiff, tongue-in-cheek pomposity. "It seems to me the College might well set an example of moderation."

Royce seconded. "After all, we've been in a sort of business compact with the young man. It's hardly fair to deny all our debts to him. I'm afraid that if we expelled him this might penalize his future prospects disproportionately. There's the matter of the sporting-goods store, for example. . . ."

Dolly Dowling dismissed such merciful visions. He lowered his chin into his open collar, adjusted the famous dimple in his right cheek that looked like a hole for a rivet and said, "You know, Dean, Barker's not going to have a store in this town."

"Perhaps that was only another rumor. . . ."

"The boys with the capital asked me. I told them what you know as well as I. I said to them, 'The kid's a bum.' They were naturally wavering anyhow, and I can see it's not an easy thing to decide, you don't know Tommy, whether in a couple years there's more advantage having up there a name the kids will recognize they want a new catcher's mitt or a fishing pole *or* disadvantage, always counting their change twice because they remember he was sentenced to a year in prison."

"Suspended," George said. "You know the sentence has been suspended." He was trying to recover his breath. He blinked as if he were trying to hold Dowling in focus—or perhaps retrieve from beyond this present some vision of justice and right. He had thought, probably, that he yielded to no one in his harsh abhorrence of what Tommy had done. He was being one-upped by the very man who had made a giant leap into prominence from Tommy's dishonest shoulders. He had lived a long time. He was not yet prepared to believe a colleague could be so merciless.

"Given the *facts*," Dolly said. "I might not have known how to decide myself. It'd be a tossup." He went on happily, "But I was in a position to know his *character*. Enterprise—the kid hasn't got it. He doesn't even like to play basketball. He doesn't get any fun out of it. He plays because he can and maybe there is and maybe there isn't a place for him in pro ball. So I said to these fellows, 'He's a bum. Why don't you gentlemen buy some oil-well stock or something really *safe*, like a nice uranium mine out in the country if you've got too much money you don't know what to do with it?' They'll thank me one day." When he finished speaking his dimple popped like a suction cup, one of those by which a sea creature attaches itself to a slimy stone.

"You've . . . already told them this?" George asked. He began to turn alternately red and white. He closed his eyes awhile. When he opened them, unfortunately he still saw Dowling. He tried a time or two to speak. Finally he said, "Yes. Young Barker is a bum. It was Wellford that made him one." He spoke rather loudly, so his words boomed around the presidential office, where they were secluded on this spring night. He added, as if it were a mournful afterthought, "Wellford . . ." As if, while it might often have occurred to him that the College fell short of its possibilities, he had never really grasped before that it might be a huge machinery for evil.

Through this exchange, Mooney had been restlessly drifting

around the room, fiddling with Venetian blinds and fingering the paneled walls as if looking for escape. Royce thought of another time when it was said that his hat and gloves had been on the desk top, ready for departure. That had not been many years ago. But a great deal was different now. The grand design, insofar as it was an administrative one, depending on prosperity, was near to accomplishment now. A shoo-in. That other time it had been only a gamble. Mooney was not going to quit now.

But he had been having high feelings in the weeks since the news broke. He had known pressure and, one supposed, stirring self-examinations. And now he cried out in hysterical anger, "I consider it despicable to use that term about any human being." He crouched and shouted into their astounded faces like a spitting cat, "From the time I've come to this college I've been aware of undemocratic sentiments lodged in high places. I've fought them openly and I've fought them indirectly. It's so easy to look down, if you've got a reputable name, and sneer. . . .

"I found everyone fixed in a pattern that lets you point the finger and say 'This boy is a bum because he comes from a poor family and used to mow lawns.' Or, 'That girl shouldn't have a college education because she can't afford to dress as well as some.' I'll say this to anyone's face: I honor Tommy Barker for coming out of Bronkley. He showed *it can be done*. He was opening the way for thousands. Where did we fail him? Where did *we* go wrong? That's the question. There are plenty who say, 'Shame on you' to Tommy.

"Look!" he shouted, his cheeks flaming. "Our great friend Henry Worth called me as late as yesterday and peremptorily ordered me to 'get rid' of Tommy. You might as well know I just as peremptorily told him to *stick it up his ass*." He followed this obscenity with a shrill, demonic hee-haw that made George Hand's jaw drop and his eyes narrow with the suspicion that they had, in addition to the obvious problem, a deranged president to cope with. Mooney himself was a little shaken, as if he had only heard the full scope of his passion when the walls echoed it back to him. A little quieter, he went on, "I won't join the pack of jackals that wants to drag him down for one slip. I won't, because I've maneuvered and I've begged —I'm supposed to be the president, but I've crawled on my belly— to make this place more democratic. I have the Whitman ideal. I believe an education is the prerogative of every boy and girl we can open the doors to, and Tommy Barker furthered that goal."

This Wagnerian extremity, a great upheaval of temperament where some coolness was obviously required, was all that Mooney seemed willing just now to contribute. Yet, uproarious as he had been, Royce could not help thinking that Mooney was putting on a show for them, that in the very explosion of pent-up feelings the man was all the time thinking of something else. It was very weird. About to get stranger yet.

"Me, I'd as soon clear out," Tommy said when Royce talked to him. "I don't think I give a damn."

Without blinking his friendly eyes, Royce told him that Northern Idaho College of Education was not only a fine institution in a pleasant western setting but that it would be glad to accept him as a candidate for a B.A. with a major in physical education, all his credits from Wellford to be honored in full. At the end of the fall semester he would have the degree that Wellford would rather prefer not to give.

"What for?" Tommy asked, without resentment. "I'm not going to use a degree for anything. I'd just as soon stay home."

"All right. But what are you going to do in the long run?"

Tommy nodded his agreement that there was a problem. Only it did not seem to be his. They might have been talking about youth in general, and Tommy had no opinions on youth in general. "I might go to Korea," he said abstractly.

"You understand that it's President Mooney's wish not to be vindictive in any way. He still wants you to have a good career."

"I understand that," Tommy said soberly. It seemed to him natural that people should not wish to be vengeful toward a boy who had made One False Step. Whatever was presented to him seemed natural enough. O.K.

"My own feeling is that even if you waited for a while—a couple of years—before resuming your studies here at Wellford, you might encounter embarrassments."

Now Tommy grinned a little as if to say, oh, boy, he understood *that*. "I been laying low. I don't go downtown much. Kids ask me questions."

"But my own strong advice is for you to finish somewhere as quickly as you can. When this blows over you may find a degree is more value to you than you can guess now."

"I'd as soon forget about it," Tommy said. "I don't give a damn."

He did not go to Korea.

He went back to Bronkley and holed up with his family. A year or two later he became a partner in a saloon in Peoria. In the saloon, on a dim wall above a bowling game, hung the vast tinted photograph of Tommy that had so briefly graced the new fieldhouse. If it was not more at home there, maybe Tommy was more at ease to have it there. His name was not exploited in the new venture. He was a quiet, hard-working partner and as he toiled and reminisced behind the bar the outsize photograph could remind him and all who got to know him of that heroic other world that it was all right to think about and listen to on TV, but which was just too damn much trouble for a guy to keep up with. In the same way that picture wasn't really him, he hadn't been himself *up there*.

It was indeed, for those who thought their thoughts in administrative jargon, a season of Retrenchment.

In spite of a whopping scandal, all was not lost. How could it be? There were nearly three thousand tuition-paying students darting hither and thither through the early spring sunshine. They were not about to pawn their books and go home to farm and factory because someone named Barker had betrayed their good name (pretty factitious anyhow: who steals our good name steals trash). There were three hundred-odd faculty members. They were not going to become bricklayers, nor surrender their disciplines, nor give up the good fight for higher salaries next year because they had been in some abstract way shamed before the huge eye of the Republic.

No, sir, in the time-honored way of faculties they were going to lick their chops and deplore overemphasis on athletics. Too late for honor, they were going to express to each other their long-withheld suspicions about the way basketball was managed at Wellford— and honorably give their semester tests and hand out grades when June came round. There were close to four hundred full- or part-time employees on the College payroll. They were not going to emigrate. They were going to go on keeping accounts, cooking in the cafeterias, dispensing linen in the dormitories, passing news releases to the papers, directing traffic on the parking lots, and planning new buildings for new students. More coming every year.

But Retrenchment . . . everyone knew it was time for that.

Truly shaken to his soul by the scandal, George Hand pleaded most earnestly with Mooney to cut back the athletic program. That phase was finished, he argued. The pioneer days were over. What was now to be worked for was triumph in the subtler game of going for big endowments, bleeding the foundations (why not a foundation-relations office in New York, a splendid modern room where a Wellford representative could offer to foundation men the amenities to which they were accustomed while he pleaded Wellford's need?); a more smoothly coordinated administration, with the lines of command finally drafted to assure Mooney's relief from tedious details; and committees for engaging faculty talents in administrative problems—and to provide a safety valve for faculty frustrations.

What he really wanted, down under all his glittering proposals, was Dolly Dowling's head. And he got what he took to be a firm commitment that Dowling would be fired. At any rate, he told Royce that Mooney had so promised, telling it with a conspiratorial breathlessness suggesting that firing Dowling was going to be as ticklish a business as firing the chief of secret police in a precarious dictatorship. Someone had better be standing behind Dowling when he got the word. . . .

That scene never materialized. Apparently Dowling also went privately and urgently to the top. Mooney never revealed what the coach's whole argument was. Part of it seemed to be that if he went, sports editors everywhere would be informed that Milton Bosky,

Fergie Hump, and Keith Buckley—that grand trio of cage stars he had brought with him to back up Tommy Barker's play—had long since used up their college eligibility under different names at San Jose, Atlanta, and Portland before they ever went on the hardwood for Wellford.

"He also thinks," Mooney said cajolingly to Royce, "that big basketball's come to our house to stay, like Little Orphant Annie." A cute and pensive smile pursed his lips. The jewels of his eyes nearly disappeared under his lids. "I wonder if, in a year or two—supposing Dolly left—George wouldn't perhaps *expect* some use to be made of the fieldhouse. Wouldn't, in a word, want to go on as before."

"I think he might," Royce said—because he did indeed think this was so, and if he had further thoughts on the matter they had not been asked for. It was his habit with Mooney to give no more than was demanded.

"In a word, we're sort of stuck with what we've started," Mooney said. He brooded picturesquely on the melancholy of that circumstance. Sighed. "We can't get out."

Only, Royce remembered, Tommy Barker had.

"Can you help me make George see reason?" Mooney asked. Sitting on the edge of Royce's desk, swinging a plump, well-tailored leg, he was playing the poor rich boy—there had been more and more of that lately in the mode of his relations with Royce; it was an act that took the place of any real ripening in their friendship or association—requesting one more indulgence from a sober uncle. "You can make him see we're too near what we've worked for to let it come apart at the seams."

"Close to the erotic university?" Royce laughed.

Mooney looked around as if afraid they were being overheard. He remembered the night on the Morgans' porch when such terms had been used, but that was hardly what he had been thinking of.

"To a university program," he said prissily. "Oh, we're going to make it in spite of my blunder in offending Henry Worth—and a lot of other blunders you know about and have had the courtesy not to throw in my face, Royce."

"You really told Henry . . . ?"

"His face is turned away from us." The Old Testament heaviness pronounced so pertly was touching enough. What it fully meant was Mooney's secret.

"Have George or Dowling been to Henry?"

Mooney shook his head. "I think neither one has dared. But they might go—either one—unless we can patch things up among ourselves. Again, I can't believe this is a matter of life or death. I'm merely going back to something I think you believe—that if a course is decided, it's better to implement it in harmony."

"Have I said that?" Royce asked with a start. Then it seemed to him that of course he had. His whole life here with the College, his marriage, too, amounted to a statement of that principle. Only it was something of a jolt to find that Mooney—who was known to be so cunning at seizing the opportunities of any moment and those aspects of character that were crucial to it—should also have been able to sum up the meaning of his years. To sum them up before Royce had them squared for himself. Again the advantage went to swiftness.

"I suppose that's exactly what I have believed," Royce said. Smiling, he said, "So I'm caught with it. It appears I do agree with you. *Ergo,* I'll tell George so. Make him 'see reason.' "

"Of course I mean 'put the squeeze on him,' " Mooney said—to take away the curse of meaning exactly that by stating it as a joke. "As for this awful business of eligibility, Royce, I swear I knew nothing about it. I was as shocked to hear about it as you are." He shrugged—perhaps at the risk of scandal on scandal that it had brought to them. "But I'll tell you. I believe that Dolly's years of beating the law are behind him."

"Why shouldn't they be?"

"And he's a good, aggressive coach."

Royce Morgan *saw* the means by which Wellford was being transformed. So to himself he might, he must, whisper, "It's all a fraud. It's all a fraud." As clearly as little Mrs. Burke—and no more clearly —he saw how the worth of education was called in question by the methods that advanced it. And there were times when he indulged a private frenzy to drive the money-changers out of the temple—or, to pull the "temple" apart.

And he refused to rock the boat for precisely the same reason he failed to command it—because in that core of a man where decision is made, he did not care enough. He no longer cared, as once—perhaps before the war and before his cold peace had been made—he would have cared.

He had a job. In a fine manner of speaking Mooney had given him a job—of compromise and balance and securing harmony— more exacting and therefore, in that way, more satisfying than any he could have designed for himself.

And he did not know—as far weaker and more vicious men than he would have known and long since blurted out—that what he was doing was wrong. He might whisper that all this was a fraud (that his marriage, too, was a fraud perpetuated and enabled to continue by his resourceful tolerance when its built-in disharmonies might long ago have wrecked it). He had only to look out of his office window and see that Wellford University was a success. The "Whitman ideal," however adulterated, twisted, parodied, hammered, whored, and misused, simply worked.

There they came every day, the students in their freshman beanies and bobby sox and porkpie hats and plaid wool skirts and shirts open at the collar. They came to learn the world's illusion, and very few before his age would guess what shabby, simple lies that illusion was founded on. But they learned so much before that wisdom could set in. What mathematician could construct the numerical equivalent of the recognitions, the additions, the qualifications, the individual shadings and modulations, the quickenings of heart and mind, the extensions and play of the mind's light that here—right here!—on the neutral surface of the planet were the unremarked circumstance of every day. To his multiplication (illusory though it might be at last) a decent man could make only one response. He must say, "More." Always that. More light in more lives more of the time, though the light sprang from darkness to which it would return.

At home, though his marriage was a fraud (by all intellectual summation its possibilities were seen as long since exhausted, now mere endurance, repetition, the hollow observation of pieties and manners without content), he had two sons now. He supposed Priss wanted to be gone. She said so as often as she pleased. In her second pregnancy she had comforted herself for weeks on end with thoughts and talk of suicide. But he held her and entertained her, foresaw and forestalled her moods when he could, sparred with her and let her buffet him when that worked. And it was just as easy to say their life was a miracle as a fraud. For each day there were the gestures of love, the recognitions, the additions, the qualifications, shadings, and modulations of animal life disciplined by mind and manners. To all that, as to the wonderful College, a decent man (who had no Faith to say otherwise; who had read Kierkegaard and knew the temptations but not the permission to become a Knight of Faith) must say, "More."

More in challenge than contrition—feeling bad one day in the seventh month of her second pregnancy—Priss had told him about her hideous little affair with LeCoeur. The whole thing had come out, the wonderfully complex, pointless coyote-in-a-cage rationalizations of an artist monkeying with life. He had listened with smiling disgust. As she had intended, he had learned to know more in these years about the kinds of pain, and to know that it is not always appropriately measured by degree. Some kinds of pain are straightforward, straight to the heart. There are others at their worst in being loathsome and crooked, though slight, like those which pass the novocaine block from a dentist's drill. He was not immune to those. She found what must be his last vulnerabilities, and shook him with the horror of finding himself able, finding himself disgustingly strong enough, to take them without being knocked down. Even strong enough to live with the knowledge that she always hurt him most out of frustrated love. She tried to mislead him from his chosen course because she loved him—a doubly frustrated Delilah who tried to betray him into being Samson so she could get on with her proper business of delivering him to the Philistines. She still hoped lovingly for the great and sundering gesture from him. But love and survival posed different requirements. He denied her love its wish so it could go on being, however frustrated, at least love. He kept the cage locked so the caged hawk would never learn for herself there was no sequel to liberty. And he wondered how long he would postpone her desire.

All his life was a patching and postponement. He did not see what else he might do. He was not the first good man who preferred injustice to disorder. That was the most he could say for himself in these years. The criminal (Tommy Barker) and those without responsibility (Mrs. Burke, whose number was legion) could count themselves out. He was neither of these things. He stayed.

Nevertheless he was tripped from his balance. The abyss had a false bottom after all, and without expecting to, he looked under it finally. He began to see how much farther down the depths extended one night in that spring of the basketball scandal.

He ran into Henry Worth at the Country Club. Their encounter took place toward midnight in the small Men's Bar off the corner of the dance floor. He was good-humoredly sparring off jokes about Tommy Barker with old acquaintances when Henry came in.

The older man bulled straight toward him, plainly intending to get something off his chest. Noting the approach, Royce thought (and would think again afterward, trying to establish some frame of reason, motive, sanity itself around what Henry actually said there) he was enraged by the way the basketball scandal might collapse all Wellford's pending ambitions. Henry had opposed the deal with Nadige. He was dragging his feet, at least, and putting off a similar arrangement with Collins Radio and Erco Battery. In his present state of mind (after having been told to shove something, especially) he was contrarily capable of wanting somebody's head if those pending negotiations were definitely spoiled.

That much explanation of his wrath was ready-made, a pat interpretation that could be fitted to him the second he swam into the corner of one's vision.

Royce greeted him mildly and went on with his chatter. Henry ordered a drink with just a bit of the air of a man who has felt himself snubbed. He took no part in the conversation until there was a little stir and shifting around the horseshoe bar as two men said good night and left.

Then he spoke grumpily—and loudly enough to be overheard by anyone there.

"Royce, I owe you an apology."

Royce bowed slightly and waited, smiling as foolishly as a man would have to in this awkward confrontation. He had no forewarning of any offense against him. What had Henry done now?

"You'd have made the better president," Henry said. The crudeness was almost necessarily calculated, Royce thought, and he wondered if the man were simply drunk. He had never seen him so in public; there had been stories now and then about his being publicly vicious to his wife.

"I might have immodestly agreed with you," Royce said, "once upon a time." He waited a little for a response, then said, "I hope you're not letting a trivial irritation carry you too far."

"What's trivial?"

Royce said, "I suppose all of us are sore this spring about what happened to . . . our star. It's natural to vent some rage on all of us at the College who are responsible. But I think all the criticisms I've heard of President Mooney have been trivial—not to say rather ungraciously belated."

Henry nodded. "You've heard criticisms, have you?"

"A good many ridiculous things."

"*Criticism,*" Henry snorted. His inflection implied that critics were now saying Mooney had not died in a suicide pact with Eva Braun nor been cremated in Berlin as the world had been told.

Royce began to heat up. "You know well enough I'm in a position to hear a lot about him from all sorts of disgruntled people. Students, staff, townspeople . . ."

"Carole Prentice?"

Royce stiffened. In spite of the effort to keep control he stretched to his full height and seemed to tower menacingly above the shorter man. And he knew at the same time this was what Henry wanted, was playing for. Now he knew Henry was challenging him to go for broke.

"Carole not satisfied with him?" Henry asked. A money man's smile tugged the corner of his mouth, hard as death.

"This is getting quite unpleasant, Henry."

"Things have been made unpleasant for us who have some *interest* in the College. I have some interest, though only a trustee."

"Perhaps in a meeting is the place . . ."

"Where that little fruit can lie to us again about what he's up to?"

The full brutality of the question was on its face. Again the calculation from which it must have sprung and the careful placing of the key word hung after it in the silence, the hushed breathing of all who had to overhear.

Royce tried once more to hold the peace. "Well . . ."

"Way-ull . . . 'you may be right,'" Henry said. He turned on fury like a man turning on a blowtorch. "Don't tell me I may be right when I am right. *If I may presume to enlighten you* . . ."

"Please do!"

". . . I'll tell you what really rankles people. It's not whether some two-bit hoodlum from Bronkley sells out a basketball game. It's that fruit thinking that he alone is going to pass judgment. It doesn't matter what we want."

"I heard your description of him before," Royce growled. He trembled like a big dog held on the leash at a hanging. "In common decency, I think you'd better not repeat it again."

But that was just what Henry meant to repeat. Too late Royce saw the real edge of the weapon.

Henry grinned and his voice was much calmer. "Why, Royce, it's common knowledge among the men of this town," he said, "that Mooney is a bee-it quee-ah. He bleaches his hair, you know that? Christ almighty, he's fucked everyone he dared, from this kid Billy Cox to the interior decorators who did the mansion over."

There wasn't, there couldn't have been, any such common knowledge. All that was plain was that Henry Worth was prepared to spread his accusations into common belief.

And that cruel intent, the face-to-face confrontation with a cruelty his intuitions had simply never registered before, broke Royce into the world of passion. Now he was almost forty, and he had never known before that he was big and strong *so* he could kill. He meant —for one irretractable second that changed him—to kill this man.

Then he said, "Henry, not the slightest rumor to support your accusation has come to me." He blinked, and in the fraction of a second his eyes were closed he saw the blue mimeographed sheets of mad Miss Halstead's bill of particulars. Those rumors then had been weak as Miss Halstead. Now they were strong as Henry Worth and perhaps that made more difference than their truth or falsity. He was at the door of a strange world.

"I'm confident there hasn't ever been such a rumor," he said with a growl. "If I hear it, I'll know its origin. And I will come and I will *whip* you! Do you understand me? Or have you drunk too much?"

The three men drinking at the opposite side of the bar were silent as mummies. Their averted eyes were indication that they were dangling on this violence like steeplejacks dangling from safety ropes. Desperate, waiting for some heavenly fire department to come and get them down.

Then, with vast surprise—as if he were watching some newborn ungainly thing emerge from the shell of an egg, horrified equally by the emergent enormity and the fracturing, splintering shell of himself—Royce saw his own hand reach up and close on Henry Worth's tie. He tugged it a couple of times. Henry's close-cropped head bobbed like a church bell. And Royce was going to pull it down until it rang against the edge of the bar.

He was going to—and for the rest of his life he would believe he should have. But he stopped. With a gesture like ridding his hand of garbage he let go of Henry's tie.

"Gentlemen!" he said, and walked out.

At four that morning he was sitting alone in the study of his quiet house. There was a storm in him and it made him shake. More than that was hard to be sure of. Where did the wind come from that shook him? And was it laughter or disgust that gusted through his mind, self-contempt or outrage?

He was in a passion and for once he would have to look outside himself for the means to control it. The authority he had lived by, the confidence that he was beyond surprise, had failed him now.

He had been surprised, and not by what Henry had said, either, but by a conclusion that formed in his mind almost as he let go of Henry's tie.

Henry had *always* known about Mooney's perversion. Henry had deliberately accepted for president a man with the kind of debility which, in theory, would make him easy to control. Had wanted a puppet in the very simplest sense of the term. And then Mooney had been a little cagier than Henry bargained for, had been rather unpredictably successful in maintaining his independence while Henry fumed. They had gone on all this time maintaining a balance of power like two pirates on a captured ship, each threatening to blow the hull and all the sleeping passengers out of the water rather than relinquish his claim to control.

What infuriated Royce was the extent to which he had helped them both. And what he was tempted to, in his rage, was to goad them on, tell them to set the powder train and have done with the entire farce that passed for an educational institution.

Worst, he had let himself be fooled. He had justified his continuance at Wellford on the assumption that there was more smoke than fire in the hints and rumors about Mooney. And year by year he had woven his own life into the web of their lies, had committed his family and others precious to him so there was no acceptable way out for them either. He had been a Judas goat for those he supposed he was supporting.

And had he not, like Henry Worth, "always known" that Mooney was intolerable as president, known that Mooney was homosexual and known the risks that went with such a case?

He might be excused on the plea that he had no solid evidence. He could not excuse himself that way. He remembered a trivial episode now: Mooney had called in the editors of the student paper and in Royce's presence was rebuking them for not having their facts straight in a story that bore on the good repute of the College. And one of the half-sophisticated farm boys, all-repentant, eager to oblige and make up for injuries, had said, "Gee, President Mooney, you really caught us with our pants down." Royce had seen—he saw it again now, totally meaningful in its simplicity—how Mooney closed his eyes with a wince of panic and then, after a minute's hidden reflection reassured him of the naïve innocence of the boy's remark, opened them like dawning jewels of indecent mirth, reveling in how easy it is to maneuver the innocent.

At the time the play on words had been nothing to make much of. It wasn't now—except that it was a lapidary miniature of the abysmal truth that engulfed them. It stung now because his own innocence had been almost identically maneuvered. It stung more because his innocence had been, on principle, chosen by himself. It was not pure, but had about it some of the shameful smell of mere convenience. He had conspired at his own betrayal. The question now was how much of his world had been betrayed with him, through his tolerance?

Ordinarily when he drank he measured his drinking with unconscious regularity. Tonight, alone now, he was drinking like a thirsty man who has forgotten what the stuff is for.

It may have been the insult of alcohol to his nerves, but, straining to seize his situation for once in its full moral truth, he had a sudden apperception of his soul. He knew it. There it was, hanging inside his skin like testicles in a withered scrotum. It was his soul that was imperiled by the maze around him, and on the flame of alcohol he responded like a man whose balls are threatened with a kick.

The vision was very brief. He let it go on purpose, because he could not afford to hold on to it. At this peak of his intoxication he saw simply that hatred and truth had become inseparable in his life —and saw how impossible it was for Royce Morgan to live as if they had anything to do with each other.

So he sobered himself by sheer determination. He fought himself back into his old cage, until the truth with the hatred was beaten down to a level he could live with. He saw that the truth was not to be his. Very well, he still had the strength of his patience to live on. That had to be a sufficient substitute.

He did not sleep until he had ordered his feelings. And when he got up in the morning—lo, the domestic world seemed to mirror truly the order he had struggled for by himself at night.

At breakfast that morning Lot would tell him a dream. Both of them would try solemnly to understand it and then, like rich folks, laugh it away as too great a mystery to bother with.

"I was following a horse that wasn't ours up a hill," Lot would say, "and we didn't find him. But there were big trees and one of the trees turned into an owl."

"Into an *owl*?" Mother would say.

"Oh, yes."

"A wise old owl?"

"And the owl wanted me to turn into a spider."

"What did you do about that?" Royce asked, while little Sherman flirted for his attention from the high chair, and Barbara brought a Man of Distinction's breakfast to set before them on the handsome breakfast table.

"It was only a dream, so I *did*," Lot said. "I mean, *because* it was only a dream."

"I'm glad you wouldn't really think of doing it," Royce said. Not in the real world of sunny May morning would man or man-child consent to the poisonous transformations recommended in the late hours of the night. Rather, repeat the previous day, hold fast to the one saving formula of repetition, lest all evils should swarm in through the single breach.

He had been warned of Henry Worth's intent to strike. Let him get in his car, drive calmly to his office, and reflect further on what could be done to forestall it—to preserve order in the face of new impossible demands for justice.

But then, while Priss and Barbara were getting his sons away from the table and heading Lot toward school, he picked up the paper.

On the front page he read that a local man named Billy Cox had committed suicide by jumping from a viaduct in front of a train from Chicago.

From that instant he knew something that in this world could never be reduced to order.

14

HE PEELED BACK one more layer of veneer and saw how Mooney
had started his career as educator in Buchanan.

In that first summer on the campus, a frog in a brand-new puddle,
lonely as a god or a newborn baby, stripped of the props that had
made his life intelligible and his vices safe in New York, Mooney
must have swung from extremity to extremity among the possibilities of his new life.

Grandiose dreams of the good . . . Royce could not sincerely
doubt that these had fumed behind those jewely eyes. Later, in the
Morgans' stable loft, Mooney had once and for all convinced his
witness of his passionate idealism. Yes, of course. Mooney had seen
his move to the Midwest as the opening of a frontier where the
"Greek ideal" could be realized. There was not even any need to
doubt that—while one realized at the same time that the newcomer
must have recognized his frontier to be open for plunder and license
as well. Indeed the heart-warming that came with opportunities
of a constructive sort must have suffused the whole torso, activating
the lower centers, setting off gonadal aspiration as a natural accompaniment to great plans for expanding the College.

Further, Mooney must have been lonely in his new environment
during those first summer months. From Cape Cod the Morgans
had got their first picture of him through George Hand's reports.
Royce remembered his notion that it had been like seeing the man
through the wrong end of a telescope and now—oh, very belatedly
—the significance of that miniaturizing sprang to his mind. It
showed him a Mooney lonely in Illinois as some of those first ex-

plorers—LaSalle or Joliet or some forgotten fur-hunter—under the blind vastness of the prairie sky, tempted to abominations by their loneliness as often as they were scared into piety by the mighty virginity of the land.

And Mooney—knowing Mooney well after years of close observation gave one the capacity for dependable retrospect, obliged one to complete those intuitions of a far-off summer—would have twisted the pain of his loneliness into the practical recognition that he was *unobserved*. People saw him, of course. George Hand and the rest of the summer administrative staff saw him daily. As much of Buchanan as was interested saw the *new president* assuming his official tasks. But Mooney knew, would certainly have known, that these innocent watchers could no more penetrate to what he really was than the Indians or the prairie rodents could have guessed that the lone *voyageur* was there to ravish and rebuild their familiar continent.

He had appeared humble and businesslike to George Hand. Did he not take his meals at Joe Chapin's lunch wagon, "where the students eat"?

He had eaten there during a summer when all the plans that cunning and opportunity would eventually let him unfold must have seemed to him maddeningly just beyond his grasp. (Did Joliet, crouched in his stinking buckskins, gnawing at the half-cooked leg of a coon, realize with tranquillity that someday there would rise from this prairie a big, ugly city named after him, and that his fame would live forever on Conservation Commission plaques, free road maps, and in fourth-grade history books? Not on your life. Every sundown pause for revittling after the day's trek must have found him torn between the high illusion that he was fathering an unprecedented expansion of the human tribe and a dank terror of being damn well lost in the middle of nowhere.) Mooney saw what could be done with the college they were handing him. But the limitless possibilities were far away. They were a knot in his throat demanding, at least, one sympathetic ear to which they could be confided without risk of scorn.

His dream of an education whose end was love. . . . Eventually he would even risk confiding it to his great enemy Royce Morgan on a certain summer evening. By then, of course, it was already fading, turning into something a clever Mooney could speak of facetiously, into a reality so shored up with banal college procedures as to seem merely pretty. It had been nothing of the sort in July of 1946, and it took a special ear then to hear it prophesied. He had met Billy Cox in the lunch wagon.

The "Greek ideal," the Whitmanesque vision voiced through such rosy male lips. . . . Most of the diners in Joe Chapin's lunch wagon would have gone aghast with miscomprehension if Mooney had seriously uttered two syllables about the pomp that burned in his imagination.

A fair number of them would have grinned knowingly. Simple souls would have discerned what Buchanan's chivalry was too smart to be sure of—that he was a fag on the make.

Not quite everyone who encountered him in the lunch wagon was either simple or smart. The Midwest breeds its strange visionaries, too, not all of whom mature into Frank Lloyd Wrights, or Sherwood Andersons, or Vachel Lindsays, either. Village cranks, prairie-land and slum-jungle dreamers, forever independent as saints, unassimilable as mental defectives, careerists in the loopholes of a society that never quite bothers to notice how little they fit.

Billy Cox was a poet. In Chapin's lunchroom and elsewhere he lent the right ear to Mooney in Mooney's unsettled period.

Royce learned the truth of this in the days following Billy's dive from the viaduct.

In his position he had to investigate the bearing of this death on Henry Worth's charges against Mooney. Self-interest required him to find out what he could. His long-range obligations to the College coincided with self-interest, though obviously in this case no higher authority was going to appoint him to the task of finding the truth.

When he began, he could still tell himself that his inquiries were an administrative obligation. And perhaps that meant his duty was to assemble a pattern of facts which would put a lid on the reeking truth. Administration is so-called because of its techniques for in-

vestigating away from the truths that private men have to, somehow, "square up."

It may even have been his hope to establish that Billy's death had
no significant relation to what went on in classroom, chapel, dormitory, or presidential mansion at Wellford. (And, hell, he would tell
himself in later years, maybe that's what he did, effectively, establish. There was never to be a clean-cut issue of his investigation.)

But the course of his enlightenment went oddly. Truth—not to
be his—nevertheless had him by the scruff and went on separating
the man from the administrator as violently as the mechanism of
disease separates the worlds of the schizophrenic. Afterward, like
the pitiable schiz, he still had to house administrator and man in
the same hide.

The worst thing was that he looked hard enough to behold Billy
as a human being. That image developed slowly, like an image
shading into itself out of its chemical ingredients under the surface
of fluid in a photographer's tank. When it was fully there (in negative, of course) the lost boy whose name had been Billy was a mad
parody of a lost boy named Lot Morgan (son of Priss and Royce
Morgan, lost somewhere between these stars at the opposite ends of
a vast constellation). The relation between Billy Cox and President
Mooney was an intolerable parody of the relation between father
and son, just as (he saw this too as part of the indigestible lump
jammed in his craw) Mooney's dishonored dream of education with
no upper limit was a parody of the hopes Royce Morgan had been
bred to defend.

At one point, while the image was still far from definite, he
read a bunch of Billy's poems. Almost all of them were mementoes
of the places Billy had wandered, his solitary walks along the water-
fronts of Davenport, Rock Island, Dubuque, St. Louis, and Keokuk.
Or of his not-so-solitary carouses in grubby bars, the brief military
service in a Southern army camp (before, as Royce learned elsewhere, he was separated from service with a discharge neither
honorable nor dishonorable, presumably not having been taken in
sodomy but having confessed to the post psychiatrist that "some-

times" he had a yen for the boys in the shower). They memorialized the intellectual love of comrades, and the comradely salutes of his farewells to sodomite companions and occasional girls.

There was vision in them, and pathos. Royce did not read them untouched, nor without a strange reminiscent sense of the places where Billy had found his carnal loves. Royce had seen the same rivers at dawn when he was a boy, when he was sheltered by family and position as Billy never would have been nor have permitted himself to be. Here were leaves of grass, poor things. They had been clutched feverishly by a hand now dead.

Royce also found (and this came to him as knowledge, not evidential material) the unmistakable and peculiar anguish of sexual deviation—that longing merely intensified by sensual gratification, that sense of compounding one's alienation in coupling it with another's. Herein the poems were the most poignant defense of Mooney that would ever be put on paper.

Not that Mooney was named. Awe and calculation both had forbidden this. But he was there, now and then recognizable, usually just half discernible, as the dark lady of these songs.

Mooney was present in the verse in other ways besides as adored object. There was a point in Royce's reading when he said to himself, Why, these are all lies. They expressed a real condition. They told the truth about nothing. The main part of talent given to Billy was the capacity to deny the reality principle.

In a second breath Royce said to himself, Why, these are all in Mooney. The slipperiness of the language itself seemed to echo the man who had inspired more than half of them (a fraction Royce could calculate when the chronology of the relationship revealed itself). Here had been the versifying equivalent of the New Man that Mooney represented in the administrative field—as if in Billy one saw the primitive of a new culture, something loosely derivative from the arts of the past, but owing no responsibility to them. The poems were a curious howl of petulance mixed with a defiance that needed only cunning like Mooney's to give it an advantage over all slow responsibility. To read the poems was to read what Mooney himself might have said if he permitted himself unguarded expression.

The poet Billy Cox had wandered in to Chapin's lunch wagon one summer evening while Mooney was eating. The meeting between them might—without the testimony of the poems to show the fated sympathy between the two men—have seemed accidental. One could suppose that the men themselves must later have told themselves that it was the purest accident.

But meet they had to, and when they had met, Mooney discovered all too readily that he had found his proper confidant. Nothing said to the younger man would seem outlandish; no extravagance of ambition, or longing, or loneliness would seem remarkable to the incompetent visionary who had cherished the same in himself.

How their earliest conversation had gone, how, for that matter, each had recognized that the other was—in this summer and perhaps never again—*ready,* was something Royce could only guess at badly.

However it might have begun, they had taken "a little trip" to Chicago together. At dawn in some hotel south of the Loop the ideal that would someday, somehow guide the transformation of sleepy Wellford College into Wellford University was articulated from one pillow to the next. And hearing it, from lips his lips had kissed, inconstant and wayward Billy Cox had fallen constantly in love. He would go on wandering, would have his other merely sexual affairs, even get married in Buchanan and father a son (eight months old when his father went off the viaduct to meet the onrushing streamliner bound for St. Louis). But from that summer onward Billy's love was fixed forever by some conjunction of bodily thrill with the glamour of the man he had taken once.

As far as Royce could ever learn, there had been no repetition of that little trip to Chicago. Like Carole after him, Billy Cox had been content to admit that Mooney was too busy (and too highly, publicly placed) to continue the relation on the terms that had begun it. Billy had worshiped from afar. Along with the poems and half as many pencil drawings also memorializing his travels and some ideal heads of companions, he had kept a scrapbook of his courtly love.

Every speech of Mooney's reported by the press, every photograph of him on formal occasions attired in handsome formal clothes or on basketball trips with Tommy Barker (there was one pathetic shot of Mooney as he had rushed onto the floor when Tommy was hurt, trying to hoist the dazed youth up in his pudgy arms while his face pleaded to heaven like the Madonna's in a *Pietà*) or on the golf course with his Buchanan associates—the whole loving collection of the resigned adorer was gathered in a thick, expensive folder that may have been Billy's greatest work, delivered posthumously not to the world but only to Royce Morgan's troubled scrutiny.

These relics of love were loaned him a few days after the catastrophe by Billy's wife. As quietly as he could, Royce was moving through a half world of gossip, never—as far as he could tell— moving much closer to open assertion than was permitted by the formula, "Henry Worth said . . ." There seemed to be quite a few in town and around the College who had some wind of what had been charged so recklessly at the Country Club. Behind that, of course, was the residual, malignant, and by ordinaries harmless will of the people at large to believe any manner of evil about a man in a position of prominence. One knew about that. Knew it waited there like a flammable mass that might be ignited into explosion and irretrievable scandal by lack of caution.

His detective work was precautionary. He knew there was unfinished business between himself and Henry Worth. Hatred or not, he was obligated like any diplomat to prepare himself for the strictest kind of bargaining. If Henry knew something of substance that he did not, that margin of advantage had to be as nearly closed as possible.

So Royce called Miss Halstead in California. Atop the embarrassment of asking her how to confirm an allegation he had once taken (however gently, however tactfully) as evidence of her senile incompetence and hysterical need for revenge, he encountered now in her a fear that accusations were still pursuing her. She wept throughout his call. She supposed she "had heard" the story somewhere. No, she could not think who might have poured such venom in her ear. She was sorry, sorry, sorry that she had ever stooped to make the charge. Wellford had been so dear to her. She hoped she hadn't hurt the College. . . .

He called on Mrs. Cox in the apartment over a theater where she had kept the married state with Billy those times he was at home. It had about it the air of rooms occupied for a night or a week. Nothing, not even the crib from which the baby listened to their talk, seemed to be owned by anyone.

When he had convinced the girl that he was not a sneaky representative of the insurance company, she told him that Billy had been lately more depressed than usual. They had quarreled, though she superstitiously dreaded to remember it now. She thought their problems were mostly money. She was afraid that Billy had "tried to pull a deal" with someone she would not or could not name. This blackmail (as she ingenuously implied it to be) had not worked except to screw Billy closer to the necessity of taking a steady job and deeper into his melancholy.

He had gone out on the day of his suicide intending to see "Dr. Mooney."

"Dr. Mooney was a friend of his?"

"He's a good man. Interested in young people. You know, you've heard him *talk*."

"But did your husband know Dr. Mooney?"

"Oh, sure. He didn't like to embarrass him by going to his house or anything. But he knew him from when he first came to town. He straightened Billy out once before. Helped him. Billy just sort of thought he was *it*. You know, an older man . . ." Her mind drifted and she had to be brought back cruelly to answer whether she thought Billy might have intended to ask Dr. Mooney for financial help.

"Oh, *no*," she said to such preposterousness.

"You know for sure that this was not his motive?"

"Billy was scared," his wife said. "He never liked trouble."

"And was afraid he was in it?"

Mrs. Cox nodded.

"And wanted advice how to get out of it?"

"Well, *advice* . . . I don't know if he wanted advice or not. He wanted to be talked to. Bucked up, I guess."

Had wanted (as Royce would at length know, but too late for this information to supplement the manageable theory he was trying to use before he had even finished weaving it) to be told, by the very man he had tried to betray, that since he had gained nothing by treachery it shouldn't be counted against him.

Like the young men in the fable who go out to find and forestall Death, Billy found his "Dr. Mooney" that day he went looking for him. (Carole would confirm this, too late for her confirmation to throw a useful light. She had been at the mansion when young Cox arrived. She knew they had left together in Mooney's car on the afternoon of the tragedy.)

He had, of course, confessed to Mooney how he had tried to betray him by going with their secret to Henry Worth. Or wait— not how he had tried to deliver the secret for money, but rather how he had tried to get money for continuing to keep the secret. Swinging like a child on the Giant Stride of a misty playground, swung at the end of a whirling chain over the lip of death itself, the boy must have been holding on desperately to what his twisted fancy still imagined to be honor.

And if Mooney had agreed with him—as once he had agreed with Mooney, reserving no doubts against the full argument of love—then what was worth saving in his outcast life would yet be safe.

After his ride and talk with Mooney, he had gone alone to the viaduct and jumped. Talked off that bridge the way Dan'l Boone talked a squirrel out of a tree.

Part of this Royce knew when he went for his obligatory confrontation with Henry Worth. He was convinced that no one (except Mooney himself) knew more of what might concern the College than they. Therefore a settlement was possible between them—if not a final settlement, at least one that could limit the damage of revelations conceivably still to come.

218

And Henry, in an expansive mood, thought so too. "So you were going to whip my ass?" he asked as they settled down in the privacy and austere pomp of his office. "So you were convinced I was flying off half-cocked?"

"It's not pleasant to be surprised by . . . charges quite as grisly as those you made."

"You know I was mad."

"That was clear."

"I'm not mad now. Are you mad at me?" The question meant, Do you know enough now to understand the foundation of the charges?

"I believe you had a visit from a young man named Cox."

"It wasn't clear to me at the time what a nut he was"—as now the testimony of the body riven and divided by the drivers of a diesel locomotive made all clear. Failure and death were the great analysts, authorities whose verdict Henry Worth could not be moved to question. "He sounded pretty convincing." An advantage the living have over the dead, now forfeit.

Henry nodded. "I'm not in the habit of shooting off my mouth until I'm satisfied I know what I'm saying and mean to see it through. Cox wasn't the first person who gave me the story."

"Madam Farona?"

Henry's wirebrush eyebrows went up in astonishment. After a moment he grinned grudgingly. "Unfair, unfair. You seem to know a hell of a lot for a fellow who keeps his nose out of the mud. All right. Let us suppose it was Mary Farona, Fox, whatever you want to call her. Someone who knew he'd been gay. *Queer.* There's a funny story about the man who gave him the Rolls-Royce, and I will tell you some time, if you would like to hear. Those boys have an international operation. You know we're lucky that the Hungarian peerage hasn't showed up wanting to rub down the athletes. At least we can't say he's staffed the College with his former playmates. Howsomever, the point is . . ."

"The point is, you've known all along what he was. . . ."

"Well," Henry said, "why didn't you know?"

And the answer, plainly, was that if Royce had been ignorant, this area of ignorance was his choice. If, long ago, he had taken his wife's prompting, he might have gone as far as he was going now after the truth that would bring Mooney down. Let no one accuse another of condoning here. Whoever had known most had borne most, the good and the bad. Why stick at this? Or that? Or over there? If life is indivisible except by squeamishness, the squeamish man can claim only a private value in his refusal to look at the mud.

Henry said, "Maybe the point in question is whether we have now seen the end of Mooney's usefulness."

"Are you asking or trying to persuade me? I thought you'd made up your mind to go to the end in uncovering this thing."

"There is no end. There's only what we have. And you know it isn't very much. Cox is dead. Mooney's had a hell of a good scare."

"The interior decorators?"

"Interior decoration. Hell, I don't know anything about them except what I got from a sheet your Miss . . ."

"Halstead?"

". . . your Miss Halstead sent me once. I suppose she might have made that up. Don't you suppose?"

Royce supposed that Miss Halstead had been in the same Stygian boat where he now found himself: She had known the simple truth, and had been tortured toward an absurd action by her inability to reshape it legalistically or scientifically. She had choked on her knowledge. So might he.

"You accuse me of tolerating him," Henry said. He shrugged. "He was doing his job. It looked like he was keeping his nose clean in Buchanan. In case anyone—me, for example—believed Miss Halstead, he could show he was going with a nice girl. . . . Why hasn't he married Carole Prentice yet?"

"I don't know."

"Maybe now he will. I guess it would quiet things down if he did."

Cool the truth off. Heat up the lie. It was the language of the world of power, and all other language was gibberish or lament. One gibbered or lamented on his own time. They were here to talk about power and where to aim it. Henry did not understand that any better than he. He could not dodge the terms.

"You won't guess about Carole Prentice?" Henry asked. "You've been doing some very tough guessing about the rest of us. But there you won't guess. Or you won't tell me. All right. As far as I'm concerned I think it would be a smart move on his part to marry her damn quick."

"You hardly expect me to advise him that way?"

"I want to see what you'll do. I've waited a long time to see you do something on your own. Here you are, Morgan. It's your turn to do your bit. Quit backing away. Of course you're going to get dirty. You've got to remember a man can't walk but about three feet higher than his own head."

The terms of the invitation were becoming clear enough. Go take your cudgel and hit Mooney behind the ear with it while you still can. Strike—not because there is a wrong to be redressed or avenged by striking. Strike because it is profitable to strike.

It was still perfectly clear to Henry that the hour Royce must have been waiting for had come. In spite of Billy's death, which eased Mooney's position considerably, the faces of power had turned away from him. Or were ready to turn.

And yet, as Royce put it, "We have no concrete indication of any offense."

"Ah," Henry said impatiently, "if you and I both say that Billy Cox told us about a little overnight trip he took to Chicago with Mooney in '46, Mooney won't stand up to it. I'm convinced it happened."

"And this is the first I've heard of it." (True. The story, the basis for charges and assumptions was coming awkwardly, backwardly, fragmentarily, and would never be complete. As stars billions of miles apart will compose into a constellation that the human eye must recognize as the representation of a trinket, a man, or a demigod, the points of light in Mooney's hidden past were composing into the pattern whose truth he would be unable to doubt, whose factuality he could never prove.)

"And," Royce said, "I suppose you haven't asked Mooney."

"He'd lie."

The assumption was sound, perhaps, but remained an assumption still. And as the real terms of Worth's offer began to settle, Royce saw himself in a position not to establish the truth (to set it on the square basis of demonstration where any man might look at it and verify it for his own good satisfaction) but to choose what the truth was hereafter going to be.

Through the days of his investigation, Royce had avoided Mooney —a circumstance neither unusual enough to be remarked nor yet quite the usual routine, since their offices were separated by hardly more than a flight of hardwood stairs.

Then he called.

"Winfred, there's something I have to talk over with you."

No pause. "Sure. Come on up. I don't have anyone. . . ."

"Very privately."

Joking, "We'll seal the doors and turn off the microphone."

"I'd rather see you at home."

"Then come this evening to the mansion. I have an engagement with Carole, but I can arrange to postpone it. How're the children? I haven't seen Priss. . . ."

Loyal Mrs. Clifton opened the front door of the mansion for Royce at eight-thirty that evening. Her chops were drooping in disapproval or a dismay so lugubrious it had about it some hellish air of impropriety. In the midst of an easy greeting to her Royce was struck with the idea that she, this ignorant old woman, knew everything, that her narrow-minded loyalty was that of a portress at hell's gate.

"Mr. Mooney's dressing," she said.

"He was expecting me." Royce checked his watch.

"He's goin' out in half an hour. Boy's bringing the car."

"I'll wait in the living room."

"Said for you to come up."

"Are you sure?"

Mrs. Clifton was always sure of the few things entrusted to her. "To his room," she said. Since she knew Mr. Morgan was familiar with the mansion, she did not offer to guide him.

He was unaccountably breathless as he climbed the carpeted stairs toward the room where his father had died. How many times as a boy had he been summoned up the same steps for a kindly, windy reproof or Chesterfieldian advice on manners? At the worst of those times, in the most childish of his remorses and misgivings, he had never dreaded authority as he dreaded it tonight.

Authority then had been orderly and mild, however mysterious it might have been to his inexperience. Now the authority that waited him was . . . well, not Mooney's authority, of course, but the authority of leering chaos that used Mooney for its representative.

It annoyed him wickedly that he should be the one who trembled in his approach to the confrontation, for he was coming as interrogator if not accuser, or, indeed, as executioner. He was the one supported by the decorum of the community, hypothetically outraged by a mode of conduct and the strong indication of specific offenses. Henry Worth would support him if he said to Mooney the one word—"Git!"

Nevertheless, his breath was short and his mouth dry with apprehension as, for the first time in many years, he let himself into the master bedroom. It was dim and rosy with indirect lighting. His nostrils caught the smell of talcum and after-shave lotion and perhaps of incense. On the wall where his father had kept a Western painting by Frederic Remington there was now a big black and white rubbing from a Chinese tomb, dragons rearing in heraldic combat.

Mooney was not in the room. Royce heard the sound of running water and Mooney's voice called to him through the bathroom door. "Royce? Is it you, Royce? I'll be with you in a minute, sir. Fix yourself a drink. You'll find liquor in the cabinet between the windows."

The water hissed and rumbled on and on. More than enough, one would think, to fill a bathtub. Turning from the liquor cabinet, Royce saw the keyhole of the bathroom door suddenly turn bright as something dark on the other side was removed from it.

"Bring your drink and come in," Mooney invited. His tone was hysterically merry.

Considering the nature of his mission, Royce declined. How discuss accusations of homosexuality with a man reclining naked in the luxury of a hot tub? "I'll wait," he said. He sat wearily in an easy chair well distant from the bed where Mooney's clothes were laid out.

"Sorry my schedule is so tight," Mooney called from beyond the door. "Change of plans. Carole and I are off to Winnetka tonight. We're going to visit some of her relatives. If you have something urgent on your mind, shouldn't we discuss it right now?"

"As soon as possible," Royce said. "As a matter of fact, when you've heard me, you may feel you should not go away this weekend."

After a while Mooney said, "Mmmmm." He was thinking hard as he wallowed in the scented water. Presently he called in a thin, anxious voice, "Can you give me an inkling?" Then, at once, he began to splash loudly as if, after all, he were trying to drown out the answer.

"Billy Cox."

From behind the bathroom door came a prolonged series of bubbling sounds. Royce could no more suppress the fantasy that Mooney had put his head under water to drown himself than he could rationally believe any such thing was happening.

"The youth who committed suicide in such a grisly way. Terrible. I read about it."

"I mean your friend Billy Cox."

The sound of droplets cascading, as if a miniature hippo were rearing out of a swamp. "I perceive that you've been talking to Henry Worth."

"And to Mrs. Cox. And to the police, the coroner, and several others."

"Police?"

"They gathered up the body."

"Of course. Of course. Mrs. Cox?"

"He was married," Royce said. "The poor devil had a child."

"Royce, I can imagine what Worth might have said. You know as well as I that he's out to get me. I've heard what he's been hinting. He hasn't a nickel's worth of evidence. None." If Mooney was so sure of that, then Billy Cox must have convinced him.

"I expect he hasn't," Royce said.

"Then why . . . ?" The incompleted question was plaintive as a child's. Now clearly Mooney was delaying his appearance, as if convinced the closed door gave him some substantial protection. He sighed through it. "Are you, my friend? Out to get me?"

"Things have to be squared up."

"Then we're all right."

"We're in great trouble."

"Henry's not such a *fool* as to go to the other trustees with his allegations. His motives for slandering me, Royce, make a sordid story. It seems that Mrs. Worth has learned about Henry and my old friend Mary . . . Magda Farona. I swear I had nothing to do with bringing those two together nor with informing Mrs. Worth about what happened. But Henry is convinced I told his wife, you see. I might have been wise to so do."

Royce made a face of disgust and said nothing. He was swept with the absurdity of making faces at a closed door.

"Henry's not a man to fool with," Mooney said in a shrill voice, as if warning his friend. "He's going to punish me now by character assassination."

"I don't think Henry has decided yet what he'll do."

"Then," Mooney said, "then . . . you hold the balance, I suppose. Is that it?"

That might be it. And as he held a balance, he was held in a balance, and the invisible hand that held them in a balance was held in balance, and nowhere was there any stable ground where a just man could practice his specialty without feeling that right tipped the balance for wrong, wrong for right, and both for an all-inclusive chaos.

"I'm glad to have you for my judge," Mooney said.

225

"At the moment, I can't help feeling that you owe me some strictly honest answers to some grim questions. There's no time left for half-truth."

"Oh." Again a ring of thought seemed to girdle the syllable like the rings of Saturn. Then there was another suspension of silence between them as Mooney toweled himself dry.

Then he opened the door and stepped naked into the bedroom, stark naked, as if he were inviting Royce to look and be damned. His pudgy body shone rosily, concentrating the rosiness of the light. Against the incandescence of the bathroom door he stood with the supreme arrogance of one so practiced in weakness that he was defended by all its tricks. He was naked—and took even that for an advantage when others seemed to have failed him. His miniature penis dangled in its web of hair like a dial's arrow resting on zero.

"My answer to all the lies being circulated—and to you, sir—is that Carole and I are going to be married very soon. We're going to Winnetka to tell her relatives. When we come back, we'll announce it in Buchanan."

Apparently he meant the shock of his announcement to be devastating, to sweep resistance out of his way. The immediate effect was to appall Royce, and he said so.

"You're appalled that Carole would marry a . . . a . . . a . . . ?"

"I'm appalled that you consider that an answer to specific allegations against you." No, that wasn't the truth. What made Royce tremble with rage was that Mooney would consider the answer good enough for *him*. It might indeed be good enough to serve Mooney's purposes with others suspending judgment.

"Charges?" Mooney did not quite dare sneer. What might have begun as a sneer turned into a squeak of wounded indignation. "That I once befriended a degenerate boy named Billy Cox? That I may have listened without laughing when he said he wished to be a poet? Oh, my, oh, my . . . if things have come to that. . . . The only threat I see is that I have incurred the wrath of a small-town tyrant who doesn't mind making the vilest charges against me at a moment when the future of the University—all you and I have dared hope for—trembles in the balance. I swear that is the only answer I'll make—to you or anyone else. Make of it what you can."

"Well, it isn't enough. I'll try to listen fairly to whatever you have to say, but I know part of the truth about you and Billy Cox. That one time or another you and he . . ."

Mooney reached for his pants. A wondering smile spread on his face. "Royce, Royce, I've always counted on you to tell me off when I'm wrong. . . ."

Silence. The disproportion of measure was too glaring, the old glib formula inadequate as a cord string to hold back a rockslide.

"You have great influence with Carole," Mooney said. "Are you going to tell her I'm a . . ."

Royce waited to learn what name Mooney had for a homosexual. None, apparently. None to use now.

Mooney seemed more troubled now, driven by the other's solemnity to search for a solemn basis for treaty. He said, "So you've been investigating me. Well, I've been investigating you. I've learned about you from Carole. And what I've learned—I say it with all respect, believe me—is just how much responsibility you feel for what . . . for what she's become."

"I don't see that Carole's involved in this just now," Royce said.

Mooney laughed at him. "She's let me see everything. You know as well as I that she's not a strong woman. She's teetering on the verge of alcoholism, if not something worse. Mental collapse! There, I've said it. So she's turned to me. Has come to me because I offer her something.

"Go ahead. Destroy that. If you go to her and say that I'm a . . . She'll believe you because you're Royce Morgan and cannot tell a lie. Sorry, I too respect your integrity, but . . . She'll believe you. And then what? Do you want her back? You want to wreck her? Do you want her on your hands? Is that what you want? Tell me what you want."

"I want you to tell me the truth."

Mooney reeled with astonishment, for once perfectly genuine. "You expect me to confess?" He had thought—it was the humble-arrogant keystone of his whole position in Wellford—that Royce

Morgan saw through him too well to expect that. "Tell Carole whatever you want about what I am. Go on. Make it all up yourself." But he still didn't really expect the other man to make up lies. He was beginning to glimpse an escape route, wondering how much loot he could take with him as he fled.

It was a game with him. In this awful, stinking, threatening, embarrassing impasse, Mooney still saw no alternative to playing life like a game. Therein, still, under the ax or not, was his advantage.

Which Royce understood. In no sense were they talking man to man. Even here, even now, nimbleness remained for Mooney the supreme substitute for virtue.

Slowly Royce said, "I don't suppose I would tell Carole you were —or had been, in the past—a homosexual. I doubt if it would in itself be so shattering to her as you've suggested. It might be shattering to her if there were a big local scandal. She knows enough about you to rest in her private evaluation. But if you force me to go to Carole I'd tell her . . ."

"There won't be a local scandal unless you decide on it," Mooney said resentfully. Whether he was through denying he had been to bed with Billy Cox or not depended on how things worked out. One could certainly rely on him to stop denying it if he were never again accused of it.

". . . I'd tell her you killed Billy," Royce said, hatred roaring into speech for once in his long association with Mooney.

Mooney blinked. Then, quite visibly, he started to relax. He had been putting on one after another garment as they battled. Now he was ready to go to the mirror and tie his tie.

He was in the clear now. Royce might have pinned him with an accusation of homosexuality. The graver charge simply flew over his head like a blast of wind from a cannon shooting blanks.

"You'd been—is the word 'lovers'?—and you brushed him out of the world when he threatened to embarrass you. That's what horrifies me."

"A manner of speaking," Mooney said. "You're talking wildly and I have no responsibility for his death. Well, a general responsibility, yes. No man is an island, is he? And I'll admit to being horrified too. I'd known the boy slightly, yes, and the train and all . . . It's gruesome." He finished tying his tie.

Royce stood up, rising to his full height with difficulty, turning to march slowly toward the door like a ponderous blind man.

"Oh, don't tell me what you plan to do," Mooney cried bitterly after him. "I suppose you and that Henry Worth have something cooked up."

"Nothing."

"If you're going to ruin me, maybe I can't stop you. Only, I beg you not to hurt Carole any more than necessary. You see, whatever you believe, I love Carole. I love her."

Royce kept walking. At the head of the stairs Mooney came running up to him. His face was twisted in an appeal, and it struck Royce that the oddly superhuman authority that had showed in his nakedness was all vanished from him. "You forced me into a fight I didn't want," Mooney said. He was panting a little, in a mixture of small dreads, stripped of the foul brightness and calm he had shown when another man might have raged or cowered.

"You force me," Royce said. "I came here to find some way to go on. You force me to tear things down."

"Well, for God's sake don't come in here and go out like a bad impersonation of the avenging angel. Look, I haven't been myself. I don't know what I'm saying half the time these days. I didn't mean to be offensive. I'm scared. You knew I was scared. For Carole, too. Maybe this isn't the time for us to get married. Royce, you and I will both go to her together . . ."

"That's absurd."

"No. No it isn't. You can tell her whatever you want about me and give me a chance to explain and you a chance to cool off a little and . . . you said I killed him. Now you know he went off that viaduct alone."

"Still, I think you killed him."

They were moving down the stairs together, and Mrs. Clifton's shadow was flickering momentarily across the carpet below. Mooney lowered his voice. "This goes beyond all bounds, Royce. It isn't like you to say things so wild, so extreme. This business comes up.

Accusations are made against me. You might well wonder. It's your character to want to know what's what, but . . . I've always valued your good opinion and I'd like a chance to straighten this up."

"You never had it," Royce said.

As he got out of the house he gasped like a man suffocating. He hoped there was still time, under the implacable wheeling of the night stars, to determine at last, once and for all, what action, of those still possible, might really be his own.

In the last hour he had shucked off any lingering notion that he could solve his riddles by any sort of administrative monkeying. It mattered nothing to him any more whether Mooney went or stayed. All that mattered was how he could resolve his own life within the net of unacceptable alternatives Mooney had draped on him.

PART FOUR

15

ROYCE MORGAN had come home from the war with no Purple Hearts to show what had happened on Saipan. (As a matter of fact he was given a Silver Star for his service as liaison officer there.) In moments of great challenge he always afterward remembered this:

He was aboard a carrier seven or eight miles off the green shore, representing General Greave, whose brigade had already landed. Before long he too would go ashore, and as he waited to be carried over there he was more terrified than he could have found language to admit. He could not have said exactly what it was he expected to happen on the island. The battle was already joined, and the possibility of wounds or death was there. But something else seemed to tease his mind with its prospect—some violence of the soul for which he was not prepared, and for which a man could not be prepared, as he was prepared to accept even his own death.

He was standing late one afternoon on the flight deck, watching the green hills half down on the horizon. The headwind was warm. The sea had a curious purple cast in a color generally leaden, as if its depths were a luminous red obscured by surface layers of partial opacity. Other elements of the great fleet were strung out behind the carrier toward Guam.

At this distance from the island there was no sign at all of a human enemy. There could be, in the minds of staff officers like him, no doubt of victory in the assault. But still he knew that the forces with which he had come were about to engage in something "unbearable." That word, in its full force, was very distinct to him as he stood on the wallowing slab of the deck.

For a minute or two—the duration was brief, the force of certainty literally uncanny—he believed the deck was his old raft anchored in the river below his aunts' house, *that it was night,* and that Carole Prentice was alone with him there. The scale of the carrier was transformed, or perhaps Carole was, for the instant of the hallucination, immensely inflated. She lay the whole width of the deck. She was relaxed in the ease of her trust in him. She propped the weight of her immense head on a naked forearm. She seemed to be there on purpose to offer him the choice of staying safe with her on that bobbing ark—hiding in some regressive cowardice, as he interpreted the vision in his rejection of it—or of going free toward the green shore on the horizon where the unbearable thing was to be accomplished.

He was neither then nor later a believer in the occult. He had no concern about his mental stability. He always thought his mind as resistant to disease as his body, and he was one of those who have never been sick a day in their lives.

So he dismissed this warning image of Carole, went over to Saipan to do his duty—and smiled afterward about the slipping of mental cogs that he had experienced.

Of what came later on the island, he remembered sitting on a green hillside, chowing with some correspondents and some other headquarters officers who had just come back with him from the line.

His unfired carbine lay beside him. As he ate, his mess kit rested on boots spotted with blood and flakes of tissue that were probably intestinal. When he had run through a cane field an hour before, with machine-gun fire clipping the stalks in a capricious harvest, he had stepped in what was left of a Japanese soldier. Whether that man had been close to a shell burst or had committed suicide by exploding a grenade in his trousers, there was little left intact of him between shoulders and knees.

Royce was not bothered by the stuff on his boots. Only, he recalled a wry sentiment of embarrassment founded on the distinction between stepping on a body and stepping in one. It seemed that somehow (had the nature of things provided a way) he ought to beg pardon for intruding into that disarray of guts that the little soldier surely would not have wanted strangers to see.

While one level of his mind fumbled like bruised fingers trying to seize this obligation of manners, the high, refined part of his consciousness was trying to puzzle out why one of Greave's regiments had caved in during the night, requiring a morning of extraordinary effort to establish flank contact with the Marines on their right.

It was no real concern of his that the regiment had "disgraced the Division colors" by its night panic. But why had they? The question was ineluctable. You answered it or gave up the hope of seeing life whole.

Under such an air cover as the Pacific had not seen before, after hours of preparation by the Long Toms and 105s on the beach, preceded by tanks that blasted out strong points and eliminated whatever remained of Japanese light artillery, flanked by a bushy-tailed division of Marines raring to advance, this regiment not only balked the orders of the division commander—in their collective disorder they had frustrated prediction itself. Command had never considered them a first-rate outfit. They were so many arms and legs equipped with a certain quantity of firepower. Not much was expected of them. But they had capriciously made havoc of the whole invisible bridge of statistics reaching from the Pentagon to this shore.

When they broke contact with the Marines (and with the enemy as well) the fleet had moved in to fire over them, an all-night barrage to prevent the Japanese from exploiting this inexplicable dissolution. The barrage, as Royce had found in the course of that morning, had made things worse, compounding panic instead of bolstering morale.

Royce understood of this what he had to—last night he and the terrified men had heard clearly what mankind had been trying to ignore through the darkening years of the century. They heard the death of the personal will in the gratuitously excessive salvoes. What the guns of the fleet meant to say was that neither courage nor cowardice nor even blood counted any more. Forces were and man was not, because in the new ontology of warfare (cold or hot) men were no more than forces in a component of forces spilling toward ends that man no longer dared conceive.

Even to forget that afterward—to forget it for all practical purposes, so one could smile at his sons and be decent or loving to his womenfolk—was not the prerogative of the human will. The forces themselves obscured themselves in the illusion of a subsequent peace.

And perhaps not the least terrifying of his perceptions at high noon on Saipan was that real despair need have no emotional accompaniment at all. The nerves do not tingle and the knees can stay quite stiff while the soul accepts its nullification. The capacity to grieve or tremble is lost by compliances that obscure its ever having existed.

So, later in the war, when the news came of Hiroshima and Nagasaki, Royce was unluckily complacent about it. It was as if these events were not news to him at all, only confirmations, like a death for which he had sorrowed in advance. In an odd, fatal rote he repeated his absence from his mother's funeral—at least he felt he was doing the same thing and was again deeply uneasy. He was spared the acute anguish suffered by a good many intellectuals and military men of his acquaintance—the shock wave of panic spread by the Bomb—because he already knew, from Saipan, what it meant. Exempt when no man dared to be.

He had been questioned by the abyss. He had failed to answer, and it seemed for a while he was going to be let off. Now he had to make his reply to Mooney.

He did not try to dodge by the expedient of pretending that what was to be done now was a College problem. Whether Mooney stayed or was brought down had become immaterial. How Royce Morgan walked in the slippery places was all that counted. It was his trial and not Mooney's.

He found nothing to trust for himself except a plan so quixotically foolish as to be unprecedented in his life. That is, he decided to desert his wife and children and take Carole away.

It rather stunned him that he should even have considered this recklessness seriously. Yet he was totally committed to it before he even hinted it to Carole.

His determination settled during the weekend that she and Mooney were in Winnetka telling her relatives about their plans to marry. The decision was made almost simultaneously with the admission of the possibility to his consciousness, all in one lucid hour of solitude while he was walking home from the campus, while he stopped in the neighborhood store to buy a roll of caps for Lot and a green balloon for Sherman—conceived his plan, checked it out with the highest authorities of his conscience, and accepted it, quite as if Sycamore Street were the road to his chosen Damascus.

Melon-colored slices of sundown flared through the trees, meaning nothing, but he took them for a sign.

He fingered the little yellow sack of evening gifts in his pocket; thought once, Of course I can't really do such a thing. Then thought, No, but *I* can. Like a temporizing prime minister who has failed to prevent a war, he could abdicate in favor of another self, the warrior self he had always repudiated.

No commandment was given him. *I* heard one. *I* would surely sacrifice my sons because God would surely tell me to if there was a God. He could still smile at the audacity of his thought as if it were frivolous. Frivolous or not, his determination for it was steely.

While he was helping Lot fit the roll of caps into a nickel-plated gun (Sherman was climbing delightedly up his broad back while he knelt to Lot's height) he thought, Yes, but I'm going away.

"You've had a good day," Priss said to him suspiciously. "Why are you smiling?"

"Because I've had a good day," he said. On Sycamore Street he had made the great leap for his life. He smiled—not without pity for all of them—to think that Priss would adore, in the abstract, what he was going to do for Carole. It was the great leap she had always wanted him to make for her. And he might have made it, too, if the occasion had ever called for it. He had not been unwilling. But occasions are no respecters of persons. So Priss would have to adore and be cheated in the same consequence.

"Ah, don't tell me if it's a secret," Priss said. "My life is so full of intellectual stimulation, heaven knows I don't need a husband who tells me what's really going on in his mind."

"We know each other so well," he said. "I never feel I have to explain my thoughts. That's all."

"True," she said. "True. I suppose I know without asking. I merely like the sound of adult voices. Lot, don't shoot that thing in here."

The boy had crept up behind her and was holding the barrel of his revolver close to her neck. He grinned knowingly and went outside. They heard the sound of his sly executions exploding back and forth on the porch.

"Yes, I know you've got some new formula for thinking about Mooney and Carole and it soothes you," Priss said with resignation —as if she knew exactly what it was and might be just waiting like himself to see the formula tested.

As soon as he heard that Mooney and Carole were back from Winnetka, Royce went to her house to tell her what they had to do. He found her out in the back garden, setting geraniums in soil still crumbly damp from the weekend rain.

She looked lumpy and gross to him as she crouched among the plants in her pale smock—as if he had not really seen her for many years and was now, for the first time, surprised not to find her still the girl he might have married. When she heard his call and stood up with red face and dark brown smudges on her arms, her eyes apologized for not being what he expected. He smelled the whiskey on her breath along with the kindly, wizened scent of geraniums.

"I was coming over to your house tonight," she said. "I called Priss and asked if I might."

"I know. Priss told me you were back."

"I have something to tell you."

"That you're going to marry Winfred?"

"Oh. Well. Don't you think . . . he might have let me know he'd already told you?" She began to pull off her dirty red gloves. She tried to smile as if congratulations were in order, then admitted this was Royce and explanations might be due him. If not, why was he frowning so severely?

She led him into the big house, almost as familiar as his own, though it had been many years since he had allowed himself to take the freedom of it as he had once. Tonight he was aware of the changes in the house. They came to his eyes vividly, as in the garden he had been vividly aware of the changes in Carole, almost as though he had not seen these rooms for fifteen years.

"What happened to the old rosewood piano?" he asked. He remembered a girl with taffy-colored hair hunched on the piano stool watching the metronome with a kind of stiff terror while her loose fingers went blindly across the keys.

She laughed that he had never asked before, that he remembered it at all. "You didn't think I'd keep the signs of my disgrace?" Her piano lessons had meant four years of duty to that insuperable metronome whose message she never understood. A total failure to advance. "Ten years ago—I guess it's ten—I gave it to the Helgeson girl. Vivian Helgeson? She had real promise. She got married. Ooof, it's hot in here. Shall we sit outside after all? I'll bring drinks."

He waited for her on the screened side porch where one or two or three—he couldn't remember how many, only the persistence of the situation—of Deirdre's maids used to bring them cookies and milk and then later Cokes and sandwiches when they came back on the bus or on their bikes from afternoons at the swimming pool.

She had washed and quickly changed to a white dress before she appeared with their drinks. Her face was set confidently as if she had now framed her explanation of why she was going to marry again. He didn't give her time to use it.

"You can't," he said. "You can not marry Winfred Mooney. Come on away with me, Carole. Marry me. That's the only right way to end our lives and I think you know it."

"Oh."

She opened her eyes as if searching for a huge mirror in which she could see them both at once and reassure herself that, after all, they were a graying man in a well-tailored summer suit leaning toward a plump, middle-aged woman still sweated from gardening. There was no mirror. She saw an ageless pair, no wiser than they had ever been.

" 'End our lives.' Well, I should think . . ." she began. It was the girl's duty to cool the boy off. She had always meant to, had never managed with Royce.

"I don't understand," she said. In the swift crumpling of her attempt to pass this off as a joke he felt her settling, yielding to his male superiority *exactly* as she had settled beneath him on the floor of his aunt's bedroom, and he knew a minute of terrible thanksgiving, as if time had truly been remitted and now into his wiser hands a chance to be loyal was given back to him. All the king's horses and all the king's men had, after all, after time had played its destructive joke, pulled off a miracle. The humpty-dumpty urn was in his hands again because he had the courage to seize it. Now there was no turning back. Cowardice and uncertainty had burned their own bridges. There was nothing left but the way of recklessness.

She frowned as if she had learned Lot's frown. Her mouth shaped to a pale, round flower of anxiety. "I don't understand what you mean about . . . well, Priss and the children." He could have laughed loud at her omission of Mooney's name. She was his.

"I'm prepared to leave them," he said.

"Lot and Sherman?" She shook her head in a kind of excited horror, as though some smell of blood were stimulating her erotically and she couldn't help it.

He was looking squarely at them. He had never seen his sons plainer than now—in a summer scene where Lot was teasing his younger brother, both of them naked beside a blue plastic pool Priss had filled for them in the shade by the stable, Lot wiry and reedlike, though strong in the shoulders, feinting and evading the little boy's square-bodied, butting charge, both laughing as if they knew some antique joke never to be put in words, their weaving bodies like honey marble against a verdure that only memory could color so deep a green.

"I'm their father," he said in the compelling voice of his trance. "I

240

can be their father in leaving them." As once upon a time I was your husband in leaving you, there on that bed in Chicago. I can reclaim them as I'm learning—help me learn!—to reclaim you now.

He saw how the miracle was done. How it would have to be done. Just how exorbitant the requirement of faith and strength would have to be to bring it off. But caution forbade him to cite his desertion of her as the model for his desertion of his sons. "I can be their father in leaving them. At any rate, it isn't clear what Priss would want to do about them. I mean, under such circumstances as I contemplate. Always—since the war, rather—Priss has been straining at the leash to go and find what she thinks she's missing. You know it's true that she might leave me if I didn't leave her. And she might prefer to leave the children with us. Let them come to us sometime."

Expediently he tried to bolster his argument. It might have stood—enough to take Carole, at least—if he had given no indication that it needed bolstering, that it required the support of practical solutions. She had been his. Now he was losing her again. As he felt her draw back he felt himself recover the mundane sanity which had ruined them. Again his decision became silly.

But it was his decision still and he refused to countenance its silliness. He had seen how their flight might work. Even when the vision fled, they might follow it. He would not be put off now by seeing how silly he still was. A schoolman trying to convert himself into Noah, naturally he would be reminded often enough that a deluge does not by itself teach a man how to build an ark.

"I think we're drunk," Carole said. She lifted her glass to her mouth now and drank heavily. She was providing an excuse for what had been so recklessly said, locking the barn door against this talk of stealing horses.

"Besides," she said with a good-natured chuckle, "it might spoil some of Winfred's plans."

"That's exactly what he has."

"Plans? I know. I know. I know, Royce. Who would marry me for my talents and sweet disposition?"

"I'm going to."

"You'd marry me because you thought it was right."

"Well?" Something in her grimace of remorse made him ask her to complete the thought.

"Well, I'd've let you do that once. Oh, if you'd ever thought it *was* right."

"Doing right is important to a man. What's more important?"

"But people who try to do the right thing always mess things up worse than anyone." It was true. No one had a better right to say that to him than Carole. Yet it angered and frightened him that he heard Mooney's voice in her comment, denouncing truth and high feeling along with fanaticism. If she had earned cynicism, by the same token she deserved to be rescued from it.

"I'm not sure you know all about Winfred's plans," he said sternly. "I'm sure he has a strong affection for you, yes, but beyond that— someone has to help you see beyond—there are ugly imperative reasons for his choice of this time to marry."

Then he would not let her get them another drink until he had told her—as concretely as he could; not altogether concretely because his own knowledge was not of that sort—about Mooney and Billy Cox, about Henry Worth's maneuver to shoot Mooney down.

He did not stress any repugnance he might have felt about Mooney's homosexuality. He didn't go so far as to repeat his intuition that Mooney had "killed" the young man. Yet it was not by these reticences that he failed to persuade her. It was rather that she was still too deeply moved by his offer to leave his sons for her to be much concerned about Mooney or herself either. She was watching Royce's mouth, not listening, really, to his words.

Still some part of her mind took the gist of his disclosures. She heard him name Mooney as though naming some part of himself he wished to disclaim. "The damnable part of it is . . . in getting rid of Cox he has covered his trail pretty well." They both heard his voice break in that sentence as neither of them remembered its breaking.

She nodded. "You're the only authoritative . . ."

"Authoritarian!"

". . . witness against him."

"No. I'm not a witness. I'm just certain. There's not much more than a thick sticky cloud of rumor. For him to be married might blow the cloud away."

"Will that be enough?" she asked—as if swaying to the temptation of being of service, whatever the cause.

"No one knows at this point. Worth is ready to chuck him. Winfred has some high cards to play. He's been lucky before. A good deal depends on where I throw my weight, that's plain. You can imagine the temptation is very strong to tie the can on him."

"I can imagine that! He's never liked you, darling."

"By going away with you I'll resist that temptation. I want him to have what he's earned. What they've made of Wellford."

"I thought you approved. Of some of it."

"I never saw an alternative. I hate it. If I have a soul my soul hates it. I haven't stayed around to glut on his leavings."

"Oh," she said. The evening was gathering around the house like the wrapper put on a bird cage at the end of a day, coming out of the elms like something dense and impenetrable, not to be clawed away by the frenzy of tiny and blunted talons. "Oh. I'm part of his leavings too."

He wanted to get the words back in her mouth. True or untrue, they didn't matter. Her enunciation of them was a successful step of evasion. "I wasn't maneuvering for any confession from you," he said.

But confession was her dodge. Now she insisted on filling their glasses again. Sitting a little closer to him than she had before, *enjoying* it—at least feeling morbidly familiar with it—she took the privilege of confessing. "You never did me . . . *wrong*. Maybe you wanted to think so. I suppose I made you think so. I can't let you believe that any more. Even the first time, you know, virginity thing . . ."

"Wasn't the first, but . . ."

"Was the first. Well, really was. Wasn't the only. I mean, while you were away at school. Sometimes. Other boys. *Ones who didn't like you.*"

"If that's true . . ."

"It is true. I used to imagine I was protecting you from them."

"My God."

"It's true I really wasn't ever very strong. Even before you made up your mind to it, decided to *face it*—which I was too weak to do— I knew I wasn't. Priss is. She's strong enough. I . . . well, afterward, whatever man I married—not so *very* many"—she laughed—"I'd kind of let myself go and be whatever they wanted me to be. It's not all nice to remember. I should have tried to do more with my own life, I know."

"What you're trying to say . . ."

"What I'm trying to say is there never was any little old Carole Prentice that Royce Morgan was responsible for. That was all in your head. So . . ."

"So you're going ahead to marry Mooney to protect me from him."

"No. No, no, no. You're trying to beat me with words. This time *I* want to do what's right. Priss wants me to marry him. Maybe that's more important than the . . . rumors."

"There isn't any little old Priss Morgan you're responsible for."

"That's all in my head," she conceded, nodding, conceding one minor point only. Her good teeth shone white in the dusk. Not in a smile. He could make out a familiar settlement, half determination and half giving up, in the lines around her mouth. "I can't do what you want, Royce."

"You can't marry Winfred."

She crouched toward him, begging. "When you told me your story, you said there were things *I* might not know about. There are things you don't know." She fought her obligation to explain like a dumb animal fighting the halter, then said with quick flippancy, "I've been putting out for Win for a couple of years, so . . . Longer than that. Been . . ."

"I knew that. Priss knew. Don't you see, she'd make sure I did?"

Her face showed a small surprise but not the relief of surprise. She didn't need his words. There was an image of Royce Morgan in her mind. It was before that image she must humble herself. And bring it down, too, in the wreck of her humility.

"He can't be, what you say, gay, because . . . Well, a woman knows."

"Gentle Carole, you can't know by that."

"He knows how to please a woman," she said stubbornly.

"It's not my argument that he may have had homosexual relations with Billy Cox and therefore is permanently out of the running. I won't countenance his *using* people—the way he used Cox. The sex part might even deserve understanding. But not the ruthlessness. He put the boy away when it was convenient."

"Are you sure he did? I know he had a long talk with Cox the other day when the boy came to bother him."

"Oh."

"What?"

"He told me a different story. That he hadn't seen Cox. So what makes you sure of one thing falls in place and confirms something else for me. Carole. Slow up a minute. Are we really talking to each other? Then . . . then ignore everyone and answer the question I came with. Will you go away with me? Try to make a life. *Try* . . ."

He felt her obedience again, the slackening of body and will that he could always have when he wanted to pay the price for it. He felt his old terror of being responsible for the totality of another's will.

She asked: "You . . . need . . . me?"

He could not make himself say that he did. He was willing to lie but could not assure himself that was, for this particular instant, the right lie. "Part of the misery of being Royce Morgan is to love without needing. No."

"Misery?" She kindled with the word. If he was miserable he was in need . . . But she said, "You need your boys."

"I love you."

"Oh, yes," she said. As if that didn't count any more. As though the knowledge of his love had lain forever like some ornamental cast-iron dog of mastiff size on the lawn outside. She was so used to passing it each day she never expected it to stand up and bark. The issue must be settled without whistling to it.

He tried to guess the direction in which her thoughts were wandering and to head them off. "You mustn't believe that Winfred will necessarily be saved if you marry him. The lightning might still strike. What use would he have for you then?"

She took this as a reflection on her shortcomings. His arguments could only add to her confusion. They could immobilize her—if that was what he wanted. Of course it was not.

"Don't think I haven't had my doubts. But, Royce, don't you see? For a long time I've had to get what *I* could out of my life. He offers something. All right, I don't know if we'll go through with it. It hasn't been announced in the papers yet."

"You'd go through with it if it had been?" The scathe of his voice stung her like the end of a rope on her shoulders. It was the kind of sting he had given her too often in the far-off years of their intimacy, the kind that could be given without trying, a vile portent for their future together.

"I'm not quite that weak," she said. "But . . . not everybody thinks like you."

"Thank God?"

"No. Not 'thank God,' but others might think I'd done the right thing. He's respected, even if the reasons are wrong. I have to make some sense out of my life. These last few years . . . I don't know what I am any more except an old, fat drunk. Whore too, I guess. Why? People always gave me whatever I asked for. Deirdre showed me how I could have been somebody if I'd wanted to. Why didn't I?"

Now it was dark enough for her to cry, the darkness like a permission. The tears on her face flowed on a scale to match the scale of her mistake. It was her life that was the mistake, a gigantic flower of error. Only, she had never meant harm to anyone. If *that* was the source of her mistake, she could weep for it but not renounce it. And when she had wept for it, she would accept it and go on carrying it like an ungainly, ludicrous cross, right on out to the end of her days.

With that lingering, irresolute farewell in his ears, he started down the sidewalk toward his car. He had been spared. Again. The man he was supposed to be could not afford another exemption.

He felt his long legs swing like crutches. The humid elm leaves rustled the sound of a Pacific swell. All common sense and all experience confirmed that his attempt had been made too late. Something clear as his father's voice said to him: *Let her go. Let her continue the huge, consistent mistake, or you will go mad.* At some point in its wrestling with inevitability, the mind had to uncouple or be permanently spoiled, like a spring stretched too far.

He was close to his car when he realized it was too late for choice. He bared his teeth, turned, and ran back to where the choice had been.

Now—mad or not, or just not yet—he tried to storm the unyielding past. He ranted and bullied Carole. He plied her with liquor and sentimentalities. Deirdre had been unable to wait for this reunion, but had foreseen it, hadn't she? They who had outlived her must not betray her still another time.

He shouted down or stifled her diminishing protests that Priss was waiting for her, for him. "You're not going there to see her gloat! I've stood by too long, excusing her because she's gifted and misused her gifts. You've got to understand she doesn't wish you well," he said.

He cursed Mooney.

He disdained to enumerate Mooney's faults. The man was evil. Evil.

Pliantly she conceded this. But what else was wrong with him?

Nothing. Does there have to be more?

Nothing. So nothing much had been said against him, and here at the last ditch of their struggle it could still be said of him that "he knew how to please."

On requirement so could Royce Morgan. Had he not, for years, pleased the most exigent of women, with tricks and firmness of the flesh that made even the metaphysical frigidity in the woman's soul stand in abeyance? Before that, had he not pleased this woman in the sense she had intended when she spoke of Mooney? Upright and often he had. Had always known he could again at the last resort.

"Royce, you're out of your mind!"

So be it. He was, nevertheless, in her pants.

"We're out of our minds!" she muttered. A sort of low, wild

whistle of horror played over the words, like heat lightning at the edge of heavy clouds. "We're out of our minds!"

They were not yet out of their clothes.

But would be, willy-nilly, and very soon, too, unless she found the magic incantation to free herself, for he intended no less than rape, a rape of the past, an Orphean plunge into the tomb between her thighs. He smelled the odor of tombs from where his hand was delving as he ground her into the couch—the smell of tropic lagoons where their youth had died.

It was part of her charity—therefore a trick of her evasion—that she would not let him rape her. She must save him from that crime, too, and charitably cheat him of the crime's winnings.

"If you need me . . ." she muttered. And yielded limply. She accepted his knee wedging hers apart, as if this were part of the celebration of her recent engagement. She let his hand play those tricks of arousal that Priss had taught him.

"Upstairs," he ordered, wild as a Hun, savage in his fear that compassion might make him incapable.

"Might as well for a sheep," she murmured, now suddenly swept away in a froth of giggles, as if drunker than she really was.

She denied him the chance to commit a rape that might have altered his life, but since she permitted him the first and only adultery during his marriage to Priss, he need not have feared himself incapable of carrying it through. As they undressed—turned away from each other as if intentionally ignoring the purpose of their being here—he wanted her as simply as on the day he had once seduced her child-self. *Needed* her . . . Yes, for a few minutes he needed her.

But already, when she lay naked on her dark bed, waiting for him to come to her, the intrusions of experience began to distinguish the one occasion from the other. He could make out the fat hump of her belly distorted to one side by its own weight like the misshapen urn she had left in the studio for Mooney to find. The spill of her vast breasts, her physical dissoluteness, looked intentional—like a vengeance taken on him for daring to remember her otherwise. And he had the curious idea that this was Priss's vengeance, paid to her in full measure.

"Take pity on an old woman," someone crooned from the bed.

He did.

He tried to give her something. His erotic competence, so serviceable to Priss, so trained in the stable of her creative lusts, should have been his to dispose where love and pity wanted to dispose them. If they rose from this passion bound even tighter in the chains he had tried to throw off, still he wanted them to have that moment of mindlessness, of materiality which one conceives as a substitute for eternity. He thumped her like a champion. He teased and filled her. He lay with his mouth on the large beads she had not removed when she undressed and imagined them reclining so on the side of an urn, oblivious to the snickers of historians watching through the glass of a museum case. Like a rider at the hurdle who imagines in the long upward poise of the jump that he is lifting his eight-times-heavier horse by the sheer strength of his exaltation, he fantasied that he was lifting her with him.

Then, in his orgasm, he knew exactly how Orpheus must have felt upon discovering himself all alone outside the mouth of hell. She had not followed. Whatever his intent, she had intended only to give him the old-time, tried-and-true consolation for what could never be. That was all.

He had to say something, and he couldn't. That was the greatest embarrassment of all—to lie there wet and be unable to get enough moisture into his mouth to say that now they must go through with his plan for getting away.

"You . . . pleased me," she said with infinite tenderness. "Beautiful, Royce. Beautiful."

He thought she meant he was beautiful, and of course he could not comment on that.

"What time is it?" she asked. "Is there still time . . . ?"

He hushed her with a kiss, since, of course, she had meant to ask if there was still time to whisk into their clothes and get to Priss, pretending that nothing had happened.

Then he lay there awhile believing that Priss wouldn't care. Now she wouldn't care. A while before he had realized she wished him impotent in this encounter (which, of course, for years, she had foreseen—had, perhaps, even demanded). He had not been technically impotent. Not at all. He had been someone's stallion—only not his own.

Beaten again, he tried again. After this bed there would be no mortal ground for another trial. He summoned strength and passion (or at least the desperation of a man floundering after a raft in the night ocean) to mount again. Then through hours of ebbing hope (or minutes; the clocks of hell have no figures on their dials) while he bobbed like a castaway, he simultaneously saw himself diminishing in the scale of his own perspective, like an abandoned survivor watched out of sight by the observer on a search plane. Carole yielded everything that did not count.

Only, when she was finally satisfied of his satisfaction, she guided him to that small, uncostly service by which, he guessed, a conscientious Mooney pleased her. She took it with a beggar's gratitude and said now she knew how much he loved her.

Then they lay there a long time, scarcely daring to touch. Their animal selves were poisoned by what they knew. It was like a death for both of them and they knew they must not admit it.

At last Carole said, "Well, you've paid him back. He'd swallow his tongue if he knew."

"We've given him something to think about," Royce said with castrating self-mockery. His bodily impulses were exhausted. Now only his will could rally against defeat, like the compass needle on a sunken ship, still pointing north in its watertight case, fathoms down. He said, "He'll have more to think about than this. *Now* you'll come away with me. We will be married, Carole."

"I can't think now. Will Priss know?"

"You mean, how will I tell her? I think it won't be hard. She can let me go now."

"I mean about tonight. We're both . . . awfully late."

"There'll be no need to go into details for her." Priss would have known the details years ago. All she had waited for was a confirmation of her insight, a grounding that would reassure her faith in her vision. She would even have known that she—not they—was now free to pack her bags and go.

"She'll know. And I'm her friend," Carole lamented. "Oh, God. It would be easy if I didn't love . . . her."

"She won't hold it against you. She won't hold anything against anybody." Not now. Not since she had exactly the kind of revenge she had thirsted for. That they should fail each other. "If she could have, Priss would have wanted to bless us both."

That was true, also, and one more among the tangle of reasons why Carole must refuse him. But he could find no remorse for saying it. She had plenty of reasons without this one, anyway.

"Yes," Carole said, rousing herself. "Yes, my darling. I'll have to trust what you tell me, and what you want. We will go away and be married. Down the sunset trail together. Yes. We'll save something. We'll have the boys someday. Tell me where and how. Only go home now. I'll call Priss and make up some lie. I won't be over tonight. Want to sleep. Wouldn't be better you go home now? Please! Tomorrow know."

Then she slept. He could not believe for a little that her sleep was real. Then he realized it was the only thing she could reasonably have done. He was grateful that she could do it.

Quietly as a thief he went down the carpeted stairs that jutted toward the front door between the living room, unchanged since Deirdre's childhood, and the more modern parlor.

At the foot he stopped, sensing another presence in the dense air of the house. Over by the ornamented Victorian mantel, invisible now, though the mirror above it picked up a few street lights patterned by curtains, the red coal of a cigarette glowed at chair-arm level. He stood watching the coal move like a living jewel, a terrible eye watching him, a rosy throat expanding to swallow him.

"Well?" Winfred Mooney asked amiably.

When Royce fled, Mooney went upstairs to claim what was his own.

16

Sixteen days later Carole and Mooney were married in the Grace Episcopal Church of Buchanan. During those sixteen days neither Priss nor Royce laid eyes on the bride-to-be.

"Which is a little odd, to say the least," Priss said. Was it not just as odd that, after she had read of the engagement in the paper, she had made no attempt to reach her friend by telephone? "We're playing our cards close to our chests these days, aren't we?" Discreetly she forebore to comment that Carole was the only one among them who could do that while still playing them at arm's length.

Discretion had settled on Priss like an acute physical change since the night Royce came home inexplicably late. Pointedly she failed to ask what had kept him. She didn't even mention that Carole had meant to call that evening. Plainly enough her mind was busy with the news of the wedding. She was not sharing her thoughts. Now she knew something so precious that it deserved to be written down, and she said she was busy with her "novel" again.

Her spoken comments about the wedding were never more or less than flip. "Well timed to coincide with the ceremonies ending a scholastic year," she said. "I must say it's *transcendently* tactful of her not to ask me to be a bridesmaid." About Carole's picture in the paper—what is called a bust shot—she said, "None of his detractors will be able to claim the bride is in drag."

Royce smiled and declined to ask what she meant by that observation. He lacked heart even to guess how much—or for how long—she had known of Mooney's incentive for marriage now. Day by day he found communication between them thinning, like a film of ice thawing over waters that certainly ran deep and hopefully would remain still. He operated on the principle that she knew everything about his attempt with Carole. Therefore he felt justified in maintaining a deanish detachment in speaking of that lady. Priss matched the detachment with an impenetrable slyness.

At the church, as the ceremonies began, she noted that Henry Worth was not among those present. "But I feel his blessing," she said. "After all, this is such an addition to our image."

"Ssssh!" Lot whispered beside her. "It's started, Mother. Talk later." He had wanted to come to the wedding because . . . well, because whatever else he knew, some signals in the air at home had told him there was to be something stranger than fairy tales about it. Once upon a time he had imagined Carole bound to a pottery wheel. He had come to see what they were making of her now. "Talk later!" he whispered savagely to his impudent mother.

"I never will," she said.

What was there, hereafter, to say? In the midst of solemn music and decorum, Royce felt his flesh crawling like some blind, amputated thing that might as well be scrambling among the feet of the crowd, searching for an altar at which it could pray. Prayer, perhaps. Comment? No. The ceremony must put an end to the dialogue of right and wrong he had sustained within himself for so many years, just as it would put an end to curiosities about Billy Cox. This sealed the past like a tomb. He would not hear from it again any voice that said, "I'm bleeding." For that relief he had to be grateful.

Yes, all expectation to the contrary, he was relieved when the minister pronounced those two man and wife. The music soared up in turbulent assurance. All was ended. All was begun. *How comely it is and how reviving* . . . It was Carole's triumph to have given him full liberty at last. Had she intended it so, in the pinch played more cunningly than any of them to bring this about? Even her silence of these last days calculated? Now there was no need to conjecture. His liberty was liberty from such riddles.

With Lot and Priss trailing handsomely beside him, he went forward to congratulate the happy couple. His hand met Mooney's, firm and frank. Their eyes met. No secrets there. All open. They shook hands like honorable and trustworthy strangers embarking on a brand-new enterprise.

There were real tears when the women embraced. They were saying goodbye to each other, disowning a mystical sisterhood which had tormented both, already missing their torment.

"Now you can kiss the bride," Lot said to his father with a troubled smile.

For some reason, the comment set Mooney off into peals of exuberant, well-nigh hysterical laughter. His face was round and red and he was bent at the waist by his fit of amusement when a photographer for the student newspaper set off his flash and caught him. Laughing, just like that.

That picture in the paper delighted everyone who saw it. It said about Mooney what language could never express so well.

Years later—many years later, so long afterward that the perspective of judgment could seem like the perspective of infinity—it would seem to Royce that Mooney was laughing because he knew that in losing Carole, Priss also was lost.

Mooney *knew* that?

Oh, well, he didn't *know*. . . . Of course Mooney wasn't very smart. What the long-range perspective showed was that Mooney never had to know things, he *was* things. A walking, talking event, blood brother to accident and things "just happening," to the primal clash and collision of destinies that didn't have to be self-conscious, because self-consciousness would not have made them any more intelligible. His laughter wasn't *from* knowing that now Royce could kiss his life goodbye. Rather—one was tempted to think from the arctic perspective of old age—his laughter was the mockery of events themselves, laughing at people who tried to nudge them into happier patterns, or even patterns that the heart could bear.

At any rate—it would be a recollection sometime, finally mingling and fusing with the moment of Mooney's hilarity in the church— Priss did divorce him.

There was time enough between Carole's marriage and his divorce for Priss to muddy the water and say such things as: "We've been divorcing since the day we got married. Can't you see that, Royce?"

He couldn't see it. He was weary and he didn't want to see it. What he had seen, and that was quite as far as he wanted to stretch a chaos of circumstances into a unified and intelligible pattern, was that the unbroken glide toward divorce had begun exactly when Carole was disposed of. He had been brave enough to think once, and only once, that his marriage to Priss and his fatherhood of Lot and Sherman could be preserved by deserting them—preserved, at least, like successes embalmed in history, the successes of gamblers who quit while they were ahead—as history tells us people can do, though no one who watched a life out to its end ever saw it accomplished.

After that brave thought was twisted out of his head, it turned out he had been right. Afterward Priss simply wasn't interested in him any more. Well, interested, then . . . but only as she was interested in those arts that had, one after another, failed to take her to that unworldly peak which they themselves had taught her to conceive. The expectation of a miracle was gone. Priss always had and always would follow the scent of a miracle. Nothing less.

She stayed around for a few years. Her hands had not lost the craft of marriage any more than they had lost the craft of music, painting, or ceramics. She stayed around long enough to offer Buchanan the façade of an impeccable divorce. Others divorcing later in this town would be hard put to live up to the style of the Morgans.

Toward the end, Priss spent more time away from her husband, her family, and Buchanan. About these absences Buchanan knew as much as it should—that she had increasing interests in New York and Chicago—and Buchanan wouldn't have been surprised at the proposition that these interests involved a man or two. Or three or four. Several. Mrs. Morgan was a stylish, beautiful woman, and no one with any sense ever took her to be a woman kept from what she wanted by provincial mores.

She flaunted exactly nothing. Even her children had what they needed most of her—love and play and company and care, sometimes; at other times that image of speed and flight and poise they could hold as a talisman against the boredom of growing up in Buchanan.

She got away, that is, as Royce had known *he should* go when he meant to skip with Carole—as Lot had seen somebody ought to fly when he thought of the trumpeter swan.

From the perspective of age, justice obliged one to admit she achieved her divorce with consummate art. Could she have given her boys any inheritance better than that image to live with through the time of their lives?

Only Royce had to witness the trail of broken glass that she left behind in imitation of stardust, the incoherences and inconsistencies that even she became unable to admit.

Through the years of their divorce dialectic, Priss returned, like a bride going home to Mother, to a core argument—that because her husband had never "given" himself to her (given totally and without reservation, she meant), she was doomed in Buchanan to remain forever unfulfilled, a spinster mother of two bright, demanding boys— boys who had deserved a truly married woman as mother.

To which Royce answered, "I can understand that. You've convinced me that you're talking about something real. Only why do you want to?"

"Convince you? So I'll be justified in your all-judging eyes."

"If they judge they don't condemn."

"Ah. To condemn would be to give yourself, wouldn't it?"

"I can understand that, too. Maybe some people have the right to condemn. And I haven't."

"Too many people depend on you," she mocked.

It was true. Many people depended on him, some for a lot, some for a little. His carcass was his own, but how could he dispense one person's rights on it in favor of another's claim? Particularly after his failure with Carole, he felt himself neutral, merely the guardian of himself appointed to umpire the shareholder's rights. "You're even jealous of the children," he admonished.

She would not deny it. "I'm capable of that. Go on, condemn me for it."

He shrugged and could not. "Priss, I hear you. Do you know that I do hear? What you think you've been cheated of in your life with me could hardly be more plain. But the question remains: Who could have given you more of what you need than I? If you know or knew a man . . ."

She raged at this tacit offer of freedom. "You fool, you fool. No one. It was only you who could have given it, and you wouldn't."

"I never knew how."

"You didn't know how! That's right, God help me. You didn't know how. Castrated by conscience while still a boy! Every apey little student in his hot rod knows how and every coed knows it in her bones. That faggot Billy Cox knew how to give himself to his wife, and to Mooney, too. Don't tell me this is hearsay."

Royce shook his head. "I believe," he said wearily.

"And even Mooney knows how to give himself to Carole. That despicable, rotten, little cunt of a man knows how to give himself. And you don't."

"I hear your words."

"But you don't hear me."

"I can't grasp it. Hereditary inability. I can't understand unless you help me. You're talking like a frustrated woman and I can't see you that way. If it's sexual . . ."

" 'Sex-you-all!' It was never that. Oh, you're the perfect stud when you have to be."

"You believed that was the important thing."

"You *let* me believe it."

"If you wanted to . . ."

"Damn you. It isn't a husband's role to be permissive. You shouldn't have let me."

"Then I'll beat you."

"Just you try!" Then she smiled fearfully at him as they surveyed their stalemate, two explorers at the world's end, staring out over the flat, white expanse of nothingness. "You always listened and you never heard," she said. "It was *me* trying to call you. You couldn't hear."

"Then I can't."

"I know. I know you can't. Then lock me up, Royce. You'd better lock me up because there's no telling what I'll do now. It's your civic duty to protect the world at large from me."

"Whatever you do will be beautiful."

There was something worse than a scream—he heard the note often in those years—in the crying melody of her voice. "I *am* beautiful. Or I was. And you couldn't take my beauty, Royce, you wouldn't have it. It's drying up. Isn't that worse for you to watch? Just say yes."

"Yes."

"You never watered it. It won't last forever."

"Of course we're aging. You have a different kind of beauty now than when I married you."

"God, he thinks there are different kinds," she said with dry, almost jolly mockery. "No real husband thinks that. He doesn't see different kinds. He doesn't see at all. He takes what's there and uses it up. You try to preserve people like cut flowers. Pouring water on them."

"Yes," he said. He stretched and yawned. "I've never talked to you —never since I met you—when you haven't extended or cleared my vision."

"Said the dean."

"You can't believe that I'm content with my life, that I have not only my family and my work but an increasing sense that the way things have worked out was how they should have worked out. If I've taken so little from you, why is it that I have so much?"

"Said the vulture. Not everyone brags about thriving on a diet of leftovers. I'm going to New York and have larks' tongues."

"Go," he said cheerfully, with an indulgence suitable for a restless daughter.

She's missing the scent of Carole in my life, he thought despairingly. Like a hunting animal bewildered in a jungle suddenly odorless, she would range far and wide at a gallop, scourging her other senses in an effort to regain the precious, hateful track she had lost.

Not that Carole Mooney—"The First Lady of Wellford," as

George Hand cornily, sincerely called her—was so hard to keep track of. *That* Carole was around, doing a pretty good job with her corny First Lady role.

The Mooneys went to Europe for the summer after their marriage. Mrs. Mooney returned to report that the Louvre was "great." The view of Florence from Fiesole was "fine." She looked tired from her travels, but her well-wishers remarked that she had lost weight. They took that as a good sign. In Buchanan now she had nothing but well-wishers. People who had disliked Mooney with or without reason could sincerely say that they liked "the Mooneys." If Mooney had married the woman for a very special, timely reason, it turned out there were many good reasons for the marriage visible in retrospect.

They sold Deirdre's house in town that fall. But rather than take up a settled residence in the presidential mansion on the campus, they bought a big old house on the river bluffs about twenty miles south of town. This, the Widmark house, had been a showplace in the nineteenth century, one of the great houses put up by Civil War profiteers of the state. While it had never been allowed to deteriorate completely, the newlywed Mooneys set out to make it a real pleasure dome. Their new life was going to be gay—as innocent Buchanan used the word.

Their remodeled house (Royce understood at second hand, preferring to limit his contacts with the Mooneys to necessary collegiate functions) would be a kind of cross between Grossinger's and Berchtesgaden. The Mooneys would live there most of the year among flowers and antiques, enjoying the privacies of wealthy eccentrics in semiretirement. *Eccentrics*—because the pose and the way of life they passed into immediately on their return from Europe gave it to be understood that Mooney *never had* tried to present himself as the merely garden variety of college president. He was a rare bird. The new image of playboy–country squire had the merit of evolving smoothly from earlier suspicions that he was queer while dropping the pejorative associations. Not queer, you know. Not even odd. But a very individual sort of individual . . .

Let it seem, as it seemed to most of Buchanan, that Mooney had after all used his presidency as a steppingstone to marrying money. (Far better than letting it seem he had married money to escape tar and feathering.) He had sought and found a way of life that not every Tom, Dick, or Harry could have conceived. At the Mooneys' chosen distance from Buchanan they could be caught in definitive glimpses—of Carole bonneted and prim out in the formal gardens they were restoring from old plans, of Mooney as the amateur yachtsman of inland waters, wearing a white cap of the Abercrombie and Fitch navy over his increasingly round, pink face, piloting his new launch up and down the river from their boathouse.

Let it seem, too, that it was a good thing for Carole to remain a certain distance from the University. For, while the older generation might recall that she had always been rather "awkward with people" and not really adept as a hostess, the younger knew that she drank too much. (Far better this interpretation than to let even herself guess the secret ministry she was performing on her new husband. The times when she could have suggested to Father London that she would marry Mooney to get him out of the road were all but forgotten in her new enthusiasms. She had forgotten her original motive, and that was good.)

They were half removed from their former lives. Yet, from the time they established their exurban domicile, a wish contradictory to exile was evident. They prepared the house for waves of company. They would keep horses and dogs. There were to be, on adjacent grounds, shooting blinds for duck-hunters. (What better place to get an endowment from Philistine industrialists than in the deathly chill of a duck blind, sharing a pint of bourbon on a November morning? Presently Mooney was reputed to have taken fifteen thousand from a St. Louis blood-sport enthusiast one morning there.) There was a new garage to house two station wagons and a jeep, besides Mooney's aging Rolls-Royce.

Alongside the old house they built a very modern swimming pool, enclosed by a high wall. The pool was heated from the main heating system of the estate and could be used in all but the coldest weather.

The house itself was furnished as a luxury hotel. For Mooney, in his narrow-gauge clairvoyance, had come to the truth that the social possibilities of the academic life had never yet, in this country, been fully exploited. Carole's money—which never forgot its motive in respect to Winfred Mooney—kept teaching him how he could rise above the Wellford presidency—like a funny, jewely-eyed sparrow mounting upward from the back of a stuffed eagle.

Carole, then, by no means dropped out of the Morgans' view after her marriage. It was rather that Priss had no real appetite for comedy. She had lost the scent of tragedy here in Buchanan, and was ranging elsewhere.

In 1954 she spent three months in the East. First she had taken the boys with her for the holidays at her father's while Royce traveled west and south for two conventions, scouting for faculty. Then she sent the boys back to Chicago by plane in time for Royce to pick them up there and get them to school when it resumed.

"She's on one of her kicks," Lot said.

"She'll have some shopping to do. She's spent so much time with you these last two weeks."

"Yes, she did. We had fun," Lot said. "It isn't just that."

"You mean she was unhappy?" Lot was thirteen now. There were not many family secrets that could be kept from him. Only there was no adequate common vocabulary for sharing them, and discussion with him veered quickly into opacity.

"She was happy enough," he insisted. "She's on one of her *kicks.*"

"Well, don't frown about it. She'll be home when she's ready to come. We'll miss her, but I suppose we can get along."

"We'll get along," Lot said reassuringly. Sherman felt no need to comment or even to register his mother's absence. He was a wonderfully self-sufficient boy; all he needed was the day to be alive in. He loved Buchanan. He fitted into it as his father had once hoped that Lot might—which was gratifying and dismaying at the same time, since where in this formula of anticipation and fulfillment was Lot's place? *Outside.* Outside of all the relationships that appeared to be his natural due, excluded but not relieved of responsibility, as if somehow he contrived to be responsible for every one of the defaulted promises in his parents' lives, in Carole's, even in the life of the legendary man on the street of Buchanan—an uncomplaining little Atlas carrying the immense globe of what had failed to be.

If you asked him about the well-being of anyone at all, he would automatically affirm that they were happy—just as it was his habit to insist that *he* was happy—but in his affirmation he was, of course, dismissing the matter of happiness as unimportant. As if he had been commissioned to a constant guard against something potentially worse than unhappiness.

Yes, his shrewd eyes had seen that his mother was happier than she mostly was at home. He probably understood as well as anyone what she had stayed in New York to find.

"A way to bear it," she said in a letter to Royce. That was what she was looking for. She left it to him to discern the unnamed thing she had to bear.

"I'm not so much asking for your approval," she wrote. "I'm not really asking for 'freedom,' which is both too much and too little to ask a dear husband to give you. I'm trying to start—something—my life?—over again lower down. On a lower scale so it won't top out so prematurely. (*Top out.* Isn't that an expression you corn-growers use in Buchanan County? Or is it something that lumbermen adopted from the analogy of Priss London's life?) As you used to say, all you really needed was to be born again."

Had Royce ever said that? Not in his own person, as far as he could recall. He supposed that Priss had been giving him lines in her incessant, silent dialogue for years. Which was to suppose that, in her absence, Priss had about as much of him on her hands as she had ever had in his presence.

Her letter failed to specify in what line she was trying to start lower down. It sounded a little as if she meant to open a settlement house, defy the police in Ban the Bomb demonstrations, or take nurse's training.

"You need not worry that I'm doing anything to compromise the family position or honor. . . ."

As if he would conceivably worry about that. He was never tempted to wonder which things came first in his life. If he had only had a way to *put* first things first . . . Well, he had his heart, and there—nowhere else—the order stayed perfect as a crack battalion on parade. Around him, values scattered like rabbits in panic.

"And anyway, I'll be home soon."

In February she wrote more flippantly. "Am entrepreneuring now. You may remember Tom LeCoeur, who used to be in the Art Department. He has now given up All for the Village Life and is a painter more boring than most. But a couple of his friends, both Midwestern, poor dears, are Promising. Have been giving them a mad whirl on E. Tenth St. and uptown. Father's friends have helped while I made them Careers. All phony (careers) but they are not. And human manipulation is my unquestioned forte. Home soon. Glad to hear the boys are doing so well. (I'm not glad. I resent it deeply. How dare they prosper without me?) I love you but can't bear it."

Then there was a series of increasingly cheerful notes climaxed by her homecoming in March. She arrived in a state of depression more bitter than Royce had ever seen in her, not so much outwardly haggard as inwardly exhausted. "I've tried everything in this last month," she announced to Royce in their cozy, late-at-night privacy, drinking with him in his study, the door locked, the children warranted to be asleep upstairs. "I'm not a Lesbian either."

"I could have told you that."

"And cheated me of two weeks of experience. Uh uh. Experience must have *some* value. No?"

"The learned fathers disagree."

This reminded her of something else. "Renata said I must become a Catholic. It was an absurd discussion. Her knee pumping into me while she argued how much good it had done her. They're so absurd."

Royce saw the plump white ends of his fingers tremble in the lamplight reflected from a walnut table top. They looked like an inverted plumage ruffled by a wind he could not feel. If she was preparing to shock him by some detail of her experience, it was no use. Only his fingers would tremble.

"It appears you've priced yourself beyond salvation's means," he said genially.

"You've spoiled me for easier games," she said. "The Mooneys, how are they?"

"Well, I believe. I try not to observe too closely."

"You and Winfred can really work together?"

He shrugged. "It appears so. The appearance will do."

Now she was studying some occult proposition. Enjoying him as the ultimate confidant, hating him that they could not have a more innocent relationship. "It's so weird that we have to act out what *should* be happening to *them*," she said. "Who're the victims on this merry-go-round?"

"Were you trying to act out what should have happened to them? In New York?"

"I was . . . trying to be your wife," she said strangely. "I'm not the only one who's priced himself out of reach of salvation. You've got yourself into a very odd predicament, old boy. Why didn't you come after me?"

"To New York?"

"Where else? To hell? I was doing my very best to be Eurydice, to see if I could tempt you. You didn't move."

Uneasily he said, "If I'd come . . . what? We'd have had this talk —word for word we've said this evening—in some hotel there. What advantage?"

"Just to see you scamper," she said weakly, spitefully.

After a while he said, "I might have come. Don't suppose I didn't think of it. I tried to break the code of every letter you wrote. But then . . . But then, as you may recall, I've never been quite at ease for taking you *away* from New York in the first place. For asking you to give me children you didn't entirely want."

"So you tried—try—to buy me off by letting me do what I want!"

"I mean to pay my debts when I can. You may be right. 'I owe a cock to Asclepius.'"

"Your father read that to you from a goddamned book," she wailed. "Oh, you goddamned imitation Socrateses! You don't have any cocks of your own. You keep giving them to someone else and saying, 'Here, take my cock and use it for me.' That's what you did with Mooney when you handed over the college. And when you handed over Carole."

"I . . . handed her over?"

"Where is she? Oh, I know you tried to persuade her not to, but you wouldn't . . ."

"There's nothing in this world I would do 'at all costs.' "

". . . offer to leave me and run off with her when you could have."

"No," he said carefully. "Of course I wouldn't have done that."

"You just couldn't want any woman at all costs, or the College either," she said. "So now, after all these years you're nothing, nothing, nothing. Not quite that, I didn't mean that, Royce. You're good and your back is strong so they'll go on using you. But still you're nothing because you might have been so much more."

"I'm nothing at the College," he said.

"So you're not the father to your boys you meant to be. You meant at least to give them what your father gave you."

"Yes. I'm not."

"You lost *us,* Carole and me, because you wouldn't face the cost of admitting what we are."

"I don't understand."

She laughed richly. "You don't understand that we're women. That we like to be pinched and kicked and humiliated. It lets us know we're women."

"Women, yes. But you're more complex than that."

"We're educated? Don't you understand that you can't educate women? You can't, that's just your silly job. They'll fight you with everything they have. Lies. Pretenses. Flattery to blind you. You thought all along you were educating me, with your goddamn patience and your wit and your tolerance. You'd let me lie around with a gang of Lesbians, wouldn't you? You mustn't be that tolerant, Royce. You can only kill women that way. The way your father killed your mother so he could have his beautiful sexless relationship with Deirdre Prentice that cut off his son's cock eventually and wasn't so beautiful either when it killed her of cancer. . . ."

He meant to say that it had taken a long, long time to kill Deirdre.

But suddenly he was trembling all over, too uncertain to make any reply at all. He heard—not the screech of a neurotic woman who happened to be his wife—but the pure tongue of a maenad, far more ancient than either of them.

"Go on," he said.

"You could only have saved Carole at the price of admitting what she is."

"I knew she was a woman."

"Filth, in the Morgan view. The 'unclean vessel,' as you sometimes say, laughing but not really laughing. You mean it and won't admit it, so you try to educate the dirt out of them. You can't admit that you didn't wrong Carole when you took her maidenhead. She said, 'I'm bleeding,' and God help you, you poor fool, you thought you had to atone for that. Women know they're supposed to bleed. That's why they're made the way they are. To bleed."

"Go on."

"*You* go on. Tell me how you tried to persuade Carole not to marry Mooney."

"I . . . told her what I knew about him."

"I know you screwed her. Why are you lying to me now? You're afraid to get down in the dirt with me and face me the way a man has to face a woman."

Now he leaned forward heavily, like a man bracing himself to lift a load that can be managed only by the coordination of all his muscles. "You're quite wrong," he said. "I'm afraid this is only your sick fantasy."

She smiled from white lips, straining as hard as he. "You think I'm trying to trap you? You couldn't be more wrong."

"I think . . . I think you're trying to find a justification for leaving me."

"Well, now . . . Well, it's finally been said."

"And I'm going to keep you."

"At all costs?"

"I don't know what they are yet."

"Evasion," she scoffed.

266

"Not as far as I can see. There's only one way in which I claim to be different from . . ."

"From whom? Say it for once."

"From you. From Mooney. From Carole."

"From all the people you never trusted to make sense out of their lives if they didn't listen to you."

"Maybe. The difference I meant is that I can wait for what I want."

"You can wait until you've turned to stone. God, it's too much to be in love with a statue. I might as well have married that portrait of your father."

"Wait with me," Royce said.

"I stuck around to see if the knight would save the princess. I don't have all the time you do. I'm being called."

"You have a family here. They're calling you."

"Isn't it funny I can hardly hear them any more?"

They quarreled then, argued, fought over matters too perilous for argument. But there was no decision. In the following weeks they said many things that left no margin for accommodation. But since this was talk, was there not reason to suppose it would wear itself out in talk?

Again Royce was aware of the queer enigma—that his whole family and himself were apparently happy. Morning to night they found things to do with gusto and a flair for doing them. They went all together to the circus one Saturday. Priss took the boys mushrooming. With Royce she visited faculty friends. The two of them appeared at Wellford's Spring Prom. "Your good looks and my new clothes," Royce quoted when the students were noticeably admiring.

At this *low* level their lives were affluent indeed. But in reality . . . Still, which of the contradictory truths about them was the real?

It would be Lot who was, in his characteristically oblique style, decisive for them. One night early in May while the rest of them were still at dinner, he stole the family car and disappeared.

They heard the motor start and Royce saw its blue top gliding past the dining room windows before it came to him that it was their car and should not have been moving at all. He got to the porch too late to see who was driving it, but Lot was missing—no calls upstairs or around the stable or in the neighboring lawns drew a response from him, and after a while it seemed all too certain that he was in the car.

Alone? Since it was Lot, they must conclude he was alone.

But could he drive the car at all? As far as Royce knew, the boy had never even attempted to put it in motion before. Of course he had watched all these years while his father operated it. Getting it started was no great task.

Driving it was something else. But was, unfortunately, just predictably enough within his capacity to make a major collision thinkable.

Yes, there was danger, and something had to be done about it, some all-important and low-level search to bring him back alive. But, besides that, there was the meaning of this flight. Royce and Priss searched each other's faces in a wild surmise of guilt. All their quarrels, all the trouble between them had been hidden from the boy. Nothing real was hidden.

"I'm going to call the police," Royce said.

"It isn't fair to him," Priss insisted. "We'll go look for him. I'll get the McClintocks' car."

"Look where?" Perhaps the most alarming thing to Royce was that even Sherman was worried. Sherman was accustomed to absolute faith in his brother's word and ability. Now he was staring wide-eyed, demanding a miracle from his parents.

"Out by the river," he suggested. "In the grove where he takes his pellet gun sometimes."

"He might go there to think," Priss agreed. She went hurrying across the lawn to borrow the neighbors' car. While she was gone, Royce called the police.

"Thirteen?" the desk sergeant said. "The kid's going to be in lots of trouble. There's not only operating without a license, there's . . ."

"Bring him in," Royce said.

Of course he and Priss were reminded of the day Lot had soiled himself in the first grade. Of course they could take no comfort whatsoever in remembering how their panic before had ended relatively well. Problems go on and on, but circumstances never repeat.

They did not find him in the grove to which Sherman directed them. When they came back to the house he had not returned.

"Do you want to . . . ?" Royce began.

"Call Carole's? Yes. I'll call," Priss said. Royce watched her face begin to blaze with fury and frustration as the conversation went on between the women.

"Now she's going out on the road to look," Priss groaned when she hung up. She would not have minded the call to Carole if it had really produced news of Lot. It was too much that Carole should be told of it to no purpose.

She bullied Royce into the neighbors' car and they drove again for an hour—down through town and back, to the cloverleaf approach on the new highway to Chicago, to the city park where the circus had been. At least the driving seemed to calm Priss. Finally, when Royce said, "We're doing no good, going around in such circles," she agreed to go home and wait for a call from the police.

That is, she permitted him to turn the car in that direction. Her seething, her anxiety—and beyond that all the overinterpretation of Lot's *meaning* in giving them this fright—were settling inwardly. It almost seemed to cease to matter to her whether they really found the boy safe or not. She was disengaging from the day-to-day reality where physical safety and happiness counted.

Only three blocks from their house, as they swung toward it again, they saw the red top light of a police car near the curb. Then, ahead of the police car, they saw their own machine with no one in it.

Lot was sitting in the rear seat of the police car. A moon-faced policeman was lecturing him. "Now you've caused your dad a lot of trouble and you're lucky, oh, you're lucky that we caught you before you ran into someone and someone might have been killed. Now tomorrow you and your dad will have to come down to the court. . . ."

Lot's head hung from shoulders that all at once seemed too frail for his thirteen years. His face, under the domelight, was utterly expressionless. Without looking at his father and mother, maybe without knowing yet that they had run up, he said, "I almost made it home."

That was where he had been heading when he ran away. Yes, of course. No need to explain further to either of his parents, since each knew the pattern so well. But here was another of them who had not made it.

"But he would have made it," Priss said, later that night when the boys were in their room. "It was you who called the police."

It was he, too, who had denied her certainty when she asked about his persuasion of Carole. She had known the truth, had nothing to pin it to. A scruple of caution, *the* scruple which now they saw as a constant in his life, had forbidden him to risk the confirmation his wife demanded. In the moment when he had to decide to lie or not he had been afraid she would use the truth to break from him while it was still his duty to hold her. So he had refused her certainty. And . . . "you can't do that to a woman, Royce." It was not her voice now that told him this. Eye to eye with her, he saw it. By blocking her flight he had blocked her way home.

"He'd have made it if I'd had the courage not to call them," he said, his voice carrying no inflection of the grief that was in the circumstance itself. "It's awfully hard for me to be brave with someone else's blood."

"Can't you learn from this?"

"No. No. Of course not. Next time . . ."

"Next time it might be different? Real blood? Next time the police would save him from breaking his neck? You'd be wrong even if he did."

"I can't change my bet now. I always will have to do what I did tonight."

"Then . . ."

"We're both right. So you'd better get away from me."

"Yep."

She went back to New York alone again that summer. She met some people who were in politics and some others who raced small yachts to Bermuda, and, according to her letters, was briefly passionate about both occupations.

After this departure she came back to Buchanan only for short visits and for her divorce.

17

"I LIE all the time," Lot said complacently. His tennis sneakers were set squarely two feet apart on the gleaming paint of the porch floor as he stirred the glider back and forth and manipulated the handle of his racket like the control stick of a primitive airplane.

Royce said, "I'm not sure whether that's a boast or a confession. And given the inherent logical paradox, I'm not sure, even, that I'm intended to believe it."

"A mere statement of fact. Dutifully reported. I lie a great deal of the time. That better?"

"I suspect I'm being baited. If I hand down a ruling on the morality of lies, what will you do with it?"

The game between them was very old, very familiar. There had been a simpler variant of it when Lot was quite young. Now that he was seventeen his eyes glittered with much the same excitement, and his face set in the same repose that his father had observed on such sparring occasions ten years before.

"I'd add it to what I already know of your character."

"Of course," Royce said. "Therefore I suppose I would do well to keep my opinion to myself, assume you're trying to confess, and await details."

"It would be comfortable to say I got my lying tendency from Mother."

"But highly disrespectful."

"Oh, yes. That's why—another reason—why I'd never actually say such a thing. I think I finally have Mother's character perfectly figured out. Wait . . ."

With a cricket leap, vaulting on his racket, he whisked from the porch where he had found his father reading. Elbows and ankles swirled behind him through the door like tag ends of rope from an awkwardly tied package, and Royce heard the crimp of rubber soles on the wax of the stairway inside.

Well, he reflected, Lot had recently been given a significant closeup of his mother's characteristic stance in life, a situation which, at her age, *might* arguably be taken as summative. He had visited her for a week in Easthampton, where she was living with a man twelve years younger than herself, who wrote upstairs while she wrote downstairs. He wrote plays. She continued with her novel "about Buchanan," which in these years was getting poetically shorter after having been prosaically longer. Lot reported that she was wearing her hair in a "very severe style" and that the pair of them had become expert trapshooters. He conveyed, without actually describing it, a domestic scene in which Priss was simultaneously mother, sister, and mistress to the young man, a triple function in which she was "happy enough"—assuming that that mattered. At any rate, and for the time being, she had discovered another way to "bear it."

"Here," Lot said, landing like a pelican in the glider he had just vacated. From his room he had brought a translation of the *Duino Elegies*. "Can I read you?" And he read, with just enough of a scraping tremble in his young voice to make it clear how true he thought his discovery: " 'Angel, if there were a place we don't know, and there on some ineffable carpet, the lovers who never quite bring off their feats here, could show their bold lofty figures of heart swings, their towers of ecstasy . . .' "

"That seems to explain everything."

Lot pondered a minute, just a little deflated. "You're back on your line that explanations never do any good."

"Heavens!" Had he said that to the boy? Had Lot gleaned that most demoralizing of educational platitudes from the abundant talk of the last few years, talk which Royce believed neutral in its balance between optimism and despair? This neutrality was his truth, though if Priss had needed to see it as castration—had got some good from choosing the other term—then that was her truth and she was welcome to it. He could not issue as open a welcome to Lot to construe this neutrality as cynicism. "At the very least," he said, "I do believe that explanations—poetry, this poetry of yours, science, even magic if you want to throw that in—are good in themselves even if they do no good. The truth about anything at all is aesthetically satisfying. . . ." But his voice was as theatrical as the sentiment itself, artfully pedantic, throaty, *deanish*—and he wondered if his life's work had not, after all, transformed him subtly so his thoughts must always come tainted or sapped with artifice. He knew he was counting on some meaningless advantage of age or simple showmanship, academic variety, here to make his meaning prevail. Was it thus that what should have been authoritative became, however mild its tone, authoritarian? He only knew that if this alteration were taking place, or had taken place, he was powerless to prevent it.

"I suppose I lie because explanations don't do any good. About Mother, I only mean it's hard to figure out what I *got* from her and what I've learned by watching her over the years. I think she's aesthetically satisfying . . ."

"Ah, yes." But now Royce's mind repaired the sin of its academic cheerfulness by recalling those explanations—of Tommy Barker, Billy Cox, Winfred Mooney, and Carole—which had been by no means fit to decorate a hypothetical urn, which could only have been accommodated by a moral system in which unredeemable ugliness might be compensated for.

". . . and does give me the feeling that in the right world she'd be just right, like Rilke's acrobats."

What was due such an explanation? Fatherly and again academic pride in a son who grasped the poem so familiarly? Fatherly anxiety that the grasp of such a thought might justify lying, which, however poetically undertaken, might lead on to the worst practical consequences? Man-to-man gratitude for the confirmation of a delicate discrimination on which he had based his moral decision to let Priss go?

"I'm not trying to, you know, say that my lies are *all right*— I'm not asking you to judge them either, Dad, don't be scared.

They're not even a pale imitation of what I think her kick is. It's a nasty adolescent habit with me, and it's fun. It's necessary with some people. Marya, for instance."

The persistent romance through Lot's prep school days had been with a Buchanan girl so stunningly unattractive that even Sherman —who neither questioned nor imitated what his brother did ordinarily—had raised a question of propriety. He had forced an agreement from their father. Marya Stohlcroft was a pig. Sherman took it as an affront to the family that Lot went on courting her.

Marya was a tall, dun girl with a knifelike nose and hair like hemp. She was less attractive at seventeen than she had been at fourteen when Lot first began to appear with her in tow. She was barrel-chested without noticeable breasts, and the skin above her bobby sox always looked rough as coarse sandpaper. Her unappealing exterior was coupled with a monster's vanity.

She read everything she could lay her hands on about the aids to feminine beauty. She tried the tricks and talked about them as if they weren't, with her, conspicuous failures. And this lack of appropriate humility seemed rather to delight Lot than to appall him.

Her awful hair was set once a week at the beauty parlor, though her parents could hardly afford the luxury. She was odorless as stone, and the most discreet eye shadow set off her glassy, fault-finding eyes, even early on those mornings when she stopped by the Morgan house to fetch Lot for tennis. She had been heard to say that while she supposed it was unhealthy and *all that,* she "thought about love all the time."

Long ago Royce had concluded that Lot cultivated this girl for the same reasons that, since puberty, he had dressed with calculated drabness. He never shined his shoes nor permitted them to be shined. In winter his nearly invariable costume was a blazer, unpressed black slacks, and gray-brown shoes. In summer he went without the blazer and wore suntan pants. Back and forth to prep school he carried a trunk full of good clothes. Royce knew they were seldom worn. Marya was part of his costume.

"Dad," Sherman had reported once, "do you know what I heard that jerk say in the kitchen? She asked Lot if he was 'hungaberry.'

Really. She was hanging on the refrigerator door and she said, 'Are you hungaberry? I am.' "

Plainly a pig, and it was hard to be precisely sure why Lot considered her a person worth lying to. But during this present summer his friendship with her had been intensified. Lot was, as well as a reader of Rilke, a frenzied jazz drummer. Almost as soon as he came home from school this year he had gotten a job playing with a small combo that operated through the center of the state. Either he took Marya with him when they played jobs in Rock Island, Peoria, or Springfield, or she was apt to follow after him in the old Chevy convertible that she and a girl friend owned.

Maybe Lot encouraged this attendance because he was much the youngest of the musicians in the band. He was also the most alienated and sophisticated of the bunch. Of course he wanted to keep it that way. With Marya sitting all by herself at a table near the bandstand—and it was unthinkable that she would pick up friends or make friends with the rest of the band (two of them were colored and she was relentlessly suspicious of Negroes)—he had an excuse for avoiding the camaraderie of the other musicians. It was a wholesome, fatherly thought to suppose that light social drinking with Marya might also be an excuse for avoiding sessions when he would be expected to smoke pot, but Royce knew his son too well to suppose Lot needed an excuse for using it or not using it. That was an area of decision that the boy would reserve exclusively for himself, since no one else could be hurt by his choice.

The lies on which Lot had recently been feeding his hideous consort appeared to be mostly about the other musicians and the "syndicate" that controlled a lot of the joints in which they played. Without any real merriment he explained, "She thinks Stanislas has a white wife here in Buchanan." Stanislas was the piano-player, a vast coffee-colored man who had been Lot's connection in getting his summer job. "She's dying to find out who it is, because she also thinks it's someone of some prominence who passes for a widow."

Why should Marya have been given this misinformation? (In literal truth Stanislas was not only monogamous but something of

276

a moral fanatic and an object of some derision to the band for his easygoing chastity.) Because it probed at her infamous prejudices against inferior races—not that the lie was intended to be educational or could conceivably bring her around to a more enlightened view, but merely because it would get her excited, would cause a kind of musical jangle and discord in her personality. It was a form of "putting her on"—a pastime that was its own reward.

For about the same ineffable reasons Marya had been led to believe that the joints in which she sat frequently waiting for Lot to be through were well-disciplined whorehouses policed by syndicate men whose eyes never left her while she sipped her Cokes.

"The other night we were in Barker's place, over in Peoria . . ."

"Wait," Royce said. "Tommy Barker?"

"Wellford's pride," Lot confirmed. "And he still has that ghastly picture of himself up on the wall by the bar, with spotlights. He came over to our table and was doing some putting on himself. About how he happened to get made the scapegoat, though everyone believes he actually took money to throw the big game."

"He knew who you were?"

"Well, sure. Why else would he bother, really? Embarrassed?"

No. Royce was not. Neither personally nor officially. The decision to let Lot go with the band this summer had not been made without foresight of the possible inadvertencies that might arise. As once before, would call the police if Lot seemed to be in real trouble. Otherwise the boy had been given a free rein.

"I suppose he'd talked to Alex"—the bandleader—"or someone. Anyway, yes, he did know who I was. And yes, I suppose he expected me to pass along his complaint."

"It's possible you shouldn't."

"You don't want to know?"

"I'm . . . not sure I want to hear it from you."

"Yeah. Well, it doesn't seem like anything that would have to be acted on. *My* lies aren't. Well, the gist of his story is that he knew something on Mooney, something that had happened in New York while they were in there for the tournament. For which, to keep him quiet about, I mean, Herr Mooney framed him with the gamblers. Did he?"

"No. Tommy took the bribe. Out of his own simple sense of right and wrong, he took it."

"But the other?"

"Did he say what the other was?"

"I got the gist. I don't believe that Marya did. Even when friend Barker began hinting at what goes on now out at the Mooneys', among what he calls the 'longhairs' they entertain. You know Marya thinks about love all the time. She thought he meant *girls*."

Royce had to smile a little. His son so wise, and still confounding shrewd insight with knowledge, still imagining that because he had seen the outer limits of the truth of human possibility, he knew all the deviousness of sin and responsibility. "Scandalous *enough* for our Marya," Royce said. "My faith in you suggests you didn't enlighten her further."

"You're the educator in the family. I encouraged her to believe it was girls because she did better with that possibility. All the way home she was fantasizing how we'd use our knowledge to get Mooney out of the way and make you president."

Royce began to laugh—not a very pretty laugh—at the image of the two kids whisking through a summer night with the top down on Marya's convertible, parodying a scene from his own memory, repeating like some ridiculous destiny the vain scheme that had once made life tolerable for Priss. Priss would not like the imitation. For her sake, truly, he was grateful she was out of this tiresomely turning cycle.

"Of course," Lot said, "I made it clear to our sweetheart that becoming president wasn't your game, what with your already being the head of the Syndicate here in the Midwest, and that you'd always found it to your advantage to sort of play behind the scenes."

"Thank you for defending my image with your friends."

"End result: it's got Marya all hot to go out there sometime to the Mooneys' and see all this sinning with her own eyes. I promised I'd take her. I like to make her feel like a big shot. Do you think I could arrange it with Carole?"

"You haven't seen much of Carole for a while."

"What's between us is eternal."

A matter for laughter, if one had the heart: In these days it was evident to Royce from his point of observation that the sheer mysterious grind of time was going to accomplish what neither lovely Priss nor awful Marya after her could accomplish by their schemes. Untoppled, Mooney was fading out of the Wellford picture.

It is well-nigh intolerable for anyone—and women in particular—to believe that alternations of power "just happen." "Something has to be done," we say. Of course, in truth, something always is being done, and what leads on to the ends we dread or desire is not often what we expected to be effective.

It was Mooney's last success, in an unbroken line of successes, that faded him out of Royce's way. The final phase of the dream he had brought with him from the old days in New York was to provide a base for a kind of academic Smart Set.

In the time of his greatest enthusiasm for Wellford, he had often spoken of "an institute for advanced studies" as the true mark of class distinction among American universities—and someday Wellford could advertise one, he hoped. But he must have realized this would not be in his time, so he had contrived a substitute, made possible by Carole's money and their new estate in the country.

Leaving the routine of the College more and more to Royce, he devoted himself to what was by now a whole group of yearly conferences—the formal cover for a national freemasonry of intellectual *bon vivants,* boozers, malcontents, black sheep, utopians, cranks, and academicians otherwise in advance of their time.

In 1954 he initiated at Wellford (more exactly, at his and Carole's estate down the river) the Underdeveloped Countries Parley. For its initiation he wheedled a fat grant from a foundation and thereafter dispensed what it could buy each year with the lavish hand of a professional host.

Delegates came to this largest of his conferences from all over Central America, England, San Francisco, and New York. The first year there were one hundred and twelve of them. Later, even more.

Two-thirds of the visitors were housed in campus dormitories and with the more sporting element of the faculty. The rest stayed with the night and day festivities at the Mooney estate.

After conference sessions in Wellford Chapel and the new Bing Auditorium (Bing Glass and Aluminum of Alton) or panel discussions in the basement rooms of the Student Union, the delegates and the *jeunesse dorée* of the faculty drank foundation booze at the Mooneys' and swam in the heated outdoor pool until the small hours of the morning. There was a constant motorcade hauling the participants between the campus and their busy playground.

From its first convocation onward, the Parley was one of Mooney's greater successes with the local newspaper and with the student body in general. Students were excused from classes for the weeks of the festivities. From the talks by distinguished free-loaders of various nationalities they were made pleasantly to feel that "something should be done" about the underdeveloped countries of the world.

There was no doubt at all that the delegates appreciated the frolic and anticipated their invitations to come back the next year. Some enjoyed it so much they stayed on with the Mooneys from fall until midwinter, and in 1957 it was said that two Latin-Americans were still there in the spring when the time came around for the Living Arts Conference which Mooney sponsored with the assistance of another foundation. Dancers, musicians, painters, sculptors, and writers made up the Bacchic troop assembled for this rite of Wellford's academic spring.

And in such hubbub Mooney, at least, of the actors in this story, went beyond Lot's haunting formula for the rest. The others might be "happy enough." Mooney was very happy. Year by year his jeweled eyes got more dazzling, the sign of some inner harmony beyond any practical accounting. He was relaxing in his life as in a hammock. Things had worked out for him. Always. Without fail. Only one thing seemed still to be a token of his bondage to the pact that had brought him success. That was his bleached hair.

A story had come back to Wellford through Friedlander of Political Science. On a grant in Japan during the summer of 1957, the Friedlanders had gone one summer day to a big-league ball game.

They were surprised to see a few rows in front of them the president of Wellford and his wife. With the disadvantage of looking at them from behind, neither of the Friedlanders had been able to make a certain identification for a while—and this was because the man beside Mrs. Mooney had crew-cut hair. The hair was a dark roan shade, somehow cinderish and coarse and not at all consistent with the presidential features they remembered.

Of course the natural hair was not much of a disguise and pretty soon Mrs. Friedlander said of course they must speak to the Mooneys.

Professor Friedlander weighed the proprieties carefully. "No," he said. "I think . . . I'm sure it wouldn't be appreciated."

And no doubt he was right, for when the Mooneys came back from their round-the-world jaunt of that summer, once again the elegant white pompadour waved above the pink face and happy eyes.

No one of the inner circles at Wellford who heard Friedlander's odd report made much of it. There was no need to. By this time the general attitude toward Mooney was gratitude for what he had done for Wellford, matched by a gratitude for fading out of the way now that it was done.

Discerning it on every hand around him, respecting the temper of judgment on which it was based—the Wellford community could not well be accused of stupidity or shallowness, though it might go on forever innocent of certain facts while it formed its consensus—Royce would not refuse to accept this attitude for his own.

He had let the Billy Cox matter drop back into limbo without pressing it to a consequence. Here also the reasons why he should have let it rest were becoming clearer in after years than at the time the action—or the default of an action he might have taken—was chosen. Still, from that sordidness a few sparks might flare up from time to time. Witness Lot's chance encounter with Tommy Barker in Peoria. No matter any more. Every new glow would drift away on the fortunate wind that kept bringing them their even annual rainfall of prosperity.

Silly little witches like Marya Stohlcroft might believe that sin was the chief attraction for the delegates at the Mooney estate. Against such adolescent fantasy—and one must reckon with how much Marya *hoped* to feel like a big shot by discovering wickedness —one could set the tiresome, reassuring, and mature conviction that Mooney was too slothful in his happiness to risk it any more.

Yes, why not be grateful to Mooney? He was not the first nor the last among human leaders to strike benefits from the rock of men's shabbier motives. Personally lucky, had he not also been lucky for Wellford? There must be many people around—men of dependable judgment, too—who felt about Mooney the way a trapper feels when he takes a valuable pelt from a loathsome animal.

And what was clear to Mooney's inheritors—few of them sorry to see him fading from the picture—was that the Wellford he left them was going to be in good shape. In 1954, with the addition of a School of Radio Engineering and a School of Fine and Applied Arts (the first subsidized by an Iowa firm, the second by an auto manufacturing company in Detroit, both investments secured by Mooney) the trustees had formally begun to call Wellford a university. Out of the scrambling and jockeying of the postwar years it had found its rank among the mills, greater and smaller, that would purvey the staples of education that the time and the exploding population demanded. The informed consensus held it to be a good and growing school, somewhat given to promotional high jinks, but sound in root and branch. Mooney's contributions were not, in the long run, misinterpreted. He was credited in educational circles for giving the school the base of enrollment, building, and "national visibility" that an institution needed to "keep its head above water." More tacitly, the working part of the University— faculty and students busy with their proper disciplines—were acknowledged to deserve a ranking in "the upper third" of some educationalist scale or another.

The age of small, internal empire-building had come. Dolly Dowling went on year by year consolidating the athletic empire. Basketball first, of course, but each year he put more professional teams on the gridiron and diamond. That "trim gentleman" Dr. Bojac had made a tiny empire out of the Music, Theater, and Art De-

282

partments and got them recognized as a semi-autonomous "school" within the university to boot. After a long time of living in the College doghouse with hardly a recognizable job to call his own, four-square Jeff Parker was making an empire out of the Campus Police and the parking lots they supervised. By sheer persistence, inertia, hanging on, he was managing to turn acre after acre of campus green into meticulously divided asphalt, and parking revenues were now a stabilized part of the institutional budget.

And all that could be interpreted as a positive good. George Hand thought it was. At the time of his retirement in 1955 he said to Royce, "I have the notion that Mooney has been the last true president of Wellford. The last to give any personal tone or direction to the place."

Then he added the sum of his recent observations. "He's fading as fast as I am, though in a different way. You'll have his office sooner or later."

"By merely outlasting him?" Royce laughed. It seemed, in its simplified form, a shameful way to come into his inheritance.

"By outlasting him, yes," George said, as if all along he had seen clearly how this was to come about. "We've conserved something through his time, Royce, in the grand old, true sense of conservatism. Wellford is still an educational institution in spite of the fieldhouse and a new library still scandalously short of books. We did our best, Royce, and can be proud."

"We did our best"—it was a little shocking that he should have kept that formula intact from the hour when they had faced the news of Mooney's election.

It was more shocking to observe—as Royce must—that when the old man was retired with honor, his sense of dishonor began to proclaim itself in everything but his optimistic talk. Within three weeks of leaving his job he developed ulcers—*the* ulcers, one supposed, that he had been postponing for forty-five years while he took the lean with the fat in his management. The ulcers were some indication that he was busier with self-judgment than he should have been in the little time left him.

A neighbor saved him from asphyxiation or burning himself to death in bed when he fell asleep with a lighted cigarette in his hand.

He suffered a slight stroke. His speech got ugly.

He fell on the ice while carrying groceries home. In his proneness to accident the turmoil of dissatisfaction he had hidden well so long was almost indecently exposed. It was a bad sign, like Mooney's crew-cut roan hair. Like that accidental exposure in a Japanese ball park, it meant nothing that practical prophets could seize on.

Anyway, at worst, George could still say to Royce, "There's always and always the groundswell of young people coming on. If we've failed to complete our task, they'll finish it for us. This week I hobbled past the art building. I saw some pretty girls painting the cherry trees. I stopped to sit awhile and watch them. It gave me heart. Those girls still want something. They haven't quit yet."

Alas, there were hours—neither few nor so many that they had any visible effect on his temper or conduct—when Royce was forced to conclude that what those girls probably wanted was justice. Not that they would say so. How would they know what they wanted? They squeezed their lovely greens out of the tubes, and while the phantom spring teased their eyes, they matched those greens with those of the rolling campus yards. They looked like harmless enough creatures, in their beauty. But when you brought them right down to it—when in any sense of that ambiguous idiom a man mounted them like a husband and tried to match his need with that sweetness, what he found was that the bitches wanted justice.

It was like a dream, and not a good dream, either, to realize they wanted not only that their lives should be nice, be comfortable, be rich and full, but that all the luxuries should have been procured for them in ways they could admire. Rub *their* noses in the truth that Wellford's palmy days came right out of a dung heap of cupidity, hypocrisy, money perversion, perversion of ideals, and (somewhere along the crazy line) simple old sex perversion, and . . . of course they would demand blood.

Let George Hand—who "had no *expertise*" in certain matters—imagine the female was sweet and malleable and ignore the wild animal demands that lay beyond his expert manipulation and accounting. Not everyone could get off with so false a vision.

The last time Royce had talked with Priss she had shown him once again what the female demanded when she got tired of her tame arts. She had returned to the old theme, not so much adding to it as connecting it with more aspects of his life, so he would not have the illusion that he had preserved some successes pure in the general waste of his hopes.

"Royce, my adored," she said. "Before you leave me again, I want to hear you say one thing you always wouldn't give me. Say, 'I'm going to be president of Wellford.' Give me one good reason why you first took me out there."

Playfully, honestly, he tried to sum up the present trend of the University, Mooney and himself. "It appears that if I live long enough . . ."

"Not 'it appears.' 'I'm going to be.' "

"I'm going to be president of Wellford."

" 'At all costs.' "

"*Not* at all costs. I told you I'd wait. That's as far as I go."

"It will have to be at all costs. It's your university, Royce, the real thing, all but the roofs and the walls. All right, I believe you know what you're talking about when you say Mooney's drifting off to Valhalla. You'll still have to take it at all costs. Don't you *see?*"

He smiled and couldn't answer for a little while. She was not coming back to him. Yet it would have been a great kindness to them both if he could have said honestly what she wanted to hear.

"I'll have it in my own time," he said.

Then she cried, and they both understood all too well why she was crying.

She wanted justice. She knew—what woman didn't when you brought them to the full possession of their knowledge, when you *educated* them?—that justice was blood. If he had only given her Mooney's blood . . . but Carole's along with it.

Impossible. He would not. Never. Not now.

But he thought of that ugly little Marya riding through starlight in her convertible, opening her mouth to taste the wind, getting the smell of blood and justice and mixing them all up with her prejudiced notions of right and wrong.

And of Lot, riding beside the witch, hearing her say they knew something to get Mooney with. Having to decide—no man and no father to help him—whether the woman deserved it or not. Lying to her, putting her on. For how long?

The bright girls would always find out. Especially if you let them come to college. Then there would be the cry and the howling.

18

"I just don't think it's so much," Marya Stohlcroft said.

"What's not how much?" Lot wondered, frowning and grinning at her at the same time.

"I don't happen to think it's so *much,* is all. All these people pretending to be somebody. And they're not. They're really not."

Such was the end of trying to please Woman. Marya had wanted for a long while to come to one of the fabled parties at the Mooneys', when the delegates to the Living Arts Conference were letting their hair down after a hard wrestle with the dilemmas thrust on them by Mass Culture, a day full of panel discussions and lectures before Wellford students.

It had been no trick to arrange their visit with Carole. She was fuzzily delighted that he was "bringing a young lady." She had not seen him for a long time, now that he was away at school so much. She thought about him *so* often, she had said, with an emphasis that gave him uncomfortably to understand she was still identifying him as a ten-year-old, a wonderful little boy who sometimes flew with her . . . though she had not been at the controls of a plane for almost half his lifetime. "There'll be an awful crowd, but you and I will find a corner and talk. And I so want to meet your young lady friend." She might, at that, Lot had concluded coldly, supposing that Carole Mooney was the one person he had ever known who would simply not recognize Marya's piggishness. (That same piggishness was and always had been well understood by him. His father and brother had been late to grasp what he had seen full and clear before he ever asked Marya for their first Coke date. Only, his Dad and Sherman were handicapped with the view that a person ought to follow after what was pleasant in this life. He had always—insofar as he could define *always*—known better. Temperamentally he might have preferred to date a one-legged girl without a nose, but that would have been ostentatious.)

So here they were, at ten o'clock at night in Carole's house, standing awkwardly as the stumps that Marya physically resembled anyhow, amid the melodious chatter and tambourine laughter of the relaxing performers.

Carole had indeed greeted them when they came in and had effusively praised Marya's ratty hair. But she had led them to no corner for no talk about old times. Her gaze was jumping from their faces even as she brought them from the front door into her throng, as if she were wanted a dozen other places by people who might find the service unsatisfactory unless she were nimble.

That was it, Lot thought. She was the hostess, but she managed to scamper so gracelessly to everyone's beck and call that she might have been a servant anxious about her job.

At the moment that Marya completed her survey of the guests and found them not much, Carole was opening lockers built on either side of an enormous window and handing out bathing suits to a group that intended to try the pool.

"They're going *swimming*," Marya said between her teeth.

"You can go if you want to. Carole probably has your size suit."

"I will *not*!"

"I said 'suit.' You don't need to squawk so. No one suggested you swim in your pelt."

"I didn't say anyone suggested it." They'd better not. "It's only April! The ninth of April!" It was implicit in her tone that people who swam before Memorial Day were worse deviants than if they had bathed nude. Of course she could see that beyond the big window—a sort of proscenium for the rites of the Mooneys' pool—the green, floodlit water was steaming like a geyser. The four or five guests who had led the movement to the pool seemed to find the April air brisk but the water warm. Even at the range from which Lot and Marya watched, the green flash of their teeth was visible in sybaritic smiles as they splashed and hopped.

But Marya's eyes were deceiving her. She might see only some middle-aged actors, poets, musicians, faculty members, painters, and dancers having a silly and proper good time among the luxuries the Mooneys provided. But she knew—pig and witch—what carnality was afoot. How could you tell what sculptor's hands were on what poetess's bottom under the tricky surface of the water? Or what all that noisy laughter meant as more people dashed from the house in the suits that Carole provided? Maybe she was relying more on Lot's fibs about what went on here than on any visual evidence. Anyway, she knew these people were *not much* and what they were doing was not right.

The crawl of fingertips in the crook of his elbow, and Lot stiffened with a kind of shiver. "You're with Julio?" a fat voice said from behind his left shoulder. He spun around into the most expectant of smiles, a broad, round yellow face soft as a pit of quicksand. A man of dimples and twinkling eyes and hair like sheepskin, an expectant man. So, naturally, Lot intended to say that he was with Julio and find out what that meant.

But President Mooney rescued him—if that was the right term for it—by catching his other elbow almost at the same moment. One felt he might have been watching and have seen the other man approach.

"This is Lot Morgan," he said, dimpling and making *his* eyes twinkle. "He's the son of our Dean Morgan, whom I introduced you to this afternoon. Dr. Mott, with the Art Institute, you know, Lot."

"Mott and Lot," the man laughed, making the joke reverberate soddenly. He got a handkerchief from his trousers and wiped his lips.

"Pleased to meet you," Lot said. "This is Miss Stohlcroft. President Mooney. Dr. Mott."

"Carole told me you were coming." Mooney took Marya's hand and stroked it gently with both his. "I saw you come in, you young folks, but I was occupied at the moment and couldn't greet you. I'm delighted. Yes, delighted. Mott, you must have mistaken Mr. Morgan for James Beal."

"Of course. Of course I did. James dances with Julio," Mott explained to Marya, who would have been shocked by that intelligence if she were not too bewildered to sort it into any meaning at all. Lot thought she was about to curtsy and meant to kick her if she did.

A sudden avalanche of music swept the room. One of the guests had started the record player. When the volume was reduced to normal, Mott was saying, ". . . grace of youth. Of course very little resemblance at all. I've never actually met James, though I've seen him dance a time or two."

"Lot's mother was a dancer," Mooney said, and though his tone was unctuous, it was not altogether free from mockery, as if he were enjoying some nuance of this conversation imperceptible to the others. "James Beal, I believe, is in with the others swimming."

"Oh." Mott's eyes darted toward the big window.

"Why don't you join them?" Mooney asked. "Mrs. Mooney will find you a suit. The water is agreeable, though you might doubt it. Go ahead."

Mott sighed. "I shall not," he said. "There are certain pleasures which my age . . ." Nevertheless, careless and magnetized, he drifted away from them toward the window from which he might glimpse the dancer's body and the sullen, dark face of his obsession.

"Mott's mixed up with the *quattrocento*," Mooney said in a confidential tone. "I'm afraid he took rather a drubbing on the panel this afternoon when he mixed with a couple of our hotheaded abstract expressionists. Poor old fellow."

Which expression of compassion did not prevent him from watching Mott's progress closely, from narrowing his eyes and nodding when Mott prowled outside the window and lowered his bulk into a beach chair near the pool.

"You kids enjoy yourselves," Mooney said. "There's Coke on the table beside the punch bowl. Lots of good things to nibble."

He stroked Marya's beautified hand again and hurried away. He did not go directly out to the pool. They saw him pause near Carole's shoulder and ask an abrupt question, get an answer that did not quite please him.

But in a while he had stationed himself on the side of the pool opposite Mott's chair. So the two of them watched, beaming influences telepathically down into the water where a white body in black trunks sported, unaware of the homage paid it, expressionless as a seal in the North Atlantic wastes.

Presently a sculptor did pinch a poetess in the murky, steaming shadows. She screamed and flung herself almost out of the water. Then all the swimmers screamed and began to climb out.

The host was quick and extended a helping hand to James Beal as he clambered dripping up the ladder. Mr. Beal smiled at him.

"I still wish you had taken Coke," Marya said to Lot.

"In cola veritas," he said, hypocritically complimenting her for having been wiser in her preference of drinks. "You know, Marya, I always ought to do what you do, but it never seems that way."

"You're drunk and it's two o'clock."

"Not drunk and it's only one-fifteen."

"And funny things are happening here and I don't think you'll be able to take me home."

They were sitting together on the bottom step of the wide stairway of the house, one that went up from a parlor adjacent to the room with the big window. Now in this room and the other one a few couples were dancing. A few people were moving like pilgrims around the buffets and the liquor table. But mostly—and the crowd was larger now than it had been three hours before—they were relaxed in voluble groups on the furniture and the rugs. The hum of their cumulative voices suggested everyone was feeling smarter and more comfortable than ever during their public colloquies, that they were collectively on the threshold of discoveries that would change their culture

Of all this presumptively valuable talk Lot and Marya had no share at all. They might as well have been Hansel and Gretel in a witch's house where the furniture gave off a babble of human sounds.

Gretel was nervous about everything. Hansel was using the host's Scotch—he scorned the punch—to prepare himself for . . . well, for the truth that would come if he waited long enough.

"You're so smart," she sneered helplessly, "but you don't have any idea of what's going on here."

"Bores. The bores are boring each other." He gestured with his glass around the room at the crowd. "There's got to be a lot of that before we get to the real—"

"I told you what I saw in the kitchen. President Mooney had his arm around Carole Mrs. Mooney's neck, and he was just pouring this cup full of *stuff* into her mouth."

"Coffee."

"If it was coffee, where is she?"

"If it was booze, why pour it into her? She can do that herself."

"You know why."

"Marya, I've overpersuaded you. Dear heart, you think I know all. See all. And you're not far from . . . what were you doing in the kitchen?"

"Snooping," she said with a loutish little giggle, trying to win him with frankness.

"For abominations. If you want to see abominations, go to the downstairs bathroom. Someone heaved in the tub."

"Really!"

"I think it was Dr. Mott, letting go of the *quattrocento*." He looked around carefully. After his fourth drink his vision had narrowed to a long tunnel. To make out a recognizable face he had to get it squarely in the end of that tunnel. He did not see Dr. Mott. Then he looked for Mooney. He did not see Mooney either.

A couple going upstairs had to steer around him and Marya. The man, who happened to be the sculptor who had pinched the poetess in the pool, rested his hand a minute on Lot's shoulder and smiled down at him before going up the carpeted stairs. Marya watched the backs of the climbing couple.

"They're just going for their coats," Lot said disgustedly. "You have a rotten foul mind."

"Then you just better go find *our* coats and take me home."

"You said I was too drunk to drive. So take your car. Go home."

"No," she said angrily. But she got to her feet, smoothed her skirt, and, with a kind of sidling hobble, passed around the side of the room and out the door that led to the downstairs hall.

Since he was sure she was not going to the bathroom after his description, he supposed she might really be mad enough to get the car and leave him here. Well, if she did, that was fine. He would stay here through the night. Carole—the thought passed confidently through his mind though there had been no particular intimacy or even chatter between them tonight—would be gratified to have him under her roof. He would ask her for a room presently. Or if she had really passed out and was sleeping, he would find himself a room. He didn't know the house, but it was big enough, even with all their guests. Somewhere in it he would find a place to lie down. A little closet was all he needed. A little closet was all he wanted.

He was roused slightly by a yipping from the next room. Through the broad doors he saw some people in bathing suits, either coming in from a dip or preparing for one more before they called it a night. He considered going in with them himself. Without Marya there to bait, everything around him was a boredom that showed no signs of termination. *Quattrocento* and abstract expressionism, Lowell and Roethke, Poulenc and Milhaud, academic politics and the art rackets —he had heard enough about them to know he had heard all he wanted to. The conversation that sustained the evening for all the others here was not for him. He had come to see behind the mask that play of inhuman power that moved all these talking dolls—and to bring Marya, of course. He thought of what Marya had seen in the kitchen. And he envied her. For what he had come to see was Mooney put a stranglehold on his wife and force her jaws apart while he poured booze into her gullet. Marya had seen what only he could deal with. "For I am the resurrection and the life," he said. Himself pitted against the mess of all that existed.

He never felt himself quite real in any social situation. It was as if no education that might be laid on him would ever truly modify the identification made—most likely—in some private play of his childhood, some wintry dusk when he had crouched behind the

293

barricade of gray banisters on their porch and understood himself to be the lone sentinel posted against the long-ousted dragons of the land. Most of the time he could not maintain this identification. Which meant he could not assemble himself so that his identity was palpable enough to reassure him. So he hid himself—in lies and masquerades and filial politeness and all the rest of the tedium of day after day.

Sometimes drink would purify away enough of this dross to make him sensitive. Then, if he was lucky—in his own style of being lucky—his long wait was rewarded, in some twisted sense of reward, by a stir at the edge of the night wilderness, so he knew the monsters were there and his long vigil not in vain.

The hint of Carole's being tormented reminded him who he was, as the sound of gunfire would remind a soldier. In the glow of her anguish his existence made sense.

Then, at the height of his unspeakable ecstasy, Marya's shocked face loomed large at the end of his tunnel of vision. She was saying what someone in a dream might have said to him.

"Come on. We've got to go call the police." She tugged at his arm and grimaced, a child with a bitter taste in her mouth.

"Ssssh." But there was no need to quiet her. She had whispered the words moistly into his ear. "What now?"

"President Mooney is down behind the furnace kissing a woman."

What Marya had been doing in the basement was a gratuitous question. She was his eyes, his carnal eyes. Who but a born fanatic could have spied so well for him? And then so happily have misunderstood what she saw, leaving him alone to deal with it.

He tried to laugh. He meant to laugh as a means of dismissing her, now that she had brought the concrete news his imagination needed. But it would have taken someone more clever to make the laugh come. He could go back and forth between their world and his, but sometimes he was a little slow, and just now he was very far over in his own.

Marya said, "That's why he gave his wife the *stuff*. The woman isn't wearing anything but black briefs."

He bumped her lips away from his ear when he shook his head.

He reached for her arm and missed. She was already on her way, taking *his* discovery out to scatter it like fire in a dry wheatfield.

"Wait," he said. "Wait. Not a woman . . ."

She turned her head. At the end of the tunnel he saw her face change like something dropped into a tank of acid, not so much seeming to lose all its familiar outlines as for the small relationships of color, shape, and value to alter in simultaneous transformation. It was the metamorphosis of a child shrew into an armed goddess.

Then she was physically gone from the room. It seemed to him— after all, he was very drunk—that she was whooshed away into the night by supernatural allies. For when he had staggered after her to the parking lot, her convertible had also been made to disappear.

Maybe he hadn't run after her as swiftly as he thought. He saw a pair of headlights topping the next ridge. He thought it was probably Marya. And in the fresh air he could guess that she would not stop this time until she had driven clear out of his life.

Let her go then. He had neither loved nor despised her. He had only found her necessary for a while. She was his probe into the common world, his most useful link with it. Now that she had found what he was fishing for there, she was free to go where she pleased.

He had no intention of going back into the Mooneys' house. Now he knew all that was happening there. The dragons were in plain sight, and the sentinel who had heard them stirring invisibly knew all at once that he had neither an army behind him nor any need for one. For the dragons hadn't come to breathe fire on this prospering countryside; they had come to sit down at the table with everyone else and be useful civil servants. What difference did it make that Mooney was a fag who was torturing his wife to death—as long as it worked? He knew what his father knew: that it worked. That it had always worked, this or something like this.

So you put down your arms, knowing them useless. You let things happen, because they were going to, anyhow. Only, you watched and you were not part of it. As his father had never been . . .

He cut around the big house and walked through the restored gardens behind and climbed a little hill. There, among a clump of elms, sitting on a log from which the house and grounds were all visible, he waited for the morning to come. He did not know or care how long that would be. It felt familiar just to be waiting. Lot thought, That's what he always did, not hoping even, just waiting. Knowing it was going to come out neither good nor bad, just less than it had to be, than it had to be for whoever was here to endure it.

For a while, sitting there by himself, he was with his father as he probably wouldn't ever be again and certainly never had been before.

While he sat there for what must have been three hours, he saw several of the cars leave the parking area. The party was gasping out. One by one the lights inside the house were turned off. At last it slept and he was still awake.

The morning star hung like an ornament on his right. The shape of the nearby trees and farther hills became definite against a light that was milky and uncertain. He heard a crow calling down by the river. He rose shakily to his feet as if to bless what wouldn't be changed by his blessing or his curse either.

And then he heard the grind of motors—half a dozen he thought—on the sloping road that led to Mooney's front gate.

There were actually only five cars. They came onto the grounds with their lights off. He made no real attempt to count the men who leaped from them and ran for Mooney's front door. There were more than twenty.

He was running, too, already sure that he was too late—not so sure just what it was he had waited all night to do. Perhaps only to see Marya's judgment enacted. Perhaps to save Carole if he could.

He got in one of the back doors in time to hear a chair go through the big window by the pool. Through a door ajar he saw the flicker of men passing at a run and heard them—most of them—lumber up the muted stairs to the second floor.

Now there was a stir and mutter from that floor. When he went up the back stairs he heard the peeping alarm of roused guests as they came to their doors to see what was crowding the halls.

Then his way was blocked. There was just no chance of clawing or dancing his way through the press of bodies. He heard the splat of a fist and saw someone catapulted back into the guest room from which he had been trying to emerge.

Then the crowding bodies crowded back against him. From a door near the end of the hall a little group emerged. President Mooney of Wellford, James Beal of New York, dancer. Their arms were twisted behind them by Tommy Barker, basketball player, also of Wellford, and two big-jawed packing-house workers.

President Mooney's lower lip was bleeding.

James Beal's eyes were rolled back so that hardly more than the whites showed.

"They was in bed together," Tommy Barker said.

19

EVEN MARYA STOHLCROFT had realized you couldn't call the police about what she had seen in the basement. But if there was one thing clear to her prejudices and her character, it was that somebody had to be called. Something had to be done.

From the first phone booth she came to she called Peoria. She was in luck. It was the hour of glory in Tommy Barker's saloon. Workers from the packing house and the Caterpillar plant, veterans who no longer remembered the war before midnight, sports-lovers, the discontented and the strong were in fellowship and harmony of mind when this girl called out of the night, got Barker himself on the wire, and told him that the man who'd let him take the rap for *everything* could not only be caught red-handed but in a situation fraught with opportunities for loud breakage. There were windows to break and abominations to be stamped out. The heroic convoy was on its way within an hour of the call.

Of course Tommy Barker was lucky that night, too. Dr. Mott might have nudged out his host in their competition for the dancer's favors. Mooney or the dancer might have been awake, might have had time to cover up or hide when they heard the glass break downstairs. No such luck. They were well and truly caught, if not actually in *flagrante* then merely fallen back from it into sated dreams.

Mooney had the luck he deserved. Fortunately for him, daylight had come and with it some confusion to the vigilante spirit of his attackers. In the pure enthusiasm of darkness they had intended to castrate him if they caught him in guilt. By dawn's early light they were satisfied to cuff him around, toss him into one of his station wagons with his dancing friend, and tell the two of them to "git."

Mooney understood them to imply a permanence in this command. It was learned later that he did not stop driving until he reached the geographic center of Greenwich Village. Until his whereabouts were known for sure to interested officials of the University, it was said that he had "gone back where he came from"—a formula in some ways more apposite than his new address in James Beal's apartment on Bleecker Street.

And Carole? It was her fortune to sleep through the whole fracas. Purposely and playfully, Mooney had poured enough gin down her throat to kill a weaker woman. She woke sick at one o'clock to an altered world. Her last husband was gone for good and her old sweetheart was, to all intents and purposes, president of Wellford University.

The mace he had not taken up before was in Royce's hands. Willy-nilly he used it. So at all costs, at the cost of everything that could have been personally sustaining to him, he made himself president. What once might have been done with bloody justice, for justice, in the sweet name of justice or even of fierce personal indignation, was accomplished in Mooney's new embarrassment by firm and adroit administration—as Priss would have said, "Too late to have any meaning."

The first necessity of administration was to block the story of Mooney's discomfiture from the newspapers. Let Mooney's scattering guests tell far and wide what they saw and heard in the upstairs corridor that morning. Far and wide, in such cases, is far better than near and concentrated. Neither the *Courier-Sentinel* nor any other paper in the state moved to cover the story.

Tommy Barker had to be told how valuable his silence was to himself.

"We've known each other a long time," Royce said to him, in tones no less authoritarian for being so mild. "From the time you used to mow lawns for my aunts I've been concerned about how you'd wind up. Now you've let loose a whirlwind you're going to have to help me quiet down."

Tommy nodded gravely. He would always want it to be understood that he had acted soberly, on the basis of the facts, for all that was good and decent. "We'll be satisfied if Mooney stays away," he said.

"I don't know who 'we' is," Royce said. "*You* will be satisfied if we don't prosecute for assault, breaking and entering, inciting to riot, *and* arrange for you to serve your suspended sentence for throwing a basketball game. Furthermore, you will lose your liquor license and—"

"I want to do what's right," Tommy said, still not untruthfully. "I don't want to hurt the University's good name, after all I've done for it."

In those first days of Mooney's absence a combination of quarantine and gag was established on prospective bearers of gory tidings inside as well as outside the University. The last few meetings of the Living Arts Conference were held on schedule—muted and denatured, to be sure. Delegates who had been hot for rebellion and spitting on the cultural flag of the Establishment were heard to tell their audiences that the chief hope of the Arts was, like the Rotary Club, to be of service to the community.

Royce, who once again had most of the dirty linen in his own grip, had to tell the proximate truth to the senior faculty. It was therefore inconceivable that their wives did not hear it, individually, from them. But for once the faculty wives didn't scatter their information as recklessly as was their habit. It may have been that the very enormity of the Mooney story awed the natural gossips into silence, as natural pessimists would be subdued by the onset of nuclear war or bubonic plague.

There was also some element of consideration for "poor Carole Mooney" in this self-censorship. Thus, at least, she served. . . .

Throughout the time of trouble Royce established, in the eyes of the trustees, once and for all, his fitness as Mooney's successor. The masterpiece of his administrative maneuvering was to put a good face on Mooney's departure by wangling his appointment with the government as "chief consultant for the Inter-American Curricular Correlation Committee."

Told of this gambit, Henry Worth, connoisseur of the slick deal, was momentarily dumfounded. "You're *not* going to flub our dead-head off on someone else? The bastard ought to be in prison and you know it."

"No," Royce said. "I'm not going to do that. I'm going to turn the clock back to 1946 and make all of us at Wellford brave enough and farsighted enough—or perhaps just modest enough—to live with our own virtues and faults, so we won't stake everything on get-rich-quick schemes. Is that what you want me to do?"

"But it's not right."

"Be careful of thoughts like that. A man can't walk but about three feet off the ground, remember? Stick to that common sense."

Henry laughed. "It's just not right. Here we're rewarding the devil when anyone can see he ought to be made to pay for what he did."

"Anyone—and everyone—must see as little as possible," Royce reminded him. "I haven't found it my task to make anything different from what it was destined to be. If I'm of any value at all it's in holding solid to whatever I find to be still workable. I played my part in supporting Mooney for whatever he was worth to us. I want to play that game out to the end without changing the rules."

"Better to light candles than curse the dark," Henry said.

"Dear God, don't twist. Let's be men and admit we're doing wrong. And don't press me, please, for what I really believe would be right. I'm offering a practical solution. For those who want it. For the University."

"Sure," Henry said, still laughing. Age was making him more tolerant—in some sense of that abused word. At the time of the Billy Cox affair he had still believed he knew what power was for—to knock in the heads of those who offend you. Now this thin, simple vision of its purposes was worn through, and he had let himself drift into comfortable cynicism. "If you can get away with it . . . it's *cute*, Royce. Sell them our dead horse."

"Do you suppose others are so much wiser and better than we that they'll know he's a dead horse? Mooney may do great things for the Americas."

"Sell him if you can," Henry said. He kept on laughing, like a man who intends to die laughing.

Against this rainy day at Wellford, Royce had hoarded throughout the country respect for his opinions and integrity. His word was good with men who were in a position to tip the balance in favor of Mooney's candidacy. And it was a species of consolation—some sort of reconciliation with the uses of time—to reflect that so smooth a transition could not have been managed if Mooney had been ditched when he persuaded Billy Cox to dive from the viaduct.

When Mooney's mail began to reach him in Greenwich Village he responded to the plan with an apparently undimmed self-confidence. "As you know, I've been restless at Wellford," he wrote. *Restless* . . .

With Royce's support, he sold himself again. And that was good for the new Wellford. It just would not have done to let the outgoing president settle permanently among the dives of Bleecker Street.

Altogether, Mooney's severance was a masterpiece. When the student chairman of the Convocation Board asked, in all good faith, whether President Mooney would "be back from his trip" in time to take his usual place in the academic processional, the Wellford administration knew its success. If its story was not essentially or fully believed, still they had compelled one and all to *act* as if it were pure truth. That is what educational administration aims at, and that is good. What might have happened in the night at Mooney's estate was refuted by the fact that the University had its business to go on with as usual. Ships of state and even lesser institutions never have and never will fly dirty linen from their flagstaffs.

But—as if this were a constant disequilibrating factor in the local moral economy—there was of course a question of how Carole must act.

It was agreed—and Royce agreed—that she was behaving as handsomely as anyone could ask. She was immediately cooperative when something was required of her—as in putting Royce first in touch with her fugitive husband. (He had needed money, naturally, or she might never have heard from him herself.) On her own initiative she moved back into the presidential mansion on the campus for the remaining weeks of the spring semester. She made social appearances, tailored and smiling (and sober), like the wife of a man truly called to service in a field broader than Wellford's. It was understood that she would be leaving to join Winfred Mooney sometime during the summer months.

"But she doesn't want to leave," Lot Morgan said to his father. Lot was home from school for the summer. One of his first days home was spent with Carole, having the talk that had never materialized the night things fell apart.

"Did she say so? That flatly?" Royce needed to know.

"She didn't say one way or the other."

"Then we have no right to assume she doesn't want to go."

"I know we haven't."

Royce had no compulsion to refute his son's assertion. More than anything he wanted to warn Lot against knowledges that stood square in the path of necessity. In his view Carole had to go. Not merely to keep up appearances for the University's sake. "She's made her choice," he said.

"Still she doesn't want to," Lot said. There was a strange agitation in his voice, usually under cautious control.

"We have to respect people's decisions—the big ones—even if we know carrying them out may be painful for them and for us. That's one of the best ways we have of respecting people. It would be terrible if we gave it up for the sake of compassion."

"Yes," Lot said. "Yes, that's all right for someone like Mother. I know just what you mean. But Carole . . ."

"Is it justified to assume she's an exception to a good general rule? Is it fair to her?"

"'I never ask if things are justified," Lot said.

There. There it was. The terrible presumption of youth, too blinding to be looked at steadily, too hot to hold in the naked hand —the presumption that love might or can override justice.

My son . . . let it go, my son. It will kill you.

"Well," Royce said heartily. "Don't try to think her thoughts for her, and wait a little to see how she shapes her feelings. There's some time yet. A few weeks, I suppose. And don't imagine we—I—anyone in Buchanan is going to put her on her train if she doesn't want to leave."

"No," Lot said. "Don't do anything to *make* her go."

Once again that summer Carole filled Royce's life. Not that he saw her often, nor that his thoughts were constantly busy with her. It was rather as if in prehistoric time a stream bed had been formed, had lain dry, domesticated, and nearly empty. Now it was again in flood, and the flood was the medium in which he swam. When he thought about the pass to which they had come, he was inclined to call this environment his *responsibility*. When awareness of it came on him in troublesome intuitions he simply named it Carole.

He neither avoided her nor sought her out in her time of decision. He was trying to be scrupulously neutral—out of respect, as he had told Lot. (And Priss's remembered counsel jeered in his ears: "You mustn't respect a *woman*.")

Nevertheless, respect enabled him to distinguish a figure of some dignity—who was Carole—from what a compassionate psychologist would have found to be only the clash of cloudy desperations, the nervous decrepitude of the booze-hungry flesh—which was also Carole. Enabled him to admire Carole in her climate of ruin and to say, in partial truth at least, that she was magnificent there.

He would have thought it splendid for her simply to stand on her feet and let neutral eyes (how could she ever guess how much they knew of the truth?) look at her face. She did far better than that. If one could not say she rose to this occasion, she took all the pressure of it without appearing to notice. Because, of course, there was no more illusion to make sense of her life. In charity one could hope that in the years of her marriage there must have been interludes of pleasure and peace. Some hours, surely, left to themselves, she and Mooney must have stood together on that gracious lawn they had restored, looking over the river, possessing themselves at the center of time past and to come, envious of no one while the moment lasted.

Hindsight must find such interludes the exception rather than the rule—interludes of discretion, respite from the real purposes of the marriage. For hindsight made clear enough that Mooney's sexual indulgences had never truly ceased from the time he assumed the presidency. Worse, it showed that Carole's wifely task had not been so much to divert his appetite toward the normal as to willfully provide a screen for his continuing abnormalities. It was there the mind wished to halt, at her conscious and apparently deliberate connivance in what—one would assume—should have cheated her more than anything else. If he knew how to "please women," as had once been so dismayingly suggested, then surely women were—this woman was—more estranged from the common codes of life than the wildest guesses dared to declare.

Why had she gone on with him to this appallingly bitter end? For his own sake Royce would not have dared to ask her, let alone for hers. He merely registered that in the hardest hours she appeared serene.

In one less than satisfying, frank conversation early in that summer, she said to Royce, "I thought I could help him."

"I'm sure you did help. Help isn't always sufficient."

"But it has to be," she said, not quite understanding him, relying even yet on what she had grown up believing.

"All of us young Protestants were taught that. But perhaps it doesn't have to be."

"You have some other religious idea? I don't understand." That was the final point, of course. She did not and had not and would not understand. "I thought at least we could get by," she said in reference to the sum of her motives for her marriage.

"We *will*," Royce promised faithlessly. "We're going to be old now, Carole. All of us. There's still no reason why our old age has to be spoiled by what has been wrong up to now. You'll be traveling a lot from now on. That kind of life may suit you—and Winfred—better than being tied to an unchanging rock like Wellford."

"You don't hate him?" she wanted to know.

"There's no use in that."

"Maybe I'm the one you ought to hate," she said. "I've never seen very well what I did to your life. Something . . . ?" She wanted to have left her mark, wanted not to have. There was a strange quaver in her voice, like the note of an innocent appalled by the guess that innocence can be murderous. "I wanted to stay out of the road so you'd have every chance to get things straightened out again with Priss."

"You mean when I asked you to go away with me and you married Winfred instead?"

"Yes."

She was lying. But he wanted her to have the lie, to hold on fast to it for the rest of her life.

"I'll always respect you for that," he said.

He was there if she needed him, he told himself. For whatever she needed. This was his willingness. But here, too, he was denied, and it was Lot who saw the end of her confusion.

Lot had been her darling, too, and once upon a time—for what was even then old time's sake—had sat on her knee while she sang the way the gentleman rode, trittity-trottity-trot and how the farmer rode, hobble-de-hoy, hobble-de-hoy. Better than anyone else he could remember how the funny, lolling, graceless manner of the farmer had been her natural way—how she hoped to "get by" in holding herself to be always a little less than others were willing to credit. So she had Lot with her very often through the month of June.

In July she went east and spent some weeks with Mooney. Early in August she came back to Buchanan, at last buckling down—according to Lot—to the job of packing and moving their things out of the mansion.

Royce told himself he would certainly call before she left. If, even now, she had something more to say to him or anything to ask, he was going to be at her disposal. Day by day he put off his visit. Lot was there ahead of him. It seemed like an intrusion into business no longer his to complicate the intimacy between the boy and the woman. All in all, Lot spent six afternoons with her, not all of them at the mansion. They drove around town and over the countryside, looking at things they remembered seeing together. They went to the airport, but of course Carole no longer flew.

Royce was afraid only that Lot, in mistaken candor, might say things to her that would wound unnecessarily. He asked, one evening, what they were finding to talk about. Was Carole mentioning her plans?

Lot's answer, not exactly rude, was, "Nothing."

"You can't spend so much time talking about nothing."

"Carole and I can. Honestly, we don't *say* much to each other."

"But you communicate."

"Oh, yeah."

"Well, since you're occasionally quite articulate with me, can you transpose into words what it is that you and Carole *don't* talk about?"

"You," Lot said.

Royce shook himself as if he had taken a dazing blow. "You shouldn't," he said.

"We wonder why it turned out you never had anybody you could love."

"Why . . . ! Why, I've loved you all."

His strange son would not accept this. "You gave everyone their chance to love you. I mean, you're the kind of person that can be loved. None of the rest of us is. You supported us."

"Well . . ." Incredible that there could be so much embarrassment for a father belatedly surprised by a trick of words. "Well, I hope so!" He blurted his hope like a confession. He had given what he could. What had he denied them all? "Maybe in some abstract way you're right. But I've *thought* I loved you."

"That's just it," the boy said with a sort of calm and fatal quiet. "You can't ever know about the things that count most, can you?" And yet he left it implied that he knew all too well where his father had succeeded, and what he had paid for his success in failures.

That afternoon, alone at home when the boys went downtown, Royce climbed to the loft of the stable where the skeletal glider wing still hung. He supposed his impulse was to prayer, but he could only think—the immense review of a life in which no demand had been neglected and nothing had come out handsomely.

And the worst . . . the worst of it was that the burden of responsibility for Carole, which was altogether his, was falling on Lot. If he had loved in Lot's sense of the word, he would have gone to her before this, discarded sense, discarded the past, made no plans, refused the common sense of foreseeing consequence. He would have said, "Forgive"—and would have added to her confusion at a time when his duty was to minimize it. He had gone to her once and offered everything. The lesson of that time was not altered by pondering it over again.

There was nothing for him to do. He knew that, and for the last time in his life, he cried like a boy.

On the following day Lot went to the mansion again. He found Carole upstairs that afternoon in a bedroom amid a scattering of open trunks that looked no closer to being packed than they had on his last visit. He knew when he came in that she had been drinking a good deal. He said later that she seemed "already out of Buchanan. Gone."

They talked for a few minutes about the schedule of her immediate future. She meant to be in New York for September and October. Then the Mooneys would sail for Rio after the first of November. She said she was pleased with the prospect of being on the water. The voyage, at least, was attractive to her.

She remembered an album of photographs that Winfred had particularly asked her to make sure of. Photographs of their place down the river. She had not been able to find them and she asked Lot if he would hunt for them in the library downstairs. She was agitated when she talked about the missing album, and he got the notion that she was afraid of some punishment if it did not turn up.

So it pleased him considerably when he found the album without any trouble. It was in plain sight on one of the lower shelves from which the other books had already been removed. But when he climbed up to the bedroom again, she had a small revolver in her hand and all her attention was concentrated on that.

"Here, Lot," she said. "You men know all about these things. I came across it in a drawer and I don't know if it's loaded or not. Show me. Show me how it works."

Without a question or the slightest discomposure of his face he explained the mechanism and offered to take the bullets out of the cylinder. He spilled them into his palm. She took them from his hand one by one, carefully but rather greedily, like a child counting pieces of candy.

"Now there's something else I wanted from the library," she said gaily. "A North High School annual from my time. There's a silly thing about me in the class prophecy, and my picture. I'll show you. It would be bound in blue and gold. I think it's on the shelf beside the fireplace. Will you find it, please?"

He left her without hesitation or a single question. He was about halfway down the stairs when he heard the shot that killed her.

Of course he had known what she meant to do. He had approved it, as, long ago, he had approved the shape of clay they were molding her into on his mother's wheel, or as, at the party, he had approved what Marya could not stand to witness. In their silent, well-understood communication he had offered to let her lean on his distrust of the world when she fired, offered to live so she might be eternally excused.

The spoken dialogue between them had meant less than nothing. But he remembered it word for word and told it with admirable control at the police station.

No, he told the police, she had said nothing that suggested a suicide attempt. Of course he had known her thought as if it were painted in block letters on the wallpaper. If he had been allowed by his inflexible code, he could have explained to their incomprehension exactly how the butt of the gun had felt to her moist palm, the great shock of glee and the good-humored joy that burst when the bullet entered her temple. For this is the way the farmer had always ridden. Hobble-de-hoy—away! you know.

Yes, he told them, he understood that he might have prevented a tragedy if he had been smarter. But she had seemed in such good spirits, unmistakably more cheerful than other times when he had talked to her lately.

No, she had not spoken of her husband or any troubles with him.

Yes, he realized that *he* was in trouble and they had very little to go on besides his word about how it happened. But his word was exact, unadorned, and more reliable than anything else the survivors had for interpretation. He would not ask them to share with him the burden of mystery he had so calmly taken now on himself.

He told them what they might have seen and heard if they had been where he was. The coroner's report confirmed his account. The police found only Carole's fingerprints on the bullets and the exploded cartridge. The angle of penetration made it nearly certain the wound was self-inflicted. The powder burns on her face showed the weapon had been rested in contact with her skin.

Royce got to the station while they were still questioning his son. He had nothing to contribute. He was only here to support. That much at least had to be understood. That much was sure.

As they were leaving the station, he tried to put his arm around Lot's shoulders. The boy flinched away, spun and faced him from a small, insuperable distance. The thin pencil lines of his frown meant hatred. It was as if they had been drawn there long before—one might as well say, In the womb, as the womb's protest against its violation.

Now he will accuse me, Royce thought. He will say for his mother, You lost us, and for Carole, You drove us away.

He'll accuse me because, after all, that's what Priss and I brought him to Buchanan to do. Only the event proves real intentions. The event is here.

When the accusation came he would not ask forgiveness, because he might as well howl or beat his head on these stone steps, and he would not do those things because he was Royce Morgan.

"She wanted to leave," Lot said. "You weren't forcing her to do what she didn't want to do."

"I wasn't," Royce said. "Of course *I* wasn't."

He hooked his arm on this last crag of truth and held on—not for dear life, but only for the dignity required to survive in his ultimate role. There was no way back. He must cling to the stone until its substance became his.

Spared the accusation he had a right to expect, he still tried to read his son's face. He thought it said, If you aren't there any more, where am I?

"So much blood," Lot said aloud.

20

Behold the man.

The president of Wellford University is standing in the September sunlight on the chapel steps. Flanking him on left and right are the deans of the University and the new chancellor. And these men appear not so much awesome as benign (or maybe just harmless) to the nearly one thousand freshmen assembled on the grass in front of them. The disposition of men and boys and girls has about it some quality of the simplest make-believe, wherein the president deserves his hierarchical place merely by virtue of being taller than the others. (He is also older than most, though two of the deans surpass his age by three and seven years. His hair is whiter than most. Like President Mooney before him, President Morgan has whitened his hair for his job, though not with bleach.)

Wearing his academic robes and cap, this President Morgan looks, to casual eyes, very much like the portrait of his father that hangs in the fieldhouse. (Royce thinks, I am taller than he, but perhaps I cast a smaller shadow.)

The freshmen, whom he must formally welcome in a moment, loaf in front of him in a mass dense at the center and looser toward the edges, like the mass of a spiral nebula somewhere in the unnamed reaches of space. Such faces of boys and girls as he can distinguish from the mass appear dismayingly purposeless. They are neither pleased nor displeased to be here, but stand like conscripts levied from one apathy to serve another. One dares no judgment about them except that they are healthy and—given the earliness of the hour and the distractions that go with their recent arrival on campus—reasonably attentive.

They are massed here because a printed schedule told them to gather. And yet Royce knows that they are waiting for him to give them, if he can, some reason for being here that might go beyond the mere inertia of compliance, the habits of their house-training. Of course they are not conscious of waiting for this. Not three out of the whole crowd would admit they expected anything from this ceremony. By and large they would be more disposed to think they were doing their elders a service by coming.

To the left of the chapel steps the Wellford Band stands in semi-military uniforms, blowing and thumping heartily. The music, at least, offers promises that Royce dare not repeat in the common tongue. Those innocently blaring horns promise the sky! Put on muscle, lads (the horns would say). Sack the library and the laboratories like vandals and you're up there! Not just on top of the heap of dogs, but free and away from your tedious childhoods, miles above the traps of love and money that took your parents. You're a race of infant giants . . . says the band. What a reckless man it took to write such notes on a musical staff!

Somewhere, lost in the crowd and probably closer to its periphery than its center, are Royce's sons. For Lot it is his last day in Buchanan before he drives east to begin his college year. Royce suspects the boy has not come to hear him speak but rather to *see* him—as if spectacle alone could be trusted in that frightful strictness to which he has committed himself. To those measuring eyes Royce has nothing to offer except the image of a man who held straight on in faithfulness to a tricky, twisting, ambiguous role.

The band concludes its blare of irresponsible promises. By now Royce ought to be sure of what he will say to the freshmen. Yet he is waveringly tempted to speak from the heart. If he did so he would tell them all to go home before it was too late. Run, run, run, run, run—my little ones. Oh, generation of pink-cheeked rabbits, scamper back to the small-town nests and intellectual briar patches you came from. Scamper in sun and shade while you can. The luckless night is almost on us.

But it is his *role*—and therefore his choice; he makes no distinction now between his office and his personal will—not to speak from the heart.

He has a joke ready. That will do for a beginning. From there he can perhaps go on to familiarize them with the physical institution. (He could tell them why the fieldhouse is the largest building here and why there is now more parking area, almost, than campus green. It is because you wanted it so, dearly beloved, and a man named Mooney understood how dear convenience was to us all.)

But how go on from there? How explain the way the visible university expresses both the flaw and the dynamic wish of each heart? How polish the unreflecting surface of the visible world until it mirrors them and the generations who have preceded them here? It might be that if all could see themselves clearly—gesture, tone, desire, and mere displacement of air and movement from one place to another in the impudence of their passage—that alone might justify their lives.

But he has no art to show them themselves, nor have they art to hear if he could. He needs someone with him, and he is reminded that might have been his wife Priss. After all, she was to supply the art that might have validated his stubborn purposes.

Priss's reflection was needed. But recently her novel "about us all in Buchanan" came to Royce's desk. She had not mailed it herself. That would have been, for her, too direct a communication. She would expect him to understand best if the message were oblique, coming from far away. The book was mailed by her publisher—a man who must have known its readers would be few.

Others besides Royce in Buchanan have waited for her novel with varying shades of impatience, because they had the illusion that she might at length offer them a simple formula for understanding Mooney's epoch and Carole's death. All are going to be disappointed. In the slim, arty book, reality has been transposed into symbols so opaque that the human content is nearly impossible to discern. In its pages a white and a black horse prance through the rare waterholes of a dry creekbed. Two women ride on the back of an enormous cat. Light poles and silos protrude from the rich Midwestern landscape like a horde of monumental phalli. Virgins and matrons are "impaled"—one of the author's favorite words—on every convexity larger than a thimble. Fathers and sons are lost in gulleys, caves, and cisterns of the jealously female earth. Children turn into spiders because owls tell them to.

No doubt there is truth in Priss's art. Perhaps her cryptography contains the whole truth as no other words or actions could speak it. It is doubtful if anyone can dig it out.

Poor Cassandra, who was Royce Morgan's wife. She spoke plain on a few occasions. If he had been quick enough, he might have heard her in time. But there is nothing in her book comparable to the clarity he heard occasionally as a living voice, warning him against Mooney at the same time she showed him the necessity for servitude. At best her book lacks pity and pain for blood shed, and only these could now make sense of the time that brought her husband to this moment.

Her book is not for those who lived through the last decade and a half. Furthermore—and quite properly—it is certain to be kept on the locked shelves of the Wellford library, where its erotic flavor (the one obvious element in the midst of evasiveness) can do no damage to these still undamaged young. *Primum non nocere.* While there is no better law, let that be the law: If you can't help, don't hurt. . . .

Let her costly vision lie again in prison, like valuable metal dug out of the earth and then returned to vaults in the earth for storage. Royce, at least, is not the man to tell these children what she meant, by her art, to declare. Perhaps someday Lot will decipher and make public the curious code of love in which she chose to write.

The moment of necessity has come. The chancellor is introducing the president—whose august robes Royce Morgan is wearing.

And in this moment Morgan has what he bargained for. He sees himself reflected by the natural and human scene he confronts. He sees himself standing like a provincial bronze statue, presiding over a Wasteland on which the great bombs have already fallen. (A statue made by an earnest, literal, single-minded, out-of-fashion sculptor; a Wasteland still brimming with poisoned milk and honey.)

The multitude is listening.

And he will speak.